PRINTED IN THE
UNITED STATES OF AMERICA

THE BENT TWI[G]

BY

DOROTHY CANFIELD

WITH

INTRODUCTION AND NOTES

BY

MARIAN W. SKINNER
The Katharine Gibbs School
Boston

NEW YORK
HENRY HOLT AND COMPANY

Colle[ge]

CONTENTS

PAGE

INTRODUCTION
    DEVELOPMENT OF THE ENGLISH NOVEL . . . vii
    MRS. FISHER: LIFE, WORKS, ESTIMATE . . . x

THE BENT TWIG

BOOK I

IN ARCADIA

CHAPTER
   I   SYLVIA'S HOME 3
  II   THE MARSHALLS' FRIENDS 12
 III   BROTHER AND SISTER 26
 IV   EVERY ONE'S OPINION OF EVERY ONE ELSE . . 38
  V   SOMETHING ABOUT HUSBANDS 44
 VI   THE SIGHTS OF LA CHANCE 53
 VII   "WE HOLD THESE TRUTHS TO BE SELF-EVIDENT..." 70
VIII   SABOTAGE 92
 IX   THE END OF CHILDHOOD 103

BOOK II

A FALSE START TO ATHENS

   X   SYLVIA'S FIRST GLIMPSE OF MODERN CIVILIZATION . 113
  XI   ARNOLD'S FUTURE IS CASUALLY DECIDED . . . 123
 XII   ONE MAN'S MEAT 131
XIII   AN INSTRUMENT IN TUNE 138
XIV   HIGHER EDUCATION 145
 XV   MRS. DRAPER BLOWS THE COALS 153
XVI   PLAYING WITH MATCHES 165
XVII   MRS. MARSHALL STICKS TO HER PRINCIPLES . . 179
XVIII   SYLVIA SKATES MERRILY ON THIN ICE . . . 192

iii

Contents

CHAPTER		PAGE
XIX	As a Bird out of a Snare	206
XX	"Blow, Wind; Swell, Billow; and Swim, Bark!"	217
XXI	Some Years During Which Nothing Happens .	232

BOOK III

IN CAPUA AT LAST

XXII	A Grateful Carthaginian	237
XXIII	More Talk Between Young Moderns . . .	250
XXIV	Another Brand of Modern Talk	261
XXV	Nothing in the Least Modern	273
XXVI	Molly in Her Element	284
XXVII	Between Windward and Hemlock Mountains .	301
XXVIII	Sylvia Asks Herself "Why Not?" . . .	312
XXIX	A Hypothetical Livelihood	322
XXX	Arnold Continues to Dodge the Renaissance .	333
XXXI	Sylvia Meets with Pity	341
XXXII	Much Ado	354
XXXIII	"Whom God Hath Joined . . ."	364
XXXIV	Sylvia Tells the Truth	370
XXXV	"A Milestone Passed, the Road Seems Clear"	384
XXXVI	The Road Is Not so Clear	392
XXXVII	". . . His wife and children perceiving it, began to cry after him to return; but the man put his fingers in his ears and ran on, crying, 'Life! Life Eternal!'"	400
XXXVIII	Sylvia Comes to the Wicket Gate	409
XXXIX	Sylvia Drifts with the Majority	418

BOOK IV

THE STRAIT PATH

XL	A Call from Home	431
XLI	Home Again	440
XLII	"Strange that we creatures of the petty ways, Poor prisoners behind these fleshly bars, Can sometimes think us thoughts with God ablaze, Touching the fringes of the outer stars" . . .	448

Contents

CHAPTER   PAGE

XLIII *"Call now; is there any that will answer thee?"* .   451

XLIV *"A bruised reed will He not break, and a dimly burning wick will He not quench"* . . .   457

XLV *"That our soul may swim We sink our heart down, bubbling, under wave."* .   461

XLVI A Long Talk with Arnold   466

XLVII *"... And All the Trumpets Sounded!"* . .   479

Notes   483

Suggestions for Study   488

Topics for Themes   497

Selections for Class Reading   497

INTRODUCTION

DEVELOPMENT OF THE ENGLISH NOVEL

Narration in some form has existed ever since man was created. In fact two of the oldest traits of humankind started the novel; namely, facility in telling stories and delight in hearing stories. The stories which through the ages have been created, developed, enlarged, ramified, even duplicated, form themselves into three great groups representing the three chief ways of telling stories: the epic, the drama, the prose fiction. To the student of fiction prose narration forms itself into classes: as, the legend, the tale, the romance, the novella; and each class again subdivides, as, for example, into Arthurian romance, pastoral romance, medieval romance, picaresque romance, etc. From the early beginnings on to present day literature, the student of prose fiction finds in all these a steady though uneven advance in technique and mastery of story telling. But the novel is not found in any one of these early forms, nor in the sum total of them. They lack certain elements vital to the novel form; (1) they neither present nor develop character, (2) they are entirely objective, (3) they have loose construction and (4) they show little observation. Necessarily, however, the novel as a form had its roots in these early stories, and given these early beginnings, it came as a result of growth.

Several social institutions which recognized more clearly the value of the individual contributed to the growth of the English novel: the 18th century Coffee Houses, the rise of the newspaper, the theater with its social democracy. Moreover, in seeming contradiction to this, the decline of the drama was a spur since it left the prose fiction freer to rise to its heights without this narrative competition.

Several 17th and 18th century works contributed definitely to the emergence of the novel, in fact are rated by some as novels. The chief of these are:

1. John Bunyan's *Pilgrim's Progress* (1677). Here we have an autobiography in allegorical form with smooth plot and good dialogue.
2. Jonathan Swift's *Gulliver's Travels* (1726). Here is allegory still, with adventure and satire.
3. Sir Richard Steele and Joseph Addison's *Sir Roger de Coverley Papers* (1711-1712). Here we find character sketching and delicate humor without an allegorical frame, essays in type but very close to the novel in which the omniscient narrator tells the story.
4. Daniel Defoe's *Robinson Crusoe* (1719). Here we have again autobiography, a strong setting, and incidents no longer incredible but molded on real life.

At just what point the novel emerged as a literary form savants do not agree. But when in the middle of the 18th century, Samuel Richardson wrote his *Pamela* and Henry Fielding his *Joseph Andrews,* the novel as a form was indisputably existent. Richardson's *Pamela,* an excessively long story in letter form is overcharged with detail, elemental in coloring, but it has plot and dialogue which show a great advance, and character drawing of exceptional skill. With Fielding's works, breezy, humorous, energetic, we find the principle of the novel well established. Richardson was the first great romanticist, Fielding the first great realist of English fiction; the two, the fathers of English fiction.

Of the legion of writers following these two great names we need mention only a few. Tobias Smollett, writer of picaresque stories, Laurence Sterne with his disciple Henry Mackenzie, of sentimental works, Fanny Burney of fashionable life, Horace Walpole and Mrs. Radcliffe, writers of terror novels—each of these contributed. In the romantic period Jane Austen, after burlesquing the terror novel, gave us a Dresden-china picture of everyday life, establishing the domestic type of novel. Walter Scott raised the historical novel to a place of high importance, depicting the time rather than tracing the main historical character; he also gave us the Scottish character. Among his followers are Maria Edgeworth who gave us the Irish character, and, in America, James Fenimore Cooper who gave us the American historical novel.

It is during the Victorian Age that the novel form takes first rank in literature. Then two names stand prominent. Charles Dickens is the portrayer of the middle and lower classes in 19th century England, a romanticist, popular, imaginative, humorous, a writer of the purpose novel, contributing to the reform of schools, courts, and jails. William Makepeace Thackeray is the portrayer of the upper class in 19th century England, a realist, genial, satirical, an enviable stylist, satisfying the fastidious English student where his great contemporary fails. Of the other writers of this period George Eliot (Mary Ann Evans) stands first, the keen analyst of the working of the human mind, intellectualist, modern realist, founder of the psychological novel. In America we have Nathaniel Hawthorne to compare with her.

Many others writing at this time are now known, each chiefly for one book. Mention may be made of Charlotte Brontë, Charles Kingsley, Richard Blackmore, Wilkie Collins, and Charles Reade.

Since the 19th century the novel has continued to appear in romantic, realistic, neo-idealistic, problematic, and humanitarian garb. Always we find variety and contrast. George Meredith, with his optimism and portrayal of noble womanhood, Thomas Hardy with his fateful pessimism and brooding, Egdon Heath setting, Joseph Conrad with his tang of the sea, Herbert George Wells with his glimpse of a desired mechanical future, Rudyard Kipling with his journalistic style, Arnold Bennett with his subdued treatment of the commonplace, Robert Louis Stevenson with his sympathy and charm, George Bernard Shaw with his egoism and sneer. In America, a country now so large that not only setting but also character and plot may differ according to the section portrayed, we find novelists tending to confine their works to portraying life in that part of America which they know best. Thus we get the novelist of local color. We have for examples Mary Wilkins Freeman treating of New England, and Joel Chandler Harris of the South.

More novels are being published now than ever before. Among the thousands, a score may live through the decades, maybe through the centuries. We are too near chronologically for proper perspective and must hesitate to assume a prophet's rôle. One statement may be made, however, with assurance. Immortality waits not for that book which is written to reap a golden harvest by satisfying public demand, but for that one which, burning with living truth, with the sincerity and best effort of a big and understanding heart and mind, carries its message in sanity and tolerance to the universal human heart and discriminating mind.

DOROTHY CANFIELD FISHER

Can a woman at the same time be a home-maker and have a professional career? If the answer is "no," Mrs. Dorothy Canfield Fisher is the exception that proves the rule; if the answer is "yes," she is a shining example. Still in early middle age, she has won international fame as a novelist, short story writer, translator, educator, and war-worker. She is at the same time an exemplary wife and mother, helper and friend. Many things have contributed to make this combination possible. Her educational advantages have been unusual, resulting in broad interests and wide sympathies, in varied abilities and efficiencies; her experiences include life in the Middle West and in New England, in Paris, and in Rome.

Dorothy Canfield was born in Kansas, the daughter of a college president and his artist wife. She traveled much and studied widely, mastering, for example, seven languages. She received her doctor's degree from Columbia University and was for a while with the Horace Mann School in New York. In 1907 she married John Redwood Fisher, the captain of the Columbia University football team.

Mrs. Fisher has always loved people. Recognizing that contact with people would be impossible in a metropolis, Mr. and Mrs. Fisher sought a place apart, where they could really live, could meet and touch the lives of others, and concentrate on those things which bring the solid satisfactions of life. What more natural than that they should choose the inherited Vermont acres which had been the old family home since 1762? It was a place which through the years had given to generation after generation of her family, happy childhood days and intermittently adult hours of happy renewal and reminiscence. Here they came with a feeling of " coming home to live." Here, with her husband, her daughter Sally, and her son Jimmie, she still lives a happy home life of accomplishment. Here she eschews bridge, movies, and cross-word puzzles and finds her recreation in out-of-door sports, her work and pleasure in the home and at her writing table. Here too, she watches the growth of the thriving young forest of 40,000 pine trees which she and Mr. Fisher have planted with their own hands.

Since trees can be left to grow without cultivation, it has been possible to interrupt this idyllic life frequently for life in France. Mrs. Fisher feels for France a love that is comparable to that of Browning for Italy, an affection that is

deep, sincere, and understanding, but which does not super-
sede a passionate love for her native land, its customs and
ideals. Even when in France, Mrs. Fisher shows her American democracy by having her children attend the French
public schools. One such interruption came during the
World War, when Mr. and Mrs. Fisher were in France for
three years of war-work. While there she edited a magazine for soldiers, often running the press with her own
hands; she started reading rooms; she organized home and
day nurseries for the children of munition workers; she ran
a camp on the edge of the war zone; she took care of
refugees; and—perhaps her greatest service—she founded
an establishment for printing in Braille that the blinded
soldiers also might read.

Previously Mrs. Fisher had made a lengthy visit in Rome
where she met Madame Montessori, became interested in her
new method of child training, and by translations and original
books on the subject introduced the Montessori system to
the American public.

Mrs. Fisher's less significant works include articles for
French as well as American magazines, besides textbooks
for school use, suggestions for training of children, and
translations. She is best known, however, for her novels
and short stories. Those most liked are *The Squirrel Cage*
(1912), *Hillsboro People* (1915), *The Bent Twig* (1915),
Understood Betsy (1917), *Home Fires in France* (1918),
The Day of Glory (1919), *The Brimming Cup* (1921),
Rough Hewn (1922), *Raw Material* (1923), and *The Home-
Maker* (1924). A number of these have been translated into
foreign languages; *The Bent Twig,* for example, appears
not only in French, but in Danish and Swedish as well.

Honors have not passed Mrs. Fisher by. She has been
a member of the Vermont State Board of Education, 1921-
1923; in 1921 Middlebury College gave her the degree of
Doctor of Letters; and in 1922 the University of Vermont

and Dartmouth College did the same. Mrs. Fisher holds the distinction of being the only woman upon whom Dartmouth College has to date conferred a degree.

As a writer Mrs. Fisher's position is enviable. Her command of the English language, her phrasing, her composition, her technique are of high quality. Her stories are full of emotional pull without being sentimental, she finds dramatical significance in the ordinary happenings, her plots are well woven and motivated, her settings artistically used, her characters truthful portraits. But her fame will be founded more definitely upon her message of sane and ideal Americanism. On this rests " the essence of her greatness and her significance for literature of to-day and to-morrow." To be sure she portrays the spirit of the French race as well as she does the expressionless New England type. But her heart is in the American settings, she knows the American people, and she especially knows and loves the ways of homes in small communities. Her fresh, buoyant optimism is coupled with clear insight into problems, generous sympathy, broad understanding, and a fine, high-spirited democracy that breaks all barriers of age, culture, race, social conditions.

THE BENT TWIG

at Mother from time to time to make sure she was getting it right; and ever afterwards the mention of the Argonauts brought up before Sylvia's eyes the picture of her mother that day, sitting very straight, her strong brown fingers making an occasional mark on the papers, as she turned them over with a crisp rustle, her quiet face bent, in a calm fixity of attention, over the pages.

Before they knew it, the work was done, Father had come for the papers, and showed Sylvia one more twist in the acrobatic stunt they were learning together. She could already take his hands and run up to his shoulders in one squirrel-like dash; but she was to learn the reverse and come down on the other side, and she still got tangled up with which foot to put first. So they practised whenever they had, as now, a minute or two to spare.

Then Judith was set to play with her blocks like the baby she still was, while Sylvia and Mother had a lesson in reading. Sylvia could remember the very sound of Mother's clear voice as she corrected a mistake. They were reading a story about what happened to a drop of water that fell into the brook in their field; how, watering the thirsty cornfields as it flowed, the brook ran down to the river near La Chance, where it worked ever so many mills and factories and things. Then on through bigger and bigger rivers until it reached the Mississippi, where boats rode on its back; and so on down to the ocean. And there, after resting a while, it was pumped up by the sun and made into a cloud, and the wind blew it back over the land and to their field again, where it fell into the brook and said, " Why, how-de-do, Sylvia—you still here?"

Father had written the story, and Mother had copied it out on the typewriter so it would be easy for Sylvia to read.

After they had finished she remembered looking out of the window and watching the big white clouds drift across the pale bright April sky. They were full of hundreds of drops of water, she thought, that were going to fall into hundreds of other brooks, and then travel and work till they reached the sea, and then rest for a while and begin all over again. Her dark eyes grew very wide as she watched the endless procession of white mountains move across the great arch of the sky. Her imagination was stirred almost painfully, her mind expanding with the effort to take in the new conception of size, of great numbers, of the small place of her own brook, her own field in the hugeness of the world. And yet it was an ordered hugeness full of comforting similarity! Now, no matter where she might go, or what brooks she might see, she would know that they were all of one family, that the same things happened to them all, that every one ended in the ocean. Something she had read on a piece of paper made her see the familiar home field with the yellow water of the little creek, as a part of the whole world. It was very strange. She tried to tell Mother something of what was in her mind, but, though Mother listened in a sympathetic silence, it was evident that she could make nothing out of the incoherent account. Sylvia thought that she would try to tell Father, the next chance she had. Even at seven, although she loved her mother passionately and jealously, she was aware that her father's mind was more like her own. He understood some things that Mother didn't, although Mother was always, always right, and Father wasn't. She fell into silence again, standing by her mother's knee, staring out of the window and watching the clouds move steadily across the sky doing their share of the world's work for all they looked so soft and lazy. Her mother did not break in on this meditative contemplation. She took up her sewing-basket and began busily to sew buttons on a small pair of half-finished nightdrawers. The sobered child beside her, gazing up at the blue-and-white infinity of the sky, heard faintly and distantly, for the first time in her life, the whirring reverberations of the great mystic wheel of change and motion and life.

Then, all at once, there was a scraping of chairs overhead in Father's study, a clattering on the stairs, and the sound of a great many voices. The Saturday seminar was over. The door below opened, and the students came out, Father at the head, very tall, very straight, his ruddy hair shinin in the late afternoon sun, his shirt-sleeves rolled up over his arms, and a baseball in his hand. "Come on, folks," Sylvia heard him call, as he had so many times before. "Let's have a couple of innings before you go!" Sylvia must have seen the picture a hundred times before, but that was the first time it impressed itself on her, the close-cut grass of their yard as lustrous as enamel, the big pine-trees standing high, the scattered players, laughing and running about, the young men casting off their coats and hats, the detached fielders running long-legged to their places. At the first sound of the voices, Judith, always alert, never wasting time in reveries, had scampered down the stairs and out in the midst of the stir-about. Judith was sure to be in the middle of whatever was going on. She had attached herself to young Professor Saunders, a special favorite of the children, and now was dragging him from the field to play horse with her. Father looked up to the window where Sylvia and Mother sat, and called: "Come on, Barbara! Come on and amuse Judith. She won't let Saunders pitch."

Mother nodded, ran downstairs, coaxed Judith over beyond first base to play catch with a soft rubber ball; and Sylvia, carried away by the cheerful excitement, hopped about everywhere at once, screaming encouragement to the base runners, picking up foul balls, and sending them with proud importance back to the pitcher.

So they all played and shouted and ran and laughed, while the long, pale-golden spring afternoon stood still, until Mother held up her finger and stopped the game. "The baby's awake!" she said, and Father went bounding off. When he came back with the downy pink morsel, everybody gathered around to see it and exclaim over the tiny fat hands and hungry little rosebud mouth. "He's starved!" said Mother. "He wants his supper, poor little Buddy! He doesn't want a lot of people staring at him, do you, Buddy-baby?" She snatched him out of Father's arms and went off with him, holding him high over her shoulders so that the sunshine shone on his yellow hair, and made a circle of gold around his flushed, sleepy face. Then everybody picked up books and wraps and note-books and said, " Good-by, ' Perfessor ! ' " and went off.

Father and Sylvia and Judith went out in the garden to the hotbed to pick the lettuce for supper and then back in the kitchen to get things ready. When Mother was through giving Buddy his supper and came hurrying in to help, Sylvia was proud that they had nearly everything done—all but the omelet. Father had made cocoa and creamed potatoes—nobody in the world could make creamed potatoes as good as his—and Sylvia and Judith had between them, somewhat wranglingly, made the toast and set the table. Sylvia was sure that Judith was really too little to be allowed to help, but Father insisted that she should try, for he said, with a turn in his voice that made Sylvia aware he was laughing at her, " You only learned through trying, all those many years ago when you were Judith's age ! "

Mother put on one of her big gingham aprons and made the omelet, and they sat down to the table out on the veranda as they always did in warm weather. In La Chance it begins to be warm enough for outdoor life in April. Although it was still bright daylight for ever so long after the sun had set, the moon came and looked at them palely over the tops of the trees.

After supper they jumped up to " race through the dishes," as the family catchword ran. They tried to beat their record every evening and it was always a lively occasion, with Mother washing like lightning, and Father hurrying to keep up, Sylvia running back and forth to put things away, and Judith bothering 'round, handing out dry dish-towels, and putting away the silver. She was allowed to handle that because she couldn't break it. Mother and Judith worked in a swift silence, but a great deal of talking and laughing went on between Sylvia and her father, while Buddy, from his high-chair where he was watching the others, occasionally broke out in a loud, high crow of delight. They did it all, even to washing and hanging out the dish-towels, in eleven and a half minutes that evening, Sylvia remembered.

Then she and Judith went to sit on the porch on the little bench Mother had made them. They tried to see who could catch the first glimpse of the evening star every evening. Mother was putting Buddy to bed and Father was starting the breakfast cereal cooking on the stove. After a while he went into the living-room and began to play something on the piano, something full of deep, swaying chords that lifted Sylvia's heart up and down as though she were floating on the water. The air was full of the moist fragrance of spring. When the music held its breath for a moment you could hear the bedtime note of sleepy birds in the oaks. Judith, who did not care much for music, began to get sleepy and leaned all her soft, warm weight against her big sister. Sylvia for the first time in her life was consciously aware of being very happy. When, some time later, the evening star shone out through the trees, she drew a long breath. " See, Judith," she cried softly and began to recite,

" Star-light, star-bright,
First star I've seen tonight——"

She stopped short—it was Aunt Victoria who had taught her that poem, the last time she had come to see them, a year ago, the time when she had brought Sylvia the pink silk dress, the only dress-up dress with lace and ribbons on it Sylvia had had up to that time. As suddenly as the evening star had shone out, another radiant vision flashed across Sylvia's mind, Aunt Victoria, magnificent in her lacy dress, her golden hair shining under the taut silk of her parasol, her white, soft fingers gleaming with rings, her air of being a condescending goddess, visiting mortals . . .

After a time Mother stepped out on the porch and said, " Oh, quick, children, wish on the shooting star."

Judith had dropped asleep like a little kitten tired of play, and Sylvia looked at her mother blankly. " I didn't see any shooting star," she said.

Mother was surprised. "Why, your face was pointed right up at the spot."

"I didn't see it," repeated Sylvia.

Mother fixed her keen dark eyes on Sylvia. "What's the matter?" she asked in her voice that always required an answer. Sylvia wriggled uncomfortably. Hers was a nature which suffers under the categorical question; but her mother's was one which presses them home. "What's the matter with you?" she said again.

Sylvia turned a clouded face to her mother. "I was wondering why it's not nice to be idyllic."

"*What?*" asked her mother, quite at a loss. Sylvia was having one of her unaccountable notions.

Sylvia went to lean on her mother's knee, looking with troubled eyes up into the kind, attentive, uncomprehending face. "Why, the last time Aunt Victoria was here—that long time ago—when they were all out playing ball—she looked round and round at everything—at your dress and mine and the furniture—*you* know—the—the uncomfortable way she does sometimes—and she said, 'Well, Sylvia —nobody can say that your parents aren't leading you a very idyllic life.'"

Mother laughed out. Her rare laugh was too sudden and loud to be very musical, but it was immensely infectious, like a man's hearty mirth. "I didn't hear her say it—but I can imagine that she did. Well, what *of* it? What if she did?"

For once Sylvia did not respond to another's mood. She continued anxiously, "Well, it means something perfectly horrid, doesn't it?"

Mother was still laughing. "No, no, child, what in the world makes you think that?"

"Oh, if you'd heard Aunt Victoria *say* it!" cried Sylvia with conviction. Father came out on the veranda, saying to Mother, "Isn't that crescendo superb?" To Sylvia he said, as though sure of her comprehension, "Didn't you like the ending, dear—where it sounded like the Argonauts all striking the oars into the water at once and shouting?"

Sylvia had been taught above everything to tell the truth. Moreover (perhaps a stronger reason for frankness), Mother was there, who would know whether she told the truth or not. "I didn't hear the end."

Father looked quickly from Sylvia's face to her mother's. "What's the matter?" he asked.

"Sylvia was so concerned because her Aunt Victoria had called our life idyllic that she couldn't think of anything else," explained Mother briefly, still smiling. Father did not smile. He sat down by Sylvia and had her repeat to him what she had said to her mother. When she had finished he looked grave and said: "You mustn't mind what your Aunt Victoria says, dear. Her ideas are very different from ours."

Sylvia's mother cried out, "Why, a child of Sylvia's age couldn't have taken in the significance of——"

"I'm afraid," said Father, "that Sylvia's very quick to take in such a significance."

Sylvia remained silent, uncomfortable at being discussed, vaguely ashamed of herself, but comforted that Father had not laughed, had understood. As happened so frequently, it was Father who understood and Mother who did the right thing. She suddenly made an enigmatic, emphatic exclamation, "Goodness *gracious!*" and reaching out her long arms, pulled Sylvia up on her lap, holding her close. The last thought of that remembered time for Sylvia was that Mother's arms were very strong, and her breast very soft. The little girl laid her head down on it with a contented sigh, watching the slow, silent procession of the stars.

CHAPTER II

THE MARSHALLS' FRIENDS

ANY one of the more sophisticated members of the faculty of the State University at La Chance would have stated without hesitation that the Marshalls had not the slightest part in the social activities of the University; but no one could have called their life either isolated or solitary. Sylvia, in her memories of childhood, always heard the low, brown house ringing with music or echoing to the laughter and talk of many voices. To begin with, a good many of Professor Marshall's students came and went familiarly through the plainly furnished rooms, although there was, of course, in each year's class, a little circle of young people with a taste for social distinctions who held aloof from the very unselect and heterogeneous gatherings at the Marshall house.

These young aristocrats were, for the most part, students from the town itself, from La Chance's " best families," who through parental tyranny or temporary financial depression were not allowed to go East to a well-known college with a sizable matriculation fee, but were forced to endure four years of the promiscuous, swarming, gratuitous education of the State University. All these august victims of family despotism associated as little as possible with the common rabble of their fellow-students, and accepted invitations only from such faculty families as were recognized by the inner circle of the town society.

The Marshalls were not among this select circle. Indeed, no faculty family was farther from it. Every detail of the Marshalls' life was in contradiction not only to the standards and ideals of the exclusive " town set," but to those of their own colleagues. They did not live in the right part of town. They did not live in the right sort of a house. They did not live in the right sort of a way. And consequently, although no family had more visitors, they were not the right sort of visitors.

This was, of course, not apparent to the children for a good many years. Home was home, as it is to children. It did not seem strange to them that instead of living in a small rented house on a closely built-up street near the campus in the section of the city occupied by the other faculty families, they lived in a rambling, large-roomed old farmhouse with five acres of land around it, on the edge of the West Side. They did not know how heartily this land-owning stability was condemned as folly by the rent-pay-ing professors, perching on the bough with calculated impermanence so that they might be free to accept at any moment the always anticipated call to a larger salary. They did not know, not even Sylvia, for many years, that the West Side was the quite unfashionable part of town. It did not seem strange to them to see their father sweeping his third-floor study with his own hands, and they were quite used to a family routine which included housework for every one of them. Indeed, a certain amount of this was part of the family fun. " Come on, folks ! " Professor Marshall would call, rising up from the breakfast table, " Tuesday—day to clean the living-room—all hands turn to ! " In a gay helter-skelter all hands turned to. The lighter furniture was put out on the porch. Professor Marshall, joking and laughing, donned a loose linen overall suit to protect his " University clothes," and cleaned the bare floor with a big oiled mop ; Mrs. Marshall, silent and swift, looked after mirrors, windows, the tops of bookcases, things hard for children to reach ; Sylvia flourished a duster ; and Judith and Lawrence out on the porch, each armed with a whisk-broom, brushed and whacked at the chairs and sofas. There were no rugs to shake, and it took but an instant to set things back in their places in the clean-smelling, dust-less room.

This daily drill, coming as it did early in the morning,

usually escaped the observation of any but passing farmers, who saw nothing amiss in it; but facetiously exaggerated reports of its humors reached the campus, and a certain set considered it very clever to lay bets as to whether the Professor of Political Economy would pull out of his pocket a handkerchief, or a duster, or a child's shirt, for it was notorious that the children never had nursemaids and that their father took as much care of them as their mother.

The question of clothes, usually such a sorely insoluble problem for academic people of small means, was solved by the Marshalls in an eccentric, easy-going manner which was considered by the other faculty families as nothing less than treasonable to their caste. Professor Marshall, it is true, having to make a public appearance on the campus every day, was generally, like every other professor, undistinguishable from a commercial traveler. But Mrs. Marshall, who often let a good many days pass without a trip to town, had adopted early in her married life a sort of home uniform, which year after year she wore in one form or another. It varied according to the season, and according to the occasion on which she wore it, but it had certain unchanging characteristics. It was always very plain as to line, and simple as to cut, having a skirt neither full nor scant, a waist crossed in front with a white fichu, and sleeves reaching just below the elbow with white turn-back cuffs. As Mrs. Marshall, though not at all pretty, was a tall, upright, powerfully built woman, with a dark, shapely head gallantly poised on her shoulders, this garb, whether short-skirted, of blue serge in the morning, or trailing, of ruby-colored cashmere in the evening, was very becoming to her. But there is no denying that it was always startlingly and outrageously unfashionable. At a time when every woman and female child in the United States had more cloth in her sleeves than in all the rest of her dress, the rounded muscles of Mrs. Marshall's arm, showing through the fabric of her sleeves, smote shockingly upon the eye of the ordinary observer, trained to the American habit of sheep-like uniformity of appearance. And at the time when the front of every woman's waist fell far below her belt in a copiously blousing sag, Mrs. Marshall's trim tautness had in it something horrifying. It must be said for her that she did not go out of her way to inflict these concussions upon the brains of spectators, since she always had in her closet one evening dress and one street dress, sufficiently approximating the prevailing style to pass unnoticed. These costumes lasted long, and they took in the long run but little from the Marshall exchequer: for she wore them seldom, only assuming what her husband called, with a laugh, her "disguise" when going into town.

For a long time, until Sylvia's individuality began to assert itself, the question of dress for the children was solved, with similar ease, by the typical Marshall expedient, most heartily resented by their faculty acquaintances, the mean-spirited expedient of getting along comfortably on inadequate means by not attempting to associate with people to whose society their brains and cultivation gave them the right—that is to say, those families of La Chance whose incomes were from three to five times that of college professors. The Marshall children played, for the most part, with the children of their neighbors, farmers, or small merchants, and continued this humble connection after they went into the public schools, where their parents sent them, instead of to "the" exclusive private school of town. Consequently the plainest, simplest clothes made them indistinguishable from their fellows. Sylvia and Judith also enjoyed the unfair advantage of being quite unusually pretty little girls (Judith being nothing less than a beauty), so that even on the few occasions when they were invited to a children's party in the faculty circle their burnished, abundant hair, bright eyes, and fresh, alert faces made up for the plainness of their white dresses and thick shoes.

It was, moreover, not only in externals like clothes that the childhood of Sylvia and Judith and Lawrence differed from that of the other faculty children. Their lives were untouched by the ominous black cloud familiar to academic households, the fear for the future, the fear which comes of living from hand to mouth, the dread of " being obliged to hand in one's resignation," a truly academic periphasis which is as dismally familiar to most faculty children as its blunt Anglo-Saxon equivalent of " losing your job " is to children of plainer workpeople. Once, it is true, this possibility had loomed up large before the Marshalls, when a high-protection legislature objected loudly to the professor's unreverent attitude towards the tariff. But although the Marshall children knew all about this crisis, as they knew all about everything that happened to the family, they had had no experience of the anxious talks and heartsick consultations which would have gone on in any other faculty household. Their father had been angry, and their mother resolute—but there was nothing new in that. There had been, on Professor Marshall's part, belligerent, vociferous talk about " freedom of speech," and on Mrs. Marshall's a quiet estimate that, with her early training on a Vermont farm, and with the high state of cultivation under which she had brought their five acres, they could successfully go into the truck-farming business like their neighbors. Besides this, they had the resource, extraordinary among University families, of an account in the savings-bank on which to fall back. They had always been able to pay their debts and have a small surplus by the expedient of refusing to acknowledge a tenth part of the social obligations under which the rest of the faculty groaned and sweated with martyr's pride. Perfidiously refusing to do their share in the heartbreaking struggle to " keep up the dignity " of the academic profession, they were not overwhelmed by the superhuman difficulties of that undertaking.

So it happened that the Marshall children heard no forebodings about the future, but only heated statements of what seemed to their father the right of a teacher to say what he believed. Professor Marshall had gone of his own initiative to face the legislative committee which was " investigating " him, had quite lost his temper (never very securely held in leash), had told them his highly spiced opinion of their strictures on his teaching and of the worth of any teacher they could find who would submit to them. Then he had gone home and put on his overalls. This last was rather a rhetorical flourish; for his cosmopolitan, urban youth had left him ineradicably ignorant of the processes of agriculture. But like all Professor Marshall's flourishes it was a perfectly sincere one. He was quite cheerfully prepared to submit himself to his wife's instruction in the new way of life.

All these picturesque facts, as was inevitable in America, had instantly reached the newspapers, which, lacking more exciting news for the moment, took that matter up with headlined characterizations of Professor Marshall as a "martyr of the cause of academic freedom," and other rather cheap phrases about "persecution" and "America, the land of free speech." The legislative committee, alarmed, retreated from its position. Professor Marshall had not "been obliged to hand in his resignation," but quite the contrary, had become the hero of the hour and was warmly complimented by his colleagues, who hoped to profit by an action which none of them would have dared to imitate. It had been an exciting drama to the Marshall children as long as it lasted. They had looked with pride at an abominable reproduction of their father's photograph in the evening paper of La Chance, and they had added an acquaintance with the manners of newspaper reporters to their already very heterogeneous experience with callers of every variety; but of real anxiety the episode had brought them nothing.

As to that same extraordinary assortment of visitors at the Marshall house, one of the University co-eds had said facetiously that you met there every sort of person in the world, from spiritualists to atheists—everybody except swells. The atheist of her dictum was the distinguished and misanthropic old Professor Kennedy, head of the Department of Mathematics, whose ample means and high social connections with the leading family of La Chance made his misanthropy a source of much chagrin to the faculty ladies, and who professed for the Marshalls, for Mrs. Marshall in particular, a wrong-headed admiration which was inexplicable to the wives of the other professors. The faculty circle saw little to admire in the Marshalls. The spiritualist of the co-ed's remark was, of course, poor foolish Cousin Parnelia, the children's pet detestation, whose rusty clothes and incoherent speech they were prevented from ridiculing only by stern pressure from their mother. She always wore a black straw hat, summer and winter, always carried a faded green shopping bag, with a supply of yellow writing paper, and always had tucked under one arm the curious, heart-shaped bit of wood, with the pencil attached, which spiritualists call "planchette." The Marshall children thought this the most laughable name imaginable, and were not always successful in restraining the cruel giggles of childhood when she spoke of planchette's writing such beautiful messages from her long-since-dead husband and children. Although he had a dramatic sympathy for her sorrow, Professor Marshall's greater vivacity of temperament made it harder for him than for his wife to keep a straight face when Cousin Parnelia proposed to be the medium whereby he might converse with Milton or Homer. Indeed, his fatigued tolerance for her had been a positive distaste ever since the day when he found her showing Sylvia, aged ten, how to write with planchette. With an outbreak of temper, for which he had afterwards apologized to his wife, he had forbidden her ever to mention her damn unseemly nonsense to his children again. He himself was a stout unbeliever in individual immortality, teaching his children that the craving for it was one of the egotistic impulses of the unregenerate human heart.

Between the two extremes represented by shabby, crack-brained Cousin Parnelia and elegant, sardonic old Professor Kennedy, there were many other habitual visitors at the house—raw, earnest, graceless students of both sexes, touchingly grateful for the home atmosphere they were allowed to enter; a bushy-haired Single-tax fanatic named Hecht, who worked in the iron-foundries by day, and wrote political pamphlets by night; Miss Lindström, the elderly Swedish woman laboring among the poor negroes of Flytown; a constant sprinkling from the Scandinavian-Americans whose well-kept truck-farms filled the region near the Marshall home; one-armed Mr. Howell, the editor of a luridly radical Socialist weekly paper, whom Judith called in private the "old puss-cat" on account of his soft, rather weak voice and mild, ingratiating ways. Yes, the co-ed had been right, one met at the Marshalls' every variety of person except the exclusive.

These habitués of the house came and went with the greatest familiarity. As they all knew there was no servant to answer the doorbell, they seldom bothered to ring, but opened the door, stepped into the hall, hung up their wraps on the long line of hooks, and went into the big, low-ceilinged living-room. If nobody was there, they usually took a book from one of the shelves lining the room and sat down before the fire to wait. Sometimes they stayed to the next meal and helped wash up the dishes afterwards. Sometimes they had a satisfactory visit with each other, two or three callers happening to meet together before the fire, and went away without having seen any of the Marshalls. Informality could go no further.

The only occurrence in the Marshall life remotely approaching the regularity and formality of a real social event was the weekly meeting of the string quartet which Professor Marshall had founded soon after his arrival in La Chance.

It was on Sunday evening that the quartet met regularly for their séance. Old Reinhardt, the violin teacher, was first violin and leader; Mr. Bauermeister (in everyday life a well-to-do wholesale plumber) was second violin; Professor Marshall played the viola, and old Professor Kennedy bent his fine, melancholy face over the 'cello. Any one who chose might go to the Marshall house on Sunday evenings, on condition that he should not talk during the music, and did not expect any attention.

The music began at seven promptly and ended at ten. A

little before that time, Mrs. Marshall, followed by any one who felt like helping, went out into the kitchen and made hot coffee and sandwiches, and when the last chord had stopped vibrating, the company adjourned into the dining-room and partook of this simple fare. During the evening no talk was allowed except the occasional wranglings of the musicians over tempo and shading, but afterwards, every one's tongue, chastened by the long silence, was loosened into loud and cheerful loquacity. Professor Marshall, sitting at the head of the table, talked faster and louder than any one else, throwing the ball to his especial favorite, brilliant young Professor Saunders, who tossed it back with a sureness and felicity of phrase which he had learned nowhere but in this give-and-take. Mrs. Marshall poured the coffee, saw that every one was served with sandwiches, and occasionally when the talk, running over every known topic, grew too noisy, or the discussion too hot, cast in one of the pregnant and occasionally caustic remarks of which she held the secret. They were never brilliant, Mrs. Marshall's remarks—but they were apt to have a dry humor, and almost always when she had said her brief say, there loomed out of the rainbow mist of her husband's flashing, controversial talk the outlines of the true proportions of the case.

After the homely feast was eaten, each guest rose and carried his own cup and saucer and plate into the kitchen in a gay procession, and since it was well known that, for the most part, the Marshalls " did their own work," several of the younger ones helped wash the dishes, while the musicians put away the music-racks and music, and the rest put on their wraps. Then Professor Marshall stood at the door holding up a lamp while the company trooped down the long front walk to the gate in the hedge, and turned along the country road to the cross-roads where the big Interurban cars whizzed by.

All this happened with that unbroken continuity which was the characteristic of the Marshall life, most marking them as different from the other faculty families. Week after week, and month after month, this program was followed with little variation, except for the music which was played, and the slight picturesque uncertainty as to whether old Reinhardt would or would not arrive mildly under the influence of long Sunday imbibings. Not that this factor interfered at all with the music. One of Sylvia's most vivid childhood recollections was the dramatic contrast between old Reinhardt with, and without, his violin. Partly from age, and partly from a too convivial life, the old, heavily veined hands trembled so that he could scarcely unbutton his overcoat, or handle his cup of hot coffee. His head shook too, and his kind, rheumy eyes, in their endeavor to focus themselves, seemed to flicker back and forth in their sockets. The child used to watch him, fascinated, as he fumbled endlessly at the fastenings of his violin-case, and put back the top with uncertain fingers. She was waiting for the thrilling moment when he should tuck the instrument away under his pendulous double chin and draw his bow across the strings in the long sonorous singing chord, which ran up and down Sylvia's back like forked lightning.

This was while all the others were tuning and scraping and tugging at their pegs, a pleasant bustle of discord which became so much a part of Sylvia's brain that she could never in after years hear the strumming and sawing of an orchestra preparing to play, without seeing the big living-room of her father's house, with its low whitewashed ceiling, its bare, dully shining floor, its walls lined with books, its shabby, comfortable furniture, the whole quickened by the Promethean glow from the blaze in the grate and glorified by the chastened passion of the singing strings.

The two Anglo-Saxon professors were but able amateurs of their instruments. Bauermeister, huge, red, and impassive, was by virtue of his blood, a lifelong training, and a musical ancestry, considerably more than an amateur; and old Reinhardt was the master of them all. His was a history which would have been tragic if it had happened to any but Reinhardt, who cared for nothing but an easy life, beer, and the divine tones which he alone could draw from his violin. He had offered, fifty years ago in Vienna, the most brilliant promise of a most brilliant career, a promise which had come to naught because of his monstrous lack of ambition, and his endless yielding to circumstance, which had finally, by a series of inconceivable migrations, landed him in the German colony of La Chance, impecunious and obscure and invincibly convinced that he had everything worth having in life. " Of vat use? " he would say, even now, when asked to play in public—" de moosic ist all—and dat is eben so goodt here mit friends." Or, " Dere goes a t'ousand peoples to a goncert—maybe fife from dat t'ousand lofes de moosic—let dose fife gome to me—and I play dem all day for noding!" or again, more iconoclastically still,—when told of golden harvests to be reaped, " And for vat den? I can't play on more dan von fioleen at a time—is it? I got a good one now. And if I drink more beer dan now, I might make myself seeck!" This with a prodigiously sly wink of one heavy eyelid.

He gave enough music lessons to pay his small expenses, although after one or two stormy passages in which he treated with outrageous and unjustifiable violence the dawdling pupils coming from well-to-do families, he made it a rule to take no pupils whose parents employed a servant, and confined himself to children of the poorer classes, among whom he kept up a small orchestra which played together twice a week and never gave any concerts. And almost since the arrival of the Marshalls in La Chance and his unceremonious entrance into the house as, walking across the fields on a Sunday afternoon, he had heard Professor Marshall playing the Doric Toccata on the newly installed piano, he had spent his every Sunday evening in their big living-room.

He had seen the children appear and grow older, and adored them with Teutonic sentimentality, especially Sylvia, whom he called his " Moonbeam brincess," his " little ellfen fairy," and whom, when she was still tiny, he used to take up on his greasy old knees and, resting his violin on her head, play his wildest fantasies, that she might feel how it " talk'l to her bones."

In early childhood Sylvia was so used to him that, like
the others of her circle, she accepted, indeed hardly noticed,
his somewhat startling eccentricities, his dirty linen, his
face and hands to match, his shapeless garments hanging
loosely over the flabby corpulence of his uncomely old body,
his beery breath. To her, old Reinhardt was but the queer
external symbol of a never-failing enchantment. Through
the pleasant harmonious give-and-take of the other instruments, the voice of his violin vibrated with the throbbing
passion of a living thing. His dirty old hand might shake
and quaver, but once the neck of the fiddle rested between
thumb and forefinger, the seraph who made his odd abiding-
place in old Reinhardt's soul sang out in swelling tones and
spoke of heavenly things, and of the Paradise where we
might live, if we were but willing.

Even when they were quite little children, Sylvia and
Judith, and later, Lawrence, were allowed to sit up on Sunday evenings to listen to the music. Judith nearly always
slept steadily; and not infrequently after a long day of outdoor fun, stupefied with fresh air and exercise, Lawrence,
and Sylvia too, could not keep their eyes open, and dozed
and woke and dozed again, coiled like so many little kittens
among the cushions of the big divan. In all the intensely
enjoyed personal pleasures of her later youth, and these
were many for Sylvia, she was never to know a more utter
sweetness than thus to fall asleep, the music a far-off murmur in her ears, and to wake again to the restrained, clarified ecstasy of the four concerted voices.

And yet it was in connection with this very quartet that
she had her first shocked vision of how her home-life
appeared to other people. She once chanced, when she was
about eight years old, to go with her father on a Saturday
to his office at the University, where he had forgotten some
papers necessary for his seminar. There, sitting on the
front steps of the Main Building, waiting for her father,
she had encountered the wife of the professor of European
History with her beautiful young-lady sister from New
York and her two daughters, exquisite little girls in white

serge, whose tailored, immaculate perfection made Sylvia's heart heavy with a sense of the plebeian inelegance of her own Saturday-morning play-clothes. Mrs. Hubert, obeying an impulse of curiosity, stopped to speak to the little Marshall girl, about whose queer upbringing there were so many stories current, and was struck with the decorative possibilities of the pretty child, apparent to her practised eye. As she made the kindly intended, vague remarks customarily served out to unknown children, she was thinking: "How *can* any woman with a vestige of a woman's instinct dress that lovely child in ready-made, commonplace, dark-colored clothes? She would repay any amount of care and thought." "So you take music-lessons too, besides your school?" she asked mechanically. She explained to her sister, a stranger in La Chance: "Music is one of the things I *starve* for, out here! We never hear it unless we go clear to Chicago—and such prices! Here, there is simply *no* musical feeling!" She glanced again at Sylvia, who was now answering her questions, fluttered with pleasure at having the beautiful lady speak to her. The beautiful lady had but an inattentive ear for Sylvia's statement that, yes, lately Father had begun to give her lessons on the piano. With the smoothly working imagination coming from a lifetime of devotion to the subject, Mrs. Hubert was stripping off Sylvia's trite little blue coat and uninteresting dark hat, and was arraying her in scarlet serge with a green velvet collar—"with those eyes and that coloring she could carry off striking color combinations—and a big white felt hat with a soft pompon of silk on one side—no, a long, stiff, scarlet quill would suit her style better. Then, with white stockings and shoes and gloves—or perhaps pearl-gray would be better. Yes, with low-cut suède shoes, fastening with two big smoked-pearl buttons." She looked down with pitying eyes at Sylvia's sturdy, heavy-soled shoes which could not conceal the slender, shapely feet within them—"but, what on earth was the child saying?——"

"——every Sunday evening—it's beautiful, and now I'm

getting so big I can help some. I can turn over the pages for them in hard places, and when old Mr. Reinhardt has had too much to drink and his hands tremble, he lets me unfasten his violin-case and tighten up his bow and——"

Mrs. Hubert cried out, "Your parents don't let you have anything to do with that old, drunken Reinhardt!"

Sylvia was smitten into silence by the other's horrified tone and hung her head miserably, only murmuring, after a pause, in damning extenuation, "He's never so *very* drunk!"

"Well, upon my word!" exclaimed Mrs. Hubert, in a widely spaced, emphatic phrase of condemnation. To her sister she added, "It's really not exaggeration then, what one hears about their home life." One of her daughters, a child about Sylvia's age, turned a candid, blank little face up to hers, "Mother, what is a drunken reinhardt?" she asked in a thin little pipe.

Mrs. Hubert frowned, shook her head, and said in a tone of dark mystery: "Never mind, darling, don't think about it. It's something that nice little girls shouldn't know anything about. Come, Margery; come, Eleanor." She took their hands and began to draw them away without another look at Sylvia, who remained behind, drooping, ostracised, pierced momentarily with her first blighting misgiving about the order of things she had always known.

CHAPTER III

BROTHER AND SISTER

A FULLER initiation into the kaleidoscopic divergencies of adult standards was given Sylvia during the visits of her Aunt Victoria. These visits were angelic in their extreme rarity, and for Sylvia were always a mixture of the beatific and the distressing. Only to look at Aunt Victoria was a bright revelation of elegance and grace. And yet the talk around table and hearth on the two or three occasions when the beautiful young widow honored their roof with a sojourn was hard on Sylvia's sensitive nerves.

It was not merely that a good deal of what was said was unintelligible. The Marshall children were quite accustomed to incessant conversations between their elders of which they could gather but the vaguest glimmering. They played about, busy in their own absorbing occupations, lending an absent but not wholly unattentive ear to the gabble of their elders, full of odd and ridiculous-sounding words like Single-tax, and contrapuntal development, and root-propagation, and Benthamism, and Byzantine, and nitrogenous fertilizers, and Alexandrine, and chiaroscuro, and surviving archaisms, and diminishing utility—for to keep up such a flood-tide of talk as streamed through the Marshall house required contributions from many diverging rivers. Sylvia was entirely used to this phenomenon and, although it occasionally annoyed her that good attention was wasted on projects so much less vital than those of the children, she bore it no grudge. But on the rare occasions when Aunt Victoria was with them, there was a different and ominous note to the talk which made Sylvia acutely uneasy, although she was quite unable to follow what was said. This uncomfortable note did not at all come from mere difference of opinion, for that too was a familiar element in Sylvia's world. Indeed, it seemed to her that everybody who came to the Marshall house disagreed with everybody else about everything. The young men, students or younger professors, engaged in perpetual discussions, carried on in acrimonious tones which nevertheless seemed not in the least to impair the good feeling between them. When there was nobody else there for Father to disagree with, he disagreed with Mother, occasionally, to his great delight, rousing her from her customary self-contained economy of words to a heat as voluble as his own. Often as the two moved briskly about, preparing a meal together, they shouted out from the dining-room to the kitchen a discussion on some unintelligible topic such as the " anachronism of the competitive system," so loudly voiced and so energetically pursued that when they came to sit down to table, they would be quite red-cheeked and stirred-up, and ate their dinners with as vigorous an appetite as though they had been pursuing each other on foot instead of verbally.

The older habitués of the house were no more peaceable and were equally given to what seemed to childish listeners endless disputes about matters of no importance. Professor La Rue's white mustache and pointed beard quivered with the intensity of his scorn for the modern school of poetry, and Madame La Rue, who might be supposed to be insulated by the vast bulk of her rosy flesh from the currents of passionate conviction flashing through the Marshall house, had fixed ideas on the Franco-Prussian War, on the relative values of American and French bed-making, and the correct method of bringing up girls (she was childless), which needed only to be remotely stirred to burst into showers of fiery sparks. And old Professor Kennedy was nothing less than abusive when started on an altercation about one of the topics vital to him, such as the ignoble idiocy of the leisure-class ideal, or the generally contemptible nature of modern society. No, it was not mere difference of opinion which so charged the air during Aunt Victoria's rare visits with menacing electricity.

As a matter of fact, if she did differ in opinion from her brother and his wife, the children would never have been able to guess it from the invariably restrained tones of her fluent and agreeable speech, so different from the outspoken virulence with which people in that house were accustomed to defend their ideas. But, indefinable though it was to Sylvia's undeveloped powers of analysis, she felt that the advent of her father's beautiful and gracious sister was like a drop of transparent but bitter medicine in a glass of clear water. There was no outward sign of change, but everything was tinctured by it. Especially was her father changed from his usual brilliantly effervescent self. In answer to the most harmless remark of Aunt Victoria, he might reply with a sudden grim sneering note in his voice which made Sylvia look up at him half-afraid. If Aunt Victoria noticed this sardonic accent, she never paid it the tribute of a break in the smooth surface of her own consistent good-will, rebuking her brother's prickly hostility only by the most indulgent tolerance of his queer ways, a tolerance which never had on Professor Marshall's sensibilities the soothing effect which might have seemed its natural result.

The visit which Aunt Victoria paid them when Sylvia was ten years old was more peaceable than the one before it. Perhaps the interval of five years between the two had mellowed the relationship; or more probably the friction was diminished because Aunt Victoria arranged matters so that she was less constantly in the house than usual. On that occasion, in addition to the maid who always accompanied her, she brought her little stepson and his tutor, and with characteristic thoughtfulness refused to impose this considerable train of attendants on a household so primitively organized as that of the Marshalls. They all spent the fortnight of their stay at the main hotel of the town, a large new edifice, the conspicuous costliness of which was one of the most recent sources of civic pride in La Chance. Here in a suite of four much-decorated rooms, which seemed unutterably elegant to Sylvia, the travelers slept, and ate most of their meals, making their trips out to the Marshall house in a small, neat, open carriage, which, although engaged at a livery-stable by Mrs. Marshall-Smith for the period of her stay, was not to be distinguished from a privately owned equipage.

It can be imagined what an event in the pre-eminently stationary life of the Marshall children was this fortnight. To Judith and Lawrence, eight and four respectively, Aunt Victoria's charms and amenities were non-existent. She was for Judith as negligible as all other grown-ups, save the few who had good sense enough to play games and go in swimming. Judith's interest centered in the new boy, whom the Marshalls now saw for the first time, and who was in every way a specimen novel in their limited experience of children. During their first encounter, the well-groomed, white-linen-clad boy with his preternaturally clean face, his light-brown hair brushed till it shone like lacquer, his polished nails and his adult appendage of a tutor, aroused a contempt in Judith's mind which was only equaled by her astonishment. On that occasion he sat upright in a chair between his stepmother and his tutor, looking intently out of very bright blue eyes at the two gipsy-brown little girls in their single-garment linen play-clothes, swinging their tanned bare legs and feet from the railing of the porch. They returned this inspection in silence—on Sylvia's part with the keen and welcoming interest she always felt in new people who were well-dressed and physically attractive, but as for Judith with a frankly hostile curiosity, as at some strange and quite unattractive new animal.

The next morning, a still, oppressive day of brazen heat, it was suggested that the children take their guest off to visit some of their own favorite haunts to "get acquainted." This process began somewhat violently by the instant halt of Arnold as soon as they were out of sight of the house. "I'm going to take off these damn socks and shoes," he announced, sitting down in the edge of a flower-bed.

"Oh, don't! You'll get your clean suit all dirty!" cried Sylvia, springing forward to lift him out of the well-tilled black loam. Arnold thrust her hand away and made a visible effort to increase his specific gravity. "I hope to the Lord I *do* get it dirty!" he said bitterly.

"Isn't it your best?" asked Sylvia, aghast. "Have you another?" "I haven't anything but!" said the boy savagely. "There's a whole trunk full of them!" He was fumbling with a rough clumsiness at the lacing of his shoes, but made no progress in loosening them, and now began kicking at the grass. "I don't know how to get them off!" he cried, his voice breaking nervously. Judith was down on her knees, inspecting with a competent curiosity the fastenings, which were of a new variety.

"It's *easy!*" she said. "You just lift this little catch up and turn it back, and that lets you get at the knot." As she spoke, she acted, her rough brown little fingers tugging at the silken laces. "How'd you ever *get* it fastened," she inquired, "if you don't know how to *un*fasten it?"

"Oh, Pauline puts my shoes on for me," explained Arnold. "She dresses and undresses me."

Judith stopped and looked up at him. "Who's Pauline?" she asked, disapproving astonishment in her accent.

"Madrina's maid."

Judith pursued him further with her little black look of scorn. "Who's Madrina?"

"Why—you know—your Aunt Victoria—my stepmother—she married my father when I was a little baby—she doesn't want me to call her 'mother' so I call her 'Madrina.' That's Italian for——"

Judith had no interest in this phenomenon and no opinion about it. She recalled the conversation to the point at issue with her usual ruthless directness. "And you wouldn't know how to undress yourself if somebody didn't help you!" She went on loosening the laces in a contemptuous silence, during which the boy glowered resentfully at the back of her shining black hair. Sylvia essayed a soothing remark about what pretty shoes he had, but with small success. Already the excursion was beginning to take on the color of its ending,—an encounter between the personalities of Judith and Arnold, with Sylvia and Lawrence left out. When the shoes finally came off, they revealed white silk half-hose, which, discarded in their turn, showed a pair of startlingly pale feet, on which the new boy now essayed wincingly to walk. " Ouch! Ouch! OUCH! " he cried, holding up first one and then the other from contact with the hot sharp-edged pebbles of the path, " How do you *do* it? "

" Oh, it always hurts when you begin in the spring," said Judith carelessly. " You have to get used to it. How old are you? "

" Ten, last May."

" Buddy here began going barefoot last summer and he's only four," she stated briefly, proceeding towards the barn and chicken-house.

After that remark the new boy walked forward with no more articulate complaints, though his face was drawn and he bit his lips. He was shown the chicken-yard—full of gawky, half-grown chickens shedding their down and growing their feathers—and forgot his feet in the fascination of scattering grain to them and watching their fluttering scrambles. He was shown the rabbit-house and allowed to take one of the limp, unresponsive little bunches of fur in his arms, and feed a lettuce-leaf into its twitching pink mouth. He was shown the house-in-the-maple-tree, a rough floor fixed between two large branches, with a canvas roof over it, ensconced in which retreat his eyes shone with happy excitement. He was evidently about to make some comment on it, but glanced at Judith's dark handsome little face, unsmiling and suspicious, and remained silent. He tried the same policy when being shown the children's own garden, but Judith tracked him out of this attempt at self-protection with some direct and searching questions, discovering in him such ignorance of the broadest division-lines of the vegetable kingdom that she gave herself up to open scorn, vainly frowned down by the more naturally civilized Sylvia, who was by no means enjoying herself. The new boy was not in the least what he had looked.

She longed to return to the contemplation of Aunt Victoria's perfections. Lawrence was, as usual, deep in an unreal world of his own, where he carried forth some enterprise which had nothing to do with any one about him. He was frowning and waving his arms, and making stabbing gestures with his fingers, and paid no attention to the conversation between Judith and the new boy.

"What *can* you do? What *do* you know?" asked the former at last.

"I can ride horseback," said Arnold defiantly.

Judith put him to the test at once, leading the way to the stall which was the abode of the little pinto broncho, left them, she explained, as a trust by one of Father's students from the Far West, who was now graduated and a civil engineer in Chicago, where it cost too much to keep a horse. Arnold emerged from this encounter with the pony with but little more credit than he had earned in the garden, showing an ineptness about equine ways which led Judith through an unsparing cross-examination to the information that the boy's experience of handling a horse consisted in being ready in a riding-costume at a certain hour every afternoon, and mounting a well-broken little pony, all saddled and bridled, which was "brought round" to the porte-cochère.

"What's a porte-cochère?" she asked, with her inimitable air of despising it, whatever it might turn out to be.

Arnold stared with an attempt to copy her own frank scorn for another's ignorance. "Huh! Don't you even know that much? It's the big porch without any floor to it, where carriages drive up so you can get in and out without getting wet if it rains. Every house that's good for anything has one."

So far from being impressed or put down, Judith took her stand as usual on the offensive. "'Fore I'd be afraid of a little rain!" she said severely, an answer which caused Arnold to seem disconcerted, and again to look at her hard with the startled expression of arrested attention which from the first her remarks and strictures seemed to cause in him.

They took the pinto out. Judith rode him bareback at a gallop down to the swimming pool and dived from his back into the yellow water shimmering hotly in the sun. This feat stung Arnold into a final fury. Without an instant's pause he sprang in after her. As he came to the top, swimming strongly with a lusty, regular stroke, and rapidly overhauled the puffing Judith, his face shone brilliantly with relief. He was another child. The petulant boy of a few moments before had vanished. " Beat you to the springboard! " he sputtered joyously, swimming low and spitting water as he slid easily through it at twice Judith's speed. She set her teeth and drove her tough little body with a fierce concentration of all her forces, but Arnold was sitting on the springboard, dangling his red and swollen feet when she arrived.

She clambered out and sat down beside him, silent for an instant. Then she said with a detached air, " You can swim better than any boy I ever saw."

Arnold's open, blond face flushed scarlet at this statement. He looked at the dripping little brown rat beside him, and returned impulsively, " I'd rather play with you than any girl I ever saw."

They were immediately reduced to an awkward silence by these two unpremeditated superlatives. Judith found nothing to say beyond a " huh " in an uncertain accent, and they turned with relief to alarums and excursions from the forgotten and abandoned Sylvia and Lawrence. Sylvia was forcibly restraining her little brother from following Judith into the water. " You *mustn't*, Buddy! You *know* we aren't allowed to go in till an hour after eating and you only had your breakfast a little while ago! " She led him away bellowing.

Arnold, surprised, asked Judith, " 'Cept for that, are you allowed to go in whenever you want? "

" Sure! We're not to stay in more than ten minutes at a time, and then get out and run around for half an hour in the sun. There's a clock under a little roof-thing, nailed up to a tree over there, so's we can tell."

"And don't you get what-for, if you go in with all your clothes on this way?"

"I haven't any clothes *on* but my rompers," said Judith. "They're just the same as a bathing suit." She snatched back her prerogative of asking questions. "Where *did* you learn to swim so?"

"At the seashore! I get taken there a month every summer. It's the most fun of any of the places I get taken. I've had lessons there from the professor of swimming ever since I was six. Madrina doesn't know what to do with me but have me take lessons. I like the swimming ones the best. I hate dancing—and going to museums."

"What else can you do?" asked Judith with a noticeable abatement of her previous disesteem.

Arnold hesitated, his own self-confidence as evidently dashed. "Well—I can fence a little—and talk French; we are in Paris winters, you know. We don't stay in Lydford for the winter. Nobody does."

"*Everybody* goes away?" queried Judith. "What a funny town!"

"Oh, except the people who *live* there—the Vermonters."

Judith was more and more at a loss. "Don't *you* live there?"

"No, we don't *live* anywhere. We just stay places for a while. Nobody that we know lives anywhere." He interrupted a further question from the astonished Judith to ask, "How'd you happen to have such a dandy swimming-pool out of such a little brook?"

Judith, switched off upon a topic of recent and absorbing interest, was diverted from investigation into the odd ways of people who lived nowhere. "Isn't it great!" she said ardently. "It's new this summer—that's why I don't swim so very well yet. Why, it was this way. The creek ran through a corner of our land, and a lot of Father's students that are engineers or something, wanted to do something

;or Father when they graduated—lots of students do, you know—and everybody said the creek didn't have water enough and they bet each other it did, and after Commencement we had a kind of camp for a week—tents and things all round here—and Mother cooked for them—camp fires— oh, lots of fun!—and they let us children tag around as much as we pleased—and they and Father dug, and fixed concrete—say, did you ever get let to stir up concrete? It's great!"

Seeing in the boy's face a blankness as great as her own during his chance revelations of life on another planet, she exclaimed, "Here, come on, down to the other end, and I'll *show* you how they made the dam and all—they began over there with——" The two pattered along the edge hand-in-hand, talking incessantly on a common topic at last, interrupting each other, squatting down, peering into the water, pointing, discussing, arguing, squeezing the deliciously soft mud up and down between their toes, their heads close together—they might for the moment have been brother and sister who had grown up together.

They were interrupted by voices, and turning flushed and candid faces of animation towards the path, beheld Aunt Victoria, wonderful and queen-like in a white dress, a parasol, like a great rose, over her stately blond head, attended by Sylvia adoring; Mrs. Marshall quiet and observant; Mr. Rollins, the tutor, thin, agitated, and unhappily responsible; and Professor Marshall smiling delightedly at the children.

"Why, Arnold *Smith!*" cried his tutor, too much overcome by the situation to express himself more forcibly than by a repetition of the boy's name. "Why, *Arnold!* Come here!"

The cloud descended upon the boy's face. "I *will* not!" he said insolently.

"But we were just *looking* for you to start back to the hotel," argued Mr. Rollins.

"I don't care if you were!" said the boy in a sullen accent.

Sylvia and Judith looked on in amazement at this scene

of insubordination, as new to them as all the rest of the boy's actions. He was standing still now, submitting in a gloomy silence to the various comments on his appearance, which was incredibly different from that with which he had started on his travels. The starch remaining in a few places in his suit, now partly dried in the hot sun, caused the linen to stand out grotesquely in peaks and mud-streaked humps, his hair, still wet, hung in wisps about his very dirty face, his bare, red feet and legs protruded from shapeless knickerbockers. His stepmother looked at him with her usual good-natured amused gaze. "It is customary, before going in swimming, isn't it, Arnold, to take your watch out of your pocket and put your cuff-links in a safe-place?" she suggested casually.

"Good Heavens! His watch!" cried Mr. Rollins, clutching at his own sandy hair.

Professor Marshall clapped the boy encouragingly on the shoulder. "Well, sir, you look more like a human being," he said heartily, addressing himself, with defiance in his tone, to his sister.

She replied with a smile, "That rather depends, doesn't it, Elliott, upon one's idea of what constitutes a human being?"

Something in her sweet voice roused Judith to an ugly wrath. She came forward and took her place protectingly beside her new playmate, scowling at her aunt. "We were having a *lovely* time!" she said challengingly.

Mrs. Marshall-Smith looked down at the grotesque little figure and touched the brown cheek indulgently with her forefinger. "That too rather depends upon one's definition of a lovely time," she replied, turning away, leaving with the indifference of long practice the unfortunate Mr. Rollins to the task of converting Arnold into a product possible to transport through the streets of a civilized town.

Before they went away that day, Arnold managed to seek Judith out alone, and with shamefaced clumsiness to slip his knife, quite new and three-bladed, into her hand. She looked at it uncomprehendingly. "For you—to keep," he said, flushing again, and looking hard into her dark eyes, which in return lightened suddenly from their usual rather somber seriousness into a smile, a real smile. Judith's smiles were far from frequent, but the recipient of one did not forget it.

CHAPTER IV

EVERY ONE'S OPINION OF EVERY ONE ELSE

In this way, almost from the first, several distinct lines of cleavage were established in the family party during the next fortnight. Arnold imperiously demanded a complete vacation from "lessons," and when it was indolently granted, he spent it incessantly with Judith, the two being always out of doors and usually joyously concocting what in any but the easy-going, rustic plainness of the Marshall mode of life would have been called mischief. Mrs. Marshall, aided by the others in turn, toiled vigorously between the long rows of vegetables and a little open shack near by, where, on a superannuated but still serviceable cook-stove, she "put up," for winter use, an endless supply of the golden abundance which, Ceres-like, she poured out every year from the Horn of Plenty of her garden. Sylvia, in a state of hypnotized enchantment, dogged her Aunt Victoria's graceful footsteps and still more graceful, leisurely halts; Lawrence bustled about on his own mysterious business in a solitary and apparently exciting world of his own which was anywhere but in La Chance; and Professor Marshall, in the intervals of committee work at the University, now about to open, alternated between helping his wife, playing a great deal of very noisy and very brilliant music on the piano, and conversing in an unpleasant voice with his sister.

Mr. Rollins, for whom, naturally, Arnold's revolt meant unwonted freedom, was for the most part invisible, " seeing the sights of La Chance, I suppose," conjectured Aunt Victoria indifferently, in her deliciously modulated voice, when asked what had become of the sandy-haired tutor. And because, in the intense retirement and rustication of this

period, Mrs. Marshall-Smith needed little attention paid
to her toilets, Pauline also was apparently enjoying an unusual vacation.   A short time after making the conjecture
about her stepson's tutor, Aunt Victoria had added the suggestion, level-browed, and serene as always, " Perhaps he
and Pauline are seeing the sights together."

Sylvia, curled on a little stool at her aunt's feet, turned
an artless, inquiring face up to her.   " What *are* the ' sights '
of La Chance, Auntie ? " she asked.

Her father, who was sitting at the piano, his long fingers
raised as though about to play, whirled about and cut in
quickly with an unintelligible answer, " Your Aunt Victoria refers to non-existent phenomena, my dear, in order
to bring home to us the uncouth provinciality in which we
live."

Aunt Victoria, leaning back, exquisitely passive, in one
of the big, shabby arm-chairs, raised a protesting hand.
" My dear Elliott, you don't do your chosen abiding-place
justice.   There is the new Court-House.   Nobody can deny
that that is a sight.   I spent a long time the other day
contemplating it.   That and the Masonic Building are a
pair of sights.   I conceive Rollins, who professes to be
interested in architecture, as constantly vibrating between
the two."

To which handsome tribute to La Chance's high-lights,
Professor Marshall returned with bitterness, " Good Lord,
Vic, why do you come, then ? "

She answered pleasantly, " I might ask in my turn why
you stay."   She went on, " I might also remind you that
you and your children are the only human ties I have."
She slipped a soft arm about Sylvia as she spoke, and
turned the vivid, flower-like little face to be kissed.   When
Aunt Victoria kissed her, Sylvia always felt that she had,
like Diana in the story-book, stooped radiant from a shining cloud.

There was a pause in the conversation.   Professor Marshall faced the piano again and precipitated himself headlong into the diabolic accelerandos of " The Hall of the

Mountain-King." His sister listened with extreme and admiring appreciation of his talent. "Upon my word, Elliott," she said heartily, "under the circumstances it's incredible, but it's true—your touch positively improves."

He stopped short, and addressed the air above the piano with passionate conviction. "I stay because, thanks to my wife, I've savored here fourteen years of more complete reconciliation with life—I've been vouchsafed more usefulness—I've discovered more substantial reasons for existing than I ever dreamed possible in the old life—than any one in that world can conceive!"

Aunt Victoria looked down at her beautiful hands clasped in her lap. "Yes, quite so," she breathed. "Any one who knows you well must agree that whatever you are, or do, or find, nowadays, is certainly 'thanks to your wife.'"

Her brother flashed a furious look at her, and was about to speak, but catching sight of Sylvia's troubled little face turned to him anxiously, gave only an impatient shake to his ruddy head—now graying slightly. A little later he said: "Oh, we don't speak the same language any more, Victoria. I couldn't make you understand—you don't know —how should you? You can't conceive how, when one is really *living,* nothing of all that matters. What does architecture matter, for instance?"

"Some of it matters very little indeed," concurred his sister blandly.

This stirred him to an ungracious laugh. "As for keeping up only human ties, isn't a fortnight once every five years rather slim rations?"

"Ah, there are difficulties—the Masonic Building——" murmured Aunt Victoria, apparently at random. But then, it seemed to Sylvia that they were always speaking at random. For all she could see, neither of them ever answered what the other had said.

The best times were when she and Aunt Victoria were all alone together—or with only the silent, swift-fingered, Pauline in attendance during the wonderful processes of dressing or undressing her mistress. These occasions seemed to please Aunt Victoria best also. She showed herself then so winning and gracious and altogether magical to the little girl that Sylvia forgot the uncomfortableness which always happened when her aunt and her father were together. As they came to be on more intimate terms, Sylvia was told a great many details about Aunt Victoria's present and past life, in the form of stories, especially about that early part of it which had been spent with her brother. Mrs. Marshall-Smith took pains to talk to Sylvia about her father as he had been when he was a brilliant dashing youth in Paris at school, or as the acknowledged social leader of his class in the famous Eastern college. "You see, Sylvia," she explained, "having no father or mother or any near relatives, we saw more of each other than a good many brothers and sisters do. We had nobody else—except old Cousin Ellen, who kept house for us in the summers in Lydford and traveled around with us." Lydford was another topic on which, although it was already very familiar to her from her mother's reminiscences of her childhood in Vermont, Aunt Victoria shed much light for Sylvia. Aunt Victoria's Lydford was so different from Mother's, it seemed scarcely possible they could be the same place. Mother's talk was all about the mountains, the sunny upland pastures, rocky and steep, such a contrast to the rich, level stretches of country about La Chance; about the excursions through these slopes of the mountains every afternoon, accompanied by a marvelously intelligent collie dog, who helped find the cows; about the orchard full of old trees more climbable than any others which have grown since the world began; about the attic full of drying popcorn and old hair-trunks and dusty files of the New York *Tribune;* about the pantry with its cookie-jar, and the "back room" with its churn and cheese-press.

Nothing of all this existed in the Lydford of which Aunt Victoria spoke, although some of her recollections were also of childhood hours. Once Sylvia asked her, "But if you were a little girl there, and Mother was too,—then you and Father and she must have played together sometimes?"

Aunt Victoria had replied with decision, "No, I never saw your mother, and neither did your father—until a few months before they were married."

"Well, wasn't that *queer?*" exclaimed Sylvia—"she *always* lived in Lydford except when she went away to college."

Aunt Victoria seemed to hesitate for words, something unusual with her, and finally brought out, "Your mother lived on a farm, and we lived in our summer house in the village." She added after a moment's deliberation: "Her uncle, who kept the farm, furnished us with our butter. Sometimes your mother used to deliver it at the kitchen door." She looked hard at Sylvia as she spoke.

"Well, I should have thought you'd have seen her *there!*" said Sylvia in surprise. Nothing came to the Marshalls' kitchen door which was not in the children's field of consciousness.

"It was, in fact, there that your father met her," stated Aunt Victoria briefly.

"Oh yes, I remember," said Sylvia, quoting fluently from an often heard tale. "I've heard them tell about it lots of times. She was earning money to pay for her last year in college, and dropped a history book out of her basket as she started to get back in the wagon, and Father picked it up and said, 'Why, good Lord! who in Lydford reads Gibbon?' And Mother said it was hers, and they talked a while, and then he got in and rode off with her."

"Yes," said Aunt Victoria, "that was how it happened. ... Pauline, get out the massage cream and do my face, will you?"

She did not talk any more for a time, but when she began, it was again of Lydford that she spoke, running along in a murmured stream of reminiscences breathed faintly between motionless lips that Pauline's reverent ministrations might not be disturbed. Through the veil of these half-understood recollections, Sylvia saw highly inaccurate pictures of great magnificent rooms filled with heavy old mahogany furniture, of riotously colored rose-gardens, terraced and box-edged, inhabited by beautiful ladies always, like Aunt Victoria, "dressed-up," who took tea under brightly striped, pagoda-shaped tents, waited upon by slant-eyed Japanese (it seemed Aunt Victoria had nothing but Japanese servants). The whole picture shimmered in the confused imagination of the listening little girl, till it blended indistinguishably with the enchantment of her fairy-stories. It all seemed a background natural enough for Aunt Victoria, but Sylvia could not fit her father into it.

"Ah, he's changed greatly—he's transformed—he is not the same creature," Aunt Victoria told her gravely, speaking according to her seductive habit with Sylvia, as though to an equal. "The year when we lost our money and he married, altered all the world for us." She linked the two events together, and was rewarded by seeing the reference slide over Sylvia's head.

"Did you lose *your* money, too?" asked Sylvia, astounded. It had never occurred to her that Aunt Victoria might have been affected by that event in her father's life, with which she was quite familiar through his careless references to what he seemed to regard as an interesting but negligible incident.

"All but the slightest portion of it, my dear—when I was twenty years old. Your father was twenty-five."

Sylvia looked about her at the cut-glass and silver utensils on the lace-covered dressing-table, at Aunt Victoria's pale lilac crêpe-de-chine négligée, at the neat, pretty young maid deft-handedly rubbing the perfumed cream into the other woman's well-preserved face, impassive as an idol's. "Why—why, I thought——" she began and stopped, a native delicacy making her hesitate as Judith never did.

Aunt Victoria understood. "Mr. Smith had money," she explained briefly. "I married when I was twenty-one."

"Oh," said Sylvia. It seemed an easy way out of difficulties. She had never before chanced to hear Aunt Victoria mention her long-dead husband.

CHAPTER V

SOMETHING ABOUT HUSBANDS

She did not by any means always sit in the hotel and watch Pauline care for different portions of Aunt Victoria's body. Mrs. Marshall-Smith took, on principle, a drive every day, and Sylvia was her favorite companion. At first they went generally over the asphalt and in front of the costly and incredibly differing "mansions" of the "residential portion" of town, but later their drives took them principally along the winding roads and under the thrifty young trees of the State University campus. They often made an excuse of fetching Professor Marshall home from a committee meeting, and as the faculty committees at that time of year were, for the most part, feverishly occupied with the classification of the annual flood-tide of Freshmen, he was nearly always late, and they were obliged to wait long half-hours in front of the Main Building.

Sylvia's cup of satisfaction ran over as, dressed in her simple best, which her mother without comment allowed her to put on every day now, she sat in the well-appointed carriage beside her beautiful aunt, at whom every one looked so hard and so admiringly. The University work had not begun, but unresigned and harassed professors and assistants, recalled from their vacations for various executive tasks, were present in sufficient numbers to animate the front steps of the Main Building with constantly gathering and dissolving little groups. These called out greetings to each other, and exchanged dolorous mutual condolences on their hard fate; all showing, with a helpless masculine naïveté, their consciousness of the lovely, observant figure in the carriage below them. Of a different sort were the professors' wives, who occasionally drifted past on the path.

Aunt Victoria might have been a blue-uniformed messenger-boy for all that was betrayed by their skilfully casual glance at her and then away, and the subsequent direct-ness of their forward gaze across the campus. Mrs. Marshall-Smith had for both these manifestations of con-sciousness of her presence the same imperturbable smile of amusement. " They are delightful, these colleagues of your father's ! " she told Sylvia. Sylvia had hoped fervently that the stylish Mrs. Hubert might see her in this brief apothe-osis, and one day her prayer was answered. Straight down the steps of the Main Building they came, Mrs. Hubert glis-tening in shiny blue silk, extremely unaware of Aunt Vic-toria, the two little girls looking to Sylvia like fairy prin-cesses, with pink-and-white, lace-trimmed dresses, and big pink hats with rose wreaths. Even the silk laces in their low, white kid shoes were of pink to match the ribbons, which gleamed at waist and throat and elbow. Sylvia watched them in an utter admiration, and was beyond measure shocked when Aunt Victoria said, after they had stepped daintily past, " Heavens ! What a horridly over-dressed family ! Those poor children look too absurd, tricked out like that. The one nearest me had a sweet, appealing little face, too."

" That is Eleanor," said Sylvia, with a keen, painful recollection of the scene a year ago. She added doubtfully, " Didn't you think their dresses pretty, Aunt Victoria ? "

" I thought they looked like pin-cushions on a kitchen-maid's dressing-table," returned Aunt Victoria more forcibly than she usually expressed herself. " You look vastly bet-ter with the straight lines of your plain white dresses. You have a great deal of style, Sylvia. Judith is hand-somer than you, but she will never have any style." This verdict, upon both the Huberts and herself, delivered with a serious accent of mature deliberation, impressed Sylvia. It was one of the speeches she was to ponder.

Although Professor Marshall showed himself noticeably negligent in the matter of introducing his colleagues to his sister, it was only two or three days before Aunt Victoria's half-hours of waiting before the Main Building had other companionship than Sylvia's. This was due to the decisive action of young Professor Saunders, just back from the British Museum, where, at Professor Marshall's suggestion, he had been digging up facts about the economic history of the twelfth century in England. Without waiting for an invitation he walked straight up to the carriage with the ostensible purpose of greeting Sylvia, who was a great favorite of his, and who in her turn had a romantic admiration for the tall young assistant. Of all the faculty people who frequented the Marshall house, he and old Professor Kennedy were the only people whom Sylvia considered " stylish," and Professor Kennedy, in spite of his very high connection with the aristocracy of La Chance, was so cross and depressed that really his " style " did not count. She was now greatly pleased by the younger professor's public and cordial recognition of her, and, with her precocious instinct for social ease, managed to introduce him to her aunt, even adding quaintly a phrase which she had heard her mother use in speaking of him, " My father thinks Professor Saunders has a brilliant future before him."

This very complimentary reference had not the effect she hoped for, since both the young man and Aunt Victoria laughed, exchanging glances of understanding, and said to each other, " Isn't she delicious? " But at least it effectually broke any ice of constraint, so that the new-comer felt at once upon the most familiarly friendly terms with the sister of his chief. Thereafter he came frequently to lean an arm on the side of the carriage and talk with the " ladies-in-waiting," as he called the pretty woman and child. Once or twice Sylvia was transferred to the front seat beside Peter, the negro driver, on the ground that she could watch the horses better, and they took Professor Saunders for a drive through the flat, fertile country, now beginning to gleam ruddy with autumnal tints of bronze and scarlet and gold. Although she greatly enjoyed the social brilliance of these occasions, on which Aunt Victoria showed herself unexpectedly sprightly and altogether enchanting, Sylvia felt a little guilty that they did not return to pick up Professor Marshall, and she was relieved, when they met at supper, that he made no reference to their defection.

He did not, in fact, mention his assistant's name at all, and yet he did not seem surprised when Professor Saunders, coming to the Sunday evening rehearsal of the quartet, needed no introduction to his sister, but drew a chair up with the evident intention of devoting all his conversation to her. For a time this overt intention was frustrated by old Reinhardt, smitten with an admiration as unconcealed for the beautiful stranger. In the interval before the arrival of the later members of the quartet, he fluttered around her like an ungainly old moth, racking his scant English for complimentary speeches. These were received by Aunt Victoria with her best calm smile, and by Professor Saunders with open impatience. His equanimity was not restored by the fact that there chanced to be rather more general talk than usual that evening, leaving him but small opportunity for his tête-à-tête.

It began by the arrival of Professor Kennedy, a little late, delayed at a reunion of the Kennedy family. He was always reduced to bilious gloom by any close contact with that distinguished, wealthy, and much looked-up-to group of citizens of La Chance, and this evening he walked into the front door obviously even more depressed than usual. The weather had turned cool, and his imposingly tall old person was wrapped in a cape-overcoat. Sylvia had no fondness for Professor Kennedy, but she greatly admired his looks and his clothes, and his handsome, high-nosed old face. She watched him wrestle himself out of his coat as though it were a grappling enemy, and was not surprised at the irritability which sat visibly upon his arching white eyebrows. He entered the room trailing his 'cello-bag beside him and plucking peevishly at its drawstrings, and although Aunt Victoria quite roused herself at the sight of him, he received his introduction to her with reprehensible indifference. He sank into a chair and looked sadly at the fire, taking the point of his white beard in his long, tapering fingers. Professor Marshall turned from the piano, where he sat, striking A for the conscientious Bauermeister to tune, and said laughingly, " Hey there, Knight of the Dolorous Countenance, what vulture is doing business at the old stand on your liver? "

Professor Kennedy crossed one long, elegantly slim leg over the other, " I've been dining with the Kennedy family," he said, with a neat and significant conciseness.

" Anything specially the matter with the predatory rich? " queried Marshall, reaching for his viola-case.

Professor Kennedy shook his head. " Alas! there's never anything the matter with them. *Comme le diable, ils se portent toujours bien.*"

At the purity of accent with which this embittered remark was made, Mrs. Marshall-Smith opened her eyes, and paid more attention as the old professor went on.

" The last of my unmarried nieces has shown herself a true Kennedy by providing herself with a dolichocephalic blond of a husband, like all the others. The dinner was given in honor of the engagement."

Sylvia was accustomed to finding Professor Kennedy's remarks quite unintelligible, and this one seemed no odder to her than the rest, so that she was astonished that Aunt Victoria was not ashamed to confess as blank an ignorance as the little girl's. The beautiful woman leaned toward the morose old man with the suave self-confidence of one who has never failed to charm, and drew his attention to her by a laugh of amused perplexity. " May I ask," she inquired, "*what* kind of a husband is that? It is a new variety to me."

Professor Kennedy looked at her appraisingly. " It's the kind most women aspire to," he answered enigmatically. He imparted to this obscure remark the air of passing a sentence of condemnation.

Sylvia's mother stirred uneasily in her chair and looked at her husband. He had begun to take his viola from the case, but now returned it and stood looking quizzically from his sister to his guest. " Professor Kennedy talks a special language, Vic," he said lightly. "Some day he'll make a book of it and be famous. He divides us all into two kinds: the ones that get what they want by taking it away from other people—those are the dolichocephalic blonds— though I believe it doesn't refer to the color of their hair. The other kind are the white folks, the unpredatory ones who have scruples, and get pushed to the wall for their pains."

Mrs. Marshall-Smith turned to the young man beside her. "It makes one wonder, doesn't it," she conjectured pleasantly, "to which type one belongs oneself?"

In this welcome shifting from the abstract to the understandably personal, old Reinhardt saw his opportunity. "Ach, womens, beautifool and goot womens!" he cried in his thick, kindly voice. "Dey are abofe being types. To every good man, dey can be only wie eine blume, so hold and schön——"

Professor Kennedy's acid voice broke in—"So you're still in the 1830 Romantische Schule period, are you, Reinhardt?" He went on to Mrs. Marshall-Smith: "But there *is* something in that sort of talk. Women, especially those who consider themselves beautiful and good, escape being *either* kind of type, by the legerdemain with which they get what they want, and yet don't soil their fingers with predatory acts."

Mrs. Marshall-Smith was, perhaps, a shade tardy in asking the question which he had evidently cast his speech to extract from her, but after an instant's pause she brought it out bravely. "How in the world do you mean?" she asked, smiling, and received, with a quick flicker of her eyelids, the old man's response of, "They buy a dolichocephalic blond to do their dirty work for them and pay for him with their persons."

"*Oh!*" cried Mrs. Marshall, checking herself in a sudden deprecatory gesture of apology towards her sister-in-law. She looked at her husband and gave him a silent, urgent message to break the awkward pause, a message which he disregarded, continuing coolly to inspect his finger-nails with an abstracted air, contradicted by the half-smile on his lips. Sylvia, listening to the talk, could make nothing out of it, but miserably felt her little heart grow leaden as she looked from one face to another. Judith and Lawrence, tired of waiting for the music to begin, had dropped asleep among the pillows of the divan. Mr. Bauermeister yawned, looked at the clock, and plucked at the strings of his violin. He hated all talk as a waste of time. Old Reinhardt's simple face looked as puzzled and uneasy as Sylvia's own. Young Mr. Saunders seemed to have no idea that there was anything particularly unsettling in the situation, but, disliking the caustic vehemence of his old colleague's speech, interposed to turn it from the lady by his side. "And you're the man who's opposed on principle to sweeping generalizations!" he said in cheerful rebuke.

"Ah, I've just come from a gathering of the Clan Kennedy," repeated the older man. "I defy anybody to produce a more successfully predatory family than mine. The fortunes of the present generation of Kennedys don't come from any white-livered subterfuge, like the rise in the value of real estate, as my own ill-owned money does. No, sir; the good, old, well-recognized, red-blooded method of going out and taking it away from people not so smart as they are, is good enough for them, if you please. And my woman relatives——" He swept them away with a gesture. "When I——"

Mrs. Marshall cut him short resolutely. "Are you going to have any music tonight, or aren't you?" she said.

He looked at her with a sudden, unexpected softening of his somber eyes. "Do you know, Barbara Marshall, that there are times when you keep one unhappy old misanthrope from despairing of his kind?"

She had at this unlooked-for speech only the most honest astonishment. "I don't know what you're talking about," she said bluntly.

Judith stirred in her sleep and woke up blinking. When she saw that Professor Kennedy had come in, she did what Sylvia would never have dared do; she ran to him and

climbed up on his knee, laying her shining, dark head
against his shoulder. The old man's arms closed around
her. "Well, spitfire," he said, "*comment ça roule,* eh?"

Judith did not trouble herself to answer. With a gesture of tenderness, as unexpected as his speech to her
mother, her old friend laid his cheek against hers. "You're
another, Judy. *You'll* never marry a dolichocephalic blond
and make him pull the chestnuts out of the fire for you,
will you?" he said confidently.

Mrs. Marshall rose with the exasperated air of one whose
patience is gone. She made a step as though to shield her
husband's sister from the cantankerous old man. "If I
hear another word of argument in this house tonight——"
she threatened. "Mr. Reinhardt, what are these people
here for?"

The musician awoke, with a sigh, from his dazzled contemplation of his host's sister, and looked about him. "Ach,
yes! Ach, yes!" he admitted. With a glance of adoration
at the visitor, he added impressively what to his mind
evidently signified some profoundly significant tribute, "Dis
night we shall blay only Schubert!"

Sylvia heaved a sigh of relief as the four gathered in
front of the music-racks at the other end of the room,
tuning and scraping. Young Mr. Saunders, evidently
elated that his opportunity had come, leaned toward Aunt
Victoria and began talking in low tones. Once or twice
they laughed a little, looking towards Professor Kennedy.

Then old Reinhardt, gravely pontifical, rapped with his
bow on his rack, lifted his violin to his chin, and—an
obliterating sponge was passed over Sylvia's memory. All
the queer, uncomfortable talk, the unpleasant voices, the
angry or malicious or uneasy eyes, the unkindly smiling
lips, all were washed away out of her mind. The smooth,
swelling current of the music was like oil on a wound.
As she listened and felt herself growing drowsy, it seemed
to her that she was being floated away, safely away from the
low-ceilinged room where personalities clashed, out to cool,
star-lit spaces.

All that night in her dreams she heard only old Reinhardt's angel voice proclaiming, amid the rich murmur of assent from the other strings:

CHAPTER VI

THE SIGHTS OF LA CHANCE

ONE day at the end of a fortnight, Aunt Victoria and Arnold were late in their daily arrival at the Marshall house, and when the neat surrey at last drove up, they both showed signs of discomposure. Discomposure was no unusual condition for Arnold, who not infrequently made his appearance red-faced and sullen, evidently fresh from angry revolt against his tutor, but on that morning he was anything but red-faced, and looked a little scared. His stepmother's fine complexion, on the contrary, had more pink than usual in its pearly tones, and her carriage had less than usual of sinuous grace. Sylvia and Judith ran down the porch steps to meet them, but stopped, startled by their aspect. Aunt Victoria descended, very straight, her head high-held, and without giving Sylvia the kiss with which she usually marked her preference for her older niece, walked at once into the house.

Although the impressionable Sylvia was so struck by these phenomena, that, even after her aunt's disappearance, she remained daunted and silent, Judith needed only the removal of the overpowering presence to restore her coolness. She pounced on Arnold with questions. " What *you* been doing that's so awful bad? I bet *you* caught it all right! "

" 'Tisn't me," said Arnold in a subdued voice. " It's Pauline and old Rollins that caught it. They're the ones that ha' been bad."

Judith was at a loss, never having conceived that grownups might do naughty things. Arnold went on, " If you'd ha' heard Madrina talking to Pauline—say! Do you know what I did? I crawled under the bed—honest I did. It

53

didn't last but a minute, but it scared the liver out o' me."
This vigorous expression was a favorite of his.

Judith was somewhat impressed by his face and manner,
but still inclined to mock at a confession of fear. "Under
the *bed!*" she sneered.

Arnold evidently felt the horror of the recently enacted
scene so vividly that there was no room for shame in his
mind. "You bet I did! And so would you too, if you'd
ha' been there. *Gee!*"

In spite of herself Judith looked somewhat startled by
the vibration of sincerity in his voice, and Sylvia, with her
quick sympathy of divination, had turned almost as pale
as the little boy, who, all his braggart turbulence gone,
stood looking at them with a sick expression in his eyes.

"Was it in your room?" asked Judith. "I thought
Pauline's room was on the top floor. What was she doing
down there?"

"No, it was in old Rollins' room—next to mine. I don't
know what Pauline was doing there."

"What did Pauline do when Aunt Victoria scolded her?"
asked Sylvia. She had come to be fond of the pretty young
maid with her fat, quick hands and her bright, warm-
hearted smile for her mistress' little niece. One day, when
Mrs. Marshall-Smith had, for a moment, chanced to leave
them alone, Pauline had given her a sudden embrace, and
had told her: "At 'ome zere are four leetle brozers and
sisters. America is a place mos' solitary!" "What did
Pauline do?" asked Sylvia again as Arnold did not answer.

The boy looked down. "Pauline just cried and cried,"
he said in a low tone. "I *liked* Pauline! She was awful
good to me. I—I heard her crying afterwards as she went
away. Seemed to me I could hear her crying all the way
out here."

"Did she go away?" asked Judith, trying to make something coherent out of the story. Arnold nodded.

"You bet she did. Madrina turned her right out—and
old Rollins too."

" Was *he* there? What was the matter anyhow? " Judith persisted.

Arnold twisted uncomfortably, loath to continue bringing up the scene. " I d'n know what was the matter. Yes, old Rollins was there, all right. He's gone away too, the doggoned old thing—for good. That's *something!* " He added, " Aw, quit talkin' about it, can't you! Let's play! "

" It's my turn to help Mother with the tomatoes," said Judith. " She's doing the last of the canning this morning. Maybe she'd let you help."

Arnold brightened. " Maybe she would! " he said, adding eagerly, " Maybe she'd tell us another of the stories about her grandmother."

Judith snatched at his hand and began racing down the path to the garden. " Maybe she would! " she cried. They both called as they ran, " Mother, *oh,* Mother! " and as they ran, they leaped and bounded into the bright autumn air like a couple of puppies.

Sylvia's mental resiliency was not of such sturdily elastic stuff. She stood still, thinking of Pauline crying, and crying—and started aside when her aunt came out again on the porch.

" I don't find any one in the house, Sylvia dear," said Mrs. Marshall-Smith quietly. Sylvia looked up into the clear, blue eyes, so like her father's, and felt the usual magic spell lay hold on her. The horrid impression made by Arnold's story dimmed and faded. Arnold was always getting things twisted. She came up closer to her aunt's side and took the soft, smooth fingers between her two little hard, muscular hands. In her relief, she had forgotten to answer. Mrs. Marshall-Smith said again, " Where are your parents, dear? "

" Oh," said Sylvia. " Oh yes—why, Father's at the University at a committee meeting and Mother's out by the garden putting up tomatoes. Judy and Arnold are helping her."

Mrs. Marshall-Smith hesitated, looked about her restlessly, and finally raised her parasol, of a gold-colored silk, a lighter tone, but the same shade as her rich plain broadcloth costume of tan. "Shall we take a little walk, my dear?" she suggested. "I don't feel like sitting still just now—nor"—she looked down into Sylvia's eyes—"nor yet like canning tomatoes."

That walk, the last one taken with Aunt Victoria, became one of Sylvia's memories, although she never had a vivid recollection of what they saw during their slow ramble. It was only Aunt Victoria whom the little girl remembered—Aunt Victoria moving like a goddess over their rough paths and under the changing glory of the autumn leaves. She herself was a brighter glory, with her shining blond hair crowned by a halo of feathery, gold-colored plumes, the soft, fine, supple broadcloth of her garments gleaming in the sunshine with a sheen like that of a well-kept animal's coat. There breathed from all her person a faint odor of grace and violets and unhurried leisure.

Sylvia clung close to her side, taking in through all her pores this lovely emanation, not noticing whether they were talking or not, not heeding the direction of their steps. She was quite astonished to find herself on the University campus, in front of the Main Building. Aunt Victoria had never walked so far before. "Oh, did you want to see Father?" she asked, coming a little to herself.

Mrs. Marshall-Smith said, as if in answer, "Just sit down here and wait for me a minute, will you, Sylvia?" moving thereupon up the steps and disappearing through the wide front door. Sylvia relapsed into her day-dreams and, motionless in a pool of sunlight, waited, quite unconscious of the passage of time.

This long reverie was at last broken by the return of Mrs. Marshall-Smith. She was not alone, but the radiant young man who walked beside her was not her brother, and nothing could have differed more from the brilliantly hard gaze which Professor Marshall habitually bent on his sister, than the soft intentness with which young Mr.

Saunders regarded the ripely beautiful woman. The dazzled expression of his eyes was one of the remembered factors of the day for Sylvia.

The two walked down the shaded steps, Sylvia watching them admiringly, the scene forever printed on her memory, and emerged into the pool of sunshine where she sat, swinging her legs from the bench. They stood there for some minutes, talking together in low tones. Sylvia, absorbed in watching the play of light on Aunt Victoria's smooth cheek, heard but a few words of what passed between them. She had a vague impression that Professor Saunders continually began sentences starting firmly with " But," and ending somehow on quite another note. She felt dimly that Aunt Victoria was less calmly passive than usual in a conversation, that it was not only the enchanting rising and falling inflections of her voice which talked, but her eyes, her arms, her whole self. Once she laid her hand for an instant on Professor Saunders' arm.

More than that Sylvia could not remember, even when she was asked later to repeat as much as she could of what she had heard. She was resolving when she was grown-up to have a ruffle of creamy lace falling away from her neck and wrists as Aunt Victoria did. She had not only forgotten Arnold's story, she had forgotten that such a boy existed. She was living in a world all made up of radiance and bloom, lace and sunshine and velvet, and bright hair and gleaming cloth and smooth voices and the smell of violets.

After a time she was aware that Professor Saunders shook hands and turned back up the steps. Aunt Victoria began to move with her slow grace along the road towards home, and Sylvia to follow, soaking herself in an impression of supreme suavity.

When, after the walk through the beech-woods, they reached the edge of the Marshall field, they saw a stiff plume of blue smoke stand up over the shack by the garden and, as they approached, heard a murmur of voices. Mrs. Marshall-Smith stopped, furled her parasol, and sur-

veyed the scene within. Her sister-in-law, enveloped in a
large blue apron, by no means fresh, sat beside a roughly
built table, peeling tomatoes, her brown stained fingers
moving with the rapidity of a prestidigitator's. Judith
stood beside her, also attacking the pile of crimson fruit,
endeavoring in vain to emulate her mother's speed. Over
the hot, rusty stove hung Arnold, red-faced and bright-
eyed, armed with a long, wooden spatula which he continually dug into the steaming contents of an enormous
white-lined kettle. As, at the arrival of the new-comers,
Mrs. Marshall's voice stopped, he looked around and
frowned impatiently at his stepmother. " She's just got
to the excitin' part," he said severely, and to the raconteur
eagerly, " 'N'*en* what? "

Mrs. Marshall looked up at her husband's sister, smiled,
and went on,—Sylvia recognized the story as one of her
own old favorites. " Well, it was very early dawn when she
had to go over to the neighbor's to borrow some medicine
for her father, who kept getting sicker all the time. As she
hurried along across the meadow towards the stile, she
kept wondering, in spite of herself, if there was any truth
in what Nat had said about having seen bear tracks near
the house the day before. When she got to the stile she
ran up the steps—and on the top one she stood still, for
there——" She made a dramatic pause and reached for
another tray of tomatoes. Arnold stopped stirring the pot
and stood motionless, his eyes fixed on the narrator, the
spatula dripping tomato-juice all along his white trousers.
" There on the other side, looking up at her, was a bear—
a big black bear."

Arnold's mouth dropped open and his eyes widened.

" My grandmother was dreadfully frightened. She was
only seventeen, and she hadn't any kind of a weapon, not
so much as a little stick with her. Her first idea was to
turn and run as fast as she could, back home. But she
remembered how sick her father was, and how much he
needed the medicine; and then besides, she used to say, all
of a sudden it made her angry, all over, to have that great

stupid animal get in her way. She always said that nothing 'got her mad up' like feeling afraid. So what do you suppose she did?"

Arnold could only shake his head silently in an ecstasy of impatience for the story to continue. Judith and Sylvia smiled at each other with the insufferable complacence of auditors who know the end by heart.

"She just pointed her finger at the bear, and she said in a loud, harsh voice: 'Shame! Shame! Shame on you! For sha-a-ame!' She'd taught district school, you know, and had had lots of practice saying that to children who had been bad. The bear looked up at her hard for a minute, then dropped his head and began to walk slowly away. Grandmother always said, 'The great lummox lumbered off into the bushes like a gawk of a boy who's been caught in mischief.' She waited just a minute and then ran like lightning along the path through the woods to the neighbors and got the medicine."

The story was evidently over, the last tomato was peeled. Mrs. Marshall rose, wiping her stained and dripping hands on her apron, and went to the stove. Arnold started as if coming out of a dream and looked about him with wondering eyes. "Well, what-d'you-think-o'-*that?*" he commented, all in one breath. "Say, Mother," he went on, looking up at her with trusting eyes, searching the quiet face, "what do you suppose *made* the bear go away? You wouldn't think a little thing like that would scare a *bear!*"

Mrs. Marshall began dipping the hot, stewed tomatoes into the glass jars ready in a big pan of boiling water on the back of the stove. The steam rose up, like a cloud, into her face, which began to turn red and to glisten with perspiration. "Oh, I don't suppose it really frightened the bear," she said moderately, refraining from the dramatic note of completeness which her husband, in spite of himself, gave to everything he touched, and adding instead the pungent, homely savor of reality, which none relished more than Sylvia and her father, incapable themselves of achieving it. " 'Most likely the bear would have gone away of his own accord anyhow. They don't attack people unless they're stirred up." Arnold bit deeply into the solidity of this unexaggerated presentation, and was silent for a moment, saying then: " Well, anyhow, she didn't *know* he'd go away! She was a sport, all right!"

" Oh yes, indeed," said Mrs. Marshall, dipping and steaming, and wiping away the perspiration, which ran down in drops to the end of her large, shapely nose. " Yes, my grandmother was a sport, all right." The acrid smell of hot, cooking tomatoes filled the shed and spread to the edge where Sylvia and her aunt stood, still a little aloof. Although it bore no resemblance to the odor of violets, it could not be called a disgusting smell: it was the sort of smell which is quite agreeable when one is very hungry. But Sylvia was not hungry at all. She stepped back involuntarily. Mrs. Marshall-Smith, on the contrary, advanced a step or so, until she stood close to her sister-in-law. " Barbara, I'd like to see you a few minutes without the children," she remarked in the neutral tone she always had for her brother's wife. " A rather unpleasant occurrence—I'm in something of a quandary."

Mrs. Marshall nodded. " All right," she agreed. " Scatter out of here, you children! Go and let out the hens, and give them some water!"

Arnold needed no second bidding, reminded by his stepmother's words of his experiences of the morning. He and Judith scampered away in a suddenly improvised race to see who would reach the chicken-house first. Sylvia went more slowly, looking back once or twice at the picture made by the two women, so dramatically contrasted— her mother, active, very upright, wrapped in a crumpled and stained apron, her dark hair bound closely about her round head, her moist, red face and steady eyes turned attentively upon the radiant creature beside her, cool and detached, leaning willow-like on the slender wand of the gold-colored parasol.

Professor Marshall chanced to be late that day in coming home for luncheon, and Aunt Victoria and Arnold had returned to the hotel without seeing him. His wife remarked that Victoria had asked her to tell him something, but, acting on her inviolable principle that nothing must interfere with the cheerful peace of mealtime, said nothing more to him until after they had finished the big plate of purple grapes from her garden, with which the meal ended.

Then Judith vanished out to the shop, where she was constructing a rabbit-house for the latest family. Sylvia took Lawrence, yawning and rubbing his eyes, but fighting desperately against his sleepiness, upstairs for his nap. When this task fell to Judith's lot it was despatched with business-like promptness, but Lawrence had early discovered a temperamental difference between his two sisters, and Sylvia was seldom allowed to leave the small bed until she had paid tribute to her ever-present desire to please, in the shape of a story or a song. On that day Buddy was more exacting than usual. Sylvia told the story of Cinderella and sang, " A Frog He Would a-Wooing Go," twice through, before the little boy's eyes began to droop. Even then, the clutch of his warm, moist fingers about her hand did not relax. When she tried to slip her fingers out of his, his eyelids fluttered open and he tightened his grasp with a wilful frown. So she sat still on the edge of his bed, waiting till he should be really asleep.

From the dining-room below her rose the sound of voices, or rather of one voice—her father's. She wondered why it sounded so angry, and then, mixed with some unintelligible phrases—" turned out on the street, in trouble—in a foreign land—Good God! " she caught Pauline's name. Oh yes, that must be the trouble. Mother was telling Father about Pauline—whatever it was she had done—and he was as mad about it as Aunt Victoria had been. If Aunt Victoria's voice had sounded like that, she didn't wonder that Arnold had hidden under the bed. If she could have moved, she, too, would have run away, although the idea that she ought to do so did not occur to her. There had been no secrets in that house. The talk had always been for all to hear who would.

But when she tried again to slip her hand away from Buddy's the little boy pulled at it hard, and half opening his eyes, said sleepily, "Sylvie stay with Buddy—Sylvie stay——" Sylvia yielded weakly, said: "Yes—sh! sh! Sister'll stay. Go to sleep, Buddy."

From below came the angry voice, quite loud now, so that she caught every queer-sounding word—"righteous indignation indeed! What else did *she* do, I'd like to know, when she wanted money. The only difference was that she was cold-blooded enough to extract a legal status from the old reprobate she accosted."

Sylvia heard her mother's voice saying coldly, "You ought to be ashamed to use such a word!" and her father retort, "It's the *only* word that expresses it! You know as well as I do that she cared no more for Ephraim Smith than for the first man she might have solicited on the street —nor so much! God! It makes me sick to look at her and think of the price she paid for her present damn Olympian serenity."

Sylvia heard her mother begin to clear off the table. There was a rattle of dishes through which her voice rose impatiently. "Oh, Elliott, why be so melodramatic always, and spoil so much good language! She did only what every girl brought up as she was, would have done. And, any-how, are you so very sure that in your heart you're not so awfully hard on her because you're envious of that very prosperity?"

He admitted, with acrimony, the justice of this thrust. "Very likely. Very likely!—everything base and mean in me, that you keep down, springs to life in me at her touch. I dare say I do envy her—I'm quite capable of that—am I not her brother, with the same——"

Mrs. Marshall said hastily: "Hush! Hush! Here's Judith. For Heaven's sake don't let the child hear you!"

For the first time the idea penetrated Sylvia's head that she ought not to have listened. Buddy was now soundly asleep: she detached her hand from his, and went soberly along the hall into her own room. She did not want to see her father just then.

A long time after, Mother called up to say that Aunt Victoria had come for her afternoon drive, and to leave Arnold. Sylvia opened the door a crack and asked, "Where's Father?"

"Oh, gone back to the University this long time," answered her mother in her usual tone. Sylvia came down the stairs slowly and took her seat in the carriage beside Aunt Victoria with none of her usual demonstrative show of pleasure.

"Don't you like my dress?" asked Aunt Victoria, as they drove away. "You don't even notice it, and I put it on 'specially to please you—you're the one discriminating critic in this town!" As Sylvia made no answer to this sally, she went on: "It's hard to get into alone, too. I had to ask the hotel chambermaid to hook it up on the shoulders."

Thus reminded of Pauline, Sylvia could have but inattentive eyes for the creation of amber silk and lace, and brown fur, which seductively clad the handsome body beside her.

Mrs. Marshall-Smith gave her favorite a penetrating look. "What's the matter with you, Sylvia?" she asked in the peremptory note which her sweet voice of many modulations could startlingly assume on occasion. Sylvia had none of Judith's instant pugnacious antagonism to any peremptory note. She answered in one imploring rush of a question, "Aunt Victoria, why should *Father* be so very mad at Pauline?"

Mrs. Marshall-Smith looked a little startled at this direct reference to the veiled storm-center of the day, but not at all displeased. "Oh, your mother told him? Was he so very angry?" she asked with a slight smile.

"Oh, dreadfully!" returned Sylvia. "I didn't *mean* to listen, but I couldn't help it. Buddy wouldn't go to sleep and Father's voice was so loud—and he got madder and madder at her." She went on with another question, "Auntie, who was Ephraim Smith?"

Aunt Victoria turned upon her in astonishment, and did not, for a moment, answer; then: "Why, that was the name of my husband, Sylvia. What has that to do with anything?"

"Why didn't Pauline like him?" asked Sylvia.

Mrs. Marshall-Smith replied with a vivacity of surprise which carried her out of her usual delicate leisure in speech. "*Pauline?* Why, she never saw him in her life! *What* are you talking about, child?"

"But, Father said—I thought—he seemed to mean——" Sylvia halted, not able to remember in her bewilderment what it had been that Father had said. In a blur of doubt and clouded perceptions she lost all definite impression of what she had heard. Evidently, as so often happened, she had grown-ups' affairs all twisted up in her mind.

Aunt Victoria was touched with kindly amusement at the little girl's face of perplexity, and told her, dismissing the subject: "Never mind, dear, you evidently misunderstood something. But I wonder what your father could have said to give you such a funny idea."

Sylvia gave it up, shaking her head. They turned into the main street of La Chance, and Aunt Victoria directed the coachman to drive them to "the" drug store of town, and offered Sylvia her choice of any soda water confection she might select. This completed the "about-face" of the mobile little mind. After several moments of blissful anguish of indecision, Sylvia decided on a peach ice-cream soda, and thereafter was nothing but sense of taste as she ecstatically drew through a straw the syrupy, foamy draught of nectar. She took small sips at a time and held them in the back of her mouth till every minute bubble of gas had rendered up its delicious prickle to her tongue. Her consciousness was filled to its uttermost limits with a voluptuous sense of present physical delight.

And yet it was precisely at this moment that from her subconscious mind, retracing with unaided travail a half-forgotten clue, there sprang into her memory a complete phrase of what her father had said. She gave one more suck to the straw and laid it aside for a moment to say in quite a comfortable accent to her aunt: "Oh yes, now I remember. He said she didn't care for him any more than for the first man she might have solicited in the street." For an instant the words came back as clearly as though they had just been uttered, and she repeated them fluently, returning thereupon at once to the charms of the tall, foam-filled frosted glass.

Evidently Aunt Victoria did not follow this sudden change of subject, for she asked blankly, "*Who? Who didn't care for who?*"

"Why, I supposed, Pauline for Ephraim Smith. It was that that made Father so mad," explained Sylvia, sucking dreamily, her eyes on the little maelstrom created in the foaming liquid by the straw, forgetting everything else. The luxurious leisure in which she consumed her potation made it last a long time, and it was not until her suction made only a sterile rattling in the straw that she looked up at her aunt to thank her.

Mrs. Marshall-Smith's face was averted and she did not turn it back as she said, "Just run along into the shop and leave your glass, Sylvia—here is the money."

After Sylvia took her seat again in the carriage, the coachman turned the horse's head back up the Main Street. "Aren't you going to the campus?" asked Sylvia in surprise.

"No, we are going to the hotel," said Aunt Victoria. She spoke quietly, and seemed to look as usual, but Sylvia's inner barometer fell fast with a conviction of a change in the emotional atmosphere. She sat as still as possible, and only once glanced up timidly at her aunt's face. There was no answering glance. Aunt Victoria gazed straight in front of her. Her face looked as it did when it was being massaged—all smooth and empty. There was, however, one change. For the first time that day, she looked a little pale.

As the carriage stopped in front of the onyx-lined, palm-decorated, plate-glass-mirrored "entrance hall" of the expensive hotel, Aunt Victoria descended, motioning to Sylvia not to follow her. "I haven't time to drive any more this afternoon," she said. "Peter will take you home. And have him bring Arnold back at once." She turned away and, as Sylvia sat watching her, entered the squirrel-cage revolving door of glass, which a little boy in livery spun about for her.

But after she was inside the entrance hall, she signified to him that she had forgotten something, and came immediately out again. What she had forgotten surprised Sylvia as much as it touched her. Aunt Victoria came rapidly to the side of the carriage and put out her arms. "Come here, dear," she said in a voice Sylvia had never heard her use. It trembled a little, and broke. With her quick responsiveness, Sylvia sprang into the outstretched arms, overcome by the other's emotion. She hid her face against the soft, perfumed laces and silk, and heard from beneath them the painful throb of a quickly beating heart.

Mrs. Marshall-Smith held her niece for a long moment and then turned the quivering little face up to her own grave eyes, in which Sylvia, for all her inexperience, read a real suffering. Aunt Victoria looked as though somebody were hurting her—hurting her awfully—Sylvia pressed her cheek hard against her aunt's, and Mrs. Marshall-Smith felt, soft and warm and ardent on her lips, the indescribably fresh kiss of a child's mouth. "Oh, little Sylvia!" she cried, in that new, strange, uncertain voice which trembled and broke, "Oh, little Sylvia!" She seemed to be about to say something more, said in fact in a half-whisper, "I hope—I hope——" but then shook her head, kissed Sylvia gently, put her back in the carriage, and again disappeared through the revolving door.

This time she did not turn back. She did not even look back. After a moment's wait, Peter gathered up the reins and Sylvia, vaguely uneasy, and much moved, drove home in a solitary state, which she forgot to enjoy.

The next morning there was no arrival, even tardy, of the visitors from the hotel. Instead came a letter, breaking the startling news that Aunt Victoria had been called unexpectedly to the East, and had left on the midnight train, taking Arnold with her, of course. Judith burst into angry expressions of wrath over the incompleteness of the cave which she and Arnold had been excavating together. The next day was the beginning of school, she reminded her auditors, and she'd have no time to get it done! Never! She characterized Aunt Victoria as a mean old thing, an epithet for which she was not reproved, her mother sitting quite absent and absorbed in the letter. She read it over twice, with a very puzzled air, which gave an odd look to her usually crystal-clear countenance. She asked her husband one question as he went out of the door. "You didn't see Victoria yesterday—or say anything to her?" to which he answered, with apparently uncalled-for heat, "I did *not!* I thought it rather more to the purpose to try to look up Pauline."

Mrs. Marshall sprang up and approached him with an anxious face. He shook his head: "Too late. Disappeared. No trace."

She sat down again, looking sad and stern.

Professor Marshall put on his hat with violence, and went away.

When he came home to luncheon there was a fresh sensation, and again a disagreeable one. He brought the astounding news that, at the very beginning of the semester's work, he had been deserted by his most valuable assistant, and abandoned, apparently forever, by his most-loved disciple. Saunders had left word, a mere laconic note, that he had accepted the position left vacant by the dismissal of Arnold's tutor, and had entered at once upon the duties of his new position.

Professor Marshall detailed this information in a hard, level voice, and without further comment handed his wife Saunders' note. She read it rapidly, this time with no perplexity, and laid it down, saying to her husband, briefly, " Will you kindly remember that the children are here? "

Judith looked at Sylvia in astonishment, this being the first time that that well-worn phrase, so familiar to most children, had ever been heard in the Marshall house. Why shouldn't Father remember they were there? Couldn't he *see* them? Judith almost found the idea funny enough to laugh at, although she had not at all in general Sylvia's helpless response to the ridiculous. Sylvia did not laugh now. She looked anxiously at her father's face, and was relieved when he only answered her mother's exhortation by saying in a low tone: " Oh, *I* have nothing to say. It's beyond words! "

Luncheon went on as usual, with much chatter among the children. Some time later—in the midst of a long story from Lawrence, Mrs. Marshall herself brought up the subject again. Buddy was beginning to struggle with the narrative form of self-expression, and to trip his tongue desperately over the tenses. He had just said, " And the rabbit *was* naughty, didn't he was? " when his mother exclaimed, addressing her husband's grim face, " Good Heavens, don't take it so hard, Elliott."

He raised an eyebrow, but did not look up from the pear he was eating. " To be responsible, as I feel I am, for the pitching into a *cul-de-sac* of the most promising young——"

His wife broke in, " *Responsible!* How in the world are *you* responsible! " she added quickly, as if at random, to prevent the reply which her husband was evidently about to cast at her. " Besides, how do *you* know?—one never knows how things will turn out—she may—she may marry him, and he may have a life which will give him more leisure for investigation than if——"

Professor Marshall wiped his lips violently on his napkin and stood up. " Nothing would induce her to marry him—or any one else. She's extracted from marriage all she wants of it. No, she'll just keep him trailing along, in an ambiguous position, sickened and tantalized and fevered, till all the temper is drawn out of him—and then he'll be dropped."

He turned away with an impatient fling of his head. His wife stood up now and looked at him anxiously. "Go play us something on the piano," she urged. This was not a common exhortation from her. She cared very little for music, and with her usual honesty she showed, as a rule, a very passive attitude towards it.

Professor Marshall glanced at her with a flash of anger. "Sometimes you count too much on my childishness, Barbara," he said resentfully, and went out of the door without further words.

Decidedly the discomposing effect of Aunt Victoria's visit lasted even after she had gone away. But the next day was the beginning of the school term, the busy, regular routine was taken up, Sylvia was promoted to the 5A grade, and at home Father let her begin to learn the Pilgrim's Chorus, from Tannhäuser.

Life for the eager little girl moved quickly forward at its usual brisk pace, through several years to come.

CHAPTER VII

"WE HOLD THESE TRUTHS TO BE SELF-EVIDENT . . ."

THE public school to which the Marshall children went as soon as they were old enough was like any one of ten thousand public schools—a large, square, many-windowed, extravagantly ugly building, once red brick, but long ago darkened almost to black by soft-coal smoke. About it, shaded by three or four big cottonwood-trees, was an inclosed space of perhaps two acres of ground, beaten perfectly smooth by hundreds of trampling little feet, a hard, bare earthen floor, so entirely subdued to its fate that even in the long summer vacation no spear of grass could penetrate its crust to remind it that it was made of common stuff with fields and meadows.

School began at nine o'clock in the morning and, as a rule, three-fourths of the children had passed through the front gate twenty or thirty minutes earlier. Nobody knew why it should be considered such a hideous crime to be "tardy," but the fact was that not the most reckless and insubordinate of the older boys cared to risk it. Any one of the four hundred children in any public school in the city preferred infinitely to be absent a day than to have the ghastly experience of walking through deserted streets (that is, with no children on them), across the empty play-ground frighteningly unlike itself, into the long, desolate halls which, walk as cat-like as one might, resounded to the guilty footsteps with accusing echoes. And then the narrow cloakroom, haunted with limp, hanging coats and caps and hats, and finally the entry into the schoolroom, seated rank on rank with priggishly complacent schoolmates, looking up from their books with unfriendly eyes of blame at the figure of the late-comer.

All over that section of La Chance, during the hour between half-past seven and half-past eight in the morning, the families of school children were undergoing a most rigorous discipline in regularity and promptness. No child was too small or too timid to refrain from embittering his mother's life with clamorous upbraidings if breakfast were late, or his school-outfit of clothes were not ready to the last button, so that he could join the procession of schoolward-bound children, already streaming past his door at a quarter past eight. The most easy-going and self-indulgent mother learned to have at least one meal a day on time; and the children themselves during those eight years of their lives had imbedded in the tissue of their brains and the marrow of their bones that unrebelling habit of bending their backs daily to a regular burden of work not selected by themselves—which, according to one's point of view, is either the bane or the salvation of our modern industrial society.

The region where the school stood was inhabited, for the most part, by American families or German and Irish ones so long established as to be virtually American; a condition which was then not infrequent in moderate-sized towns of the Middle West and which is still by no means unknown there. The class-rolls were full of Taylors and Allens and Robinsons and Jacksons and Websters and Rawsons and Putnams, with a scattering of Morrisseys and Crimminses and O'Hearns, and some Schultzes and Brubackers and Helmeyers. There was not a Jew in the school, because there were almost none in that quarter of town, and, for quite another reason, not a single negro child. There were plenty of them in the immediate neighborhood, swarming around the collection of huts and shanties near the railroad tracks given over to negroes, and known as Flytown. But they had their own school, which looked externally quite like all the others in town, and their playground, beaten bare like that of the Washington Street

School, was filled with laughing, shouting children, ranging from shoe-black through coffee-color to those occasional tragic ones with white skin and blue eyes, but with the telltale kink in the fair hair and the bluish half-moon at the base of the finger-nails.

The four hundred children in the Washington Street School were, therefore, a mass more homogeneous than alarmists would have us believe it possible to find in this country. They were, for all practical purposes, all American, and they were all roughly of one class. Their families were neither rich nor poor (at least so far as the children's standards went). Their fathers were grocers, small clerks, merchants, two or three were truck-farmers, plumbers, carpenters, accountants, employees of various big businesses in town.

It was into this undistinguished and plebeian mediocrity that the Marshall children were introduced when they began going to school.

The interior of the school-building resembled the outside in being precisely like that of ten thousand other graded schools in this country. The halls were long and dark and dusty, and because the building had been put up under contract at a period when public contract-work was not so scrupulously honest as it notably is in our present cleanly muck-raked era, the steps of the badly built staircase creaked and groaned and sagged and gave forth clouds of dust under the weight of the myriads of little feet which climbed up and down those steep ascents every day. Everything was of wood. The interior looked like the realized dream of a professional incendiary.

The classrooms were high and well-lighted, with many large windows, never either very clean or very dirty, which let in a flood of our uncompromisingly brilliant American daylight upon the rows of little seats and desks screwed, like those of an ocean liner, immovably to the floor, as though at any moment the building was likely to embark upon a cruise in stormy waters.

Outwardly the rows of clean-faced, comfortably dressed,

well-shod American children, sitting in chairs, bore
no resemblance to shaven-headed, barefooted little Ara-
bian students, squatting on the floor, gabbling loud un-
comprehended texts from the Koran; but the sight of
Sylvia's companions bending over their school-books with
glazed, vacant eyes, rocking back and forth as a rhythmical
aid to memorizing, their lips moving silently as they repeated over and over, gabblingly, the phrases of the
printed page, might have inclined a hypothetical visitor
from Mars to share the bewildered amusement of the
American visitors to Moslem schools. Sylvia rocked and
twisted a favorite button, gabbled silently, and recited
fluently with the rest, being what was known as an apt
and satisfactory pupil. In company with the other children she thus learned to say, in answer to questions, that
seven times seven is forty-nine; that the climate of Brazil
is hot and moist; that the capital of Arkansas is Little
Rock; and that "through" is spelled with three misleading
and superfluous letters.

What she really learned was, as with her mates, another
matter—for, of course, those devouringly active little minds
did not spend six hours a day in school without learning
something incessantly. The few rags and tatters of book-
information they acquired were but the merest fringes on
the great garment of learning acquired by these public-
school children, which was to wrap them about all their
lives. What they learned during those eight years of sitting still and not whispering had nothing to do with the
books in their desks or the lore in their teachers' brains.
The great impression stamped upon the wax of their
minds, which became iron in after years, was democracy—
a crude, distorted, wavering image of democracy, like
every image an ideal in this imperfect world, but in its
essence a reflection of the ideal of their country. No
European could have conceived how literally it was true
that the birth or wealth or social position of a child made
no difference in the estimation of his mates. There were
no exceptions to the custom of considering the individual

on his own merits. These merits were often queerly enough imagined, a faculty for standing on his head redounding as much, or more, to a boy's credit as the utmost brilliance in recitation, or generosity of temperament, but at least he was valued for something he himself could do, and not for any fortuitous incidents of birth and fortune.

Furthermore there lay back of these four hundred children, who shaped their world to this rough-and-ready imitation of democracy, their families, not so intimately known to each other, of course, as the children themselves, but still by no means unknown in their general characteristics; four hundred American families who were, on the whole, industrious, law-abiding, who loved their children, who were quite tasteless in matters of art, and quite sound though narrow in matters of morals, utterly mediocre in intelligence and information, with no breadth of outlook in any direction; but who somehow lived their lives and faced and conquered all the incredible vicissitudes of that Great Adventure, with an unconscious, cheerful fortitude which many an acuter mind might have envied them.

It is possible that the personal knowledge of these four hundred enduring family lives was, perhaps, the most important mental ballast taken on by the children of the community during their eight years' cruise at school. Certainly it was the most important for the sensitive, complicated, impressionable little Sylvia Marshall, with her latent distaste for whatever lacked distinction and external grace, and her passion for sophistication and elegance, which was to spring into such fierce life with the beginning of her adolescence. She might renounce, as utterly as she pleased, the associates of her early youth, but the knowledge of their existence, the acquaintance with their deep humanity, the knowledge that they found life sweet and worth living, all this was to be a part of the tissue of her brain forever, and was to add one to the conflicting elements which battled within her for the mastery during all the clouded, stormy radiance of her youth.

The families which supplied the Washington Street School being quite stationary in their self-owned houses, few new pupils entered during the school-year. There was, consequently, quite a sensation on the day in the middle of March when the two Fingál girls entered, Camilla in the "Fifth A" grade, where Sylvia was, and Cécile in the third grade, in the next seat to Judith's. The girls themselves were so different from other children in school that their arrival would have excited interest even at the beginning of the school-year. Coming, as they did, at a time when everybody knew by heart every detail of every one else's appearance from hair-ribbon to shoes, these two beautiful exotics, in their rich, plain, mourning dresses were vastly stared at. Sylvia's impressionable eyes were especially struck by the air of race and breeding of the newcomer in her class. Everything about the other child, from her heavy, black hair, patrician nose, and large dark eyes to her exquisitely formed hands, white and well-cared-for, seemed to Sylvia perfection itself.

During recess she advanced to the new-comer, saying, with a bright smile: "Aren't you thirsty? Don't you want me to show you where the pump is?" She put out her hand as she spoke and took the slim white fingers in her own rough little hand, leading her new schoolmate along in silence, looking at her with an open interest.

She had confidently expected amicable responsiveness in the other little girl, because her experience had been that her own frank friendliness nearly always was reflected back to her from others; but she had not expected, or indeed ever seen, such an ardent look of gratitude as burned in the other's eyes. She stopped, startled, uncomprehending, as though her companion had said something unintelligible, and felt the slim fingers in her hand close about her own in a tight clasp. "You are so very kind to show me this pump," breathed Camilla shyly. The faint flavor of a foreign accent which, to Sylvia's ear, hung about these words, was the final touch of fascination for her. That instant she decided in her impetuous, enthusiastic heart that

Camilla was the most beautiful, sweetest, best-dressed, loveliest creature she had ever seen, or would ever see in her life; and she bent her back joyfully in the service of her ideal. She would not allow Camilla to pump for herself, but flew to the handle with such energy that the white water gushed out in a flood, overflowing Camilla's cup, spattering over on her fingers, and sparkling on the sheer white of her hemstitched cuffs. This made them both laugh, the delicious silly laugh of childhood.

Already they seemed like friends. " How do you pronounce your name ? " Sylvia asked familiarly.

" Cam-eela Fingál," said the other, looking up from her cup, her upper lip red and moist. She accented the surname on the last syllable.

" What a perfectly lovely name ! " cried Sylvia. " Mine is Sylvia Marshall."

" That's a pretty name too," said Camilla, smiling. She spoke less timidly now, but her fawn-like eyes still kept their curious expression, half apprehension, half hope.

" How old are you ? " asked Sylvia.

" Eleven, last November."

" Why, my birthday is in November, and I was eleven too ! " cried Sylvia. " I thought you must be older—you're so tall."

Camilla looked down and said nothing.

Sylvia went on : " I'm crazy about the way you do your hair, in those twists over your ears. When I was studying my spelling lesson, I was trying to figure out how you do it."

" Oh, I don't do it. Mattice does it for us—for Cécile and me—Cécile's my sister. She's in the third grade."

" Why, I have a sister in the third grade too ! " exclaimed Sylvia, much struck by this second propitious coincidence. " Her name is Judith and she's a darling. Wouldn't it be nice if she and Cécile should be good friends *too !* " She put her arm about her new comrade's waist, convinced that they were now intimates of long standing. They ran together to take their places at the sound of the bell; all during the rest of the morning session she smiled radiantly at the new-comer whenever their eyes met.

She planned to walk part way home with her at noon, but she was detained for a moment by the teacher, and when she reached the front gate, where Judith was waiting for her, Camilla was nowhere in sight. Judith explained with some disfavor that a surrey had been waiting for the Fingál girls and they had been driven away.

Sylvia fell into a rhapsody over her new acquaintance and found to her surprise (it was always a surprise to Sylvia that Judith's tastes and judgments so frequently differed from hers) that Judith by no means shared her enthusiasm. She admitted, but as if it were a matter of no importance, that both Camilla and Cécile were pretty enough, but she declared roundly that Cécile was a little sneak who had set out from the first to be " Teacher's pet." This title, in the sturdy democracy of the public schools, means about what " sycophantic lickspittle " means in the vocabulary of adults, and carries with it a crushing weight of odium which can hardly ever be lived down.

" *Judith,* what makes you think so? " cried Sylvia, horri- fied at the epithet.

" The way she looks at Teacher—she never takes her eyes off her, and just jumps to do whatever Teacher says. And then she looks at everybody so kind o' scared—'s'if she thought she was goin' to be hit over the head every minute and was so thankful to everybody for not doing it. Makes me feel just *like* doin' it! " declared Judith, the Anglo- Saxon.

Sylvia recognized a scornful version of the appealing expression which she had found so touching in Camilla.

" Why, I think it's sweet of them to look so! When they're so awfully pretty, and have such good clothes—and a carriage—and everything! They might be as stuck-up as *any*thing! I think it's just *nice* for them to be so sweet! " persisted Sylvia.

" I don't call it bein' sweet," said Judith, " to watch Teacher every minute and smile all over your face if she

looks at you and hold on to her hand when she's talkin' to
you! It's silly!"

They argued all the way home, and the lunch hour was
filled with appeals to their parents to take sides. Professor
and Mrs. Marshall, always ready, although occasionally
somewhat absent, listeners to school news, professed themselves really interested in these new scholars and quite
perplexed by the phenomenon of two beautiful dark-eyed
children, called Camilla and Cécile Fingál. Judith refused
to twist her tongue to pronounce the last syllable accented,
and her version of the name made it sound Celtic. "Perhaps their father is Irish and the mother Italian or Spanish," suggested Professor Marshall.

Sylvia was delighted with this hypothesis, and cried out
enthusiastically, "Oh yes—Camilla *looks* Italian—like an
Italian princess!"

Judith assumed an incredulous and derisive expression
and remained silent, an achievement of self-control which
Sylvia was never able to emulate.

The Fingál girls continued to occupy a large space in
Sylvia's thoughts and hours, and before long they held a
unique position in the opinion of the school, which was
divided about evenly between the extremes represented by
Sylvia and Judith. The various accomplishments of the
new-comers were ground both for uneasy admiration and
suspicion. They could sing like birds, and, what seemed
like witchcraft to the unmusical little Americans about
them, they could sing in harmony as easily as they could
carry an air. And they recited with fire, ease, and evident
enjoyment, instead of with the show of groaning, unwilling
submission to authority which it was etiquette in the Washington Street School to show before beginning to "speak
a piece."

They were good at their books too, and altogether, with
their quick docility, picturesqueness, and eagerness to please,
were the delight of their teachers. In the fifth grade,
Sylvia's example of intimate, admiring friendship definitely
threw popular favor on the side of Camilla, who made every

effort to disarm the hostility aroused by her too-numerous gifts of nature. She was ready to be friends with the poorest and dullest of the girls, never asked the important rôles in any games, hid rather than put forward the high marks she received in her studies, and was lavish with her invitations to her schoolmates to visit her at home.

The outside of this house, which Mr. Fingál had rented a month or so before when they first moved to La Chance, was like any one of many in the region; but the interior differed notably from those to which the other children were accustomed. For one thing there was no "lady of the house," Mrs. Fingál having died a short time before. Camilla and Cécile could do exactly as they pleased, and they gave the freedom of the house and its contents lavishly to their little friends. In the kitchen was an enormous old negro woman, always good-natured, always smelling of whiskey. She kept on hand a supply of the most meltingly delicious cakes and cookies, and her liberal motto, " Heah, chile, put yo' han' in the cookie-jah and draw out what you lights on!" was always flourished in the faces of the schoolmates of the two daughters of the house.

In the rest of the house, filled with dark, heavy, dimly shining furniture, reigned Mattice, another old negro woman, but, unlike the jolly, fat cook, yellow and shriveled and silent. She it was who arrayed Camille and Cécile with such unerring taste, and her skilful old hands brushed and dressed their long black hair in artful twists and coils.

Here, against their own background, the two girls seemed more at their ease and showed more spontaneity than at school. They were fond of "dressing up" and of organizing impromptu dramatizations of the stories of familiar books, and showed a native ability for acting which explained their success in recitations. Once when the fun was very rollicking, Camilla brought out from a closet a banjo and, thrumming on its strings with skilful fingers, played a tingling accompaniment to one of her songs. The other little girls were delighted and clamored for more, but she put it away quickly with almost a frown on her sweet face, and for once in her life did not yield to their demands.

"Well, I think more of her for that!" remarked Judith, when this incident was repeated to her by Sylvia, who cried out, "Why, Judy, how *hateful* you are about poor Camilla!"

Nothing was learned about the past history of the Fingáls beyond the fact, dropped once by the cook, that they had lived in Louisiana before coming to La Chance, but there were rumors, based on nothing at all, and everywhere credited, that their mother had been a Spanish-American heiress, disinherited by her family for marrying a Protestant. Such a romantic and picturesque element had never before entered the lives of the Washington Street schoolchildren. Once a bold and insensitive little girl, itching to know more of this story-book history, had broken the silence about Mrs. Fingál and had asked Camilla bluntly, "Say, who *was* your mother, anyway?" The question had been received by Camilla with whitening lips and a desperate silence—ended by a sudden loud burst of sobs, which tore Sylvia's heart. "You mean, horrid thing!" she cried to the inquisitor. "Her mother isn't dead a year yet! Camilla can't bear to talk about her!"

Once in a great while Mr. Fingál was visible,—a bald, middle-aged man with a white, sad face, and eyes that never smiled, although his lips often did when he saw the clusters of admiring children hanging about his daughters.

Judith held aloof from these gatherings at the Fingál house, her prejudice against the girls never weakening, although Cécile as well as Camilla had won over almost all the other girls of her grade. Judith showed the self-contained indifference which it was her habit to feel about matters which did not deeply stir her, and made no further attempts to analyze or even to voice her animosity beyond saying once, when asked to go with them on a drive, that she didn't like their "meechin' ways,"—a vigorous New England phrase which she had picked up from her mother.

About a month after the Fingál girls entered school, the project of a picnic took form among the girls of the Fifth A grade. One of them had an uncle who lived three or four miles from town on a farm which was passed by the Inter-urban trolley line, and he had sent word that the children could, if they liked, picnic in his maple woods, which over-hung the brown waters of the Piquota river. There was to be no recess that day in Five A, and the grade was to be dismissed half an hour earlier than usual, so that the girls could go out on the trolley in time to get the supper ready. The farmer was to bring them back by moonlight in his hay-wagon.

The prospect seemed ideal. Five A hummed with ex-citement and importance as the various provisions were allotted to the different girls and the plans talked over. Sylvia was to bring bananas enough for the crowd; one of the German-American girls, whose father kept a grocery-store, promised pickles and olives; three or four together were to make the sandwiches, and Camilla Fingál was to bring along a big bag of the famous rich and be-raisined cookies that lived in the " cookie-jah." Sylvia, who always enjoyed prodigiously both in anticipation and in reality any social event, could scarcely contain herself as the time drew near with every prospect of fair weather.

The morning of the day was clear and fine, a perfect ex-ample of early spring, with silvery pearls showing on the tips of the red-twig osiers, and pussy-willows gleam-ing gray along the margins of swampy places. Sylvia and Judith felt themselves one with this upward surge of new life. They ran to school together, laughing aloud for no reason, racing and skipping like a couple of spring lambs, their minds and hearts as crystal-clear of any shadow as the pale-blue, smiling sky above them. The rising sap beat in their young bodies as well as in the beech-trees through which they scampered, whirling their school-books at the end of their straps, and shouting aloud to hear the squirrel's petulant, chattering answer.

When they came within sight and hearing of the school-house, their practised ears detected (although with no hint of foreboding) that something unusual had happened. The children were not running about and screaming, but standing with their heads close together, talking, and talking, and talking. As Judith and Sylvia came near, several ran to meet them, hurling out at them like a hard-flung stone: "Say—what d'ye think? Those Fingál girls are niggers!"

To the end of her life, Sylvia would never forget the rending shock of disillusion brought her by these blunt words. She did not dream of disbelieving them, or of underestimating their significance. A thousand confirmatory details leaped into her mind: the rich, sweet voices—the dramatic ability—the banjo—the deprecatory air of timidity—the self-conscious unwillingness to take the leading position to which their talents and beauty gave them a right. Yes, of course it was true! In the space of a heartbeat, all her romantic Italian imaginings vanished. She continued to walk forward mechanically, in an utter confusion of mind.

She heard Judith asking in an astonished voice, "Why, what makes you think so?" and she listened with a tortured attention to the statement vouchsafed in an excited chorus by a great many shrill little voices that the Fingáls' old cook had taken a little too much whiskey for once and had fallen to babbling at the grocery-store before a highly entertained audience of neighbors, about the endless peregrinations of the Fingál family in search of a locality where the blood of the children would not be suspected—"an' theah motheh, fo' all heh good looks, second cousin to Mattice!" she had tittered foolishly, gathering up her basket and rolling tipsily out of the store.

"*Well*—" said Judith, "did you ever!" She was evidently as much amazed as her sister, but Sylvia felt with a sinking of the heart that what seemed to her the real significance of the news had escaped Judith.

The Five A girls came trooping up to Sylvia.—"Of course we can't have Camilla at the picnic."—"My uncle wouldn't want a *nigger* there."—"We'll have to tell her she can't come."

Sylvia heard from the other groups of children about them snatches of similar talk.—"Anybody might ha' known

it—singin' the way they do—just like niggers' voices."—
"They'll have to go to the *nigger* school now."—"Huh!
puttin' on airs with their carriage and their black dresses—
nothin' but niggers!" The air seemed full of that word.
Sylvia sickened and quailed.

Not so Judith! It had taken her a moment to understand
the way in which the news was being received. When she
did, she turned very pale, and broke out into a storm of
anger. She stuttered and halted as she always did when
overmastered by feeling, but her words were molten. She
ignored the tacit separation between children of different
grades and, though but a third-grader, threw herself passionately among the girls who were talking of the picnic,
clawing at their arms, forcing her way to the center, a raging, white-faced, hot-eyed little thunderbolt. "You're the
meanest low-down things I ever heard of!" she told the
astonished older girls, fairly spitting at them in her fury.
"You—you go and s-sponge off the Fingáls for c-c-cakes
and rides and s-s-soda water—and you think they're too
l-l-lovely for w-words—and you t-t-try to do your hair just
the way C-C-Camilla does. They aren't any different to-day
f-f-from what they were yesterday—are they? You make
me sick—you m-m-make m-m-me——"

The big bell rang out its single deep brazen note for the
formation of lines, and the habit of unquestioning, instant
obedience to its voice sent the children all scurrying to their
places, from which they marched forward to their respective
classrooms in their usual convict silence. Just as the line
ahead was disappearing into the open door, the well-kept,
shining surrey drove up in haste and Camilla and Cécile,
dazzling in fresh white dresses and white hair ribbons, ran
to their places. Evidently they had heard nothing. Camilla
turned and smiled brightly at her friend as she stepped
along in front of her.

Sylvia experienced another giddy reaction of feeling. Up
to that moment, she had felt nothing but shocked and intensely self-centered horror at the disagreeableness of what
had happened, and a wild desire to run away to some quiet

spot where she would not have to think about it, where it could not make her unhappy, where her heart would stop beating so furiously. What had she ever done to have such a horrid thing happen in her world! She had been as much repelled by Judith's foaming violence as by any other element of the situation. If she could only get away! Every sensitive nerve in her, tuned to a graceful and comely order of life, was rasped to anguish by the ugliness of it all. Up to the moment Camilla came running to her place —this had been the dominant impulse in the extreme confusion of Sylvia's mind.

But at the sight of Camilla she felt bursting up through this confusion of mind, and fiercely attacking her instinct of self-preservation, a new force, unsuspected, terribly alive— sympathy with Camilla—Camilla, with her dog-like, timid, loving eyes—Camilla, who had done nothing to deserve unhappiness except to be born—Camilla, always uneasy with tragic consciousness of the sword over her head, and now smiling brightly with tragic unconsciousness that it was about to fall. Sylvia's heart swelled almost unendurably. She was feeling, for the first time in her life consciously, the two natures under her skin, and this, their first open struggle for the mastery of her, was like a knife in her side.

She sat during the morning session, her eyes on the clock, fearing miserably the moment of dismissal at noon, when she must take some action—she who only longed to run away from discord and dwell in peace. Her mind swung, pendulum-like, from one extreme of feeling to another. Every time that Camilla smiled at her across the heads of the other children, sullenly oblivious of their former favorite, Sylvia turned sick with shame and pity. But when her eyes rested on the hard, hostile faces which made up her world, the world she had to live in, the world which had been so full of sweet and innocent happiness for her, the world which would now be ranged with her or against her according to her decision at noon, she was overcome by a panic at the very idea of throwing her single self against this many-headed tyrant. With an unspeakable terror she longed to feel the safe walls of conformity about her. There was a battle with drawn swords in the heart of the little girl trying blindly to see where the *n* came in "pneumonia."

The clock crept on, past eleven, towards twelve. Sylvia had come to no decision. She could come to no decision! She felt herself consciously to be unable to cope with the crisis. She was too small, too weak, too shrinking, to make herself iron, and resist an overwhelming force.

It was five minutes of twelve. The order was given to put away books and pencils in the desks. Sylvia's hands trembled so that she could hardly close the lid.

"Turn!" said the teacher, in her tired, mechanical voice. The children turned their stubbed-toed shoes out into the aisle, their eyes menacingly on Camilla.

"Rise!" Like a covey of partridge, they all stood up, stretching, twisting their bodies, stiff and torpid after the long hours of immobility.

"Pass!" Clattering feet all over the building began moving along the aisles and out towards the cloakrooms. Every one seized his own wraps with a practised snatch, and passed on, still in line, over the dusty wooden floors of the hall, down the ill-built, resounding stairs, out to the play-ground—out to Sylvia's ordeal.

As she came out blinkingly into the strong spring sunlight, she still had reached no decision. Her impulse was to run, as fast as she could, out to the gate and down the street—home! But another impulse held her back. The lines were breaking up. Camilla was turning about with a smile to speak to her. Malevolent eyes were fixed on them from all sides. Sylvia felt her indecision mount in a cloud about her, like blinding, scalding steam.

And then, there before her, stood Judith, her proud dark little face set in an angry scowl, her arm about Cécile Fingál's neck.

Sylvia never could think what she would have done if Judith had not been there; but then, Judith was one of the formative elements of her life—as much as was the food she ate or the thoughts she had. What she did was to turn as quickly and unhesitatingly as though she had always meant to do it, put her arm through Camilla's and draw her rapidly towards the gate where the surrey waited. Judith and Cécile followed. The crowds of astonished, and for the moment silenced, children fell back before them.

Once she had taken her action, Sylvia saw that it was the only one possible. But she was upheld by none of the traditional pride in a righteous action, nor by a raging single-mindedness like Judith's, who stalked along, her little fists clenched, frowning blackly to right and left on the other children, evidently far more angry with them than sympathetic for Cécile. Sylvia did not feel angry with any one. She was simply more acutely miserable than she had ever dreamed possible. The distance to the surrey seemed endless to her.

Her sudden rush had taken Camilla so completely by surprise that not until they were at the gate did she catch her breath to ask laughingly: "What in the world's the *matter* with you, Sylvia? You act so queer!"

Sylvia did not answer, every nerve bent on getting Camilla into safety, but a little red-headed boy from the second grade, who could scarcely talk plainly, burst out chantingly, pointing his dirty forefinger at Camilla:

> "Nigger, nigger, never die,
> Black face and shiny eye,
> Curly hair and curly toes—
> *That's* the way the nigger goes!"

There was a loud laugh from the assembled children.

Camilla wavered as though she had been struck. Her lovely face turned ashy-gray, and she looked at Sylvia with the eyes of one dying.

From the deepest of her nature, Sylvia responded to that look. She forgot the crowd,—boldly, unafraid, beside herself with pity, she flung her arms about her friend's neck, hiding the white face on her shoulder. Judith ran up, blazing with rage, and pulled at Camilla's arm. "Don't give in! Don't give in!" she screamed. "Don't cry! Don't let 'em see you care! Sass 'em back, why don't you? Hit that little boy over the head! Sass them back, why don't you?"

But Camilla only shook her head vehemently and shrank away into the carriage, little Cécile stumbling after, the silent tears streaming down her face. The two clasped each other, and the surrey drove quickly away, leaving the Marshall girls standing on the curb.

Judith turned around and faced the crowds of enemies back of them. "Nasty old things!" she cried, sticking out her tongue at them. She was answered by a yell, at which she made another face and walked away, pulling Sylvia with her. For a few steps they were followed by some small boys who yelled in chorus:

> "Judith's mad and I'm glad,
> And I know what'll please her:
> A bottle of wine to make her shine,
> And two little niggers to squeeze her!"

They were beginning this immemorially old chant over again when Judith turned and ran back towards them with a white, terrible face of wrath. At the sight they scattered like scared chickens.

Judith was so angry that she was shivering all over her small body, and she kept repeating at intervals, in a suffocated voice: "Nasty old things! Just wait till I tell my father and mother!"

As they passed under the beech-trees, it seemed to Sylvia a physical impossibility that only that morning they had raced and scampered along, whirling their school-books and laughing.

They ran into the house, calling for their parents in excited voices, and pouring out incoherent exclamations. Sylvia cried a little at the comforting sight of her mother's face and was taken up on Mrs. Marshall's lap and closely held. Judith never cried; she had not cried even when she ran the sewing-machine needle through her thumb; but when infuriated she could not talk, her stammering growing so pronounced that she could not get out a word, and it was Sylvia who told the facts. She was astonished to find them so few and so quickly stated, having been under the impression that something of intense and painful excitement had been happening every moment of the morning.

But the experience of her parents supplied the tragic background of strange, passionate prejudice which Sylvia could not phrase, and which gave its sinister meaning to her briefly told story: "——and so Judith and I walked with them out to the gate, and then that little Jimmy Cohalan yelled out, ' nigger—nigger '—*you* know——"

Judith broke in, her nostrils distended, " And they never sassed back, or hit anybody or anything—just crumpled up and cried! "

Sylvia was aghast with bewilderment. " Why, I thought you were on their side! "

" Well, I *am!* " asserted Judith, beginning to stammer again. " But I don't have to *like* 'em any better, do I— because I get mad when a l-l-lot of mean, n-nasty girls that have b-b-b-been s-s-spongin' off——" She stopped, balked by her infirmity, and appealed to her parents with a silent look of fury.

" What *shall* we do, Mother? " asked Sylvia despairingly, looking up into her mother's face from the comfortable shelter of her long, strong arms. Mrs. Marshall looked down at her without speaking. It occurred to Sylvia disquietingly that her mother's expression was a little like Judith's. But when Mrs. Marshall spoke it was only to say in her usual voice: " Well, the first thing to do is to have something to eat. Whatever else you do, don't let a bad condition of your body interfere with what's going on in your mind. Lunch is getting cold—and don't talk about trouble while you're eating. After you're through, Father'll tell you what to do."

Professor Marshall made a gesture of dismay. "Good Lord, Barbara, don't put it off on me!"

His wife looked at him with smoldering eyes. "I certainly have nothing to say that would be fit for children to hear!" she said in an energetic tone, beginning to serve the baked beans, which were the main dish for the day.

After the meal, always rather hasty because of the children's short noon-hour, Sylvia and Judith went to sit on their father's knees, while he put an arm about each and, looking from one serious expectant face to the other, began his explanation. He cleared his throat, and hesitated before beginning, and had none of his usual fluency as he went on. What he finally said was: "Well, children, you've stumbled into about the hardest problem there is in this country, and the honest truth is that we don't any of us know what's right to do about it. The sort of thing that's just happened in the Washington Street School is likely to happen 'most anywhere, and it's no harder on these poor little playmates of yours than on all colored people. But it's awfully hard on them all. The best we can do is to hope that after a great many people have lived and died, all trying to do their best, maybe folks will have learned how to manage better. Of course, if grown men and women don't know how to help matters, you little girls can't expect to fix things either. All you can do is to go on being nice to Camilla and——"

Judith broke in here hotly, "You don't mean we oughtn't to *do* something about the girls being so mean to them— not letting Camilla go to the picnic and——"

"What *could* you do?" asked her father quietly, "that would make things any better for Camilla? If you were forty times as strong as you are, you couldn't make the other girls *want* Camilla at the picnic. It would only spoil the picnic and wouldn't help Camilla a bit." Professor Marshall meditated a moment, and went on, "Of course I'm proud of my little daughters for being kind to friends who are unhappy through no fault of theirs" (Sylvia winced at this, and thought of confessing that she was **very** near running away and leaving Camilla to her fate), "and I hope you'll go on being as nice to your unfortunate friends as ever——"

Judith said: "They aren't friends of mine! *I* don't like them!"

As not infrequently happened, something about Judith's attitude had been irritating her father, and he now said with some severity, "Then it's a case where Sylvia's loving heart can do more good than your anger, though you evidently think it very fine of you to feel that!"

Judith looked down in a stubborn silence, and Sylvia drooped miserably in the consciousness of receiving undeserved praise. She opened her mouth to explain her vacillations of the morning, but her moral fiber was not equal to the effort. She felt very unhappy to have Judith blamed and herself praised when things ought to have been reversed, but she could not bring herself to renounce her father's good opinion.

Professor Marshall gave them both a kiss and set them down. "It's twenty minutes to one. You'd better run along, dears," he said.

After the children had gone out, his wife, who had preserved an unbroken silence, remarked dryly, "So that's the stone we give them when they ask for bread."

Professor Marshall made no attempt to defend himself. "My dim generalities are pretty poor provender for honest children's minds, I admit," he said humbly, "but what else have we to give them that isn't directly contradicted by our lives? There's no use telling children something that they never see put into practice."

"It's not impossible, I suppose, to change our lives," suggested his wife uncompromisingly.

Professor Marshall drew a great breath of disheartenment. "As long as I can live without thinking of that element in American life—it's all right. But when anything brings it home—like this today—I feel that the mean compromise we all make must be a disintegrating moral force in the national character. I feel like gathering up all of you, and going away—away from the intolerable question—to Europe—and earning the family living by giving English lessons!"

Mrs. Marshall cried out, "It makes *me* feel like going out right here in La Chance with a bomb in one hand and a rifle in the other!"

From which difference of impression it may perhaps be seen that the two disputants were respectively the father and mother of Sylvia and Judith.

Mrs. Marshall rose and began clearing away the luncheon dishes. As she disappeared into the kitchen, she paused a moment behind the door, a grim, invisible voice, remarking, "And what we shall do is, of course, simply nothing at all!"

CHAPTER VIII

SABOTAGE

Sylvia and Judith walked to school in a profound silence. Sylvia was shrinking with every nerve from the ordeal of facing again those four hundred hostile faces; from the new and painful relations with her playmates which lay before her. She was now committed irrevocably to the cause of the Fingáls, and she felt a terrified doubt of having enough moral strength to stick to that position.

For the moment the problem was settled by their arriving at the schoolhouse almost too late. The lines were just marching into the building, and both girls barely slipped into their places in time. Sylvia noticed with relief that Camilla was absent.

All the Five A girls had paper bags or pasteboard boxes, and in the air of the Five A cloakroom was a strong smell of vinegar. Gretchen Schmidt's pickles had begun to soak through the bag, and she borrowed the cover of a box to set them in. These sounds and smells recalled the picnic to Sylvia's mind, the picnic to which she had been looking forward with such inexpressible pleasure. For an instant she was aghast to think that she had forgotten her bananas, tied up all ready at home on the sideboard. But the next instant she thought sadly that she probably would not be welcome at the picnic. She went to her seat and sat forlorn through the changing lessons of the afternoon.

The teacher ground out the half-hour lessons wearily, her eyes on the clock, as unaware of the crisis in her class as though she were in another planet. At four o'clock Sylvia filed out with the other children to the cloakroom, but there was not the usual quick, practised grab, each for his own belongings. The girls remained behind, exclaiming and lamenting. Such a clamor arose that the teacher came hurrying in, anxious for the reputation for good behavior of her class. Good behavior in the Washington Street School, as in a penitentiary, was gauged by the degree of silence and immobility achieved by the inmates.

The girls ran to Miss Miller, crying out, " Somebody's stolen our lunches,—we left them here—all our boxes and things—and they're all gone——! "

Sylvia hung back in the door to the schoolroom, apart from the others, half relieved by the unexpected event which diverted attention from her.

One of the boys who had gone ahead in the line now came back, a large cucumber stuck in the corner of his mouth like a fat, green cigar. He announced with evident satisfaction in the girls' misfortune that the steps were strewn with pickles. The bag must have burst entirely as they were being carried downstairs. Gretchen Schmidt began to weep,—" all them good pickles——! " One of the girls flew at the boy who brought the bad news. " I just bet you did it yourself, Jimmy Weaver, you an' Frank Kennedy. You boys were mad anyhow because we didn't ask you to come to the picnic."

Jimmy's face assumed the most unmistakably genuine expression of astonishment and aggrieved innocence. " Aw, you're off yer base! I wouldn't ha' gone to your darned old picnic—an' wasn't I in the room every minute this afternoon? "

" No, you weren't—you weren't! " More of the girls had come to the attack, and now danced about the boy, hurling accusations at him. " You got excused to get a drink of water! And so did Pete Roberts! You did it then! You did it then! You did——"

" Hush, children! Not so loud! " said Miss Miller. *" You'll have the Principal down here! "*

At this terrible threat the children, in spite of their heat, lowered their voices. Jimmy was beginning an angry, half-alarmed protest—" Aw, 'twas a tramp must ha' got in an' saw——" when he was pushed out of the way by a small, vigorous hand. Judith Marshall walked in, her face very pale. She was breathing hard, and through her parted lips, as though she had been running fast, her small white teeth showed like those of an enraged squirrel. "I threw your picnic things in the river," she said.

The older children recoiled from this announcement, and from the small, tense figure. Even the teacher kept her distance, as though Judith were some dangerous little animal.

"What in the world did you do that for?" she asked in a tone of stupefaction.

"Because they are n-n-nasty, mean things," said Judith, "and if they weren't going to let C-C-Camilla go to the picnic, I wasn't going to let them *have* any picnic!"

The teacher turned around to Sylvia, now almost as white as her sister, and said helplessly, "Sylvia, do you know what she's talking about?"

Sylvia went forward and took Judith's hand. She was horrified beyond words by what Judith had done, but Judith was her little sister. "Yes, ma'am," she said, to Miss Miller's question, speaking, for all her agitation, quickly and fluently as was her habit, though not very coherently. "Yes, ma'am, I know. Everybody was saying this morning that the Fingáls' mother was a negro, and so the girls weren't going to invite Camilla to the picnic, and it made Judith mad."

"Why, *she* didn't know Camilla very well, did she?" asked the teacher, astonished.

"No, ma'am," said Sylvia, still speaking quickly, although the tears of fright were beginning to stand in her eyes. "It just made her mad because the girls weren't going to invite her because she didn't think it was anyhow her fault."

"*Whose* fault!" cried the teacher, completely lost.

"Camilla's," quavered Sylvia, the tears beginning to fall.

There was a pause. "*Well*—I *never!*" exclaimed the teacher, whose parents had come from New England. She was entirely at a loss to know how to treat this unprece-

dented situation, and like other potentates with a long habit
of arbitrary authority, she covered her perplexity with a
smart show of decision. " You children go right straight
home, along out of the building this minute," she commanded. " You know you're not allowed to loiter around
after school-hours. Sylvia and Judith, stay here. *I'm
going to take you up to the Principal's office.*"

The girls and Jimmy Weaver ran clattering down the
stairs, in an agreeably breathless state of excitement. In
their opinion the awfulness of the situation had been adequately recognized by the teacher and signaled by the
equally awful expedient of a visit to the Principal's office,
the last resort in the case of the rarely occurring insubordinate boy.

Because Miss Miller had not the least idea what to say in
an event so far out of the usual routine, she talked a great
deal during the trip through the empty halls and staircases
up to the Principal's office on the top floor; chiefly to the
effect that as many years as she had taught, never had
she encountered such a bad little girl as Judith. Judith
received this in stony silence, but Sylvia's tears fell fast.
All the years of her docile school existence had trained her
in the habit of horror at insubordination above every other
crime. She felt as disgraced as though Judith had been
caught stealing,—perhaps more so.

Miss Miller knocked at the door; the Principal, stooping
and hollow-chested, opened it and stood confronting with
tired, kind eyes the trio before him—the severe woman,
with her pathetic, prematurely old face and starved flat body,
the pretty little girl hanging down her head and weeping,
the smaller child who gave him one black defiant look
and then gazed past him out of the window.

" Well, Miss Miller——? " he asked.

" I've brought you a case that I don't know what to do
with," she began. " This is Judith Marshall, in the third
grade, and she has just done one of the naughtiest things
I ever heard of——"

When she had finished her recital, " How do you know

this child did it?" asked Mr. Bristol, always his first question in cases between teachers and pupils.

" She was so brazen as to come right back and tell us so," said Miss Miller, her tone growing more and more condemnatory.

Judith's face, capable of such rare and positive beauty, had now shut down into a hard, repellent little mask of hate. Mr. Bristol looked at her for a moment in silence, and then at Sylvia, sobbing, her arm crooked over her face, hiding everything but her shining curls. " And what has this little girl to do with anything?" he asked.

" This is Sylvia Marshall, Judith's sister, and of course she feels dreadfully about Judith's doing such a dreadful thing," explained Miss Miller inelegantly.

Mr. Bristol walked back to his desk and sat down. " Well, I think I needn't keep you any longer, Miss Miller," he said. " If you will just leave the little girls here for a while perhaps I can decide what to do about it."

Thus mildly but unmistakably dismissed, the teacher took her departure, pushing Sylvia and Judith inside the door and shutting it audibly after her. She was so tired as she walked down the stairs that she ached, and she thought to herself, " As if things weren't hard enough without their going and being naughty——!"

Inside the room there was a moment's silence, filled almost palpably by Sylvia's quivering alarm, and by Judith's bitter mental resistance. Mr. Bristol drew out a big book from the shelf over his desk and held it out to Sylvia. " I guess you all got pretty excited about this, didn't you?" he said, smiling wisely at the child. " You and your sister sit down and look at the pictures in this for a while, till you get cooled off, and then I'll hear all about it."

Sylvia took the book obediently, and drew Judith to a chair, opening the pages, brushing away her tears, and trying to go through the form of looking at the illustrations, which were of the birds native to the region. In spite of her emotion, the large, brightly colored pictures did force their way through her eye to her brain, instinct in every fiber with the modern habit of taking in impressions from the printed page; and for years afterwards she could have told the names of the birds they saw during that long, still half-hour, broken by no sound but the tap-tap-tap of Mr. Bristol's typewriter. He did not once look towards them. This was partly a matter of policy, and partly because he was trying desperately to get a paper written for the next Convention of Public School Principals, which he was to address on the " Study of Arithmetic in the Seventh Grade." He had very fixed and burning ideas about the teaching of arithmetic in the seventh grade, which he longed with a true believer's fervor to see adopted by all the schools in the country. He often said that if they would only do so, the study of arithmetic would be revolutionized in a decade.

Judith sat beside her sister, not pretending to look at the book, although the rigidity of her face insensibly softened somewhat in the contagious quiet of the room.

When they had turned over the last page and shut the book, Mr. Bristol faced them again, leaning back in his swivel-chair, and said: " Now, children—all quiet? One of you begin at the beginning and tell me how it happened." Judith's lips shut together in a hard line, so Sylvia began, surprised to find her nerves steadied and calmed by the silent half-hour of inaction back of her. She told how they were met that morning by the news, how the children shouted after Camilla as she got into the carriage, how the Five A girls had decided to exclude her from the picnic, how angry Judith had been, and then—then—she knew no more to tell beyond the bare fact of Judith's passionate misdeed.

Mr. Bristol began to cross-examine Judith in short, quiet sentences. " What made you think of throwing the things into the river ? "

" I was afraid they'd get them back somehow if I didn't," said Judith, as if stating a self-evident argument.

" Where did you go to throw them in ? To the Monroe Street bridge ? "

" No, I didn't have time to go so far. I just went down

through Randolph Street to the bank and there was a boat there tied to a tree, and I got in and pushed it out as far as the rope would go and dropped the things in from the other end."

Sylvia caught her breath in terror at this recital. The Piquota river ran swift and turbid and deep between high banks at that point. "Weren't you afraid to venture out in a boat all by yourself?" asked the man, looking at Judith's diminutive person.

"Yes, I was," said Judith unexpectedly.

Mr. Bristol said "Oh——" and stood in thought for a moment. Some one knocked on the door, and he turned to open it. At the sight of the tall figure standing there in his pepper-and-salt suit, Sylvia's heart gave a great bound of incredulous rapture. The appearance of a merciful mediator on the Day of Judgment could not have given her keener or more poignant relief. She and Judith both ran headlong to their father, catching his hands in theirs, clinging to his arms and pressing their little bodies against his. The comfort Sylvia felt in his mere physical presence was inexpressible. It is one of the pure golden emotions of childhood, which no adult can ever recover, save perhaps a mystic in a moment of ecstatic contemplation of the power and loving-kindness of his God.

Professor Marshall put out his hand to the Principal, introducing himself, and explained that he and his wife had been a little uneasy when the children had not returned from school. Mr. Bristol shook the other's hand, saying that he knew of him through mutual acquaintances and assuring him that he could not have come at a more opportune moment. "Your little daughter has given me a hard nut to crack. I need advice."

Both men sat down, Sylvia and Judith still close to their father's side, and Mr. Bristol told what had happened in a concise, colorless narration, ending with Judith's exploit with the boat. "Now what would *you* do in *my* place?" he said, like one proposing an insoluble riddle.

Sylvia, seeing the discussion going on in such a quiet, conversational tone, ventured in a small voice the suggestion that Judith had done well to confess, since that had saved others from suspicion. " The girls were sure that Jimmy Weaver had done it."

" Was that why you came back and told? " asked Professor Marshall.

" No," said Judith bluntly, " I never thought of that. I wanted to be sure they knew why it happened."

The two men exchanged glances. Professor Marshall said : " Didn't you understand me when I told you at noon that even if you could make the girls let Camilla go to the picnic, she wouldn't have a good time? You couldn't make them like to have her? "

" Yes, I understood all right," said Judith, looking straight at her father, " but if she couldn't have a good time—and no fault of hers—I wasn't going to let *them* have a good time either. I wasn't trying to make them want her. I was trying to get even with them! "

Professor Marshall looked stern. " That is just what I feared, Judith, and that hateful spirit is the bad thing about the whole business." He turned to the Principal : " How many girls were going to the picnic? "

The other, with a wide gesture, disavowed any knowledge of the matter. " Good Heavens ! how should I know? "

Sylvia counted rapidly. " Fourteen," she said.

" Well, Mr. Bristol, how would this do for a punishment? Judith has worked in various ways, digging up dandelions from the lawn, weeding flower-beds, running errands—you know—all the things children do—and she has a little more than five dollars in her iron savings-bank, that she has been saving for more than a year to buy a collie puppy. Would you be satisfied if she took that money, divided it into fourteen parts, and took it herself in person to each of the girls? "

During this proposal Judith's face had taken on an expression of utter dismay. She looked more childlike, more like her years than at any moment during the interview. " Oh, *Father!* " she implored him, with a deep note of entreaty.

He did not look at her, but over her head at the Principal, who was rising from his chair with every indication of relief on his face. " Nothing could be better," he said. " That will be just right—every one will be satisfied. And I'll just say for the sake of discipline that little Judith shan't come back to school till she has done her penance. Of course she can get it all done before supper-time tonight. All our families live in the vicinity of the school." He was shaking Professor Marshall's hand again and edging him towards the door, his mind once more on his paper, hoping that he might really finish it before night—if only there were no more interruptions!

His achievement in divining the mental processes of two children hysterical with excitement, his magnetic taming of those fluttering little hearts, his inspired avoidance of a fatal false step at a critical point in the moral life of two human beings in the making—all this seemed as nothing to him—an incident of the day's routine already forgotten. He conceived that his real usefulness to society lay in the reform of arithmetic-teaching in the seventh grade, and he turned back to his arguments with the ardor of the great landscape painter who aspires to be a champion at billiards.

Professor Marshall walked home in silence with his two daughters, explained the matter to his wife, and said that he and Sylvia would go with Judith on her uncomfortable errand. Mrs. Marshall listened in silence and went herself to get the little bank stuffed full of painfully earned pennies and nickels. Then she bade them into the kitchen and gave Judith and Sylvia each a cookie and a glass of milk.

She made no comment whatever on the story, or on her husband's sentence for the culprit, but just as the three were going out of the door, she ran after them, caught Judith in her arms, and gave her a passionate kiss.

The next day was Saturday, and it was suggested that Judith and Sylvia carry on their campaign by going to see the Fingáls and spending the morning playing with them as though nothing had happened.

As they approached the house, somewhat perturbed by
the prospect, they saw with surprise that the windows were
bare of the heavy yellow lace curtains which had hung in
the parlor, darkening that handsomely furnished room to
a rich twilight. They went up on the porch, and Judith
rang the bell resolutely, while Sylvia hung a little back of
her. From this position she could see into the parlor, and
exclaimed, " Why, Judy, this isn't the right house—nobody
lives here! " The big room was quite empty, the floors bare
of the large soft rugs, and as the children pressed their faces
to the pane, they could see through an open door into a
bedroom also dismantled and deserted.

They ran around the house to the back door and knocked
on it. There was no answer. Judith turned the knob, the
door opened, and they stood in what had been unmistakably
the Fingáls' kitchen. Evidence of wild haste and confusion
was everywhere about them—the floor was littered with
excelsior, the shelves half cleared and half occupied still
with cooking supplies, a packing-box partly filled with
kitchenware which at the last moment the fugitives had
evidently decided to abandon.

The little girls stood in this silent desolation, looking
about them with startled eyes. A lean mother-cat came
and rubbed her thin, pendent flanks against their legs, purring and whining. Three kittens skirmished joyfully in the
excelsior, waylaying one another in ambush and springing
out with bits of the yellow fibers clinging to their woolly
soft fur.

" They've *gone!* " breathed Sylvia. " They've gone away
for good! "

Judith nodded, even her bold and unimaginative spirit
somewhat daunted by the ghostly silence of the house.
Sylvia tiptoed to the swinging-door and pushed it open.
Yes, there was the pantry, like the kitchen, in chaotic dis-
order, tissue paper and excelsior thick on the floor, and
entangled with it the indescribable jumble of worthless, disconnected objects always tumbled together by a domestic
crisis like a fire or a removal—old gloves, whisk-brooms,

hat-forms, lamps, magazines, tarnished desk-fittings. The sight was so eloquent of panic haste that Sylvia let the door swing shut, and ran back into the kitchen.

Judith was pointing silently to a big paper bag on the shelf. It had been tossed there with some violence evidently, for the paper had burst and the contents had cascaded out on the shelf and on the floor—the rich, be-raisined cookies which Camilla was to have taken to the picnic. Sylvia felt the tears stinging her eyelids, and pulled Judith out of the tragic house. They stood for a moment in the yard, beside a bed of flowering crocuses, brilliant in the sun. The forsaken house looked down severely at them from its blank windows. Judith was almost instantly relieved of mental tension by the outdoor air, and stooped down unconcernedly to tie her shoe. She broke the lacing and had to sit down, take it out of the shoe, tie it, and put it back again. The operation took some time, during which Sylvia stood still, her mind whirling.

For the first time in her steadily forward-going life there was a sharp, irrevocable break. Something which had been yesterday was now no more. She would never see Camilla again, she who recalled Camilla's look of anguish as though they still stood side by side. Her heart filled with unspeakable thankfulness that she had put her arms around Camilla's neck at that supreme last moment. That had not been Judith's doing. That had come from her own heart. Unconsciously she had laid the first stone in the wall of self-respect which might in the future fortify her against her weaknesses.

She stood looking up blindly at the house, shivering again at the recollection of its echoing, empty silence. The moment was one she never forgot. Standing there in that commonplace backyard, staring up at a house like any one of forty near her, she felt her heart grow larger. In that moment, tragedy, mystery, awe, and pity laid their shadowy fingers on her shining head.

CHAPTER IX

THE END OF CHILDHOOD

THAT afternoon a couple of children who came to play in the Marshall orchard brought news that public opinion, after the fashion of that unstable weathercock, was veering rapidly, and blowing from a wholly unexpected quarter. "My papa says," reported Gretchen Schmidt, who never could keep anything to herself, even though it might be by no means to her advantage to proclaim it—"my papa says that he thinks the way American people treats colored peoples is just fierce; and he says if he'd ha' known about our not letting Camilla go to the picnic, he'd ha' taken the trouble to me '*mit der flachen Hand schlagen.*' That means he'd have spanked me good and plenty."

Maria Perkins, from the limb where she hung by her knees, responded, "Yup, my Uncle Eben says he likes Judy's spunk."

"I guess he wouldn't have, if it'd ha' been his pickles!" Gretchen made a last stand against the notorious injustice of fickle adult prejudices.

But the tide had begun to turn. On Monday morning Sylvia and Judith found themselves far from ostracized, rather the center of much respectful finger-pointing on the part of children from the other grades who had never paid the least attention to them before. And finally when the Principal, passing majestically from room to room in his daily tour of inspection, paused in his awful progress and spoke to Judith by name, asking her quite familiarly and condescendingly what cities you would pass through if you went from Chicago to New Orleans, the current set once and for all in the other direction. No mention was ever made of the disappearance of the Fingáls, and the Marshall children found their old places waiting for them.

It was not long before Judith had all but forgotten the episode; but Sylvia, older and infinitely more impressionable, found it burned irrevocably into her memory. For many and many a week, she did not fall asleep without seeing Camilla's ashy face of wretchedness. And it was years before she could walk past the house where the Fingáls had lived, without feeling sick.

Her life was, however, brimming with active interests which occupied her, mind and body. There was rarely a day when a troop of children did not swarm over the Marshall house and barn, playing and playing and playing with that indomitable zest in life which is the birthright of humanity before the fevers and chills of adolescence begin. Sylvia and Judith, moreover, were required to assume more and more of the responsibility of the housework, while their mother extracted from the Marshall five acres an ever increasing largesse of succulent food. Sylvia's séances with old Reinhardt and the piano were becoming serious affairs: for it was now tentatively decided that she was to earn her living by teaching music. There were many expeditions on foot with their mother, for Mrs. Marshall had become, little by little, chief nurse and adviser to all the families of the neighborhood; and on her errands of service one of her daughters was needed to carry supplies and act as assistant. And finally, as the children grew older, and the family tradition of bookishness took hold of them, there were shelves and shelves to be devoured, a strange mixture—Thackeray, Maeterlinck, Fielding, Hakluyt, Ibsen, Dickens, Ruskin, Shaw, Austen, Molière, Defoe, Cervantes, Shakespeare,— the children dipped, or tasted or swallowed whole, according to their temperaments and the books they happened on.

When Sylvia was thirteen, almost fourteen years old, she " graduated " from the eighth grade of the public schools and was ready to enter the High School. But after a good many family councils, in most of which, after the unreticent Marshall manner, she herself was allowed to be present, it was decided not to send her to the huge new Central High School, which had cost La Chance such a big slice of its taxes, but to prepare her at home for her course at the State University. She had been growing very fast, was a little thin and white, and had been outgrowing her strength. This at least was the reason given out to inquirers. In reality her father's prejudice against High School life for adolescents was the determining cause. In the course of his University work he was obliged to visit a good many High Schools, and had acquired a violent prejudice against the stirring social life characteristic of those institutions.

Sylvia's feelings about this step aside from the beaten track were, like many of Sylvia's feelings, decidedly mixed. She was drawn towards the High School by the suction of the customary. A large number of her classmates expected as a matter of course to pass on in the usual way; but, with an uneasy qualm, half pride and half apprehension, Sylvia was beginning to feel her difference from ordinary children. She was not altogether sorry to say good-bye to her playmates, with whom she no longer had much in common. She would miss the fun of class-life, of course; but there was a certain distinction involved in being educated " differently." She might be queer, but since she was apparently fated to be queer, she might as well not be " common " as well. Finally, because she was still, at fourteen, very much of a child, the scale was tipped by her thinking what fun it would be to go down-town on errands in school hours. Charles Lamb, lost in painful wonder at his own leisure after thirty-six years of incessant office-hours, could savor no more acutely than an American school-child the exquisite flavor of freedom at an hour formerly dedicated to imprisonment.

As a matter of fact, during the next three years Sylvia's time was more constantly occupied than when there was a fixed time-limit to her studies. Her teachers were always about her, and lightly as the new yoke pressed, she wore it practically without intermission. Her immersion in the ideals, the standards, the concepts of her parents was complete, engulfing. Somebody was nearly always teaching her something. She studied history and Latin with her father;

mathematics with her mother. She learned to swim, to play tennis, to ride in the summer-time, and to skate on the frozen swimming-pool in winter, all without stirring from home. Old Reinhardt was supposed to come twice a week to give her a piano-lesson, but actually he dropped in almost every day to smoke meditatively and keep a watchful ear on her practising.

Although during those years she was almost literally rooted to the Marshall soil, watered by Marshall convictions, and fed by Marshall information, the usual miracle of irresistibly individual growth went silently and unconsciously forward in her. She was growing up to be herself, and not her mother or her father, little as any one in her world suspected the presence of this unceasingly recurrent phenomenon of growth. She was alive to all the impressions reflected so insistently upon her, but she transmuted them into products which would immensely have surprised her parents, they being under the usual parental delusion that they knew every corner of her heart. Her budding aversions, convictions, ambitions were not in the least the aversions, convictions, and ambitions so loudly voiced about her; and a good deal of her energy was taken up in a more or less conscious reaction from the family catchwords, with especial emphasis laid on an objection to the family habit of taking their convictions with great seriousness.

Her father would have been aghast if he could have felt the slightest reflection from the heat of her detestation of his favorite, Emersonian motto, which, now that he had reached five and forty, he was apt to repeat with the iteration natural to his age, rousing in Sylvia the rebellious exasperation felt by *her* age for over-emphatic moralizings.

On the occasion of one of the annual gatherings at the Marshall house of the Seniors in her father's classes, she remarked fiercely to Judith, " If Father gets off that old Emerson, ' What will you have, quoth God. Take it and pay for it,' again tonight in his speech, I'm going to get right up and scream."

Judith stared. The girls were in the kitchen, large aprons

over their best dresses, setting out rows of plates for the chicken salad which was to come after the music. "I don't see anything to scream about in that!" said Judith with a wondering contempt for Sylvia's notions.

"I'm so *sick* of it!" cried Sylvia, tearing the lettuce-leaves apart with venom. "Father never gets through any sort of a speech that he doesn't work it in—and I hate it, anyhow! It makes me feel as though somebody had banged a big door in my face and shut me up in prison."

"Well, for goodness' sakes!" cried Judith, who, at this period of their lives, had remained rather more than her three years behind Sylvia's intelligence. "How do you get all that out of *that!*"

"You haven't sense enough to know what it means, that's all!" retorted Sylvia. "It means something perfectly hateful, the way Father uses it. It means you've got to pay for every single thing you do or get in this world! It's somebody tagging you round with an account-book, seeing how big a bill you're running up. It's the perfectly horrid way Father and Mother make us do, of *always* washing up the dishes we dirty, and *always* picking up the things we drop. Seems as though I'd die happy, if I could just step out of my nightgown in the morning and *leave* it there, and know that it would get hung up without my doing it."

"Well, if that's all you want, to die happy," said Judith, the literal-minded, "I will do that much for you!"

"Oh gracious, no! That wouldn't do any good! You know I couldn't take any satisfaction letting *you* do that!" objected Sylvia peevishly, fuming and fumbling helplessly before the baffling quality of her desires. "I don't want just somebody to pick it up for me. I want it picked up by somebody that I don't care about, that I don't see, that I'd just as soon have do the tiresome things as not. I want somebody to do it, and me to feel all right about *having* them do it!"

"Well, for goodness' sakes!" Judith was reduced again to mere wonder.

Professor and Mrs. Marshall stepped into the kitchen for

a moment to see that everything was progressing smoothly. The professor had his viola in his hand and was plucking softly at the strings, a pleasant, tranquil anticipation of harmony on his face. He looked affectionately at his daughters and thought what dear good children they were. Judith appealed to her parents: " Sylvia's as crazy as a loon. She says she wants somebody to do her work for her, and yet she wants to feel all right about shirking it!"

Mrs. Marshall did not follow, and did not care. "What?" she said indifferently, tasting the chicken-salad in the big yellow bowl, and, with an expression of serious consideration, adding a little more salt to it.

But Sylvia's father understood, "What you want to remember, daughter," he said, addressing himself to his oldest child with a fond certainty of her quick apprehension, " is that fine saying of Emerson, ' What will you have, quoth—' " A raw-boned assistant appeared in the doorway. " Everybody here, I guess, Perfesser," he said.

When the girls were alone again, Sylvia stole a look at Judith and broke into noiseless giggles. She laughed till the tears ran down her cheeks and she had to stop work and go to the kitchen sink to wash her face and take a drink of water. " You never do what you say you're going to," said Judith, as gravely alien to this mood as to the other. " I thought you said you'd scream."

" I *am* screaming," said Sylvia, wiping her eyes again.

They were very familiar with the work of preparing the simple " refreshments " for University gatherings. Their mother always provided exactly the same viands, and long practice had made them letter-perfect in the moves to be made. When they had finished portioning off the lettuce-leaves and salad on the plates, they swiftly set each one on a fresh crêpe-paper napkin. Sylvia professed an undying hatred for paper napkins. " I don't see why," said Judith. " They're so much less bother than the other kind when you're only going to use them once, this way." " That's it," asserted Sylvia; " that's the very stingy, economical thing about them I hate, their *not* being a bother! I'd like to use big, fine-damask ones, all shiny, that somebody had ironed twenty minutes, every one, like those we had at Eleanor Hubert's birthday party. And then I'd scrunch them up and throw them in the laundry if there was the least speck on them."

"I wouldn't like the job of doing them up," said Judith.

"Neither would I. I'd hate it! And I wouldn't," continued Sylvia, roaming at will in her enchanted garden; "I'd hire somebody to take all the bother of buying them and hemming them and doing them up and putting them on the table. All I'd do, would be to shake them out and lay them across my lap," she went through a dainty-fingered pantomime, "and never think a thing about how they got there. That's all *I* want to do with napkins. But I do love 'em big and glossy. I could *kiss* them!"

Judith was almost alarmed at the wildness of Sylvia's imaginings. "Why, you talk as though you didn't have good sense tonight, Sylvie. It's the party. You always get so excited over parties." Judith considered it a "come-down" to get excited over anything.

"Great Scotland! I guess I don't get excited over one of these *student* parties!" Sylvia repudiated the idea. "All Father's 'favorite students' are such rough-necks. And it makes me tired to have all our freaks come out of their holes when we have company—Miss Lindström and Mr. Hecht and Cousin Parnelia and all."

"The President comes," advanced Judith.

Sylvia was sweeping in her iconoclasm. "What if he does—old fish-mouth! *He's* nobody—he's a rough-neck himself. He used to be a Baptist minister. He's only President because he can talk the hayseeds in the Legislature into giving the University big appropriations. And anyhow, he only comes here because he *has* to—part of his job. He doesn't like the freaks any better than I do. The last time he was here, I heard Cousin Parnelia trying to persuade him to have planchette write him a message from Abraham Lincoln. Isn't she the limit, anyhow!"

The girls put off their aprons and slipped into the big.

low-ceilinged living-room, singing like a great sea-shell with thrilling violin-tones. Old Reinhardt was playing the Kreutzer, with Professor Marshall at the piano. Judith went quietly to sit near Professor Kennedy, and Sylvia sat down near a window, leaning her head against the pane as she listened, her eyes fixed on the blackness outside. Her face cleared and brightened, like a cloudy liquor settling to limpidity in a crystal vase. Her lips parted a little, her eyes were fixed on a point incalculably distant. Her mind emptied itself of everything but her joy in the glorious cadences. . . .

If she had been asked what she and Judith had been talking of, she could not have told; but when, after the second movement was finished, old Reinhardt put down his violin and began to loosen his bow (he never played the presto finale), it all came back to the girl as she looked around her at her father's guests. She hated the way the young men's Adam's apples showed through their too-widely opened collars, and she loathed the way the thin brown hair of one of the co-eds was strained back from her temples. She received the President's condescending, oleaginous hand-shake with a qualm at his loud oratorical voice and plebeian accent, and she headed Cousin Parnelia off from a second mediumistic attack, hating her badly adjusted false-front of hair as intensely as ever Loyola hated a heretic. And this, although uncontrollably driven by her desire to please, to please even a roomful of such mediocrities, she bore to the outward eyes the most gracious aspect of friendly, smiling courtesy. Professor Marshall looked at her several times, as she moved with her slim young grace among his students and friends, and thought how fortunate he was in his children.

After the chicken-salad and coffee had been successfully served and eaten, one of the Seniors stepped forward with an awkward crudeness and presented Professor Marshall with a silver-mounted blotting-pad. The house was littered with such testimonials to the influence of the Professor on the young minds under his care, testimonials which his children took as absolutely for granted as they did everything else in the home life. On this occasion Sylvia was so afflicted because the young rustic appointed to make the presentation speech, forgot most of what he had planned to say, that she felt nothing but the liveliest impatience with the whole proceeding. But her father's quick heart was touched, and more than half of his usual little speech of farewell to his Seniors was an expression of thanks to them. Before he had finished the last part, which consisted of eloquent exhortations to the higher life, none the less sincerely heartfelt for being re- markably like similar speeches he had made during the last twenty years, he had quoted his favorite saying from Emer- son. Judith looked apprehensively at Sylvia; but she was not laughing. She evidently was not hearing a word her father said, being lost in the contemplation of the perfect evening costume of the newest assistant in Professor Mar- shall's department. He was a young man from Massachu- setts, fresh from Harvard, who had come West to begin his teaching that year. His was certainly the most modern dress-suit in the University faculty; and he wore it with a supercilious disregard for its perfections which greatly impressed Sylvia.

After these usual formalities were thus safely past, some one suggested a game of charades to end the evening. Amid great laughter and joking from the few professors present and delighted response from the students who found it immensely entertaining to be on such familiar terms with their instructors, two leaders began to " choose sides." The young assistant from Harvard said in a low tone to his friend, not noticing Professor Marshall's young daughter near them: " They won't really go on and *do* this fool, undignified, backwoods stunt, will they? They don't ex- pect us to join *in!* "

" Oh yes, they will," answered his friend, catching up his tone of sophisticated scorn. He too was from Harvard, from an earlier class. " You'll be lucky if they don't have a spelling-down match, later on."

"Good Lord!" groaned the first young man.

"Oh, you mustn't think all of the University society is like *this!*" protested the second. "And anyhow, we can slope now, without being noticed."

Sylvia understood the accent and tone of this passage more than the exact words, but it summed up and brought home to her in a cruelly clarified form her own groping impressions. The moment was a terribly painful one for her. Her heart swelled, the tears came to her eyes, she clenched her fists. Her fine, lovely, and sensitive face darkened to a tragic intensity of resolve. She might have been the young Hannibal, vowing to avenge Carthage. What she was saying to herself passionately was, "When *I* get into the University, I will *not* be a jay!"

It was under these conditions that Sylvia passed from childhood, and emerged into the pains and delights and responsibilities of self-consciousness.

BOOK II

A FALSE START TO ATHENS

CHAPTER X

SYLVIA'S FIRST GLIMPSE OF MODERN CIVILIZATION

ALTHOUGH there was not the slightest actual connection between the two, the trip to Chicago was always in Sylvia's mind like the beginning of her University course. It is true that the journey, practically the first in Sylvia's life, was undertaken shortly before her matriculation as a Freshman, but this fortuitous chronological connection could not account for Sylvia's sense of a deeper unity between the two experiences. The days in Chicago, few as they were, were as charged with significance for her as the successive acts in a drama, and that significance was of the substance and marrow of the following and longer passage in her life.

The fact that her father and her mother disagreed about the advisability of the trip was one of the salient points in the beginning. When Aunt Victoria, breaking a long silence with one of her infrequent letters, wrote to say that she was to be in Chicago " on business " during the last week of September, and would be very glad to have her sister-in-law bring her two nieces to see her there, Professor Marshall said, with his usual snort: " Business nothing! She never has any business. She won't come to see them *here,* that's all. The idea's preposterous." But Mrs. Marshall, breaking a long silence of her own, said vigorously: " She is your sister, and you and your family are the only

blood-kin she has in the world. I've a notion—I have had
for some time—that she was somehow terribly hurt on that
last visit here. It would be ungenerous not to go half-way
to meet her now."

Sylvia, anxiously hanging on her father's response, was
surprised when he made no protest beyond, " Well, do as
you please. I can keep Lawrence all right. She only speaks
of seeing you and the girls." It did not occur to Sylvia,
astonished at this sudden capitulation, that there might be a
discrepancy between her father's habit of vehement speech
and his real feeling in this instance.

It was enough for her, however, that they were going to
take a long journey on the train overnight, that they were
going to see a great city, that they were going to see Aunt
Victoria, about whom her imagination had always hovered
with a constancy enhanced by the odd silence concerning her
which was the rule in the Marshall house.

She was immensely stirred by the prospect. She made
herself, in the brief interval between the decision and the
beginning of the journey, a new shirt-waist of handkerchief
linen. It took the last cent of her allowance to buy the
material, and she was obliged, by a secret arrangement with
her father, to discount the future, in order to have some
spending-money in the city.

Mrs. Marshall was quite disappointed by the dullness of
Sylvia's perceptions during that momentous first trip, which
she had looked forward to as an occasion for widening the
girls' horizon to new interests. Oddly enough it was Judith,
usually so much less quick than Sylvia, who asked the intelligent questions and listened attentively to her mother's
explanations about the working of the air-brakes, and the
switching systems in railroad yards, and the harvesting of
the crops in the flat, rich country gliding past the windows.
It was quite evident that not a word of this highly instruc-
tive talk reached Sylvia, sitting motionless, absorbing every
detail of her fellow-passengers' aspect, in a sort of trance
of receptivity. She scarcely glanced out of the windows,
except when the train stopped at the station in a large town,

when she transferred her steady gaze to the people coming and going from the train. " Just look, Sylvia, at those blast-furnaces!" cried her mother as they passed through the outskirts of an industrial town. "They have to keep them going, you know, night and day."

"Oh, do they? What for?" asked Judith, craning her neck to watch the splendid leap of the flames into the darkness.

"Because they can't allow the ore to become——." Mrs. Marshall wondered why, during her conscientious explanation of blast-furnaces, Sylvia kept her eyes dully fixed on her hands on her lap. Sylvia was, as a matter of fact, trying imaginary bracelets on her slim, smooth, white wrists. The woman opposite her wore bracelets.

"Isn't it fine," remarked the civic-minded Mrs. Marshall, "to see all these little prairie towns so splendidly lighted?"

"I hadn't noticed them," said Sylvia, her gaze turned on the elegant nonchalance of a handsome, elderly woman ahead of her. Her mother looked at her askance, and thought that children are unaccountable.

There were four of the Chicago days, and such important events marked them that each one had for all time a physiognomy of its own. Years afterwards when their travels had far outrun that first journey, Sylvia and Judith could have told exactly what occurred on any given day of that sojourn, as " on the third day we were in Chicago."

The event of the first day was, of course, the meeting with Aunt Victoria. They went to see her in a wonderful hotel, entering through a classic court, with a silver-plashing fountain in the middle, and slim Ionic pillars standing up white and glorious out of masses of palms. This dreamlike spot of beauty was occupied by an incessantly restless throng of lean, sallow-faced men in sack-coats, with hats on the backs of their heads and cigars in the corners of their mouths. The air was full of tobacco smoke and the click of heels on the marble pavement. At one side was a great onyx-and-marble desk, looking like a soda-water fountain without the

silver faucets, and it was the thin-cheeked, elegant young-
old man behind this structure who gave instructions whereby
Mrs. Marshall and her two daughters found their way to
Aunt Victoria's immense and luxurious room. She was
very glad to see them, shaking hands with her sister-in-law
in the respectful manner which that lady always seemed
to inspire in her, and embracing her two tall young nieces
with a fervor which melted Sylvia's heart back to her old
childish adoration.

"What *beautiful* children you have, Barbara!" cried
Mrs. Marshall-Smith, holding Judith off at arm's length
and looking from her to Sylvia; "although I suppose I
ought not to tell them that!" She looked at Sylvia with an
affectionate laugh. "Will you be spoiled if I tell you you
are very pretty?" she asked.

"I can't think of anything but how pretty *you* are!" said
Sylvia, voicing honestly what was in her mind.

This answer caused her aunt to cry out: "Oh! Oh!
And tact too! She's meant for social success!" She left
this note to vibrate in Sylvia's ears and turned again to her
sister-in-law with hospitable remarks about the removing
of wraps. As this was being done, she took advantage of
the little bustle to remark from the other side of the room,
"I rather hoped Elliott would come with you." She spoke
lightly, but there was the tremor of feeling in her sweet
voice which Sylvia found she remembered as though it
had been but yesterday she had heard it last.

"You didn't ask him," said Mrs. Marshall, with her
usual directness.

Mrs. Marshall-Smith arched her eyebrows, dropped her
eyelids, and shook her head. "No, I didn't ask him," she
admitted, and then with a little wry twist of her lips, "But
I rather hoped he might feel like coming." She looked down
at her hands.

Mrs. Marshall surprised her daughters very much by
going across the room and kissing her husband's sister.
Mrs. Marshall-Smith took the other's strong, hard hand between her soft fingers. "That's generous in you, Barbara,"

she said, looking intently into the pitying dark eyes. "I'm human, you know."

"Yes, I know you're human," said Mrs. Marshall, looking down at her gravely. "So are we all of us. So's Elliott. Don't forget that." With which obscure reference, entirely unintelligible to the two girls, the matter was forever dropped.

The two ladies thereupon embarked upon the difficult business of laying out to the best advantage the few days before them so that every hour might be utilized for the twofold purpose of seeing each other and having the girls see the sights. Judith went to the window during this conversation, and looked down into the crowded street, the first city street she had ever seen. Sylvia sat quietly and imprinted upon her memory every item in the appearance of the two women before her, not the first time she had compared them. Mrs. Marshall was dressed in a dark-blue, well-preserved, ready-made suit, dating from the year before. It was in perfect condition and quite near enough the style of the moment to pass unnoticed. Sylvia saw nothing to be ashamed of in her mother's unaccented and neutral costume, but there was no denying that she looked exactly like any one else. What was most apparent to the discerning eye was that her garb had been organized in every detail so as to consume as little thought and effort as possible. Whereas Aunt Victoria—Sylvia's earnest and thoughtful efforts at home-dressmaking had fitted her, if for nothing else, for a full appreciation of Mrs. Marshall-Smith's costume. She had struggled with cloth enough to bow her head in respect and awe before the masterly tailoring of the rich, smooth broadcloth dress. She knew from her own experience that the perfection of those welted seams could not be accomplished by even the most intense temporary concentration of amateur forces. No such trifling fire of twigs lighted the way to that pinnacle. The workman who had achieved that skill had cut down the whole tree of his life and thrown it into the flame.

Like a self-taught fiddler at the concert of a master, Sylvia's failures had taught her the meaning of success. Although her inexperience kept her from making at all a close estimate of the literal cost of the toilet, her shrewdness made her divine the truth, which was that Mrs. Marshall-Smith, in spite of the plainness of her attire, could have clad herself in cloth-of-gold at a scarcely greater expenditure of the efforts and lives of others. Sylvia felt that her aunt was the most entirely enviable person in the world, and would gladly have changed places with her in a moment.

That was, on the whole, the note of the Chicago trip, all the dazzling lights and reflections of which focused, for Sylvia, upon Aunt Victoria's radiant person. At times, the resultant beam was almost too much for the young eyes; as, for example, on the next day when the two made a momentous shopping expedition to the largest and finest department store in the city. " I've a curiosity to see," Aunt Victoria had declared carelessly, " what sort of things are sold in a big Western shop, and besides I've some purchases to make for the Lydford house. Things needs freshening up there. I've thought of wicker and chintz for the living-room. It would be a change from what I've had. Perhaps it would amuse the children to go along?"

At this, Judith, who had a boy's detestation of shopping, looked so miserable that Aunt Victoria had laughed out, her frank, amused laugh, and said, " Well, Sylvia and I alone, then!"

" Judith and I'll go to Lincoln Park to take a walk by the lake," said Mrs. Marshall. " Our inland young folks have never seen so much water all at once."

Sylvia had been, of course, in the two substantial and well-run department stores of La Chance, when she went with her mother to make their carefully considered purchases. They always went directly to the department in question, where Mrs. Marshall's concise formula ran usually along such lines as, " I would like to look at misses' coats, size 16, blue or brown serge, moderate style, price somewhere between ten and fifteen dollars." And then they

looked at misses' coats, size 16, blue or brown serge, of the
specified price; and picked out one. Sylvia's mother was
under the impression that she allowed her daughters to
select their own clothes because, after all these defining and
limiting preliminaries, she always, with a very genuine indifference, abandoned them to their own choice between the
four or five garments offered.

Even when Sylvia, as she grew older, went by herself to
make a small purchase or two, she was so deeply under the
influence of her mother's example that she felt it unbecom-
ing to loiter, or to examine anything she knew she could
not buy. Besides, nearly all the salespeople, who, for the
most part, had been at their posts for many years, knew
her from childhood, and if she stopped to look at a show-
case of new collars, or jabots, they always came pleasantly
to pass the time of day, and ask how her little brother was,
and how she liked studying at home. She was ashamed
to show in their presence anything but a casual, dignified
interest in the goods they handled.

After these feeble and diluted tipplings, her day with
Aunt Victoria was like a huge draught of raw spirits. That
much-experienced shopper led her a leisurely course up one
dazzling aisle and down another, pausing ruthlessly to look
and to handle and to comment, even if she had not the least
intention of buying. With an inimitable ease of manner
she examined whatever took her fancy, and the languid,
fashionably dressed salesladies, all in aristocratic black,
showed to these whims a smiling deference, which Sylvia
knew could come from nothing but the exquisite tailoring of
Aunt Victoria's blue broadcloth. This perception did not in
the least lower her opinion of the value of the deference.
It heightened her opinion of the value of tailoring.

They stood by glass tables piled high with filmy and costly
underwear, such underwear as Sylvia had never dreamed
could exist, and Aunt Victoria looked casually at the cob-
web tissues which the saleswoman held up, herself hankering
in a hungry adoration of the luxury she would never touch
in any other way. Without apology or explanation, other

than Aunt Victoria's gracious nod of dismissal, they moved on to the enchanted cave where, under the stare of innumerable electric lights, evening wraps were exhibited. The young woman who served them held the expensive, fragile chiffon of the garments up in front of her black uniform, her eyes wistful and unsatisfied. Her instant of glory was over when Aunt Victoria bought one of these, exclaiming humorously about the quaintness of going from Paris to Chicago to shop. It was of silver tissue over white brocade, with a collar of fur, and the price was a hundred and thirty-seven dollars. Sylvia's allowance for all her personal expenses for a whole year was a hundred and twenty. To reach the furniture, they passed by, with an ignoring contempt, huge counters heaped with hundreds and hundreds of shirt-waists, any one of which was better than the one Sylvia had made with so much care and interest before leaving home.

Among the furniture they made a long stay. Aunt Victoria was unexpectedly pleased by the design of the wicker pieces, and bought and bought and bought; till Sylvia turned her head away in bewilderment. She looked down a long perspective of glittering show-cases filled with the minor luxuries of the toilet, the ruffs, the collars, the slipper-rosettes, the embroidered belts, the hair ornaments, the chiffon scarves, all objects diverse, innumerable, perishable as mist in tree-branches, all costly in exact ratio to their fragility. Back of her were the children's dresses, fairy-like, simple with an extravagantly costly simplicity. It occurred to Sylvia as little as to many others of the crowd of half-hypnotized women, wandering about with burning eyes and watering mouths through the shrewdly designed shop, that the great closets back of these adroitly displayed fineries might be full of wearable, firm-textured little dresses, such as she herself had always worn. It required an effort of the will to remember that, and wills weak, or not yet formed, wavered and bent before the lust of the eye, so cunningly inflamed. Any sense of values, of proportion, in Sylvia was dumfounded by the lavishness, the enormous quantities, the immense varieties of the goods displayed. She ached with covetousness. . . .

When they joined the others at the hotel her mother, after commenting that she looked rather flushed and tired, happened to ask, " Oh, by the way, Sylvia, did you happen to come across anything in serge suits that would be suitable for school-wear?"

Sylvia quivered, cried out explosively, *"No!"* and turned away, feeling a hot pulse beating through her body. But Aunt Victoria happened to divert attention at that moment. She had been reading, with a very serious and somewhat annoyed expression, a long telegram just handed her, and now in answer to Mrs. Marshall's expression of concern, said hastily, " Oh, it's Arnold again. . . . It's always Arnold!" She moved to a desk and wrote a brief telegram which she handed to the waiting man-servant. Sylvia noticed it was addressed to Mr. A. H. Saunders, a name which set dimly ringing in her head recollections now muffled and obscured.

Aunt Victoria went on to Mrs. Marshall: " Arnold hates this school so. He always hates his schools."

" Oh, he is at school now?" asked Mrs. Marshall. " You haven't a tutor for him?"

" Oh yes, Mr. Saunders is still with him—in the summers and during holidays." Mrs. Marshall-Smith explained further: " To keep him up in his *studies*. He doesn't learn anything in his school, you know. They never do. It's only for the atmosphere—the sports; you know, they play cricket where he is now—and the desirable class of boys he meets . . . *All* the boys have tutors in vacation times to coach them for the college-entrance examinations."

The face of the college professor's wife continued immovably grave during this brief summary of an educational system. She inquired, " How old is Arnold now?" learned that he was seventeen, remembered that, oh yes, he was a year older than Sylvia, and allowed the subject to drop into one of the abysmal silences for which she alone had the courage. Her husband's sister was as little proof against it as her husband. As it continued, Mrs. Marshall-Smith went through the manœuvers which in a less perfectly bred person would have been fidgeting. . . .

No one paid any attention to Sylvia, who sat confronting herself in a long mirror and despising every garment she wore.

CHAPTER XI

ARNOLD'S FUTURE IS CASUALLY DECIDED

THE next day was to have been given up to really improving pursuits. The morning in the Art Institute came off as planned. The girls were marshaled through the sculpture and paintings and various art objects with about the result which might have been expected. As blankly inexperienced of painting and sculpture as any Bushmen, they received this sudden enormous dose of those arts with an instant, self-preservatory incapacity to swallow even a small amount of them. It is true that the very first exhibits they saw, the lions outside the building, the first paintings they encountered, made an appreciable impression on them; but after this they followed their elders through the interminable crowded halls of the museum, their legs aching with the effort to keep their balance on the polished floors, their eyes increasingly glazed and dull. For a time a few eccentric faces or dresses among the other sightseers penetrated through this merciful insensibility, but by noon the capacity for even so much observation as this had left them. They set one foot before the other, they directed their eyes upon the multitudinous objects exhibited, they nodded their heads to comments made by the others, but if asked suddenly what they had just seen in the room last visited, neither of them could have made the faintest guess.

At half-past twelve, their aunt and mother, highly self-congratulatory over the educational morning, voted that enough was as good as a feast, and led their stunned and stupefied charges away to Aunt Victoria's hotel for lunch.

It was while they were consuming this exceedingly appetizing meal that Sylvia saw, threading his way towards them between the other tables, a tall, weedy, expensively dressed young man, with a pale freckled face and light-brown hair. When he saw her eyes on him he waved his hand, a largely knuckled hand, and grinned. Then she saw that it was not a young man, but a tall boy, and that the boy was Arnold. The quality of the grin reminded her that she had always liked Arnold.

His arrival, though obviously unexpected to the last degree, caused less of a commotion than might have seemed natural. It was as if this were for Aunt Victoria only an unexpected incident in a general development, quite resignedly anticipated. After he had shaken hands with everybody, and had sat down and ordered his own luncheon very capably, his stepmother remarked in a tolerant tone, "You didn't get my telegram, then?" He shook his head: "I started an hour or so after I wired you. We'd gone down to the town with one of the masters for a game with Concord. There was a train just pulling out as we went by the station, and I ran and jumped on."

"How'd you know where it was going?" challenged Judith.

"I didn't," he explained lightly. He looked at her with the teasing, provocative look of masculine seventeen for feminine thirteen. "Same old spitfire, I see, Miss Judy," he said, his command of unhackneyed phrases by no means commensurate with his desire to be facetious.

Judith frowned and went on eating her éclair in silence. It was the first éclair she had ever eaten, and she was more concerned with it than with the new arrival.

Nobody made any comment on Arnold's method of beginning journeys until Mrs. Marshall asked, "What did you do it for?" She put the question with an evident seriousness of inquiry, not at all with the rhetorical reproach usually conveyed in the formula she used.

Arnold looked up from the huge, costly, bloody beef-steak he was eating and, after an instant's survey of the grave, kind face opposite him, answered with a seriousness like her own, "Because I wanted to get away." He added after a moment, laughing and looking again at the younger

girl, " I wanted to come out and pull Judy's hair again! "
He spoke with his mouth full, and this made him entirely
a boy and not at all the young man his well-cut clothes
made him appear.

Without speaking, Judith pulled her long, smooth braid
around over her shoulder where she could protect the end
of it. Her mouth was also full, bulgingly, of the last of her
éclair. They might have been brother and sister in a common nursery.

"My! Aren't you pretty, Sylvia! " was Arnold's next
remark. " You're a regular peach; do you know it? " He
turned to the others: " Say, let's go to a show this afternoon," he proposed. " Tling-Tling's in town. I saw it in
the papers as I came in. The original company's singing.
Did you ever hear them? " he asked Sylvia. " They beat the
other road companies all hollow."

Sylvia shook her head. She had never heard the name
before, the Broadway brand of comic opera being outside
her experience to a degree which would have been inconceivable to Arnold.

There was some discussion over the matter, but in the end,
apparently because there was nothing else to do with Arnold,
they all did go to the " show," Arnold engineering the expedition with a trained expertness in the matter of ticket-
sellers, cabs, and ushers which was in odd contrast to
his gawky physical immaturity. At all the stages of the
process where it was possible, he smoked cigarettes, producing them in rapid succession out of a case studded with
little pearls. His stepmother looked on at this, her beautiful manner of wise tolerance tightening up a little, and after
dinner, as they sat in a glittering corridor of the hotel to
talk, she addressed him suddenly in a quite different tone.
" I don't want you to do that so much, Arnold," she said.
His hand was fumbling for his case again. " You're too
young to smoke at all," she said definitely. He went on
with his automatic movements, opening the case, taking out
a cigarette and tapping it on the cover. " Oh, all the fellows do," he said rebelliously, and struck a match.

Mrs. Marshall-Smith aroused herself to a sudden, low-toned, iron masterfulness of voice and manner which, for all its quietness, had the quality of a pistol shot in the family group. She said only, " Put away that cigarette "; but by one effort of her will she massed against the rebellion of his disorganized adolescence her mature, well-ripened capacity to get her own way. She held him with her eyes as an animal-trainer is supposed to cow his snarling, yellow-fanged captives, and in a moment Arnold, with a pettish gesture, blew out the match and shut the cigarette case with a snap. Mrs. Marshall-Smith forbore to over-emphasize her victory by a feather-weight of gloating, and turned to her sister-in-law with a whimsical remark about the preposterousness of one of the costumes passing. Arnold sulked in silence until Judith, emerging from her usual self-contained reticence, made her first advance to him. " Let's us all go there by the railing where we can look down into the central court," she suggested, and having a nodded permission from their elders, the three children walked away.

They looked down into the great marble court, far below them, now fairy-like with carefully arranged electric lights, gleaming through the palms. The busily trampling cohorts in sack-coats and derby hats were, from here, subdued by distance to an æsthetic inoffensiveness of mere ant-like comings and goings.

" Not so bad," said Arnold, with a kindly willingness to be pleased, looking about him discriminatingly at one detail after another of the interior, the heavy velvet and gold bullion of the curtains, the polished marble of the paneling, the silk brocade of the upholstery, the heavy gilding of the chairs. . . . Everything in sight exhaled an intense consciousness of high cost, which was heavy on the air like a musky odor, suggesting to a sensitive nose, as does the odor of musk, another smell, obscured but rancidly perceptible —the unwashed smell, floating up from the paupers' cellars which support Aladdin's palaces of luxury.

But the three adolescents, hanging over the well-designed

solid mahogany railing, had not noses sensitive to this peculiar, very common blending of odors. Judith, in fact, was entirely unconscious even of the more obvious of the two. She was as insensitive to all about her as to the too-abundant pictures of the morning. She might have been leaning over a picket fence. "I wouldn't give in to Her!" she said to Arnold, staring squarely at him.

Arnold looked nettled. "Oh, I don't! I don't pay any attention to what she says, except when she's around where I am, and that's not so often you could notice it much! *Saunders* isn't that kind! Saunders is a gay old bird, I tell you! We have some times together when we get going!"

It dawned on Sylvia that he was speaking of the man who, five years before, had been their young Professor Saunders. She found that she remembered vividly his keen, handsome face, softened by music to quiet peace. She wondered what Arnold meant by saying he was a gay old bird.

Arnold went on, shaking his head sagely: "But it's my belief that Saunders is beginning to take to dope . . . bad business! Bad business! He's in love with Madrina, you know, and has to drown his sorrows some way."

Even Judith, for all her Sioux desire to avoid seeming surprised or impressed, could not restrain a rather startled look at this lordly knowledge of the world. Sylvia, although she had scarcely taken in the significance of Arnold's words, dropped her eyes and blushed. Arnold surveyed them with the indulgent look of a rakish but good-hearted man of the world patting two pretty children on the head.

Judith upset his pose by bringing the talk abruptly back to where she had begun it. "But you *did* give in to her! You pretend you didn't because you are ashamed. She just looked you down. I wouldn't let *any*body look me down. I wouldn't give in to anybody!"

Under this attack, the man of the world collapsed into an awkward overgrown boy, ill at ease, with red lids to his eyes and premature yellow stains on two fingers of his left hand.

He shifted his feet and said defensively: "Aw, she's a woman. A fellow can't knock her down. I wouldn't let a man do it." He retreated still further, through another phase, and became a little boy, heated and recriminatory: "I'd like to know who *you* are to talk! You give in to *your* mother all the time!"

"I don't give in to my mother; I *mind* her," said Judith, drawing a distinction which Arnold could not follow but which he was not acute enough to attack other than by a jeering, "Oh, what a crawl! What's the diff?"

"And I mind her whether she's there or not! *I* do!" continued Judith, pressing what she seemed, inexplicably to Arnold, to consider her advantage.

Sylvia was vexed with them for talking so loudly and getting so red-faced and being so generally out of key with the booming note of luxury resounding about them. "Hush! hush!" she said; "don't be so silly. We ought to be going back."

Arnold took her rebuke without protest. Either something in this passage-at-arms had perversely brought a sudden impulse to his mind, or he had all along a purpose in his fantastic trip West. As they reached the two ladies, he burst out, "Say, Madrina, why couldn't I go on to La Chance and go to school there, and live with the Marshalls?"

Four amazed faces were turned on him. His stepmother evidently thought him stricken with sudden insanity and strove distractedly to select, from the heaped pile of her reasons for so thinking, some few which might be cited without too great offense to her brother's mode of life: "Why, what a strange idea, Arnold! What ever made you think of such a thing? *You* wouldn't like it!" She was going on, as in decency bound, to add that it would be also rather a large order for the Marshalls to adopt a notably "difficult" boy, when Judith broke in with a blunt divination of what was in her aunt's mind. "You'd have to wash dishes if you came to our house," she said, "and help peel potatoes, and weed the celery bed."

"I'd like it!" declared Arnold. "We'd have lots of fun."

"I *bet* we would!" said Judith, with an unexpected assent.

Mrs. Marshall-Smith laughed gently. "You don't know what you're talking about, you silly boy. You never did an hour's work in your life!"

Arnold sat down by Mrs. Marshall. "I wouldn't be in the way, *would* I?" he said, with a clumsy pleading. He hesitated obviously over the "Mother" which had risen to his lips, the name he had had for her during the momentous visit of five years before, and finally, blushing, could not bring it out. "I'd like it like anything! *I* wouldn't be . . . I'd be *different!* Sylvie and Judy seem like little sisters to me." The red on his face deepened. "It's—it's good for a fellow to have sisters, and a home," he said in a low tone not audible to his stepmother's ears.

Mrs. Marshall put out a large, strong hand and took his slack, big-knuckled fingers into a tight clasp. Mrs. Marshall-Smith evidently thought a light tone best now, as always, to take. "I tell you, Barbara"—she suggested laughingly, "we'll exchange. You give me Sylvia, and take Arnold."

Mrs. Marshall ignored this as pure facetiousness, and said seriously: "Why really, Victoria, it might not be a bad thing for Arnold to come to us. I know Elliott would be glad to have him, and so would I."

For an instant Arnold's life hung in the balance. Mrs. Marshall-Smith, gleaming gold and ivory in her evening-dress of amber satin, sat silent, startled by the suddenness with which the whole astonishing question had come up. There was in her face more than one hint that the proposition opened a welcome door of escape to her. . . .

And then Arnold himself, with the tragic haste of youth, sent one end of the scales down, weighted so heavily that the sight of his stepmother's eyes and mouth told him it could never rise again. In the little, pregnant pause, he cried out joyfully, "Oh, Mother! Mother!" and flung his arms around Mrs. Marshall's neck. It was the only time he had shown the slightest emotion over anything. It burst from him with surprising effect.

Mrs. Marshall-Smith was, as she had said, only human, and at this she rose, her delicate face quiet and impassive, and shook out the shimmering folds of her beautiful dress. She said casually, picking up her fan and evidently preparing for some sort of adjournment: " Oh, Arnold, don't be so absurd. Of course you can't foist yourself off on a family that's no relation to you, that way. And in any case, it wouldn't do for you to graduate from a co-educational State University. Not a person you know would have heard of it. You know you're due at Harvard next fall." With adroit fingers, she plucked the string sure to vibrate in Arnold's nature. " Do go and order a table for us in the Rose-Room, there's a good boy. And be sure to have the waiter give you one where we can see the dancing."

The matter was settled.

CHAPTER XII

ONE MAN'S MEAT . . .

THAT night after the Marshalls had gone back to their somewhat shabby boarding-house, " things " happened to the two people they had left in the great hotel. Sylvia and Judith never knew the details, but it was apparent that something portentous had occurred, from the number of telegrams Aunt Victoria had managed to receive and send between the hour when they left her in the evening, and eleven o'clock the next morning, when they found her, hatted and veiled, with an array of strapped baggage around her.

" It's Arnold again! " she told them, with a resigned gesture. She laid down the time-table she had been consulting and drew Mrs. Marshall to the window for a low-voiced explanation. When she came back, " I'm so sorry, dears, to cut short even by a single day this charming time together," she told the girls. " But the news I've been getting from Arnold's school—there's nothing for me to do but to stop everything and take him back there to see what can be done to patch things up." She spoke with the patient air of one inured to the sacrifices involved in the upbringing of children. " We leave on the eleven-forty— oh, I *am* so sorry! But it would have been only one day more. I meant to get you both a dress—I've 'phoned to have them sent to you."

The rest was only the dreary, bustling futility of the last moments before train-time—kisses, remarks about writing more often; a promise from Aunt Victoria to send Sylvia from time to time a box of old dresses and fineries as material for her niece's dressmaking skill ;—from Arnold, appearing at the last minute, a good deal of rather flat, well-meant chaffing, proffered with the most entire unconcern as to the expressed purpose of their journey; and then the descent through long, mirrored, softly carpeted corridors to the classic beauty of the Grecian temple where the busy men, with tired eyes, came and went hurriedly, treading heavily on their heels. Outside was the cab, Arnold extremely efficient in browbeating the driver as to the stowing away of bags, more kisses, in the general cloud of which Arnold pecked shyly at Sylvia's ear and Judith's chin; then the retreating vehicle with Arnold standing up, a tall, ungainly figure, waving a much-jointed hand.

After it was out of sight the three watchers looked at each other in a stale moment of anticlimax.

"Arnold's horrid, isn't he?" said Judith thoughtfully.

"Why, I *like* him!" opposed Sylvia.

"Oh, I *like* him, all right," said Judith.

Then both girls looked at their mother. What next . . .? They were not to have gone back to La Chance until the next night. Would this change of plans alter their schedule? Mrs. Marshall saw no reason why it should. She proposed a sightseeing expedition to a hospital. Miss Lindström, the elderly Swedish woman who worked among the destitute negroes of La Chance, had a sister who was head-nurse in the biggest and newest hospital in Chicago, and she had written very cordially that if her sister's friends cared to inspect such an institution, she was at their service. Neither of the girls having the slightest idea of what a hospital was like, nor of any other of the sights in the city which they might see instead, no objection was made to this plan.

They made inquiries of a near-by policeman and found that they could reach it by the elevated. Their encounter with this metropolitan facility for transportation turned out to be among the most memorable bits of sightseeing of their trip. Neither of the girls had ever imagined anything so lurid as the Saturday noon jam, the dense, packed throngs waiting on the platforms and bursting out through the opened doors like beans from a split bag, their places instantly taken by an even greater crowd, perspiring, fighting grimly for foot-room and expecting and receiving no other kind. Judith was fired contagiously with the spirit about her, set her teeth, thrust out her elbows, shoved, pushed, grunted, fought, all with a fresh zest in the performance which gave her an immense advantage over the fatigued city-dwellers, who assaulted their fellow-citizens with only a preoccupied desire for an approach to a breathing space, and, that attained, subsided into lurching, strap-hanging quiescence. Judith secured with ease, on all the public vehicles they utilized that day, a place on the outside edge of a platform, where she had fresh air in abundance and could hang over the grating to watch with extreme interest the intimate bits of tenement-house life which flashed jerkily by.

But Sylvia, a shuddering chip on the torrent, always found herself in the exact middle of the most crowded spot, feeling her body horrifyingly pressed upon by various invisible ones behind her and several only too visible ones in front, breathing down the back of somebody's neck, often a dirty and sweaty one, with somebody breathing hotly down the back of her own. Once as a very fat and perspiring German-American began to fight the crowd in the endeavor to turn around and leave the car, his slowly revolving bulbous bulk pushed her so smotheringly into the broad back of a negro ahead of her that she felt faint. As they left the car, she said vehemently: " Oh, Mother, this makes me sick! Why couldn't we have taken a cab? Aunt Victoria always does! "

Her mother laughed. " You little country girl! A cab for as far as this would cost almost as much as the ticket back to La Chance."

" I don't see why we came, then! " cried Sylvia. " It's simply awful! And this is a *horrid* part of town! " She suddenly observed that they were walking through a very poor, thickly inhabited street, such as she had never seen before. As she looked about her, her mother stopped laughing and watched her face with a painful attention. Sylvia looked at the tall, dingy houses, the frowzy little shops, the swarms of dirty-nosed children, shrill-voiced, with matted hair, running and whooping in the street, at the slatternly women yelling unobeyed orders to them out of half-glimpsed, cheerless interiors, smelling of cabbage and dish-water. It was Sylvia's first sight of the life of city poor, and upon her face of disgust and revulsion her mother bent a stern and anxious eye.

"See here, Sylvia!" she said abruptly, "do you know what *I* was thinking about back there in the crowd on the elevated? I was thinking that lots of girls, no older than *my* girl, have to stand that twice a day, going to earn their livings."

Sylvia chafed under the obviously admonitory tone of this. "I don't see that that makes it any easier for us if they *do!*" she said in a recalcitrant voice. She stepped wide to avoid a pile of filth on the sidewalk, and clutched at her skirt. She had a sudden vision of the white-tiled, velvet-carpeted florist's shop in a corner of Aunt Victoria's hotel where, behind spotless panes of shining plate-glass, the great clusters of cut-flowers dreamed away an enchanted life—roses, violets, lilies of the valley, orchids. . . .

"Here we are at the hospital," said Mrs. Marshall, a perplexed line of worry between her brows. But at once she was swept out of herself, forgot her seriously taken responsibility of being the mother of a girl like Sylvia. She was only Barbara Marshall, thrilled by a noble spectacle. She looked up at the great, clean, many-windowed façade above them, towering, even above the huge bulk of the gas-tanks across the street, and her dark eyes kindled. "A hospital is one of the most wonderful places in the world!" she cried, in a voice of emotion. "All this—to help people get well!"

They passed into a wide, bare hall, where a busy young woman at a desk nodded on hearing their names, and spoke into a telephone. There was an odd smell in the air, not exactly disagreeable, yet rather uncomfortably pungent. "Oh, iodoform," remarked the young woman at the desk, hearing them comment on it. "Do you get it? We don't notice it *here* at all."

Then came Miss Lindström's sister, powerfully built, gaunt, gray, with a professional, impersonal cheerfulness. The expedition began. "I'll take you to the children's ward first," said Miss Lindström; "that always interests visitors so much. . . ."

Rows on rows of little white beds and white, bloodless faces with an awful patience on them, and little white hands lying in unchildlike quiet on the white spreads; rows on rows of hollow eyes turned in listless interest on the visitors; nurses in white, stepping briskly about, bending over the beds, lifting a little emaciated form, deftly unrolling a bandage; heat; a stifling smell of iodoform; a sharp sudden cry of pain from a distant corner; somewhere a dully beating pulse of low, suppressed sobs. . . .

They were out of the children's ward now, walking along a clean bare corridor. Sylvia swallowed hard. Her eyes felt burning. Judith held her mother's hand tightly. Miss Lindström was explaining to Mrs. Marshall a new system of ventilation.

"This is one of the women's wards," said their leader, opening another swinging door, from which rushed forth a fresh blast of iodoform. More rows of white beds, each with its mound of suffering, each with its haggard face of pain. More nurses, bearing basins of curious shape, bandages, hot-water bottles, rubber tubes. There was more restlessness here than in the children's ward, less helpless prostration before the Juggernaut of disease . . . fretfulness, moans, tossing heads, wretched eyes which stared at the visitors in a hostile indifference.

"Oh, they are just putting the dressing on such an *interesting* case!" said Miss Lindström's voice coming to Sylvia from a great distance. She spoke with the glow of professional enthusiasm, with that certainty, peculiar to sincere doctors and nurses, that a complicated wound is a fascinating object.

In spite of herself Sylvia had one glimpse of horribly lacerated red tissues. . . . She gripped her hands together after this and looked fixedly at a button on her glove, until

Miss Lindström's voice announced: " It's the Embury stitch that makes that possible: we've just worked out the application of it to skin-graft cases. Two years ago she'd have lost her leg. Isn't it simply splendid! "

She said cordially as they moved forward: " Sister Selma said to treat you as though you were the Queen of Sweden, and I am! You're seeing things that visitors are *never* allowed to see."

They walked on and on interminably, past innumerable sick souls, each whirling alone in a self-centered storm of suffering; and then, somehow, they were in a laboratory, where an immensely stout and immensely jovial doctor in white linen got down from a high stool to shake hands with them and profess an immense willingness to entertain them. " . . . but I haven't got anything much today," he said, with a disparaging wave of his hand towards his test-tubes. " Not a single death-warrant. Oh yes, I have too, one brought in yesterday." He brought them a test-tube, stoppered with cotton, and bade them note a tiny bluish patch on the clear gelatine at the bottom. " That means he's a dead one, as much as if he faced the electric chair," he explained. To the nurse he added, " A fellow in the men's ward, Pavilion G. Very interesting culture . . . first of that kind I've had since I've been here." As he spoke he was looking at Sylvia with an open admiration, bold, intrusive, flippant.

They were passing along another corridor, hot, silent, their footsteps falling dully on a long runner of corrugated rubber, with red borders which drew together in the distance like the rails streaming away from a train. Behind a closed door there suddenly rose, and as quickly died away, a scream of pain. With an effort Sylvia resisted the impulse to clap her hands over her ears.

" Here we are, at the minor operating-room," said Miss Lindström, pausing. " It's against the rules, but if you want to look from across the room—just to say you've been there—" She held the door open a little, a suffocating odor of anæsthetics blew out in their faces, like a breath from a dragon's cave. Mrs. Marshall and Judith stepped forward. But Sylvia clutched at her mother's arm and whispered: "Mother! Mother! I don't think I'll go on. I feel—I feel—I'll go back down to the entrance hall to wait."

Mrs. Marshall nodded a preoccupied assent, and Sylvia fled away down the endless corridor, looking neither to the right nor the left, down repeated flights of scrubbed and sterilized marble stairs, into the entrance hall, and, like a bolt from a bow, out of it on the other side, out into the street, into the sunshine, the heat, the clatter, the blessed, blessed smell of cabbage and dish-water. . . .

After a time she went to sit down on the top step of the hospital entrance to wait. She contemplated with exquisite enjoyment the vigorous, profane, hair-pulling quarrel between two dirty little savages across the street. She could have kissed her hand to the loud-voiced woman who came scuffling to the window to scold them, clutching a dirty kimono together over a Hogarth-like expanse of bosom. They were well, these people, blood ran in their veins, their skin was whole, they breathed air, not iodoform! Her mother had pulled the string too tight, and Sylvia's ears were full of the ugly twang of its snapping.

When, at last, Judith and Mrs. Marshall came out, hand-in-hand, Sylvia sprang up to say: "What an *awful* place! I hope I'll never have to set foot in one again!" But quick as was her impulse to speech, her perceptions were quicker, and before the pale exaltation of the other two, she fell silent, irritated, rebellious, thoroughly alien. They walked along in silence. Then Judith said, stammering a little with emotion, "M-M-Mother, I want to b-b-b-be a trained n-n-nurse when I grow up."

CHAPTER XIII

AN INSTRUMENT IN TUNE

As they drew near to their boarding-house late that afternoon, very hot, very crumpled, very solemn, and very much out of tune with one another, they were astonished to see a little eager-faced boy dash out of the house and run wildly to meet them, shouting as he came.

"Why, Lawrence *Marshall!*" cried his mother, picking him up in strong arms; "how ever in the world did you get here!"

"Father brungded me," cried the child, clasping her tightly around the neck. "We got so lonesome for Mother we couldn't wait."

And then Sylvia had stamped on her mind a picture which was to come back later—her father's face and eyes as he ran down the steps to meet his wife. For he looked at his daughters only afterwards, as they were all walking along together, much excited, everybody talking at once, and hanging on everybody's arm. ". . . Yes, Buddy's right! We found we missed you so, we decided life wasn't worth it. You don't know, Barbara, what it's like without you—you don't *know!*"

Her father's voice sounded to Sylvia so loud, so gay, so vital, so inexpressibly welcome. . . . She leaped up at his face like a young dog, for another kiss. "Oh, I'm *awfully* glad you came!" she cried, wondering a little herself at the immensity of her relief. She thought that she must get him by himself quickly and tell him her side of that hospital story, before her mother and Judith began on any virtuous raptures over it.

But there was no consecutive talk about anything after they all were joyfully gathered in their ugly, commonplace

138

boarding-house bedroom. They loosened collars and belts, washed their perspiring and dusty faces, and brushed hair, to the tune of a magpie chatter. Sylvia did not realize that she and her father were the main sources of this volubility, she did not realize how she had missed his exuberance, she only knew that she felt a weight lifted from her heart. She had been telling him with great enjoyment of the comic opera they had seen, as she finished putting the hairpins into her freshly smoothed hair, and turned, a pin still in her mouth, in time to be almost abashed by the expression in his eyes as he suddenly drew his wife to him.

"Jove! Barbara!" he cried, half laughing, but with a quiver in his voice, "it's hell to be happily married! A separation is—well, never mind about it. I came along anyhow! And now I'm here I'll go to see Vic of course."

"No, you won't," said Judith promptly. "She's gone back. To get Arnold out of a scrape."

Mrs. Marshall explained further, and incidentally touched upon her sister-in-law's views of the relation between expensive boys' schools and private tutors. Her dryly humorous version of this set her husband off in a great mirthful roar, to which Sylvia, after a moment of blankness, suddenly joined a burst of her own clear laughter. At the time she had seen nothing funny in Aunt Victoria's statement, but she was now immensely tickled to remember Aunt Victoria's Olympian certainty of herself and her mother's grave mask of serious consideration of the idea. Long after her father had stopped laughing, she still went on, breaking out into delighted giggles. Her new understanding of the satire back of her mother's quiet eyes, lent to Aunt Victoria's golden calm the quaint touch of caricature which made it self-deceived complacency. At the recollection she sent up rocket after rocket of schoolgirl laughter.

Her mother, absorbed in conscientious anxiety about Sylvia's development, and deeply disappointed by the result of the visit to the hospital, ignored this laughter, nor did Sylvia at all guess that she was laughing away half the spell which Aunt Victoria had cast about her. When they went down to their supper of watery creamed potatoes, and stewed apricots in thick saucers, she was in such good humor that she ate this unappetizing fare with no protest.

"Now, folks," said Professor Marshall, after supper, "we have to go home tomorrow early, so we ought to have one more fling tonight. While I was waiting for you to come back this afternoon, I looked up what Chicago has to offer in the way of flings, and this is what I found. Here, Barbara," he took a tiny envelope out of his upper waist-coat pocket, "are two tickets for the symphony orchestra. By the greatest of luck they're giving a special concert for some charity or other, a beautiful program; a sort of musical requiem. Sylvia mustn't miss it; you take her. And here," he spun round to face Judith and Lawrence, producing another slim, tiny envelope from the other upper waistcoat pocket, "since symphony concerts are rather solid meat for milk teeth, and since they last till way after bedtime, I have provided another sort of entertainment; to wit: three seats for moving pictures of the only real and authentic Cheyenne Bill's Congress of the World's Fron-tiersmen. All in favor of going there with me, say 'Aye.'"

"Aye!" screamed Judith and Lawrence. Everybody laughed in pleased excitement and everybody seemed sat-isfied except Mrs. Marshall, who insisted that she should go to the moving pictures while the Professor took Sylvia to the concert.

Then followed the most amiable, generous wrangle as to which of the parents should enjoy the adult form of amuse-ment. But while the Professor grew more and more half-hearted in his protestations that he really didn't care where he went, Mrs. Marshall grew more and more positive that he must not be allowed to miss the music, finally silencing his last weak proffer of self-abnegation by saying peremp-torily: "No, no, Elliott; go on in to your debauch of emotion. I'll take the children. Don't miss your chance. You know it means ten times as much to you as to me. You haven't heard a good orchestra in years."

Sylvia had never been in such a huge hall as the one

where they presently sat, high, giddily high in the eyrie of a top gallery. They looked down into yawning space. The vast size of the auditorium so dwarfed the people now taking their innumerable seats, that even after the immense audience was assembled the great semicircular enclosure seemed empty and blank. It received those thousands of souls into its maw, and made no sign; awaiting some visitation worthy of its bulk.

The orchestra, an army of ants, straggled out on the stage. Sylvia was astonished at their numbers—sixteen first violins, she saw by the program! She commented to her father on the difficulty of keeping them all in tune. He smiled at her absently, bade her, with an air of suppressed excitement, wait until she had heard them, and fell to biting his nails nervously. She re-read the program and all the advertisements, hypnotized, like every one else in the audience, by the sight of printed matter. She noticed that the first number of this memorial concert was the funeral march from the Götterdämmerung, which she knew very well from having heard a good many times a rather thin version of it for four strings and a piano.

The conductor, a solitary ant, made his toilsome way across the great front of the stage, evoking a burst of applause, which resounded hollowly in the inhuman spaces of the building. He mounted a step, waved his antennæ, there was a great indrawn breath of silence, and then Sylvia, waiting with agreeable curiosity to hear how a big orchestra would really sound, gasped and held her breath. The cup of that vast building suddenly brimmed with a magical flood of pure tone, coming from everywhere, from nowhere, from her own heart as well as from outside her body. The immense hall rang to the glorious quality of this sound as a violin-back vibrates to the drawn bow. It rained down on her, it surged up to her, she could not believe that she really heard it.

She looked quickly at her father. His arms were folded tightly across his chest. He was looking frowningly at the back of the chair in front of him. It was evident that

Sylvia did not exist for him. She was detached from her wonder at his pale sternness by the assault on her nerves made by the first of those barbaric outcries of woe, that sudden, brief clamor of grief, the shouts of despair, the beating upon shields. Her heart stood still— There rose, singing like an archangel, the mystic call of the Volsung, then the yearning melody of love; such glory, such longing for beauty, for life—and then brusquely, again and again, the screaming, sobbing recollection of the fact of death. . . .

When it was over, Sylvia's breath was still coming pantingly. "Oh, Father! How—how wonderful—how——" she murmured.

He looked at her, as though he were angry with her, and yet scarcely seeming to know her, and spoke in a hard, bitter tone: "And it is *years* since I have heard one!" He seemed to cry out upon her for the conditions of his life.

She had no key for these words, could not imagine a meaning for them, and, chilled and repelled, wondered if she had heard him rightly.

The funeral march from the Eroica began, and her father's face softened. The swelling volume of tone rose like a flood-tide. The great hall, the thousands of human hearts, all beat solemnly in the grave and hopeless pulsations of the measured chords. The air was thick with sorrow, with quiet despair. No outcries here, no screams— the modern soul advancing somberly with a pale composure to the grave of its love, aware that during all the centuries since the dead Siegfried was lifted high on the shoulders of his warriors not a word of explanation, of consolation has been found; that the modern, barren self-control means only what the barbarian yells out in his open abandonment to sorrow—and yet such beauty, such beauty in that singing thread of melody—"*durch Leiden, Freude!*"

Not even the shadow of death had ever fallen across Sylvia's life, or that of her father, to explain the premonitory emotion which now drew them together like two frightened children. Sylvia felt the inexorable music beating in her own veins, and when she took her father's hand it seemed to her that its strong pulses throbbed to the same rhythm; beauty, and despair . . . hope . . . life . . . death.

At the end, " Oh, Father—oh, Father ! " she said under her breath, imploringly, struggling to free herself from the muffling, enveloping sense of imminent disaster. He pressed her hand hard and smiled at her. It was his own old smile, the father-look which had been her heart's home all her life—but it was infinitely sweeter to her now than ever before. She had never felt closer to him. There was a pause during which they did not speak, and then there burst upon them the splendid tumult of " Death and Transfiguration," which, like a great wind, swept Sylvia out of herself. She could not follow the music—she had never heard of it before. She was beaten down, over-whelmed, freed, as though the transfiguration were her own, from the pitiful barriers of consciousness. . . .

" Was the concert good ? " asked Mrs. Marshall, yawning, and reaching out of bed to kiss Sylvia sleepily. She laughed a little at their faces. " Oh, music *is* a madness ! To spend a cheerful evening listening to death-music, and then come back looking like Moses before the Burning Bush ! "

" Say, you ought to have seen the stunt they did with their lassos," cried Judith, waking in the bed on the other side of the room, and sitting up with her black hair tousled about her face. " I'm going to try it with the pinto when we get home."

" I *bet* you'll do it, too," came from Lawrence the loyal, always sure of Judith's strength, Judith's skill.

Sylvia looked at her father over their heads and smiled faintly. It was a good smile, from a full heart.

" Aunt Victoria sent our dresses," said Judith, dropping back on the pillow. " That big box over there. Mine has pink ribbons, and yours are blue."

Mrs. Marshall looked at the big box with disfavor, and then at Sylvia, now sunk in a chair, her hands clasped behind her head, her eyes dreamy and half closed.

Across the room the long pasteboard box displayed a frothy mass of white lace and pale shining ribbons. Sylvia looked at it absently and made no move to examine it. She closed her eyes again and beat an inaudible rhythm with her raised fingers. All through her was ringing the upward-surging tide of sound at the end of " Death and Transfiguration."

"Oh, go to bed, Sylvia; don't sit there maundering over the concert," said her mother, with a good-natured asperity. But there was relief in her voice.

CHAPTER XIV

HIGHER EDUCATION

To any one who is familiar with State University life, the color of Sylvia's Freshman year will be vividly conveyed by the simple statement that she was not invited to join a fraternity. To any one who does not know State University life, no description can convey anything approaching an adequate notion of the terribly determinative significance of that fact.

The statement that she was invited to join no sorority is not literally true, for in the second semester when it was apparent that none of the three leading fraternities intended to take her in, there came a late " bid " from one of the third-rate sororities, of recent date, composed of girls like Sylvia who had not been included in the membership of the older, socially distinguished organizations. Cut to the quick by her exclusion from the others, Sylvia refused this tardy invitation with remorseless ingratitude. If she were not to form one of the " swell " set of college, at least she would not proclaim herself one of the " jays," the " grinds," the queer girls, who wore their hair straight back from their foreheads, who invariably carried off Phi Beta Kappa, whose skirts hung badly, whose shoe-heels turned over as they walked, who stood first in their classes, whose belts behind made a practice of revealing large white safety-pins ; and whose hats, even disassociated from their dowdy wearers, and hanging in the cloakroom, were of an almost British eccentricity.

Nothing of this sort could be alleged against Sylvia's appearance, which she felt, as she arrayed herself every morning, to be all that the most swagger frat could ask of a member. Aunt Victoria's boxes of clothing, her own nimble fingers and passionate attention to the subject, combined to turn her out a copy, not to be distinguished from the original, of the daughter of a man with an income five times that of her father. As she consulted her mirror, it occurred to her also, as but an honest recognition of a conspicuous fact, that her suitable and harmonious toilets adorned a person as pleasing to the eye as any of her classmates.

During the last year of her life at home she had shot up very fast, and she was now a tall, slender presence, preserved from even the usual touching and delightful awkwardness of seventeen by the trained dexterity and strength with which she handled her body, as muscular, for all its rounded slimness, as a boy's. Her hair was beautiful, a bright chestnut brown with a good deal of red, its brilliant gloss broken into innumerable high-lights by the ripple of its waviness; and she had one other positive beauty, the clearly penciled line of her long, dark eyebrows, which ran up a trifle at the outer ends with a little quirk, giving an indescribable air of alertness and vivacity to her expression. Otherwise she was not at that age, nor did she ever become, so explicitly handsome as her sister Judith, who had at every period of her life a head as beautiful as that on a Greek coin. But when the two were together, although the perfectly adjusted proportions of Judith's proud, dark face brought out the irregularities of Sylvia's, disclosed the tilt of her small nose, made more apparent the disproportionate width between her eyes, and showed her chin to be of no mold in particular, yet a modern eye rested with far more pleasure on the older sister's face. A bright, quivering mobility like sunshine on water, gave it a charm which was not dependent on the more obvious prettinesses of a fine-grained, white skin, extremely clear brown eyes, and a mouth quick to laugh and quiver, with pure, sharply cut outline and deeply sunk corners. Even in repose, Sylvia's face made Judith's seem unresponsive, and when it lighted up in talk and laughter, it seemed to give out a visible light. In contrast Judith's beautiful countenance seemed carved out of some very hard and indestructible stone.

And yet, in spite of this undeniably satisfactory physical outfit, and pre-eminent ability in athletics, Sylvia was not invited to join any of the best fraternities. It is not surprising that there was mingled with her bitterness on the subject a justifiable amount of bewilderment. What *did* they want? They recruited, from her very side in classes, girls without half her looks or cleverness. What *was* the matter with her? She would not for her life have given a sign to her family of her mental sufferings as, during that first autumn, day after day went by with no sign of welcome from the social leaders of her new world; but a mark was left on her character by her affronted recognition of her total lack of success in this, her first appearance outside the sheltering walls of her home; her first trial by the real standards of the actual world of real people.

The fact, which would have been balm to Sylvia's vanity, had she ever had the least knowledge of it, was that upon her appearance in the Freshman class she had been the occasion of violent discussion and almost of dissension in the councils of the two "best" fraternities. Her beauty, her charm, and the rumors of her excellence in tennis had made a flutter in the first fraternity meetings after the opening of the autumn term. The younger members of both Sigma Beta and Alpha Kappa counseled early and enthusiastic "rushing" of the new prize, but the Juniors and Seniors, wise in their day and generation, brought out a number of damning facts which would need to be taken into consideration if Sylvia wore their pin.

There were, in both fraternities, daughters of other faculty families, who were naturally called upon to furnish inside information. They had been brought up from childhood on the tradition of the Marshalls' hopeless queerness, and their collective statement of the Marshalls' position ran somewhat as follows: " The only professors who have anything to do with them are some of the jay young profs from the West, with no families; the funny old La Rues—you know what a hopeless dowd Madame La Rue is—and Professor Kennedy, and though he comes from a swell family he's an awful freak himself. They live on a farm, like farmers, at the ends of the earth from anybody that anybody knows. They are never asked to be patrons of any swell college functions. None of the faculty ladies with any social position ever call on Mrs. Marshall—and no wonder. She doesn't keep any help, and when the doorbell rings she's as apt to come running in from the chicken house with rubber boots on, and a basket of eggs—and the *queerest* clothes! Like a costume out of a book; and they never have anybody to wait on the table, just jump up and down themselves—you can imagine what kind of a frat tea or banquet Sylvia would give in such a home—and of course if we took her in, we couldn't very well *tell* her her family's so impossible we wouldn't want their connection with the frat known—and the students who go there are a perfect collection of all the jays and grinds and freaks in college. It's enough to mark you one to be seen there— you meet all the crazy guys you see in classes and never anywhere else—and of course that wouldn't stop when Sylvia's frat sisters began going there. And their house wouldn't do at *all* to entertain in—it's queer—no rugs— dingy old furniture—nothing but books everywhere, even in their substitute for a parlor—and you're likely to meet not only college freaks, but worse ones from goodness knows where. There's a beer-drinking old monster who goes there every Sunday to play the fiddle that you wouldn't have speak to you on the street for anything in the world. And the way they entertain! My, in such a countrified way! Some of the company go out into the kitchen to help Mrs. Marshall serve up the refreshments—and everything home- made—and they play charades, and nobody knows what else —bean-bag, or spelling-down maybe——"

This appalling picture, which in justice to the young delineators must be conceded to be not in the least over- drawn, was quite enough to give pause to those impetuous and immature young Sophomores who had lacked the philo- sophical breadth of vision to see that Sylvia was not an isolated phenomenon, but (since her family lived in La

Chance) an inseparable part of her background. After all, the sororities made no claim to be anything but social organizations. Their standing in the college world depended upon their social background, and of course this could only be made up of a composite mingling of those of their individual members.

Fraternities did not wish to number more than sixteen or eighteen undergraduates. That meant only four or five to be chosen from each Freshman class, and that number of "nice" girls was not hard to find, girls who were not only well dressed, and lively and agreeable in themselves, but who came from large, well-kept, well-furnished houses on the right streets of La Chance; with presentable, card-playing, call-paying, reception-giving mothers, who hired caterers for their entertainments; and respectably absentee fathers with sizable pocketbooks and a habit of cash liberality. The social standing of the co-eds in State Universities was already precarious enough, without running the risk of acquiring dubious social connections.

If Sylvia had been a boy, it is almost certain that the deficiencies of her family would have been overlooked in consideration of her potentialities in the athletic world. Success in athletics was to the men's fraternities what social standing was to the girls'. It must be remarked parenthetically that neither class of these organizations had the slightest prejudice against high scholastic standing. On the contrary it was regarded very kindly by fraternity members, as a desirable though not indispensable addition to social standing and physical prowess.

But Sylvia was not a boy, and her fine, promising game of tennis, her excellence in the swimming-pool, and her success on the gymnasium floor and on the flying rings, served no purpose but to bring to her the admiration of the duffers among the girls, whom she despised, and the unspoken envy of the fraternity girls, whose overtures at superficial friendliness she constantly rebuffed with stern, wounded pride.

The sharpest stab to her pride came from the inevitable

publicity of her ordeal. For, though her family knew nothing of what that first year out in the world meant to her, she had not the consolation of hoping that her condition was not perfectly apparent to every one else in the college world. At the first of the year, all gatherings of undergraduates not in fraternities hummed and buzzed with speculations about who would or would not be " taken " by the leading fraternities. For every girl who was at all possible, each day was a long suspense, beginning in hope and ending in listlessness; and for Sylvia in an added shrinking from the eyes of her mates, which were, she knew, fixed on her with a relentless curiosity which was torture to one of her temperament. She had been considered almost sure to be early invited to join Alpha Kappa, the frat to which most of the faculty daughters belonged, and all during the autumn she was aware that when she took off her jacket in the cloak-room, a hundred glances swept her to see if she wore at last the coveted emblem of the "pledged " girl; and when an Alpha Kappa girl chanced to come near her with a casual remark, she seemed to hear a significant hush among the other girls, followed by an equally significant buzz of whispered comment when the fraternity member moved away again. This atmosphere would have made no impression on a nature either more sturdily philosophic, or more unimaginative than Sylvia's (Judith, for instance, was not in the least affected by the experience), but it came to be a morbid obsession of this strong, healthy, active-minded young creature. It tinged with bitterness and blackness what should have been the crystal-clear cup holding her youth and intelligence and health. She fancied that every one despised her. She imagined that people who were in reality quite unaware of her existence were looking at her and whispering together a wondering discussion as to why she was not " in the swim " as such a girl ought to be—all girls worth their salt were.

Above all she was stung into a sort of speechless rage by her impotence to do anything to regain the decent minimum of personal dignity which she felt was stripped from her by this constant play of bald speculation about whether she would or would not be considered "good enough" to be invited into a sorority. If only something definite would happen! If there were only an occasion on which she might in some way proudly proclaim her utter indifference to fraternities and their actions! If only the miserable business were not so endlessly drawn out! She threw herself with a passionate absorption into her studies, her music, and her gymnasium work, cut off both from the "elect" and from the multitude, a proudly self-acknowledged maverick. She never lacked admiring followers among less brilliant girls who would have been adorers if she had not held them off at arm's length, but her vanity, far from being omnivorous, required more delicate food. She wished to be able to cry aloud to her world that she thought nothing and cared nothing about fraternities, and by incessant inner absorption in this conception she did to a considerable extent impose it upon the collective mind of her contemporaries. She, the yearningly friendly, sympathetic, sensitive, praise-craving Sylvia, came to be known, half respected and half disliked, as proud and clever, and "high-brow," and offish, and conceited, and so "queer" that she cared nothing for the ordinary pleasures of ordinary girls.

This reputation for a high-browed indifference to commonplace mortals was naturally not a recommendation to the masculine undergraduates of the University. These young men, under the influence of reports of what was done at Cornell and other more eastern co-educational institutions, were already strongly inclined to ignore the co-eds as much as possible. The tradition was growing rapidly that the proper thing was to invite the "town-girls" to the college proms and dances, and to sit beside them in the grandstand during football games. As yet, however, this tendency had not gone so far but that those co-eds who were members of a socially recognized fraternity were automatically saved from the neglect which enveloped all other but exceptionally flirtatious and undiscriminating girls. Each girls' fraternity, like the masculine organizations, gave one big hop in the course of the season and several smaller dances, as well as lawn-parties and teas and stage-coach parties to the football games. The young men naturally wished to be invited to these functions, the increasing elaborateness of which kept pace with the increasing sophistication of life in La Chance and the increasing cost of which made the parents of the girls groan. Consequently each masculine fraternity took care that it did not incur the enmity of the organized and socially powerful sororities. But Sylvia was not protected by this ægis. She was not invited during her Freshman year to the dances given by either the sororities or the fraternities; and the large scattering crowd of masculine undergraduates were frightened away from the handsome girl by her supposed haughty intellectual tastes.

Here again her isolation was partly the result of her own wish. The raw-boned, badly dressed farmers' lads, with red hands and rough hair, she quite as snobbishly ignored as she was ignored in her turn by the well-set-up, fashionably dressed young swells of the University, with their white hands, with their thin, gaudy socks tautly pulled over their ankle-bones, and their shining hair glistening like lacquer on their skulls (that being the desideratum in youthful masculine society of the place and time). Sylvia snubbed the masculine jays of college partly because it was a breath of life to her battered vanity to be able to snub some one, and partly because they seemed to her, in comparison with the smart set, seen from afar, quite and utterly undesirable. She would rather have no masculine attentions at all than such poor provender for her feminine desire to conquer.

Thus she trod the leafy walks of the beautiful campus alone, ignoring and ignored, keenly alive under her shell of indifference to the brilliant young men and their chosen few feminine companions.

CHAPTER XV

MRS. DRAPER BLOWS THE COALS

THE most brilliant of these couples were Jermain Fiske, Jr., and Eleanor Hubert. The first was the son of the well-known and distinguished Colonel Jermain Fiske, one of the trustees of the University, ex-Senator from the State. He belonged to the old, free-handed, speech-making type of American statesmen, and, with his florid good looks, his great stature, his loud, resonant, challenging voice, and his picturesque reputation for highly successful double-dealing, he was one of the most talked-of men in the State, despite his advanced years. His enemies, who were not few, said that the shrewdest action of his surpassingly shrewd life had been his voluntary retirement from the Senate and from political activities at the first low murmur heralding the muck-raking cyclone which was to devastate public life as men of his type understood it. But every inhabitant of the State, including his enemies, took an odd pride in his fiercely debonair defiance to old age, in his grandiloquent, too fluent public addresses, and in the manner in which, despite his dubious private reputation, he held open to him, by sheer will-power, sanctimonious doors which were closed to other less robust bad examples to youth.

This typical specimen of an American class now passing away, had sent his son to the State University instead of to an expensive Eastern college because of his carefully avowed attitude of bluff acceptance of a place among the plain people of the region. The presence of Jermain, Jr., in the classrooms of the State University had been capital for many a swelling phrase on his father's part—" What's good enough for the farmers' boys of my State is good enough for my boy," etc., etc.

As far as the young man in question was concerned, he

certainly showed no signs whatever of feeling himself sacrificed for his father's advantage, and apparently considered
that a leisurely sojourn for seven years (he took both the
B.A. and the three-year Law course) in a city the size of
La Chance was by no means a hardship for a young man
in the best of health, provided with ample funds, and never
questioned as to the disposition of his time. He had had
at first a reputation for dissipation which, together with his
prowess on the football field, had made him as much talked
of on the campus as his father in the State; but during his
later years, those spent in the Law School, he had, as the
college phrase ran, " taken it out in being swagger," had
discarded his former shady associates, had two rooms in
the finest frat house on the campus, and was the only
student of the University to drive two horses tandem to a
high, red-wheeled dog-cart. His fine physique and reputation for quick assertion of his rights saved him from the
occasional taunt of dandyism which would have been flung
at any other student indulging in so unusual a freak of
fashion.

During Sylvia's Freshman year there usually sat beside
him, on the lofty seat of this equipage, a sweet-faced, gentle-
browed young lady, the lovely flower blooming out of the
little girl who had so innocently asked her mother some ten
years ago what was a drunken reinhardt. The oldest
daughter of the professor of European History was almost
precisely Sylvia's age, but now, when Sylvia was laboring
over her books in the very beginning of her college life,
Eleanor Hubert was a finished product, a graduate of an
exclusive, expensive girls' boarding-school in New York,
and a that-year's débutante in La Chance society. Her
name was constantly in the items of the society columns, she
wore the most profusely varied costumes, and she drove
about the campus swaying like a lily beside the wealthiest
undergraduate. Sylvia's mind was naturally too alert and
vigorous, and now too thoroughly awakened to intellectual
interests, not to seize with interest on the subjects she
studied that year; but enjoy as much as she tried to do, and

did, this tonic mental discipline, there were many moments when the sight of Eleanor Hubert made her wonder if after all higher mathematics and history were of any real value.

During this wretched year of stifled unhappiness, she not only studied with extreme concentration, but, with a healthy instinct, spent a great deal of time in the gymnasium. It was a delight to her to be able to swim in the winter-time, she organized the first water-polo team among the co-eds, and she began to learn fencing from the Commandant of the University Battalion. He had been a crack with the foils at West Point, and never ceased trying to arouse an interest in what seemed to him the only rational form of exercise; but fencing at that time had no intercollegiate vogue, and of all the young men and women at the State University, Sylvia alone took up his standing offer of free instruction to any one who cared to give the time to learn; and even Sylvia took up fencing primarily because it promised to give her one more occupation, left her less time for loneliness. As it turned out, however, these lessons proved far more to her than a temporary anodyne: they brought her a positive pleasure. She delighted the dumpy little captain with her aptness, and he took the greatest pains in his instruction. Before the end of her Freshman year she twice succeeded in getting through his guard and landing a thrust on his well-rounded figure; and though to keep down her conceit he told her that he must be losing, along with his slenderness, some of his youthful agility, he confessed to his wife that teaching Miss Marshall was the best fun he had had in years. The girl was as quick as a cat, and had a natural-born fencer's wrist.

During the summer vacation she kept up her practice with her father, who remembered enough of his early training in Paris to be more than a match for her, and in the autumn of her Sophomore year, at the annual Gymnasium exhibition, she gave with the Commandant a public bout with the foils in which she notably distinguished herself. The astonished and long-continued applause for this new feature of the exhibition was a draught of nectar to her embittered young heart, but she acknowledged it with not the smallest sign of pleasure, showing an impassive face as she stood by the portly captain, slim and tall and young and haughty, joining him in a sweeping, ceremonious salute with her foil to the enthusiastic audience, and turning on her heel with a brusqueness as military as his own, to march firmly with high-held head beside him back to the ranks of blue-bloomered girls who stood watching her.

The younger girls in Alpha Kappa and Sigma Beta were seizing this opportunity to renew an old quarrel with their elders in the fraternities and were acrimoniously hoping that the older ones were quite satisfied with their loss of a brilliant member. These accusations met with no ready answer from the somewhat crestfallen elders, whose only defense was the entire unexpectedness of the way in which Sylvia was distinguishing herself. Who ever heard before of a girl doing anything remarkable in athletics? And anyhow, now in her Sophomore year it was too late to do anything. A girl so notoriously proud would certainly not consider a tardy invitation, and it would not do to run the risk of being refused. It is not too much to say that to have overheard a conversation like this would have changed the course of Sylvia's development, but of such colloquies she could know nothing, attributing to the fraternities, with all an outsider's resentful overestimation of their importance, an arrogant solidarity of opinion and firmness of purpose which they were very far from possessing.

Professor and Mrs. Marshall and Lawrence and Judith, up in the front row of chairs set for the audience about the running track, followed this exploit of Sylvia's with naïvely open pride and sympathy, applauding even more heartily than did their neighbors. Lawrence, as usual, began to compose a poem, the first line of which ran,

"Splendid, she wields her gleaming sword——"

The most immediate result of this first public success of Sylvia's was the call paid to Mrs. Marshall on the day

following by Mrs. Draper, the wife of the professor of
Greek. Although there had never been any formal social
intercourse between the two ladies, they had for a good
many years met each other casually on the campus, and
Mrs. Draper, with the extremely graceful manner of assurance which was her especial accomplishment, made it seem
quite natural that she should call to congratulate Sylvia's
mother on the girl's skill and beauty as shown in her prowess
on the evening before. Mrs. Marshall prided herself on
her undeceived view of life, but she was as ready to hear
praise of her spirited and talented daughter as any other
mother, and quite melted to Mrs. Draper, although her
observations from afar of the other woman's career in La
Chance had never before inclined her to tolerance. So that
when Mrs. Draper rose to go and asked casually if Sylvia
couldn't run in at five that afternoon to have a cup of tea
at her house with a very few of her favorites among the
young people, Mrs. Marshall, rather inflexible by nature
and quite unused to the subtleties of social intercourse,
found herself unable to retreat quickly enough from her reflected tone of cordiality to refuse the invitation for her
daughter.

When Sylvia came back to lunch she was vastly fluttered and pleased by the invitation, and as she ate, her
mind leaped from one possible sartorial combination to
another. Whatever she wore must be exactly right to be
worthy of such a hostess: for Mrs. Draper was a conspicuous figure in faculty society. She had acquired,
through years of extremely intelligent manœuvering, a reputation for choice exclusiveness which was accepted even in
the most venerable of the old families of La Chance, those
whose founders had built their log huts there as long as fifty
years before. In faculty circles she occupied a unique position, envied and feared and admired and distrusted and
copiously gossiped about by the faculty ladies, who accepted
with eagerness any invitations to entertainments in her
small, æsthetic, and perfectly appointed house. She was
envied even by women with much more than her income:—

for of course Professor Draper had an independent income; it was hardly possible to be anybody unless one belonged to that minority of the faculty families with resources beyond the salary granted by the State.

Faculty ladies were, however, not favored with a great number of invitations to Mrs. Draper's select and amusing teas and dinners, as that lady had a great fancy for surrounding herself with youth, meaning, for the most part, naturally enough, masculine youth. With an unerring and practised eye she picked out from each class the few young men who were to her purpose, and proclaiming with the most express lack of reticence the forty-three years which she by no means looked, she took these chosen few under a wing frankly maternal, giving them, in the course of an intimate acquaintance with her and the dim and twilight ways of her house and life, an enlightening experience of a civilization which she herself said, with a humorous appreciation of her own value, quite made over the young, unlicked cubs. This statement of her influence on most of the young men drawn into her circle was perhaps not much exaggerated.

From time to time she also admitted into this charmed circle a young girl or two, though almost never one of the University girls, of whom she made the jolliest possible fun. Her favorites were the daughters of good La Chance families who at seventeen had "finished" at Miss Home's Select School for Young Ladies, and who came out in society not later than eighteen. She seemed able, as long as she cared to do it, to exercise as irresistible a fascination over these youthful members of her own sex as over the older masculine undergraduates of the University. They copied their friend's hats and neckwear and shoes and her mannerisms of speech, were miserable if she neglected them for a day, furiously jealous of each other, and raised to the seventh heaven by attention from her. Just at present the only girl admitted frequently to Mrs. Draper's intimacy was Eleanor Hubert.

On the day following the Gymnasium exhibition, when

Sylvia, promptly at five, entered the picturesque vine-covered Draper house, she found it occupied by none of the usual habitués of the place. The white-capped, black-garbed maid who opened the door to the girl held aside for her a pair of heavy brown-velvet portières which veiled the entrance to the drawing-room. The utter silence of this servitor seemed portentous and inhuman to the young guest, unused to the polite convention that servants cast no shadow and do not exist save when serving their superiors.

She found herself in a room as unlike any she had ever seen as though she had stepped into a new planet. The light here was as yellow as gold, and came from a great many candles which, in sconces and candelabra, stood about the room, their oblong yellow flame as steady in the breathless quiet of the air as though they burned in a vault underground. There was not a book in the room, except one in a yellow cover lying beside a box of candy on the mantelpiece, but every ledge, table, projection, or shelf was covered with small, queerly fashioned, dully gleaming objects of ivory, or silver, or brass, or carved wood, or porcelain.

The mistress of the room now came in. She was in a loose garment of smoke-brown chiffon, held in place occasionally about her luxuriously rounded figure by a heavy cord of brown silk. She advanced to Sylvia with both hands outstretched, and took the girl's slim, rather hard young fingers in the softest of melting palms. "Aren't you a *dear,* to be so exactly on time!" she exclaimed.

Sylvia was a little surprised. She had thought it axiomatic that people kept their appointments promptly. "Oh, I'm always on time," she answered simply.

Mrs. Draper laughed and pulled her down on the sofa. "You clear-eyed young Diana, you won't allow me even an instant's illusion that you were eager to come to see *me!*"

"Oh yes, I *was!*" said Sylvia hastily, fearing that she might have said something rude.

Mrs. Draper laughed again and gave the hand she still held a squeeze. "You're adorable, that's what *you* are!" She exploded this pointblank charge in Sylvia's face with

nonchalant ease, and went on with another. " Jerry Fiske
is quite right about you. I suppose you know that you're
here today so that Jerry can meet you."

As there was obviously not the faintest possibility of
Sylvia's having heard this save through her present in-
formant, she could only look what she felt, very much at
a loss, and rather blank, with a heightened color. Mrs.
Draper eyed her with an intentness at variance with the
lightness of her tone, as she continued: " I do think Jerry'd
have burned up in one flare, like a torch, if he couldn't
have seen you at once! After you'd fenced and disappeared
again into that stupid crowd of graceless girls, he kept
track of you every minute with his opera-glasses, and kept
saying: ' She's a goddess! Good Lord! how she carries
herself! ' It was rather hard on poor Eleanor right there
beside him, but I don't blame him. Eleanor's a sweet thing,
but she'd be sugar and water compared to champagne if
she stood up by you."

For a good many months Sylvia had been craving praise
with a starved appetite, and although she found this down-
pour of it rather drenching, she could not sufficiently col-
lect herself to make the conventional decent pretense that it
was unwelcome. She flushed deeply and looked at her
hostess with dazzled eyes. Mrs. Draper affected to see in
her silence a blankness as to the subject of the talk, and
interrupted the flow of personalities to cry out, with a pretense of horror, " You don't mean to say you don't know
who Jerry Fiske *is!* "

Sylvia, as unused as her mother to conversational traps,
fell into this one with an eager promptness. " Oh yes, indeed; I know him by sight very well," she said and stopped,
flushing again at a significant laugh from Mrs. Draper. " I
mean," she went on with dignity, " that Mr. Fiske has always been so prominent in college—football and all, you
know—and his father being one of our State Senators so
long—I suppose everybody on the campus knows him by
sight." Mrs. Draper patted the girl's shoulder propitiat-
ingly. " Yes, yes, of course," she assented. She added

"He's ever so good-looking, don't you think—like a great Viking with his yellow hair and bright blue eyes?"

"I never noticed his eyes," said Sylvia stiffly, suspicious of ridicule in the air.

"Well, you'll have a chance to this afternoon," answered her hostess, "for he's the only other person who's to be admitted to the house. I had a great time excusing myself to Eleanor—she was coming to take me out driving—but of course it wouldn't do—for her own sake—the poor darling —to have her here today!"

Sylvia thought she could not have rightly understood the significance of this speech, and looked uncomfortable. Mrs. Draper said: "Oh, you needn't mind cutting Eleanor out— she's only a dear baby who can't feel anything very deeply. It's Mamma Hubert who's so mad about catching Jerry. Since she's heard he's to have the Fiske estate at Mercerton as soon as he graduates from Law School, she's like a wild creature! If Eleanor weren't the most unconscious little bait that ever hung on a hook Jerry'd have turned away in disgust long ago. He may not be so very acute, but Mamma Hubert and her manœuvers are not millstones for seeing through!"

The doorbell rang, one long and one short tap. "That's Jerry's ring," said Mrs. Draper composedly, as though she had been speaking of her husband. In an instant the heavy portières were flung back by a vigorous arm, and a very tall, broad-shouldered, clean-shaven young man, in a well-tailored brown suit, stepped in. He accosted his hostess with easy assurance, but went through his introduction to Sylvia in a rather awkward silence.

"Now we'll have tea," said Mrs. Draper at once, pressing a button. In a moment a maid brought in a tray shining with silver and porcelain, set it down on the table in front of Mrs. Draper, and then wheeled in a little circular table with shelves, a glorified edition in gleaming mahogany of the homely, white-painted wheeled-tray of Sylvia's home. On the shelves was a large assortment of delicate, small cakes and paper-thin sandwiches. While she poured out the amber-colored tea into the translucent cups, Mrs. Draper kept up with the new-comer a lively mono-logue of personalities, in which Sylvia, for very ignorance of the people involved, could take no part. She sat silent, watching with concentration the two people before her, the singularly handsome man, certainly the handsomest man she had ever seen, and the far from handsome but singularly alluring woman who faced him, making such a display of her two good points, her rich figure and her fine dark eyes, that for an instant the rest of her person seemed non-existent.

"How do you like your tea, dear?" The mistress of the house brought her stranded guest back into the current of talk with this well-worn hook.

"Oh, it doesn't make any difference," said Sylvia, who, as it happened, did not like the taste of tea.

"You really ought to have it nectar; with whipped am-brosia on top." Mrs. Draper troweled this statement on with a dashing smear, saving Sylvia from being forced to answer, by adding lightly to the man, "Is ambrosia any-thing that will whip, do you suppose?"

"Never heard of it before," he answered, breaking his silence with a carefree absence of shame at his confession of ignorance. "Sounds like one of those labels on a soda-water fountain that nobody ever samples."

Mrs. Draper made a humorously exaggerated gesture of despair and turned to Sylvia. "Well, it's just as well, my dear, that you should know at the very beginning what a perfect monster of illiteracy he is! You needn't expect any-thing from him but his stupid good-looks, and money and fascination. Otherwise he's a Cave-Man for ignorance. You must take him in hand!" She turned back to the man. "Sylvia, you know, is as clever as she is beautiful. She had the highest rank but three in her class last year."

Sylvia was overcome with astonishment by this knowl-edge of a fact which had seemed to make no impression on the world of the year before. "Why, how could you know that!" she cried.

Mrs. Draper laughed. " Just hear her ! " she appealed to the young man. Her method of promoting the acquaintance of the two young people seemed to consist in talking to each of the other. " Just hear her ! She converses as she fences —one bright flash, and you're skewered against the wall— no parryings possible ! " She faced Sylvia again : " Why, my dear, in answer to your rapier-like question, I must simply confess that this morning, being much struck with Jerry's being struck with you, I went over to the registrar's office and looked you up. I know that you passed supremely well in mathematics and French (what a quaint combination !), very well indeed in history and chemistry, and moderately in botany. What's the matter with botany ? I have always found Professor Cross a very obliging little man."

" He doesn't make me see any sense to botany," explained Sylvia, taking the question seriously. " I don't seem to get hold of any real reason for studying it at all. What difference does it make if a bush is a hawthorn or not ?— and anyhow, I know it's a hawthorn without studying botany."

The young man spoke for himself now, with a keen relish for Sylvia's words. He faced her for the first time. " Now you're *shouting,* Miss Marshall ! " he said. " That's the most sensible thing I ever heard said. That's just what I always felt about the whole B.A. course, anyhow ! What's the diff ? Who cares whether Charlemagne lived in six hundred or sixteen hundred ? It all happened before we were born. What's it all *to* us ? "

Sylvia looked squarely at him, a little startled at his directly addressing her, not hearing a word of what he said in the vividness of her first-hand impression of his personality, his brilliant blue eyes, his full, very red lips, his boldly handsome face and carriage, his air of confidence. In spite of his verbal agreement with her opinion, his look crossed hers clashingly, like a challenge, a novelty in the amicable harmony which had been the tradition of her life. She felt that tradition to be not without its monotony, and her young blood warmed. She gazed back at him silently, wonderingly, frankly.

With her radiantly sensuous youth in the first splendor of its opening, with this frank, direct look, she had a moment of brilliance to make the eyes of age shade themselves as against a dazzling brightness. The eyes of the man opposite her were not those of age. They rested on her, aroused, kindling to heat. His head went up like a stag's. She felt a momentary hot throb of excitement, as though her body were one great fiddle-string, twanging under a vigorously plucking thumb. It was thrilling, it was startling, it was not altogether pleasant. The corners of her sensitive mouth twitched uncertainly.

Mrs. Draper, observing from under her down-drooped lids this silent passage between the two, murmured amusedly to herself, "Ah, now you're shouting, my children!"

CHAPTER XVI

PLAYING WITH MATCHES

THERE was much that was acrid about the sweetness of triumph which the next months brought Sylvia. The sudden change in her life had not come until there was an accumulation of bitterness in her heart the venting of which was the strongest emotion of that period of strong emotions. As she drove about the campus, perched on the high seat of the red-wheeled dog-cart, her lovely face looked down with none of Eleanor Hubert's gentleness into the envying eyes of the other girls. A high color burned in her cheeks, and her bright eyes were not soft. She looked continually excited.

At home she was hard to live with, quick to take offense at the least breath of the adverse criticism which she felt, unspoken and forbearing but thick in the air about her. She neglected her music, she neglected her studies; she spent long hours of feverish toil over Aunt Victoria's chiffons and silks. There was need for many toilets now, for the incessantly recurring social events to which she went with young Fiske, chaperoned by Mrs. Draper, who had for her old rival and enemy, Mrs. Hubert, the most mocking of friendly smiles, as she entered a ballroom, the acknowledged sponsor of the brilliant young sensation of the college season.

At these dances Sylvia had the grim satisfaction, not infrequently the experience of intelligent young ladies, of being surrounded by crowds of admiring young men, for whom she had no admiration, the barren sterility of whose conversation filled her with astonishment, even in her fever of exultation. She knew the delights of frequently "splitting" her dances so that there might be enough to go around. She was plunged headlong into the torrent of excitement which is the life of a social favorite at a large State University, that breathless whirl of one engagement after another for every evening and for most of the days, which is one of the oddest developments of the academic life as planned and provided for by the pioneer fathers of those great Western commonwealths; and she savored every moment of it, for during every moment she drank deep at the bitter fountain of personal vindication. She went to all the affairs which had ignored her the year before, to all the dances given by the " swell men's fraternities," to the Sophomore hop, to the " Football Dance," at the end of the season, to the big reception given to the Freshman class by the Seniors. And in addition to these evening affairs, she appeared beside Jerry Fiske at every football game, at the first Glee Club Concert, at the outdoor play given by the Literary Societies, and very frequently at the weekly receptions to the students tendered by the ladies of the faculty.

These affairs were always spoken of by the faculty as an attempt to create a homogeneous social atmosphere on the campus; but this attempt had ended, as such efforts usually do, in adding to the bewildering plethora of social life of those students who already had too much, and in being an added sting to the solitude and ostracism of those who had none. Naturally enough, the ladies of the faculty who took most interest in these afternoon functions were the ones who cared most for society life, and there was only too obvious a contrast between their manner of kindly, vague, condescending interest shown to one of the " rough-neck" students, and the easy familiarity shown to one of those socially " possible." The " rough-necks" seldom sought out more than once the prettily decorated tables spread every Friday afternoon in the Faculty Room, off the reading-room of the Library. Sylvia especially had, on the only occasion when she had ventured into this charming scene, suffered too intensely from the difference of treatment accorded her and that given Eleanor Hubert to feel anything but angry resentment. After that experience, she had passed along the halls with the other outsiders, books

in hand, her head held proudly high, and never turned even
to glance in at the gleaming tables, the lighted candles, and
the little groups of easily self-confident fraternity men and
girls laughing and talking over their teacups, and revenging
vicariously the rest of the ignored student-body by the calm
young insolence with which they in their turn ignored their
presumptive hostesses, the faculty ladies.

Mrs. Draper changed all this for Sylvia with a wave of
her wand. She took the greatest pains to introduce her
protégée into this phase of the social life of the University.
On these occasions, as beautiful and as over-dressed as any
girl in the room, with Jermain Fiske in obvious attendance;
with the exclusive Mrs. Draper setting in a rich frame of
commentary any remark she happened to make (Sylvia was
acquiring a reputation for great wit) ; with Eleanor Hubert,
eclipsed, sitting in a corner, quite deserted save for a funny
countrified freak assistant in chemistry; with all the " swell-
est frat men " in college rushing to get her tea and sandwiches; with Mrs. Hubert plunged obviously into acute unhappiness, Sylvia knew as ugly moments of mean satisfaction as often fall to the lot even of very pretty young
women.

At home she knew no moments of satisfaction of any
variety, although there was no disapprobation expressed by
any one, except in one or two characteristically recondite
comments by Professor Kennedy, who was taking a rather
uneasy triumph in the proof of an old theory of his as to
Sylvia's character. One afternoon, at a football game, he
came up to her on the grandstand, shook hands with Jermain Fiske, whom he had flunked innumerable times in
algebra, and remarked in his most acid voice that he wished
to congratulate the young man on being the perfect specimen
of the dolichocephalic blond whose arrival in Sylvia's life
he had predicted years before. Sylvia, belligerently aware
of the attitude of her home world, and ready to resent
criticism, took the liveliest offense at this obscure comment,
which she perfectly understood. She flushed indignantly and
glared in silence with the eyes of an angry young goddess.

Young Fiske, who found the remark, or any other made by a college prof, quite as unintelligible as it was unimportant, laughed with careless impudence in the old man's face; and Mrs. Draper, for all her keenness, could make nothing of it. It sounded, however, so quite like a dictum which she herself would have liked to make, that she cross-questioned Sylvia afterwards as to its meaning; but Sylvia lied fluently, asserting that it was just some of Professor Kennedy's mathematical gibberish which had no meaning.

In the growing acquaintance of Sylvia and Jermain, Mrs. Draper acted assiduously as chaperon, a refinement of sophisticated society which was, as a rule, but vaguely observed in the chaotic flux of State University social life, and she so managed affairs that they were seldom together alone. For obvious reasons Sylvia preferred to see the young man elsewhere than in her own home, where indeed he made almost no appearance, beyond standing at the door of an evening, very handsome and distinguished in his evening dress, waiting for Sylvia to put on her wraps and go out with him to the carriage where Mrs. Draper sat expectant, furred and velvet-wrapped. This discreet manager made no objection to Sylvia's driving about the campus in the daytime alone with Jermain, but to his proposal to drive the girl out to the country-club for dinner one evening she added blandly the imperious proviso that she be of the party; and she discouraged with firmness any projects for solitary walks together through the woods near the campus, although this was a recognized form of co-educational amusement at that institution of learning.

For all her air of free-and-easy equality with the young man, she had at times a certain blighting glance which, turned on him suddenly, always brought him to an agreement with her opinion, an agreement which might obviously ring but verbal on his tongue, but which was nevertheless the acknowledged basis of action. As for Sylvia, she acquiesced, with an eagerness which she did not try to understand, in any arrangement which precluded tête-à-têtes with Jerry.

She did not, as a matter of fact, try to understand anything of what was happening to her. She was by no means sure that she liked it, but was stiffened into a stubborn resistance to any doubts by the unvoiced objection to it all at home. With an instinct against disproportion, perverse perhaps in this case, but with a germ of soundness in it, she felt confusedly and resentfully that since her home circle was so patently narrow and exaggerated in its standard of personality, she would just have to even things up by being a little less fastidious than was her instinct; and on the one or two occasions when a sudden sight of Jerry sent through her a strange, unpleasant stir of all her flesh, she crushed the feeling out of sight under her determination to assert her own judgment and standards against those which had (she now felt) so tyrannically influenced her childhood. But for the most part she did little thinking, shaking as loudly as possible the reverberating rattle of physical excitement.

Thus everything progressed smoothly under Mrs. Draper's management. The young couple met each other usually in the rather close air of her candle-lighted living-room, drinking a great deal of tea, consuming large numbers of delicate, strangely compounded sandwiches, and listening to an endless flow of somewhat startlingly frank personalities from the magnetic mistress of the house. Sylvia and Jermain did not talk much on these occasions. They listened with edification to the racy remarks of their hostess, voicing that theoretical "broadness" of opinion as to the conduct of life which, quite as much as the perfume which she always used, was a specialty of her provocative personality; they spoke now and then, to be sure, as she drew them into conversation, but their real intercourse was almost altogether silent. They eyed each other across the table, breathing quickly, and flushing or paling if their hands chanced to touch in the services of the tea-table. Once the young man came in earlier than usual and found Sylvia alone for a moment in the silent, glowing, perfumed room. He took her hand, apparently for the ordinary handclasp of greeting, but with a surge of his blood retained it, pressing it so fiercely that his ring cut into her finger, causing a tiny drop of bright red to show on the youthful smoothness of her skin. At this living ruby they both stared fixedly for an instant; then Mrs. Draper came hastily into the room, saying chidingly, " Come, come, children! " and looking with displeasure at the man's darkly flushed face. Sylvia was paler than usual for the rest of the afternoon, and could not swallow a mouthful of the appetizing food, which as a rule she devoured with the frank satisfaction of a hungry child. She sat, rather white, not talking much, avoiding Jerry's eyes for no reason that she could analyze, and, in the pauses of the conversation, could hear the blood singing loudly in her ears.

Yet, although she felt the oddest relief, as after one more escape, at the end of each of these afternoons with her new acquaintances, afternoons in which the three seemed perpetually gliding down a steep incline and as perpetually being arrested on the brink of some unexplained plunge, she found that their atmosphere had spoiled entirely her relish for the atmosphere of her home. The home supper-table seemed to her singularly flat and distasteful with its commonplace fare—hot chocolate and creamed potatoes and apple sauce, and its brisk, impersonal talk of socialism, and politics, and small home events, and music. As it happened, the quartet had the lack of intuition to play a great deal of Haydn that autumn, and to Sylvia the cheerful, obvious tap-tap-tap of the hearty old master seemed to typify the bald, unsubtle obtuseness of the home attitude towards life. She herself took to playing the less difficult of the Chopin nocturnes with a languorous over-accentuation of their softness which she was careful to keep from the ears of old Reinhardt. But one evening he came in, unheard, listened to her performance of the B-flat minor nocturne with a frown, and pulled her away from the piano before she had finished. " Not true music, not true love, not true anydings! " he said, speaking however with an unexpected gentleness, and patting her on the shoulder with a dirty old hand. "Listen!" He clapped his fiddle under his chin and played the air of the andante from the Kreutzer Sonata with so singing and heavenly a tone that Sylvia, as helpless an instrument in his skilful hands as the violin itself, felt the nervous tears stinging her eyelids.

This did not prevent her making a long détour the next day to avoid meeting the uncomely old musician on the street and being obliged to recognize him publicly. She lived in perpetual dread of being thus forced, when in the company of Mrs. Draper or Jermain, to acknowledge her connection with him, or with Cousin Parnelia, or with any of the eccentrics who frequented her parents' home, and whom it was physically impossible to imagine drinking tea at Mrs. Draper's table.

It was beside this same table that she met, one day in early December, Jermain Fiske's distinguished father. He explained that he was in La Chance for a day on his way from Washington to Mercerton, where the Fiske family was collecting for its annual Christmas house-party, and had dropped in on Mrs. Draper quite unexpectedly. He was, he added, delighted that it happened to be a day when he could meet the lovely Miss Marshall of whom (with a heavy accent of jocose significance) he had heard so much. Sylvia was a little confused by the pointed attentions of this gallant old warrior, oddly in contrast with the manner of other elderly men she knew; but she thought him very handsome, with his sweeping white mustache, his bright blue eyes, so like his son's, and she was much impressed with his frock-coat, fitting snugly around his well-knit, erect figure, and with the silk hat which she noticed on the table in the hall as she went in. Frock-coats and silk hats were objects seldom encountered in La Chance, except in illustrations to magazine-stories, or in photographs of life in New York or Washington. But of course, she reflected, Colonel Fiske lived most of his life in Washington, about the cosmopolitan delights of which he talked most eloquently to the two ladies.

As was inevitable, Sylvia also met Eleanor Hubert more

or less at Mrs. Draper's. Sylvia had been rendered acutely self-conscious in that direction by Mrs. Draper's very open comments on her rôle in the life of the other girl, and at first had been so smitten by embarrassment as positively to be awkward, a rare event in her life: but she was soon set at ease by the other girl's gentle friendliness, so simple and sincere that even Sylvia's suspicious vanity could not feel it to be condescension. Eleanor's sweet eyes shone so kindly on her successful rival, and she showed so frank and unenvious an admiration of Sylvia's wit and learning, displayed perhaps a trifle ostentatiously by that young lady in the ensuing conversation with Mrs. Draper, that Sylvia had a fresh, healing impulse of shame for her own recently acquired attitude of triumphing hostility towards the world.

At the same time she felt a surprised contempt for the other girl's ignorance and almost illiteracy. Whatever else Eleanor had learned in the exclusive and expensive girls' school in New York, she had not learned to hold her own in a conversation on the most ordinary topics; and as for Mrs. Draper's highly spiced comments on life and folk, her young friend made not the slightest attempt to cope with them or even to understand them. The alluring mistress of the house might talk of sex-antagonism and the hatefulness of the puritanical elements of American life as much as she pleased. It all passed over the head of the lovely, fair girl, sipping her tea and raising her candid eyes to meet with a trustful smile, perhaps a little blank, the glance of whomever chanced to be looking at her. It was significant that she had the same smile for each of the three very dissimilar persons who sat about the tea-table. Of all the circle into which Sylvia's changed life had plunged her, Eleanor, the type of the conventional society bud, was, oddly enough, the only one she cared to talk about in her own extremely unconventional home. But even on this topic she felt herself bruised and jarred by the severity, the unpicturesque austerity of the home standards. As she was trying to give her mother some idea of Eleanor's character, she quoted one day a remark of Mrs. Draper's, to the effect that

"Eleanor no more knows the meaning of her beauty than a rose the meaning of its perfume." Mrs. Marshall kept a forbidding silence for a moment and then said: "I don't take much stock in that sort of unconsciousness. Eleanor isn't a rose, she isn't even a child. She's a woman. The sooner girls learn that distinction, the better off they'll be, and the fewer chances they'll run of being horribly misunderstood."

Sylvia felt very angry with her mother for this unsympathetic treatment of a pretty phrase, and thought with resentment that it was not *her* fault if she were becoming more and more alienated from her family.

This was a feeling adroitly fostered by Mrs. Draper, who, in her endless talks with Sylvia and Jermain about themselves, had hit upon an expression and a turn of phrase which was to have more influence on Sylvia's development than its brevity seemed to warrant. She had, one day, called Sylvia a little Athenian, growing up, by the oddest of mistakes, in Sparta. Sylvia, who was in the Pater-reading stage of development, caught at her friend's phrase as at the longed-for key to her situation. It explained everything. It made everything appear in the light she wished for. Above all it enabled her to clarify her attitude towards her home. Now she understood. One did not scorn Sparta. One respected it, it was a noble influence in life; but for an Athenian, for whom amenity and beauty and suavity were as essential as food, Sparta was death. As was natural to her age and temperament, she sucked a vast amount of pleasure out of this pitying analysis of her subtle, complicated needs and the bare crudity of her surroundings. She now read Pater more assiduously than ever, always carrying a volume about with her text-books, and feeding on this delicate fare in such unlikely and dissimilar places as on the trolley-cars, in the kitchen, in the intervals of preparing a meal, or in Mrs. Draper's living-room, waiting for the problematical entrance of that erratic luminary.

There was none of Mrs. Draper's habits of life which made more of an impression on Sylvia's imagination than her custom of disregarding engagements and appointments, of coming and going, appearing and disappearing quite as she pleased. To the daughter of a scrupulously exact family, which regarded tardiness as a fault, and breaking an appointment as a crime, this high-handed flexibility in dealing with time and bonds and promises had an exciting quality of freedom.

On a good many occasions these periods of waiting chanced to be shared by Eleanor Hubert, for whom, after the first two or three encounters, Sylvia came to have a rather condescending sympathy, singularly in contrast to the uneasy envy with which she had regarded her only a few months before. However, as regards dress, Eleanor was still a phenomenon of the greatest interest, and Sylvia never saw her without getting an idea or two, although it was plain to any one who knew Eleanor that this mastery of the technique of modern American costume was no achievement of her own, that she was merely the lovely and plastic material molded, perhaps to slightly over-complicated effects, by her mother's hands.

From that absent but pervasive personality Sylvia took one suggestion after another. For instance, a very brief association with Eleanor caused her to relegate to the scrap-heap of the " common " the ready-made white ruching for neck and sleeves which she had always before taken for granted. Eleanor's slim neck and smooth wrists were always set off by a few folds of the finest white chiffon, laid with dexterous carelessness, and always so exquisitely fresh that they were obviously renewed by a skilful hand after only a few hours' wearing. The first time she saw Eleanor, Sylvia noticed this detail with appreciation, and immediately struggled to reproduce it in her own costume. Like other feats of the lesser arts this perfect trifle turned out to depend upon the use of the lightest and most adroit touch. None of the chiffon which came in Aunt Victoria's boxes would do. It must be fresh from the shop-counter, ruinous as this was to Sylvia's very modest allowance for dress. Even then she spoiled many a yard of the filmy, unmanageable stuff before she could catch the spirit of those apparently careless folds, so loosely disposed and yet never displaced. It was a phenomenon over which a philosopher might well have pondered, this spectacle of Sylvia's keen brain and well-developed will-power equally concerned with the problems of chemistry and philosophy and history, and with the problem of chiffon folds. She herself was aware of no incongruity, indeed of no difference, between the two sorts of efforts.

Many other matters of Eleanor's attire proved as fruitful of suggestion as this, although Aunt Victoria's well-remembered dictum about the " kitchen-maid's pin-cushion " was a guiding finger-board which warned Sylvia against the multiplication of detail, even desirable detail.

Mrs. Hubert had evidently studied deeply the sources of distinction in modern dress, and had grasped with philosophic thoroughness the underlying principle of the art, which is to show effects obviously costly, but the cost of which is due less to mere brute cash than to prodigally expended effort. Eleanor never wore a costume which did not show the copious exercise by some alert-minded human being, presumably with an immortal soul, of the priceless qualities of invention, creative thought, trained attention, and prodigious industry. Mrs. Hubert's unchallengeable slogan was that dress should be an expression of individuality, and by dint of utilizing all the details of the attire of herself and of her two daughters, down to the last ruffle and buttonhole, she found this medium quite sufficient to express the whole of her own individuality, the conspicuous force of which was readily conceded by any observer of the lady's life.

As for Eleanor's own individuality, any one in search of that very unobtrusive quality would have found it more in the expression of her eyes and in the childlike lines of her lips than in her toilets. It is possible that Mrs. Hubert might have regarded it as an unkind visitation of Providence that the results of her lifetime of effort in an important art should have been of such slight interest to her daughter, and should have served, during the autumn under consideration, chiefly as hints and suggestions for her daughter's successful rival.

That she was Eleanor's successful rival, Sylvia had Mrs. Draper's more than outspoken word. That lady openly gloried in the impending defeat of Mrs. Hubert's machinations to secure the Fiske money and position for Eleanor; although she admitted that a man like Jerry had his two opposing sides, and that he was quite capable of being attracted by two such contrasting types as Sylvia and Eleanor. She informed Sylvia indeed that the present wife of Colonel Fiske—his third, by the way—had evidently been in her youth a girl of Eleanor's temperament. It was more than apparent, however, that in the case of the son, Sylvia's "type" was in the ascendent; but it must be set down to Sylvia's credit that the circumstance of successful competition gave her no satisfaction. She often heartily wished Eleanor out of it. She could never meet the candid sweetness of the other's eyes without a qualm of discomfort, and she suffered acutely under Eleanor's gentle amiability.

Once or twice when Mrs. Draper was too outrageously late at an appointment for tea, the two girls gave her up, and leaving the house, walked side by side back across the campus, Sylvia quite aware of the wondering surmise which followed their appearance together. On these occasions, Eleanor talked with more freedom than in Mrs. Draper's presence, always in the quietest, simplest way, of small events and quite uninteresting minor matters in her life, or the life of the various household pets, of which she seemed extremely fond. Sylvia could not understand why, when she bade her good-bye at the driveway leading into the Hubert house, she should feel anything but a rather contemptuous amusement for the other's insignificance, but the odd fact was that her heart swelled with inexplicable warmth. Once she yielded to this foolish impulse, and felt a quivering sense of pleasure at the sudden startled responsiveness with which Eleanor returned a kiss, clinging to her as though she were an older, stronger sister.

One dark late afternoon in early December, Sylvia waited alone in the candle-lighted shrine, neither Eleanor nor her hostess appearing. After five o'clock she started home alone along the heavily shaded paths of the campus, as dim as caves in the interval before the big, winking sputtering arc-lights were flashed on. She walked swiftly and lightly as was her well-trained habit, and before she knew it, was close upon a couple sauntering in very close proximity. With the surety of long practice Sylvia instantly diagnosed them as a college couple indulging in what was known euphemistically as "campus work," and prepared to pass them with the slight effect of scorn for philanderings which she always managed to throw into her high-held head and squarely swinging shoulders. But as she came up closer, walking noiselessly in the dusk, she recognized an eccentric, flame-colored plume just visible in the dim light, hanging down from the girl's hat—and stopped short, filled with a rush of very complicated feelings. The only flame-colored plume in La Chance was owned and worn by Eleanor Hubert, and if she were out sauntering amorously in the twilight, with whom could she be but Jerry Fiske,—and that meant— Sylvia's pangs of conscience about supplanting Eleanor were swept away by a flood of anger as at a defeat. She could not make out the girl's companion, beyond the fact that he was tall and wore a long, loose overcoat. Jerry was tall and wore a long, loose overcoat. Sylvia walked on, slowly now, thoroughly aroused, quite unaware of the inconsistency of her mental attitude. She felt a rising tide of heat. She had, she told herself, half a notion to step forward and announce her presence to the couple, whose pace as the Hubert house was approached became slower and slower.

But then, as they stood for a moment at the entrance of the Hubert driveway, the arc-lights blazed up all over the campus at once and she saw two things: one was that Eleanor was walking very close to her companion, with her arm through his, and her little gloved fingers covered by his hand, and next that he was not Jerry Fiske at all, but the queer, countrified "freak" assistant in chemistry with whom Eleanor, since Jerry's defection, had more or less masked her abandonment.

At the same moment the two started guiltily apart, and Sylvia halted, thinking they had discovered her. But it was Mrs. Hubert whom they had seen, advancing from the other direction, and making no pretense that she was not in search of an absent daughter. She bore down upon the couple, murmured a very brief greeting to the man, accompanied by a faint inclination of her well-hatted head, drew Eleanor's unresisting hand inside her arm, and walked her briskly into the house.

CHAPTER XVII

MRS. MARSHALL STICKS TO HER PRINCIPLES

DURING the autumn and early winter it not only happened unfortunately that the quartet played altogether too much Haydn, but that Sylvia's father, contrary to his usual custom, was away from home a great deal. The State University had arrived at that stage of its career when, if its rapidly increasing needs and demands for State money were to be recognized by the Legislature, it must knit itself more closely to the rest of the State system of education, have a more intimate affiliation with the widely scattered public high schools, and weld into some sort of homegeneity their extremely various standards of scholarship. This was a delicate undertaking, calling for much tact and an accurate knowledge of conditions in the State, especially in the rural districts. Professor Marshall's twenty years of popularity with the more serious element of the State University students (that popularity which meant so little to Sylvia, and which she so ignored) had given him a large acquaintance among the class which it was necessary to reach. He knew the men who at the University had been the digs, and jays, and grinds, and who were now the prosperous farmers, the bankers, the school-trustees, the leading men in their communities; and his geniality, vivacity, and knack for informal public speaking made him eminently fitted to represent the University in the somewhat thankless task of coaxing and coercing backward communities to expend the necessary money and effort to bring their schools up to the State University standard.

If all this had happened a few years sooner, he undoubtedly would have taken Sylvia with him on many of these journeys into remote corners of the State, but Sylvia had her class-work to attend to, and the Professor shared to the fullest extent the academic prejudice against parents who broke in upon the course of their children's regular instruction by lawless and casual junketings. Instead, it was Judith who frequently accompanied him, Judith who was now undergoing that home-preparation for the University through which Sylvia had passed, and who, since her father was her principal instructor, could carry on her studies wherever he happened to be; as well as have the stimulating experience of coming in contact with a wide variety of people and conditions. It is possible that Professor Marshall's sociable nature not only shrank from the solitude which his wife would have endured with cheerfulness, but that he also wished to take advantage of this opportunity to come in closer touch with his second daughter, for whose self-contained and occasionally insensitive nature he had never felt the instinctive understanding he had for Sylvia's moods. It is certain that the result was a better feeling between the two than had existed before. During the long hours of jolting over branch railroads back to remote settlements, or waiting at cheerless junctions for delayed trains, or gaily eating impossible meals at extraordinary country hotels, the ruddy, vigorous father, now growing both gray and stout, and the tall, slender, darkly handsome girl of fifteen, were cultivating more things than history and mathematics and English literature. The most genuine feeling of comradeship sprang up between the two dissimilar natures, a feeling so strong and so warm that Sylvia, in addition to her other emotional complications, felt occasionally a faint pricking of jealousy at seeing her primacy with her father usurped.

A further factor in her temporary feeling of alienation from him was the mere physical fact that she saw him much less frequently and that he had nothing like his usual intimate knowledge of her comings and goings. And finally, Lawrence, now a too rapidly growing and delicate lad of eleven, had a series of bronchial colds which kept his mother much occupied with his care. As far as her family was concerned, Sylvia was thus left more alone than ever before, and although she had been trained to too delicate and high a personal pride to attempt the least concealment of her doings, it was not without relief that she felt that her parents had but a very superficial knowledge of the extent and depth to which she was becoming involved in her new relations. She herself shut her eyes as much as possible to the rate at which she was progressing towards a destination rapidly becoming more and more imperiously visible; and consciously intoxicated herself with the excitements and fatigues of her curiously double life of intellectual effort in classes and her not very skilful handling of the shining and very sharp-edged tools of flirtation.

But this ambiguous situation was suddenly clarified by the unexpected call upon Mrs. Marshall, one day about the middle of December, of no less a person than Mrs. Jermain Fiske, Sr., wife of the Colonel, and Jerry's stepmother. Sylvia happened to be in her room when the shining car drove up the country road before the Marshall house, stopped at the gate in the osage-orange hedge, and discharged the tall, stooping, handsomely dressed lady in rich furs, who came with a halting step up the long path to the front door. Although Sylvia had never seen Mrs. Fiske, Mrs. Draper's gift for satiric word-painting had made her familiar with some items of her appearance, and it was with a rapidly beating heart that she surmised the identity of the distinguished caller. But although her quick intelligence perceived the probable significance of the appearance, and although she felt a distinct shock at the seriousness of having Jerry's stepmother call upon her, she was diverted from these capital considerations of such vital importance to her life by the trivial consideration which had, so frequently during the progress of this affair, absorbed her mind to the exclusion of everything else—the necessity for keeping up appearances. If the Marshall tradition had made it easier for her to achieve this not very elevated goal, she might have perceived more clearly where her rapid feet were taking her. Just now, for example, there was nothing in her consciousness but the embittered knowledge that there was no maid to open the door when Mrs. Fiske should ring.

She was a keen-witted modern young woman of eighteen, with a well-trained mind stored with innumerable facts of science, but it must be admitted that at this moment she reverted with passionate completeness to quite another type. She would have given—she would have given a year of her life—one of her fingers—all her knowledge of history—anything! if the Marshalls had possessed what she felt any decently prosperous grocer's family ought to possess—a well-appointed maid in the hall to open the door, take Mrs. Fiske's card, show her into the living-room, and go decently and in order to summon the mistress of the house. Instead she saw with envenomed foresight what would happen. At the unusual sound of the bell, her mother, who was playing dominoes with Lawrence in one of his convalescences, would open the door with her apron still on, and her spectacles probably pushed up, rustic fashion, on top of her head. And then their illustrious visitor, used as of course she was to ceremony in social matters, would not know whether this was the maid, or her hostess; and Mrs. Marshall would frankly show her surprise at seeing a richly dressed stranger on the doorstep, and would perhaps think she had made a mistake in the house; and Mrs. Fiske would not know whether to hand over the cards she held ready in her whitely gloved fingers—in the interval between the clanging shut of the gate and the tinkle of the doorbell Sylvia endured a sick reaction against life, as an altogether hateful and horrid affair.

As a matter of fact, nothing of all this took place. When the bell rang, her mother called out a tranquil request to her to go and open the door, and so it was Sylvia herself who confronted the unexpected visitor,—Sylvia a little flurried and breathless, but ushering the guest into the house with her usual graceful charm of manner.

She had none of this as a moment later she went rather slowly upstairs to summon her mother. It occurred to her that Mrs. Marshall might very reasonably be at a loss as to the reason of this call. Indeed, she herself felt a sinking alarm at the definiteness of the demonstration. What could Mrs. Fiske have to say to Mrs. Marshall that would not lead to some agitating crystallization of the dangerous solution which during the past months Mrs. Marshall's daughter had been so industriously stirring up? Mrs. Marshall showed the most open surprise at the announcement, " Mrs. Colonel Fiske to see me? What in the world——" she began, but after a glance at Sylvia's down-hung head and twisting fingers, she stopped short, looking very grave, and rose to go, with no more comments.

They went down the stairs in silence, tall mother and tall daughter, both sobered, both frightened at what might be in the other's mind, and at what might be before them, and entered the low-ceilinged living-room together. A pale woman, apparently as apprehensive as they, rose in a haste that had almost some element of apology in it, and offered her hand to Mrs. Marshall. " I'm Mrs. Fiske," she said hurriedly, in a low voice, " Jerry's stepmother, you know. I hope you won't mind my coming to see you. What a perfectly lovely home you have! I was wishing I could just stay and *stay* in this room." She spoke rapidly with the slightly incoherent haste of shy people overcoming their weakness, and glanced alternately, with faded blue eyes, at Sylvia and at her mother. In the end she remained standing, looking earnestly into Mrs. Marshall's face. That lady now made a step forward and again put out her hand with an impulsive gesture at which Sylvia wondered. She herself had felt no attraction towards the thin, sickly woman who had so little grace or security of manner. It was constantly surprising Sylvia to discover how often people high in social rank seemed to possess no qualifications for their position. She always felt that she could have filled their places with vastly more aplomb.

" I'm very glad to see you," said Mrs. Marshall in a friendly tone. " Do sit down again. Sylvia, go and make us some tea, won't you? Mrs. Fiske must be cold after driving out here from town."

When Sylvia came back ten minutes later, she found the guest saying, " My youngest is only nine months old, and he is having *such* a time with his teeth."

" Oh! " thought Sylvia scornfully, pouring out the tea. " She's *that* kind of a woman, is she? " With the astonishingly quick shifting of viewpoint of the young, she no longer felt the least anxiety that her home, or even that she herself should make a good impression on this evidently quite negligible person. Her anguish about the ceremony of opening the door seemed years behind her. She examined with care all the minutiæ of the handsome, unindividualized costume of black velvet worn by their visitor, but turned an absent ear to her talk, which brought out various facts relating to a numerous family of young children. " I have six living," said Mrs. Fiske, not meeting Mrs. Marshall's eyes as she spoke, and stirring her tea slowly, " I lost four at birth."

Sylvia was indeed slightly interested to learn through another turn of the conversation that the caller, who looked to her unsympathetic eyes any age at all, had been married at eighteen, and that that was only thirteen years ago. Sylvia thought she certainly looked older than thirty-one, advanced though that age was.

The call passed with no noteworthy incidents beyond a growing wonder in Sylvia's mind that the brilliant and dashing old Colonel, after his other matrimonial experiences, should have picked out so dull and colorless a wife. She was not even pretty, not at all pretty, in spite of her delicate, regular features and tall figure. Her hair was dry and thin, her eyes lusterless, her complexion thick, with brown patches on it, and her conversation was of a domesticity unparalleled in Sylvia's experience. She seemed oddly drawn to Mrs. Marshall, although that lady was now looking rather graver than was her wont, and talked to her of the overflowing Fiske nursery with a loquacity which was evidently not her usual habit. Indeed, she said naïvely, as she went away, that she had been much relieved to find Mrs. Marshall so approachable. " One always thinks of Uni versity families as so terribly learned, you know," she said, imputing to her hostess, with a child's tactlessness, an absence of learning like her own. "I really dreaded to come—I go out so little, you know—but Jerry and the Colonel thought I ought, you know—and now I've really enjoyed it—and if Miss Marshall will come, Jerry and the Colonel will be quite satisfied. And so, of course, will I." With which rather jerky valedictory she finally got herself out of the house.

Sylvia looked at her mother inquiringly. "If I go where?" she asked. Something must have taken place while she was out of the room getting the tea.

"She called to invite you formally to a Christmas house-party at the Fiskes' place in Mercerton," said Mrs. Marshall, noting smilelessly Sylvia's quick delight at the news. "Oh, what have I got to wear!" cried the girl. Mrs. Marshall said merely, "We'll see, we'll see," and without discussing the matter further, went back to finish the interrupted game with Lawrence.

But the next evening, when Professor Marshall returned from his latest trip, the subject was taken up in a talk between Sylvia and her parents which was more agitating to them all than any other incident in their common life, although it was conducted with a great effort for self-control on all sides. Judith and Lawrence had gone upstairs to do their lessons, and Professor Marshall at once broached the subject by saying with considerable hesitation, "Sylvia—well—how about this house-party at the Fiskes'?"

Sylvia was on the defense in a moment. "Well, how about it?" she repeated.

"I hope you don't feel like going."

"But I do, very much!" returned Sylvia, tingling at the first clear striking of the note of disapproval she had felt for so many weeks like an undertone in her life. As her father said nothing more, biting his nails and looking at her uncertainly, she added in the accent which fitted the words, "Why shouldn't I?"

He took a turn about the room and glanced at his wife, who was hemming a napkin very rapidly, her hands trembling a little. She looked up at him warningly, and he waited an instant before speaking. Finally he brought out with the guarded tone of one forcing himself to moderation of speech, " Well, the Colonel is an abominable old black-guard in public life, and his private reputation is no better."

Sylvia flushed. " I don't see what that has to do with his son. It's not fair to judge a young man by his father— or by anything but what he is himself—you yourself are always saying that, if the trouble is that the father is poor or ignorant or something else tiresome."

Professor Marshall said cautiously, " From what I hear, I gather that the son in this case is a good deal like his father."

" No, he *isn't!* " cried Sylvia quickly. " He may have been wild when he first came up to the University, but he's all right now ! " She spoke as with authoritative and intimate knowledge of all the details of Fiske, Jr.'s, life. " And anyhow, I don't see what difference it makes, *what* the Colonel's reputation is. I'm just going up there with a lot of other young people to have a good time. Eleanor Hubert's invited, and three or four other society girls. I don't see why we need to be such a lot more particular than other people. We never are when it's a question of people being dirty, or horrid, other ways ! How about Cousin Parnelia and Mr. Reinhardt ? I guess the Fiskes would laugh at the idea of people who have as many queer folks around as we do, thinking *they* aren't good enough."

Professor Marshall sat down across the table from his daughter and looked at her. His face was rather ruddier than usual and he swallowed hard. " Why, Sylvia, the point is this. It's evident, from what your mother tells me of Mrs. Fiske's visit, that going to this house party means more in your case than with the other girls. Mrs. Fiske came all the way to La Chance to invite you, and from what she said about you and her stepson, it was evident that she and the Colonel——" He stopped, opening his hands nervously.

"I don't know how they think they know anything about it," returned Sylvia with dignity, though she felt an inward qualm at this news. "Jerry's been ever so nice to me and given me a splendid time, but that's all there is to it. Lots of fellows do that for lots of girls, and nobody makes such a fuss about it."

Mrs. Marshall laid down her work and went to the heart of the matter. "Sylvia, you don't *like* Mr. Fiske?"

"Yes, I do!" said Sylvia defiantly, qualifying this statement an instant later by, "Quite well, anyhow. Why *shouldn't* I?"

Her mother assumed this rhetorical question to be a genuine one and answered it accordingly. "Why, he doesn't seem at all like the type of young man who would be liked by a girl with your tastes and training. I shouldn't think you'd find him interesting or——"

Sylvia broke out: "Oh, you don't know how sick I get of being so everlastingly high-brow! What's the *use* of it? People don't think any more of you! They think less! You don't have any better time—nor so good! And why should you and Father always be so down on anybody that's rich, or dresses decently? *Jerry's* all right—if his clothes *do* fit!"

"Do you really *know* him at all?" asked her father pointedly.

"Of course I do—I know he's very handsome, and awfully good-natured, and he's given me the only good time I've had at the University. You just don't know how ghastly last year was to me! I'm awfully grateful to Jerry, and that's all there is to it!"

Before this second disclaimer, her parents were silent again, Sylvia looking down at her lap, picking at her fingers. Her expression was that of a naughty child—that is, with a considerable admixture of unhappiness in her wilfulness.

By this time Professor Marshall's expression was clearly one of downright anger, controlled by violent effort. Mrs.

Marshall was the first one to speak. She went over to Sylvia and laid her hand on her shoulder. "Well, Sylvia dear, I'm sorry about——" She stopped and began again. "You know, dear, that we always believed in letting our children, as far as possible, make their own decisions, and we won't go back on that now. But I want you to understand that that puts a bigger responsibility on you than on most girls to make the *right* decisions. We trust you—your good sense and right feeling—to keep you from being carried away by unworthy motives into a false position. And, what's just as important, we trust to your being clear-headed enough to see what your motives really are."

"I don't see," began Sylvia, half crying, "why something horrid should come up just because I want a good time—other girls don't have to be all the time so solemn, and thinking about things!"

"There'd be more happy women if they did," remarked Mrs. Marshall, adding: "I don't believe we'd better talk any more about this now. You know how we feel, and you must take that into consideration. You think it over."

She spoke apparently with her usual calmness, but as she finished she put her arms about the girl's neck and kissed the flushed cheeks. Caresses from Mrs. Marshall were unusual, and, even through her tense effort to resist, Sylvia was touched. "You're just worrying about nothing at all, Mother," she said, trying to speak lightly, but escaped from a possible rejoinder by hurriedly gathering up her text-books and following Judith and Lawrence upstairs.

Her father and mother confronted each other. *"Well!"* said Professor Marshall hotly, "of all the weak, inconclusive, modern parents—is *this* what we've come to?"

Mrs. Marshall took up her sewing and said in the tone which always quelled her husband, "Yes, this is what we've come to."

His heat abated at once, though he went on combatively, "Oh, I know what you mean, reasonable authority and not tyranny and all that—yes, I believe in it—of course—but this goes beyond——" he ended. " Is there or is there not such a thing as parental authority? "

Mrs. Marshall answered with apparent irrelevance, " You remember what Cavour said? "

" Good Heaven! No, I don't remember!" cried Professor Marshall, with an impatience which might have been Sylvia's.

" He said, ' Any idiot can rule by martial law.' "

" Yes, of course, that theory is all right, but——"

" If a theory is all right, it ought to be acted upon."

Professor Marshall cried out in exasperation, " But see here, Barbara—here is a concrete fact—our daughter—our precious Sylvia—is making a horrible mistake—and because of a theory we mustn't reach out a hand to pull her back."

" We *can't* pull her back by force," said his wife. " She's eighteen years old, and she has the habit of independent thought. We can't go back on that now."

" We don't seem to be pulling her back by force or in any other way! We seem to be just weakly sitting back and letting her do exactly as she pleases."

" If during all these years we've had her under our influence we haven't given her standards that——" began the mother.

" You heard how utterly she repudiated our influence and our standards and——"

" Oh, what she *says*—it's what she's made of that'll count—that's the *only* thing that'll count when a crisis comes——"

Professor Marshall interrupted nastily: " When a crisis! What do you call *this* but a crisis—she's like a child about to put her hand into the fire."

" I trust in the training she's had to give her firm enough nerves to pull it out again when she feels the heat," said her mother steadily.

Professor Marshall sprang up, with clenched hands, tall, powerful, helpless. " It's outrageous, Barbara, for all your talk! We're responsible! We ought to shut her up under lock and key——"

" So *many* girls have been deterred from a mistake by being shut up under lock and key ! " commented Mrs. Marshall, with an ironical accent.

" But, good Heavens! Think of her going to that old scoundrel's—how can I look people in the face, when they all know my opinion of him—how I've opposed his being a Trustee and——"

" *Ah,*——! " remarked his wife significantly, " that's the trouble, is it? "

Professor Marshall flushed, and for a moment made no rejoinder. Then, shifting his ground, he said bitterly : " I think you're forgetting that I've had a disillusionizing experience in this sort of thing which you were spared. You forget that Sylvia is closely related to my sister."

" I don't forget that—but I don't forget either that Sylvia has had a very different sort of early life from poor Victoria's. She has breathed pure air always—I trust her to recognize its opposite."

He made an impatient gesture of exasperation. " But she'll be *in* it—it'll be too late——"

" It's never too late." She spoke quickly, but her unwavering opposition began to have in it a note of tension.

" She'll be caught—she'll have to go on because it'll be too hard to get out——"

" The same vigor that makes her resist us now will give her strength then—she's not Eleanor Hubert."

Her husband burst out upon her in a frightened, angry rush of reproach : " Barbara—how *can* you! You make me turn cold! This isn't a matter of talk—of theories—we're confronted with——"

She faced him down with unflinching, unhappy eyes. " Oh, of course if we are to believe in liberty only so long as everything goes smoothly——" She tried to add something to this, but her voice broke and she was silent. Her husband looked at her, startled at her pallor and her trembling lips, immensely moved by the rare discomposure of that countenance. She said in a whisper, her voice shaking, " Our little Sylvia—my first baby——"

He flung himself down in the chair beside her and took her hand. "It's damnable!" he said.

His wife answered slowly, with long pauses. "No—it's all right—it's part of the whole thing—of life. When you bring children into the world—when you live at all—you must accept the whole. It's not fair to rebel—to rebel at the pain—when——"

"Good God, it's not *our* pain I'm shrinking from——!" he broke out.

"No—oh no—that would be easy——"

With an impulse of yearning, and protection, and need, he leaned to put his arms around her, his graying beard against her pale cheek. They sat silent for a long time.

In the room above them, Sylvia bent over a problem in trigonometry, and rapidly planned a new evening-dress. After a time she got up and opened her box of treasures from Aunt Victoria. The yellow chiffon would do—Jerry had said he liked yellow—she could imagine how Mrs. Hubert would expend herself on Eleanor's toilets for this great occasion—if she could only hit on a design which wouldn't look as though it came out of a woman's magazine—something really sophisticated—she could cover her old white slippers with that bit of gold-tissue off Aunt Victoria's hat—she shook out the chiffon and laid it over the bed, looking intently at its gleaming, shimmering folds and thinking, "How horrid of Father and Mother to go and try to spoil everything so!" She went back to the problem in trigonometry and covered a page with figures, at which she gazed unseeingly. She was by no means happy. She went as far as the door, meaning to go down and kiss her parents good-night, but turned back. They were not a family for surface demonstrations. If she could not yield her point— She began to undress rapidly, turned out the light, opened the windows, and sprang into bed. "If they only wouldn't take things so awfully *solemnly!*" she said to herself petulantly.

CHAPTER XVIII

SYLVIA SKATES MERRILY ON THIN ICE

THE design for the yellow chiffon dropped almost literally at Sylvia's feet the next day, on the frontispiece of
a theatrical magazine left by another passenger in the street-
car in which she chanced to be riding. Sylvia pounced on
it with instant recognition of its value. It was " different "
and yet not " queer," it was artistic and yet fashionable,
and with its flowing lines it would not be hard to construct.
It was the creation of a Parisian boulevard actress, known
widely for her costumes, for the extraordinary manner in
which she dressed her hair, and for the rapidity of her
succeeding emotional entanglements. Her name meant
nothing to Sylvia. She tore out the page, folded it, and put
it for safe-keeping between the pages of her text-book of
Logic.

That afternoon she began work on it, running the long
seams up on the machine with whirring rapidity, acutely
aware of her mother's silent, uncommenting passage back
and forth through the sewing-room. With an impulse of
secrecy which she did not analyze, she did the trying-on
in her own room, craning and turning about before her
own small mirror. She knew that her mother would think
the dress was cut too low, although, as she told herself,
looking with complacency at the smooth, white, exquisitely
fine-grained skin thus disclosed, it wasn't nearly as low cut
as the dresses Eleanor Hubert wore to any little dance.
She had long felt it to be countrified in the extreme to
wear the mild compromises towards evening-dress which
she and most of the State University girls adopted, as
compared with the frankly disclosing gowns of the " town
girls " whose clothes came from Chicago and New York.

She knew from several outspoken comments that Jerry admired Eleanor's shoulders, and as she looked at her own, she was not sorry that he was to compare them to those of the other girl.

After this brief disposal of the question, she gave it no more thought, working with desperate speed to complete all her preparations. She had but a week for these, a week filled with incessant hurry, since she was naturally unwilling to ask help of her mother. Judith was off again with her father.

This absence greatly facilitated the moment of Sylvia's departure, which she had dreaded. But, as it happened, there was only her mother to whom to say the rather difficult good-bye, her mother who could be counted on never to make a scene.

About the middle of the morning of the twenty-third of December, she came down the stairs, her hand-bag in her hand, well-hatted, well-gloved, freshly veiled, having achieved her usual purpose of looking to the casual eye like the daughter of a wealthy man. She had put all of her autumn allowance for dress into a set of furs, those being something which no ingenuity could evolve at home. The rest of her outfit, even to the odd little scarlet velvet hat, with its successful and modish touch of the ugly, was the achievement of her own hands. Under its absurd and fashionable brim, her fresh face shone out, excessively pretty and very young.

Mrs. Marshall kissed her good-bye gently, not smiling at Sylvia's attempt to lighten the moment's seriousness by saying playfully, " Now, Mother, don't you be such an old worrier! " But she said nothing "uncomfortable," for which Sylvia was very grateful.

She had no sooner embarked upon the big Interurban trolley-car which was to take her to Mercerton than her attention was wholly diverted from uneasy reflections by the unexpected appearance of two of the house-party guests. Eleanor Hubert, every detail of her complicated costume exquisitely finished as a Meissonier painting, sat looking out of the window rather soberly, and so intently that she saw neither Sylvia's entrance, nor, close upon her heels, that of a florid-faced, rather heavily built young man with a large, closely shaven jaw, who exclaimed joyfully at seeing Miss Marshall, and appropriated with ready assurance the other half of her seat.

"Now, this is surely dandy! You're going to the house-party too, of course!" he cried, unbuttoning and throwing back his bright tan overcoat. "Here's where I cut Jerry out all right, all right! Wait a minute! *How* much time have we?" He appealed to the conductor as though a matter of life and death depended on the answer. "Four minutes?—here goes——" He sprang to his feet, dashed out of the car and disappeared, leaving his coat beside Sylvia. It was evidently quite new, of the finest material, with various cunningly stitched seams and straps disposed upon its surface in a very knowing way. Sylvia noted out of the corner of her eye that the address of the maker, woven into the neckband, was on Fifth Avenue, New York.

The four minutes passed—and the conductor approached Sylvia. "Your friend's coming back, ain't he?" he asked, with the tolerant, good-natured respect natural for the vagaries of expensively dressed young men who wore overcoats made on Fifth Avenue. Sylvia, who had met the young man but once before, when Jerry had introduced him as an old friend, was a little startled at having a casual acquaintance so publicly affixed to her; but after an instant's hesitation, in which she was reflecting that she positively did not even remember her "friend's" name, she answered, "Oh yes, yes, I suppose so—here he is now."

The young man bounded up on the back platform panting, holding his hat on with one hand, a large box of candy in the other. Sylvia glanced at the name on the cover. "You didn't go all the way to *Dutton's!*" she cried.

He nodded, breathless, evidently proud of his feat, and when he caught his breath enough to speak, explained, "Yepp,—it's the only place in this bum town where you can get Alligretti's, and they're the only kind that 're fit to eat." He tore open the box as he spoke, demolishing with ruthless and practised hands the various layers of fine paper and gold cord which wrapped it about, and presented the rich layer of black chocolates to Sylvia. " Get a move on and take one," he urged cordially; " I pretend I buy 'em for the girls, but I'm crazy about 'em myself." He bit into one with an air of prodigious gusto, took off his hat, wiped his forehead, and looked at Sylvia with a relish as frank as his enjoyment of the bonbon. " That's a corking hat you got on," he commented. " Most girls would look like the old Harry with that dangling thing in their eyes, but *you* can carry it off all right."

Sylvia's face assumed a provocative expression. " Did you ever make that remark to any other girl, I wonder? " she said reflectively.

He laughed aloud, eying her with appreciation, and clapping another large black chocolate into his mouth. " You're the prompt article, aren't you? " he said. He hitched himself over and leaned towards her. " Something tells me I'm goin' to have a good time at this house-party, what? "

Sylvia stiffened. She did not like his sitting so close to her, she detected now on his breath a faint odor of alcohol, and she was afraid that Eleanor Hubert would think her lacking in dignity. She regretted having succumbed to the temptation to answer him in his own tone; but, under her bravado, she was really somewhat apprehensive about this expedition, and she welcomed a diversion. Besides, the voluble young man showed not the slightest sign of noting her attempt to rebuff him, and she found quite unavailing all her efforts to change the current of the talk, the loud, free-and-easy, personally admiring note of which had the effect on her nerves of a draught of raw spirits. She did not enjoy the taste while it was being administered, but the effect was certainly stimulating, not to say exciting, and absorbed her attention so entirely that uncomfortable self-questionings were impossible. She was also relieved to note that, although the young man flung himself about in the public conveyance with the same unceremonious self-assurance that he would have shown in a lady's drawing-room, Eleanor Hubert, at the other end of the car, was apparently unaware of his presence. Perhaps she too had some grounds for uncomfortable thought, for through-out the hour's journey she continued to stare unseeingly out of the window, or to look down fixedly and rather sadly at her gloved hands.

Even through the confusion of her own ideas and plans, and the need for constant verbal self-defense against the encroaching familiarity of her companion, the notion flitted across Sylvia's mind that probably Eleanor was thinking of the young assistant in chemistry. How queer and topsy-turvy everything was, she reflected, as she bandied lively words with the lively young man at her side, continuing to eat his candies, although their rich, cloying taste had al-ready palled on her palate—here was Mrs. Hubert throw-ing Eleanor at Jerry's head, when what Eleanor wanted was that queer, rough-neck freak of an assistant prof; and here were Jerry's parents making such overtures to Sylvia, when what *she* wanted—she didn't know what she did want. Yes, she did, she wanted a good time, which was somehow paradoxically hard to attain. Something always kept spoiling it,—half the time something intangible inside her own mind. She gave the candy-box a petulant push. "Oh, take it away!" she said impatiently; "I've eaten so many now, it makes me sick to look at them!"

The donor showed no resentment at this ingratitude, holding the box on his knees, continuing to help himself to its contents with unabated zest, and to keep the conver-sation up to concert pitch: "——the only girl I ever saw who'd stop eating Alligretti's while there was one left—another proof that there's only one of you—I said right off, that any co-ed that Jerry Fiske would take to must be a unique specimen——" He did not further specify the period to which he referred by his "right off," but the phrase gave Sylvia a tingling, uncomfortable sense of having been for some time the subject of speculation in circles of which she knew nothing.

They were near Mercerton now, and as she gathered her wraps together she found that she was bracing herself as for an ordeal of some sort. The big car stopped, a little way out of town, in front of a long driveway bordered with maple-trees; she and the young man descended from one end-platform and Eleanor Hubert from the other, into the midst of loud and facetious greetings from the young people who had come down to meet them. Jerry was there, very stalwart, his white sweater stretched over his broad chest. All the party carried skates, which flashed like silver in the keen winter sun. They explained with many exclamations that they had been out on the ice, which was, so the three new-comers were assured many times, " perfectly grand, perfectly dandy, simply elegant! "

A big, many-seated sled came jingling down the driveway now, driven by no less a personage than Colonel Fiske himself, wrapped in a fur-lined coat, his big mustache white against the red of his strongly marked old face. With many screams and shouts the young people got themselves into this vehicle, the Colonel calling out in a masterful roar above the din, " Miss Marshall's to come up here with me! "

He held in his pawing, excited horses with one hand and helped Sylvia with the other. In the seat behind them sat Jerry and Eleanor Hubert and the young man of the trolley trip. Sylvia strained her ears to catch Jerry's introduction of him to Eleanor, so that she might know his name. It was too absurd not even to know his name! But the high-pitched giggles and deeper shouts of mirth from the rest of the party drowned out the words. As a matter of fact, although he played for an instant a rather important rôle in Sylvia's drama, she was destined never to know his name.

The Colonel looked back over the sleighload, shouted out " All aboard! " loosened the reins, and snapped his whip over the horses' heads. They leaped forward with so violent a spring that the front runners of the long sled were for an instant lifted into the air. Immediately all the joyful shrieking and screaming which had gone on before, became as essential silence compared to the delighted uproar which now rose from the sleigh. The jerk had thrown most of the young people over backward into each other's arms and laps, where, in a writhing, promiscuous mass, they roared and squealed out their joy in the joke, and made ineffectual and not very determined efforts to extricate themselves. Sylvia had seen the jerk coming and saved herself by a clutch forward at the dashboard. Glancing back, she saw that Jerry and Eleanor Hubert still sat upright; although the gay young man beside them had let himself go backward into the waving arms and legs, and, in a frenzy of high spirits, was shouting and kicking and squirming with the others. It was a joke after his own heart.

Colonel Fiske, so far from slackening his pace to help his young guests out of their predicament, laughed loudly and cracked his whip over the horses' ears. They went up the long, curving driveway like a whirlwind, and drew up under the porte-cochère of a very large brick-and-stone house with another abrupt jerk which upset those in the sleigh who had succeeded in regaining their seats. Pandemonium broke out again, in the midst of which Sylvia saw that Mrs. Fiske had come to the doorway and stood in it with a timid smile. The Colonel did not look at her, Jerry nodded carelessly to her as he passed in, and of all the disheveled, flushed, and laughing young people who crowded past her into the house, only Sylvia and Eleanor recognized her existence. The others went past her without a glance exclaimed at the lateness of the hour, cried out that they must go and " fix up " for lunch, and ran upstairs, filling the house with their voices. Sylvia heard one girl cry to another, " *Oh,* I've had such a good time! I've hollered till I'm hoarse! "

After luncheon, a meal at which more costly food was served than Sylvia had ever before seen, Jerry suggested between puffs of the cigarette he was lighting that they have a game of billiards. Most of the young people trooped off after him into the billiard-room, but Sylvia, after a moment's hesitation, lingered near the big wood-fire in the hall, unwilling to admit that she had never seen a billiard table. She made a pretext of staying to talk to Mrs. Fiske, who sat stooping her tall figure forward in a chair too small for her. Sylvia looked at this ungraceful attitude with strong disapproval. What she thought was that such inattention to looks was perfectly inexcusable. What she said was, in a very gracious voice: "What a beautiful home you have, Mrs. Fiske! How wonderfully happy you must be in it."

The other woman started a little at being addressed, and looked around vaguely at the conventional luxury of the room, with its highly polished floors, its huge rich rugs, its antlers on the wall, and its deeply upholstered leather chairs. When Sylvia signified her intention of continuing the talk by taking a seat beside the fire, Mrs. Fiske roused herself to the responsibility of entertaining the young guest. After some futile attempts at conversation in the abstract, she discharged this responsibility through the familiar expedient of the family photograph album. With this between them, the two women were able to go through the required form of avoiding silences. Sylvia was fearfully bored by the succession of unknown faces, and utterly unable to distinguish, in her hostess' somewhat disconnected talk, between the different sets of the Colonel's children. "This one is Stanley, Jermain's brother, who died when he was a baby," the dull voice droned on; "and this is Mattie in her wedding dress."

"Oh, I didn't know Jerry had a married sister," murmured Sylvia indifferently, glad of any comment to make.

"She's only his half-sister, a great deal older."

"But *you* haven't a daughter old enough to be married?" queried Sylvia, astonished.

"Oh—no—no. Mattie is the daughter of the Colonel's first wife."

"Oh," said Sylvia awkwardly, remembering now that Mrs. Draper had spoken of the Colonel's several marriages. She added to explain her question, " I'd forgotten that Jerry's mother was the Colonel's second wife and not his first."

" She was his third," breathed Mrs. Fiske, looking down at the pages of the album.

Sylvia repressed a " Good gracious!" of startled repugnance to the topic, and said, to turn the conversation, " Oh, who is that beautiful little girl with the fur cap?"

" That is my picture," said Mrs. Fiske, "when I was eighteen. I was married soon after. I've changed very much since my marriage." Decidedly it was not Sylvia's lucky day for finding topics of talk. She was wondering how the billiard game was progressing, and was sorry she had not risked going with the others. She was recalled by Mrs. Fiske's saying with a soft earnestness, " I want you to know, Miss Marshall, how I *appreciate* your kindness to me!"

Sylvia looked at her in astonishment, half fearing that she was being made fun of.

The other went on: " It was *very* nice of you—your staying here to talk with me instead of going off with the young people—the others don't often——" She played nervously with a gleaming pendant on a platinum chain which hung over her flat chest, and went on: " I—you have *always* seemed to me the very nicest of Jerry's friends —and I shall never forget your mother's kindness. I hope—I hope so much I shall see more of her. The Colonel thinks so too—we've liked so much having him like you." The incoherence of this did not prevent Sylvia's having a chillingly accurate grasp on its meaning. " It is the Colonel's hope," she went on painfully, " to have Jerry marry as soon as he graduates from the Law School. The Colonel thinks that nothing is so good for a young man as an early marriage—though of course Jerry isn't so very, very young any more. He—the—Colonel is a great believer in marriage——" Her voice died away into murmurs. Her long, thin throat contracted in a visible swallow.

At this point only Sylvia's perception of the other's anguished embarrassment prevented her from literally running away. As it was, they sat silent, fingering over the pages of the album and gazing unseeingly at the various set countenances which looked out at them with the unnatural glare of the photographed. Sylvia was canvassing desperately one possibility of escape after another when the door opened, and the lively young man of the trolley-car stepped in. He tiptoed to the fireplace with exaggerated caution, looking theatrically over his shoulder for a pursuer. Sylvia positively welcomed his appearance and turned tc him with a cordiality quite unlike the cool dignity witl which she had planned to treat him. He sat down on the rug before the fire, very close to her feet, and looked up at her, grinning. " Here's where I get another one on Jerry— what? " he said, ignoring Mrs. Fiske. " Old Jerry thinks he's playing such a wonderful game in there he can't tear himself away—but there'll be something doing, I guess, when he does come and finds where *I* am! " He had partaken freely of the excellent white wine served at luncheon (the first Sylvia had ever seen), and though entirely master of his speech, was evidently even more uplifted than was his usual hilarious wont. Sylvia looked down at him, and across at the weak-faced woman opposite her, and had a moment of wishing heartily she had never come. She stood up impatiently, a movement which the young man took to mean a threat of withdrawal. " Aw, *don't* go! " he pleaded, sprawling across the rug towards her. As she turned away, he snatched laughingly at her skirts, crying out, " Tag! You're caught! You're It! "

At this moment Jerry Fiske appeared in the doorway. He looked darkly at his friend's cheerful face and said shortly: " Here, Stub—quit it! Get up out of that! " He added to Sylvia, holding out his hand: " Come on, go skating with me. The ice is great."

" Are the others going? " asked Sylvia.

" Oh yes, I suppose so," said Jerry, a trifle impatiently. The young man on the floor scrambled up. " Here's one that's going, whoever else don't," he announced.

" Get yourself a girl, then," commanded Jerry, " and tell the rest to come along. There's to be eats at four o'clock."

The ice was even as fine as it had been so redundantly represented to Sylvia. Out of doors, leaning her supple, exquisitely poised body to the wind as she veered like a bird on her flying skates, Sylvia's spirits rebounded with an instant reaction into enjoyment. She adored skating, and she had in it, as in all active exercise, the half-wild pleasure of one whose childhood is but a short time behind her. Furthermore, her costume prepared for this event (Mrs. Draper had told her of the little lake on the Fiske estate) was one of her successes. It had been a pale cream broadcloth of the finest texture, one of Aunt Victoria's reception gowns, which had evidently been spoiled by having coffee spilled down the front breadth. Sylvia had had the bold notion of dyeing it scarlet and making it over with bands of black plush (the best bits from an outworn coat of her mother's). On her gleaming red-brown hair she had perched a little red cap with a small black wing on either side (one of Lawrence's pet chickens furnished this), and she carried the muff which belonged with her best set of furs. Thus equipped, she looked like some impish, slender young Brunhilde, with her two upspringing wings. The young men gazed at her with the most unconcealed delight. As she skated very well, better than any of the other girls, she felt, sweeping about the pond in long, swift curves, that she was repaid for her ignorance of billiards.

Jerry and the young man he called Stub were openly in competition for her attention, highly jocose on Stub's part and not at all so on Jerry's, whose brow did not clear at the constant crackling of the other's witticisms. On the shore burned a big fire, tended by a man-servant in livery, who was occupied in setting out on a long table a variety of sandwiches and cups of steaming bouillon. Sylvia had never encountered before a real man-servant in livery. She looked at him with the curiosity she might have shown at seeing a mediæval knight in full armor. Jerry brought her a cup of the bouillon, which was deliciously hot and strong. Experienced as she was in the prudent provisioning of the Marshall kitchen she was staggered to think how many chickens had gone into filling with that clear liquor the big silver tureen which steamed over the glittering alcohol lamp. The table was set, for that casual outdoor picnic lunch, as she could hardly have imagined a royal board.

"What beautiful things your people have!" she exclaimed to Jerry, looking at a pile of small silver forks with delicately carved ivory handles. "The rugs in the house are superb."

Jerry waved them aside as phenomena of no importance. "All of 'em tributes from Dad's loving constituents," he said, repeating what was evidently an old joke in the family. "You'd better believe Dad doesn't vote to get the tariff raised on anything unless he sees to it that the manufacturers know who they have to thank. It works something fine! Talk about the presents a doctor gets from his grateful patients! Nothing to it!"

This picturesque statement of practical politics meant so little to Sylvia's mind that she dismissed it unheard, admiring, in spite of her effort to take things for granted, the fabulous fineness of the little fringed napkin set under the bouillon cup. Jerry followed the direction of her eyes. "Yep—tariff on linen," he commented pregnantly.

The young man called Stub now sped up to them, skating very fast, and swept Sylvia off. "*Here's* where we show 'em how to do it!" he cried cheerfully, skating backward with crazy rapidity, and pulling Sylvia after him. There was a clang of swift steel on ice, and Jerry bore down upon them, the muscles of his jaw showing prominently. Without a word he thrust his friend aside, caught at Sylvia's hands, and bore her in a swooping flight to the other end of the pond, now deserted by the other skaters.

As they sped along he bent over Sylvia fiercely and said in a low, angry tone, "You don't like that bounder, do you? You *don't!*"

Sylvia was astonished at the heat of his suspicion. She had known that Jerry was not notably acute, but it had seemed to her that her dislike for his friend must be more than apparent to any one. They had reached the edge of the ice now, and Sylvia's hands were still in Jerry's, although they were not skating, but stood facing each other. A bush of osier, frozen into the ice, lifted its red twigs near them. Sylvia looked down at it, hesitating how to express her utter denial of any liking for the hilarious young man. Jerry misunderstood her pause and cried out: " Good God! Sylvia! Don't say you *do*."

Sylvia's heart gave a frightened leap. " Oh no—no—not a bit! " she said hastily, looking longingly across the pond at the group around the fire. Jerry caught his breath with a gasp and gripped her hands hard. " It makes me crazy to see you look at another fellow," he said. He forced her eyes to meet his. " Sylvia—you know—you know what I mean."

Yes, Sylvia knew what he meant. Her very white face showed that. The young man went on, pressing, masterful, confident, towering over her: "It's idiotic to speak of it now, out here—with all these people around—but it just *got* me to see you with that—I wasn't sure how I felt about you till I saw how I felt when you seemed so friendly with him, when you got off the car together. Then I knew. It made me crazy—I *wanted* you! "

Sylvia had not been able once to look away from him since he began to speak. Her mouth was a little open in her white face, her eyes fixed with a painful intensity on his. He moistened his lips with his tongue. " Sylvia—*it's all right*—isn't it? "

With no change of expression in her strained face, Sylvia nodded. As suddenly and apparently as automatically she took a backward step.

The young man made a great stride towards her—there was a sound of quick strokes on the ice and—" BOO! " shouted the hilarious young man, bursting between them at railroad speed. He executed a marvelous pirouette and

returned instantly, calling out, "Less spooning in the corners if you please—or if it's got to be, let me in!" He
was followed closely by a string of young men and girls,
playing snap-the-whip. They "snapped" just as they
reached Jerry. The end girl flew off and bumped, screaming with joy, into Jerry's arms. He looked furiously over
her head towards Sylvia, but she had been enveloped in a
ring and was being conveyed away to the accompaniment
of the usual squeals and shouts. The Colonel had come
down to take them all back, she was informed, and was
waiting for them with the sleigh.

CHAPTER XIX

AS A BIRD OUT OF A SNARE

SYLVIA dressed for dinner literally like one in a dream. Outwardly she was so calm that she thought she was so inwardly. It was nothing like so exciting as people said, to get engaged, she thought as she brushed out her hair and put it up in a big, gleaming knot. Here she had been engaged for a whole hour and a half, and was getting calmer every minute, instead of the reverse. She astonished herself by the lucidity of her brain, although it only worked by snatches—there being lacunæ when she could not have told what she was doing. And yet, as she had approached the house, sitting again beside the Colonel, she had looked with a new thrill of interest at its imposing battlemented façade. The great hall had seemed familiar to her already as she stepped across it on her way to the stairs, her feet had pressed the rugs with assurance, she had been able to be quite nonchalant about refusing the services of the maid who offered to help her dress.

It was true that from time to time she suddenly flushed or paled; it was true that her mind seemed incapable of the slightest consecutive thought; it was true that she seemed to be in a dream, peopled by crazily inconsequent images—she had again and again a vision, startlingly vivid, of the red-twigged osier beside which she had stood; it was true that she had a slight feeling of vertigo when she tried to think ahead of the next moment—but still she was going ahead with her unpacking and dressing so steadily that she marveled. She decided again from the depth of her experience that getting engaged was nothing like so upsetting an event as people made out. She thrust the last pin into her hair and tipped her head preeningly before the big triplicate mirror—the first time she had ever encountered this luxury outside of a ready-made clothes shop. The yellow chiffon came out from the trunk in perfect condition, looking like a big, silk-petaled flower as she slipped it on over her bare shoulders, and emerged above, triumphant and yet half afraid to look at herself in the mirror lest she should see that her home-made toilet had not "the right look." One glance satisfied even her jealous eagerness. It had exactly the right look—that is, it looked precisely like the picture from which she had copied it. She gazed with naïve satisfaction at the faithfulness with which her reflected appearance resembled that of the Parisian demi-mondaine whose photograph she had seen, and settled on her slim, delicately modeled shoulders the straps of shirred and beaded chiffon which apparently performed the office of keeping her dress from sliding to the floor. In reality, under its fluid, gauzy draperies, it was constructed on a firm, well-fitting, well-fastened foundation of opaque cloth which quite adequately clothed the young body, but its appearance was of a transparent cloud, only kept from floating entirely away by those gleaming straps on the shoulders, an effect carefully calculated in the original model, and inimitably caught by Sylvia's innocent fingers.

She turned herself about, artlessly surprised to see that her neck and shoulders looked quite like those of the women in the fashion-plates and the magazine illustrations. She looked at the clock. It was early yet. She reflected that she never *could* take the time other girls did in dressing. She wondered what they did. What could one do, after one's bath was taken, one's hair done, and one's gown donned—oh, of course, powder! She applied it liberally, and then wiped away every grain, that being what she had seen older girls do in the Gymnasium dressing-room. Then with a last survey of her face, unaltered by the ceremonial with the powder-puff, she stepped to the door.

But there, with her hand on the knob, she was halted by an inexplicable hesitation about opening the door and showing herself. She looked down at her bare shoulders and bosom, and faintly blushed. It was really very, very low, far lower than any dress she had ever worn! And the fact that Eleanor Hubert, that all the " swell " girls wore theirs low, did not for the moment suffice her—it was somehow different—their showing their shoulders and her showing her own. She could not turn the knob and stood, irresolute, frowning vaguely, though not very deeply disquieted. Finally she compromised by taking up a pretty spangled scarf Aunt Victoria had sent her, wrapping it about her like a shawl, in which quaint garb she went out in more confidence, and walked down the hall to the stairway. Half-way down she met Colonel Fiske just coming up to dress. Seeing one of his young guests arrayed for the evening he made her his compliments, the first words rather absent and perfunctory. But when he was aware which guest she was, he warmed into a pressing and personal note, as his practised eyes took in the beauty, tonight startlingly enhanced by excitement, of the girl's dark, shining eyes, flushed cheeks, and white neck and arms. He ended by lifting her hand, in his florid way, and pressing it to his white mustache for a very fervent kiss. Sylvia blushed prettily, meeting his hot old eyes with a dewy unconsciousness, and smiling frankly up into the deeply lined carnal face with the simple-hearted pleasure she would have felt at the kind word of any elderly man. The Colonel seemed quite old to her—much older than her father—like Professor Kennedy.

" Jerry's in the library, waiting," his father announced with a sly laugh. " I wondered at the young rascal's being dressed so far ahead of time." He turned reluctantly and went on up the stairs, leaving Sylvia to go forward to her first meeting alone with the man she had promised to marry. As she descended the long flight of stairs, her scarf, loosened by her movement, slipped unobserved in her excitement and hung lightly about her shoulders.

The door to the library was shut. She opened it with a rapidly beating heart and stood on the threshold, shyly hesitating to advance further, looking with agitation at the stalwart, handsome, well-groomed figure which stood in an attitude of impatient expectation by the window. Except for the light which came in from the electric bulb on the porch outside, the big room was in twilight. In the brilliantly lighted door-opening, she stood revealed as by a searchlight.

At the sound of the opening door, and his name spoken in a quavering voice, the young man turned, paused an instant as if blinded by the vision, and sprang forward. The door behind Sylvia swung shut, and her eyes, widening in the dusk, saw only the headlong, overwhelming rush upon her of her lover. She was enfolded strongly in muscular arms, she was pressed closer and yet closer to a powerful body, whose heat burned through the thin broadcloth, she was breathless, stunned, choked. As the man bent forward over her, clasping her to him, her flexible spine bent and her head drooped backward, her face with its flush all gone, gleaming white in the dusk. At this he rained kisses on it, on her eyes, hair, cheeks, mouth, the burning softness of his full lips seeming to leave a smear on her skin where they pressed it. Still holding her with one arm, pressed to him as though the two young bodies were gripped together by a vice, he loosened the other arm and thrust it at the back of her dress, through the flimsy gauze of her scarf, down next her body. His stiff cuff caught on the edge of her dress, and his sleeve slid up—it was his bare arm against her naked flesh. He gave a savage, smothered, gasping exclamation, pressed his fingers deeply into her side, still kissing her passionately, her neck, her shoulders, burying his hot face in her bosom.

It was the girl's body which acted, since at the first instant of the whirlwind which had broken over her, her mind had been shocked into a swooning paralysis. Only her strong, sound body, hardened by work, fortified by outdoor exercise, was ready in its every fiber for this moment. Her body bent suddenly like a spring of fine steel, its strength momentarily more than a match for his, and thrust the man from her with staggering violence. Her reaction from him was as physical a sensation as though she had bitten into a tempting fruit and found it not sweet—not even bitter—but nasty. She sickened at the sight of him.

As he caught his balance, laughing a little but not at all good-naturedly, and started back towards her with a dangerous dark face of excited anger and desire, his head-long rush was checked an instant by the fierce eyes which flamed at him from her crimson face. Even her neck and shoulders were now scarlet. She held him off for the space of a breath, giving one deep exclamation, *"Oh!"* short, sharply exhaled, almost like a blow in his face.

But his blood was up as well as hers, and after his momentary pause, he rushed forward again, his hand-some, blond face black with passion.

Sylvia stooped, gathered up her skirts, turned, burst open the door, and fled out of the room, running in her high-heeled satin slippers as she did on the track in the Gymnasium, with long, deer-like bounds. In a flash she had crossed the wide hall—which was as it happened empty, although she would not have slackened her pace for all the assembled company—and was darting arrow-like up the stairs, her torn scarf flying behind her like a banner. Her flight had been so unexpected and so swift that young Fiske did not attempt to follow her; but she reached her room, flung the door shut, and locked it with as much precipitancy as though he were on her heels, instead of standing quite still, open-mouthed, where she had left him.

The sharp crack of her slamming door, loud in the quiet house, broke the spell which held him. His mouth shut, and his clenched hands loosened from their fierce tension. He took an aimless step and drew a long breath. A moment later, quite automatically, he fumbled for his cigarette-case, and finding it, took out a cigarette and lighted it with fingers that were not steady. The familiar action and the first puff of smoke affected him like emerging from a tur-moil of darkness into the quiet and order of a well-lighted room. "Well, may I be damned!" he said to himself with the beginning of a return of his usual assurance—"the damn little spitfire!"

He walked about the room, puffing vigorously, feeling with relief his blood resume its usual rate of circulation. His head seemed to clear of a thick vapor. The startling recollection of the anger in his fiancée's eyes was fading rapidly from his mind. Now he only saw her, blushing, recoiling, fleeing—he laughed out a little, this time not angrily, but with relish. "Ain't she the firebrand!" he said aloud. He found his desire for her a hundredfold enhanced and stood still, his eyes very lustrous, feeling again in imagination the warm softness of her bosom under his lips. "Gee!" he exclaimed, turning restlessly in his pacing walk.

He was aware that some one in the room moved. "Jermain," said his stepmother's faint voice. He looked at her smiling. "Hello, Momma," he said good-naturedly, "when did *you* gum-shoe in?"

"Oh, just now," she told him, giving him an assurance which he doubted, and which he would not have valued had he known it to be true. He was perfectly indifferent as to the chance that this negligible person might have been a spectator to the scene between the son of the house and a guest. If she said anything about it, he meant to give the all-sufficing explanation that he and Miss Marshall had just become engaged. This would of course, it seemed self-evident to him, make it all right.

But Mrs. Fiske did not make any remark calling forth that information. She only said, in her usual listless manner, "Your sleeve is shoved up."

He glanced down in surprise, realizing how excited he must be not to have noticed that before, and remained for a moment silent, looking at the splendidly muscular white arm, and the large well-manicured hand. He was feeling in every nerve the reminiscence of the yielding firmness of Sylvia's flesh, bare against his own. The color came up flamingly into his face again. He moistened his lips with his tongue. "Jesus *Christ!*" he exclaimed, contemptuously careless of his listener, " I'm wild in love with that girl!" He pulled his sleeve down with a quick, vigorous gesture, deftly shot the cuff out beyond the black broadcloth, and, the picture of handsome, well-groomed youth in easy circumstances, turned again to his father's wife. "What you in here *for,* anyhow?" he asked still with his light absence of concern about anything she did or did not do.

She hesitated, looking about the room. " I thought Miss Marshall would be here. She promised to come down early to write the names on the place-cards. I thought I heard her voice."

"You did," he told her. " She came down early all right—but she went back again." He laughed, tossed his cigarette-end in the fireplace, and vouchsafing no more explanation, strolled into the billiard-room, and began to knock the balls about, whistling a recent dance tune with great precision and vivacity. He was anticipating with quickened blood the next meeting with Sylvia. As he thrust at the gleaming balls, his mouth smiled and his eyes burned.

Mrs. Fiske went upstairs and knocked at Sylvia's door. There was a rush of quick footsteps and the girl asked from the other side in a muffled voice, " Who is it?" Mrs. Fiske gave her name, and added, in answer to another question, that she was alone. The door opened enough for her to enter, and closed quickly after her. She looked about the disordered room, saw the open trunk, the filmy cascade of yellow chiffon half on and half off the bed, the torn and crumpled spangled scarf, and Sylvia herself, her hastily donned kimono clutched about her with tense hands.

The mistress of the house made no comment on this scene, looking at Sylvia with dull, faded eyes in which there was no life, not even the flicker of an inquiry. But Sylvia began in a nervous voice to attempt an explanation: "Oh, Mrs. Fiske—I—you'll have to excuse me—I must go home at once—I—I was just packing. I thought—if I hurried I could make the eight-o'clock trolley back to

La Chance, and you could send my trunk after me." Her every faculty was so concentrated on the single idea of flight—flight back to the safety of home, that she did not think of the necessity of making an excuse, giving a reason for her action. It seemed that it must be self-evident to the universe that she could not stay another hour in that house.

Mrs. Fiske nodded. "Yes, I'll send your trunk after you," she said. She drew a long breath, almost audible, and looked down at the fire on the hearth. Sylvia came up close to her, looking into her lusterless eyes with deep entreaty. "And, Mrs. Fiske, *would* you mind not telling any one I'm going, until I'm gone—*nobody* at all! It's because—I—you could say I didn't feel well enough to come down to dinner. I—if you—and say I don't want any dinner up here either!"

"Won't you be afraid to go down through the grounds to the trolley alone, at night?" asked Mrs. Fiske, without looking at her.

"Everybody will be at dinner, won't they?" asked Sylvia.

Mrs. Fiske nodded, her eyes on the floor.

Upon which, "Oh no, I won't be afraid!" cried Sylvia.

Her hostess turned to the door. "Well, I won't tell them if you don't want me to," she said. She went out, without another word, closing the door behind her. Sylvia locked it, and went on with her wild packing. When she came to the yellow chiffon she rolled it up tightly and jammed it into a corner of her trunk; but the instant afterward she snatched it out and thrust it fiercely into the fire. The light fabric caught at once, the flames leaped up, filling the room with a roaring heat and flare, which almost as quickly died down to blackened silence.

Sylvia faced that instant of red glare with a grimly set jaw and a deeply flushed face. It did not look at all like her own face.

At a quarter of eight the room was cleared, the trunk strapped and locked, and Sylvia stood dressed for the street, gloved, veiled, and furred. Under her veil her face showed still very flushed. She took up her small handbag and her umbrella and opened the door with caution. A faint clatter of dishes and a hum of laughing talk came up to her ears. Dinner was evidently in full swing. She stepped out and went noiselessly down the stairs. On the bottom step, close to the dining-room door, her umbrella-tip caught in the balustrade and fell with a loud clatter on the bare polished floor of the hall. Sylvia shrank into herself and waited an instant with suspended breath for the pause in the chatter and laughter which it seemed must follow. The moment was forever connected in her mind with the smell of delicate food, and fading flowers, and human beings well-washed and perfumed, which floated out to her from the dining-room. She looked about her at the luxuriously furnished great hall, and hated every inch of it.

If the noise was heard, it evidently passed for something dropped by a servant, for Colonel Fiske, who was telling a humorous story, went on, his recital punctuated by bass and treble anticipatory laughter from his auditors: "——and when he called her upon the 'phone the next day to ask her about it, she said *she* didn't know he'd been there at all!" A roar of appreciation greeted this recondite climax, under cover of which Sylvia opened the front door and shut it behind her.

The pure coldness of the winter night struck sharply and gratefully on her senses after the warmth and indoor odors of the house. She sprang forward along the porch and down the steps, distending her nostrils and filling her lungs again and again. These long deep breaths seemed to her like the renewal of life.

As her foot grated on the gravel of the driveway she heard a stealthy sound back of her, at which her heart leaped up and stood still. The front door of the house had opened very quietly and shut again. She looked over her shoulder fearfully, preparing to race down the road, but seeing only Mrs. Fiske's tall, stooping figure, stopped and turned expectantly. The older woman came down the steps towards the fugitive, apparently unaware of the biting winter wind on her bared shoulders. Quite at a loss, and suspiciously on her guard, Sylvia waited for her, searching the blurred pale face with impatient inquiry.

"I—I thought I'd walk with you a little ways," said the other, looking down at her guest.

"Oh no! *Don't!*" pleaded Sylvia in despair lest some one notice her hostess' absence. "You'll take a dreadful cold! With no wraps on—*do* go back! I'm not a bit afraid!"

The other looked at her with a smoldering flush rising through the ashes of her gray face. "It wasn't that—I didn't suppose you'd be afraid—I—I just thought I'd like to go a ways with you," she repeated, bringing out the words confusedly and with obvious difficulty. "*I* won't make you late," she added, as if guessing the girl's thoughts. She put a thin hand on Sylvia's arm and drew her rapidly along the driveway. For a moment they walked in silence. Then, "How soon will you reach home?" she asked.

"Oh, about a quarter to ten—the Interurban gets into La Chance at nine-fifteen, and it's about half an hour across town on the Washington Street trolley."

"In less than two hours!" cried Mrs. Fiske wildly. "In less than two hours!"

Seeing no cause for wonder in her statement, and not welcoming at all this unsought escort, Sylvia made no answer. There was another silence, and then, looking in the starlight at her companion, the girl saw with consternation that the quiet tears were running down her cheeks. She stopped short, "Oh . . . *oh!*" she cried. She caught up the other's hand in a bewildered surprise. She had not the faintest idea what could cause her hostess' emotion. She was horribly afraid she would lose the trolley. Her face painted vividly her agitation and her impatience.

Mrs. Fiske drew back her hand and wiped her eyes with her palm. "Well, I must be going back," she said. She looked dimly at the girl's face, and suddenly threw her arms about Sylvia's neck, clinging to her. She murmured incoherent words, the only ones which Sylvia could make out being, " I can't—I can't—I *can't!* "

What it was she could not do, remained an impenetrable mystery to Sylvia, for at that moment she turned away quickly, and went back up the driveway, her face in her hands. Sylvia hesitated, penetrated, in spite of her absorption in her own affairs, by a vague pity, but hearing in the distance the clang of the trolley-car's bell, she herself turned and ran desperately down the driveway. She reached the public road just in time to stop the heavy car, and to swing herself lightly on, to all appearances merely a rather unusually well-set-up, fashionably dressed young lady, presenting to the heterogeneous indifference of the other passengers in the car even a more ostentatiously abstracted air than is the accepted attitude for young ladies traveling alone. One or two of her fellow voyagers wondered at the deep flush on her face, but forgot it the next moment. It was a stain which was not entirely to fade from Sylvia's face and body for many days to come.

CHAPTER XX

"BLOW, WIND; SWELL, BILLOW; AND SWIM, BARK!"

SHE reached home, as she had thought, before ten o'clock, her unexpected arrival occasioning the usual flurry of exclamation and question not to be suppressed even by the most self-contained family with a fixed desire to let its members alone, and a firm tradition of not interfering in their private affairs. Judith had come home before her father and now looked up from her game of checkers with wondering eyes. Sylvia explained that she was not sick, and that nothing had happened to break up or disturb the house-party. "I just *felt* like coming home, that's all!" she said irritably, touched on the raw by the friendly loving eyes and voices about her. She was glad at least that her father was not at home. That was one less to look at her.

"Well, get along to bed with you!" said her mother, in answer to her impatient explanation. "And, you children—keep still! Don't bother her!"

Sylvia crept upstairs into the whiteness of her own slant-ceilinged room, and without lighting a lamp sat down on the bed. Her knees shook under her. She made no move to take off her furs or hat. She felt no emotion, only a leaden fatigue and lameness as though she had been beaten. Her mother, coming in five minutes later with a lighted lamp and a cup of hot chocolate, made no comment at finding her still sitting, fully dressed in the dark. She set the lamp down, and with swift deftness slipped out hatpins, unhooked furs, unbuttoned and unlaced and loosened, until Sylvia woke from her lethargy and quickly completed the process, slipping on her nightgown and getting into bed. Not a word had been exchanged. Mrs. Marshall

brought the cup of hot chocolate and Sylvia drank it as
though she were a little girl again. Her mother kissed
her good-night, drew the blankets a little more snugly over
her, opened two windows wide, took away the lamp, and
shut the door.

Sylvia, warmed and fed by the chocolate, lay stretched
at full length in the bed, breathing in the fresh air which
rushed across her face from the windows, feeling herself
in a white beatitude of safety and peace. Especially did
she feel grateful to her mother. " Isn't Mother *great!* " she
said to herself. Everything that had passed seemed like a
confusing dream to her, so dreadful, so terrifying that she
was amazed to feel herself, in spite of it, overcome with
drowsiness. Now the rôles were reversed. It was her
brain that was active, racing and shuddering from one
frightening mental picture to another, while her body,
young, sound, healthful, fell deeper and deeper into torpor,
dragging the quivering mind down to healing depths of
oblivion. The cold, pure air blew so strongly in her face
that she closed her eyes. When she opened them again the
sun was shining.

She started up nervously, still under the influence of a
vivid dream—strange. . . . Then as she blinked and rubbed
her eyes she saw her mother standing by the bed, with a
pale, composed face.

" It's nine o'clock, Sylvia," she said, " and Mr. Fiske is
downstairs, asking to see you. He tells me that you and
he are engaged to be married."

Sylvia was instantly wide awake. " Oh no! Oh no! "
she said passionately. " No, we're not! I won't be! I
won't see him! " She looked about her wildly, and added,
" I'll write him that—just wait a minute." She sprang out
of bed, caught up a pad of paper, and wrote hastily : " It
was all a mistake—I don't care for you at all—not a bit!
I hope I shall never have to speak to you again." " There,"
she said, thrusting it into her mother's hands. She stood
for a moment, shivering in her thin nightgown in the icy
draught, and then jumped back into bed again.

Her mother came back in a few moments, closed the windows, and opened the register. There was not in her silence or in a line of her quiet presence the faintest hint of curiosity about Sylvia's actions. She had always maintained in theory, and now at this crisis with characteristic firmness of purpose acted upon her theory, that absolutely unforced confidence was the only kind worth having, and that moreover, unless some help was necessary, it might be as well for the younger generation early to acquire the strengthening capacity to keep its own intimate experiences to the privacy of its own soul, and learn to digest them and feed upon them without the dubiously peptonizing aid of blundering adult counsel. Sylvia watched her mother with wondering gratitude. She wasn't going to ask! She was going to let Sylvia shut that ghastly recollection into the dark once for all. She wasn't going by a look or a gesture to force her helplessly responsive child to give, by words, weight and substance to a black, shapeless horror from which Sylvia with a vivid impulse of sanity averted her eyes.

She got out of bed and put her arms around her mother's neck. " Say, Mother, you are *great!* " she said in an unsteady voice. Mrs. Marshall patted her on the back.

•   " You'd better go and take your bath, and have your breakfast," she said calmly. " Judith and Lawrence have gone skating."

When Sylvia, tingling with the tonic shock of cold water and rough toweling, and rosy in her old blue sailor-suit, came downstairs, she found her mother frying pancakes for her in the kitchen blue with smoke from the hot fat. She was touched, almost shocked by this strange lapse from the tradition of self-help of the house, and said with rough self-accusation: " My goodness! The idea of *your* waiting on *me!* " She snatched away the handle of the frying-pan and turned the cakes deftly. Then, on a sudden impulse, she spoke to her mother. standing by the sink. " I came back because I found I didn't like Jerry Fiske as much as

I thought I did. I found I didn't like him at all," she said,
her eyes on the frying-pan.

At this announcement her mother's face showed pale,
and for an instant tremulous through the smoke. She
did not speak until Sylvia lifted the cakes from the pan and
piled them on a plate. At this signal of departure into the
dining-room she commented, " Well, I won't pretend that
I'm not very glad."

Sylvia flushed a little and looked towards her silently.
She had a partial, momentary vision of what the past two
months must have been to her mother. The tears stood in
her eyes. " Say, Mother dear," she said in a quavering
voice that tried to be light, " why don't you eat some of
these cakes to keep me company? It's 'most ten. You
must have had breakfast three hours ago. It'd be fun! I
can't begin to eat all these."

" Well, I don't care if I do," answered Mrs. Marshall.
Sylvia laughed at the turn of her phrase and went into
the dining-room. Mrs. Marshall followed in a moment
with a cup of hot chocolate and buttered toast. Sylvia
pulled her down and kissed her. " You'd prescribe hot
chocolate for anything from getting religion to a broken
leg!" she said, laughing. Her voice shook and her laugh
ended in a half-sob.

" No—oh no!" returned her mother quaintly. " Sometimes hot milk is better. Here, where is my share of those
cakes?" She helped herself, went around the table, and
sat down. " Cousin Parnelia was here this morning," she
went on. " Poor old idiot, she was certain that planchette
would tell who it was that stole our chickens. I told
her to go ahead—but planchette wouldn't write. Cousin
Parnelia laid it to the blighting atmosphere of skepticism
of this house."

Sylvia laughed again. Alone in the quiet house with her
mother, refreshed by sleep, aroused by her bath, safe, sheltered, secure, she tried desperately not to think of the
events of the day before. But in spite of herself they came
back to her in jagged flashes—above all, the handsome blond

face darkened by passion. She shivered repeatedly, her voice was quite beyond her control, and once or twice her hands trembled so that she laid down her knife and fork. She was silent and talkative by turns—a phenomenon of which Mrs. Marshall took no outward notice, although when the meal was finished she sent her daughter out into the piercing December air with the command to walk six miles before coming in. Sylvia recoiled at the prospect of solitude. " Oh, I'd rather go and skate with Judy and Larry! " she cried.

" Well, if you skate hard enough," her mother conceded.

The day after her return Sylvia had a long letter from Jermain Fiske, a letter half apologetic, half aggrieved, passionately incredulous of the seriousness of the break between them, and wholly unreconciled to it. The upshot of his missive was that he was sorry if he had done anything to offend her, but might he be everlastingly confounded if he thought she had the slightest ground for complaint! Everything had been going on so swimmingly—his father had taken the greatest notion to her—had said (the very evening she'd cut and run that queer way) that if he married that rippingly pretty Marshall girl he could have the house and estate at Mercerton and enough to run it on, and could practise as much or as little law as he pleased and go at once into politics—and now she had gone and acted so—what in the world was the matter with her—weren't they engaged to be married—couldn't an engaged man kiss his girl—had he ever been anything but too polite for words to her before she had promised to marry him—and what *about* that promise anyhow? His father had picked out the prettiest little mare in the stables to give her when the engagement should be announced—the Colonel was as much at a loss as he to make her out—if the trouble was that she didn't want to live in Mercerton, he was sure the Colonel would fix it up for them to go direct to Washington, where with his father's connection she could imagine what an opening they'd have! And above all he was crazy about her—he really was! He'd never had any idea what it was to be in love before—he hadn't slept a wink the night she'd gone away—just tossed on his bed and thought of her and longed to have her in his arms again——" Sylvia suddenly tore the letter in two and cast it into the fire, breathing hard. In answer she wrote, " It makes me sick to think of you! "

She could not endure the idea of " talking over " the experience with any one, and struggled to keep it out of her mind, but her resolution to keep silence was broken by Mrs. Draper, who was informed, presumably by Jermain himself, of the circumstances, and encountering Sylvia in the street waited for no invitation to confidence by the girl, but pounced upon her with laughing reproach and insidiously friendly ridicule. Sylvia, helpless before the graceful assurance of her friend, heard that she was a silly little unawakened schoolgirl who was throwing away a brilliantly happy and successful life for the queerest and funniest of ignorant notions. " What did you suppose, you baby? You wouldn't have him marry you unless he was in love with you, would you? Why do you suppose a man *wants* to marry a woman? Did you suppose that men in love carry their sweethearts around wrapped in cotton-wool? You're a woman now, you ought to welcome life—rich, full-blooded life—not take this chilly, suspicious attitude toward it! Why, Sylvia, I thought you were a big, splendid, vital, fearless modern girl—and here you are acting like a little, thin-blooded New England old maid. How can you blame Jerry? He was engaged to you. What do you think marriage *is?* Oh, Sylvia, just think what your life would be in Washington with your beauty and charm! "

This dexterously aimed attack penetrated Sylvia's armor at a dozen joints. She winced visibly, and hung her head, considering profoundly. She found that she had nothing to oppose to the other's arguments. Mrs. Draper walked beside her in a silence as dexterous as her exhortation, her hand affectionately thrust through Sylvia's arm. Finally,

Sylvia's ponderings continuing so long that they were approaching the Marshall house, in sight of which she had no mind to appear, she gave Sylvia's arm a little pat, and stood still. She said cheerfully, in a tone which seemed to minimize the whole affair into the smallest of passing incidents: " Now, you queer darling, don't stand so in your own light! A word would bring Jerry back to you now— but I won't say it will always. I don't suppose you've ever considered, in your young selfishness, how cruelly you have hurt his feelings! He was awfully sore when I saw him. And Eleanor Hubert is right on the spot with Mamma Hubert in the background to push."

Sylvia broke her silence to say in a low tone, blushing scarlet, " He was—*horrid!*"

Mrs. Draper dropped her light tone and said earnestly: " Dear little ignorant Sylvia—you don't recognize life when you see it. That's the way men are—all men—and there's no use thinking it horrid unless you're going into a convent. It's not so bad either,—once you get the hang of managing it—it's a hold on them. It's a force, like any other force of nature that you can either rebel against, or turn to your account and make serviceable, if you'll only accept it and not try to quarrel with water for running downhill. As long as she herself isn't carried away by it, it's a weapon in the hand of a clever woman. Only the stupid women get hurt by it—the silly ones who can't keep their heads. And after all, my dear, it *is* a force of nature—and you're too intelligent not to know that there's no use fighting against that. It's just idiotic and puritanic to revolt from it—and doesn't do any good besides! " She looked keenly into Sylvia's downcast, troubled face, and judged it a propitious moment for leaving her. " *Good*-bye, darling," she said, with a final pat on the shoulder.

Sylvia walked slowly into the house, her heart like lead. Her food had no savor to her. She did not know what she was eating, nor what her mother, the only one at home for lunch, was saying to her. As a matter of fact Mrs. Marshall said very little, even less than was her custom.

Her face had the look of terrible, patient endurance it had worn during the time when Lawrence had had pneumonia, and his life had hung in the balance for two days; but she went quietly about her usual household tasks.

After the meal was over, Sylvia continued to sit alone at the table, staring palely down at the tablecloth, her mind full of Mrs. Draper's illuminating comments on life, which had gone through her entire system like a dexterously administered drug. And yet that ingenious lady would have been surprised to know how entirely her attack had failed in the one point which seemed to her important, the possibility of a reconciliation between Sylvia and Jermain. The girl was deeply under the impression made by the philosophy of the older woman; she did not for the moment dream of denying its truth; but she stood granite in a perfectly illogical denial of its implications in her own case. She did not consciously revolt against the suggestion that she renew her relations to Jerry Fiske, because with a united action of all her faculties she refused utterly to consider it for an instant. She would no more have been persuaded to see Jerry again, by a consideration of the material advantages to be gained, than she could have been persuaded to throw herself down from the housetop. That much was settled, not by any coherent effort of her brain, but by a co-ordination of every instinct in her, by the action of her whole being, by what her life had made her.

But that certainty brought her small comfort in the blackness of the hour. What hideous world was this in which she had walked unawares until now! Mrs. Draper's jaunty, bright acceptance of it affected her to moral nausea. All the well-chosen words of her sophisticated friend were imbedded in the tissue of her brain like grains of sand in an eyeball. She could not see for very pain. And yet her inward vision was lurid with the beginning of understanding of the meaning of those words, lighted up as they were by her experience of the day before, now swollen in her distraught mind to the proportions of a nightmare: " It's a weapon in the hand of a clever woman—it's not so bad once you get the hang of managing it—it's a hold on men——" Sylvia turned whiter and whiter at the glimpse she had had of what was meant by Mrs. Draper's lightly evasive "it"; a comprehension of which all her "advanced" reading and study had left her mind as blankly ignorant as a little child's. Now it was vain to try to shut her thoughts away from Jermain. She lived over and over the scene with him, she endured with desperate passivity the recollection of his burning lips on her bosom, his fingers pressing into her side. Why not, if every man was like that as soon as he dared? Why not, if that was all that men wanted of women? Why not, if that was the sole ghastly reality which underlay the pretty-smooth surface of life?

And beyond this bleak prospect, which filled her with dreary horror, there rose glimpsed vistas which sent the shamed blood up to her face in a flood—if every man was like that, why, so were the men she had known and loved and trusted; old Reinhardt, who seemed so simple, what had been his thoughts when he used years ago to take her on his knee—what were his thoughts now when he bent over her to correct her mistakes on the piano?

The expression of Colonel Fiske's eyes, as he had complimented her, brought her to her feet with a shudder—but Colonel Fiske was an old, old man—as old as Professor Kennedy—

Why, perhaps Professor Kennedy—perhaps—she flung out her arms—perhaps her father—

She ran to the piano as to a refuge, meaning to drown out these maddening speculations, which were by this time tinctured with insanity; but the first chords she struck jarred on her ear like a discordant scream. She turned away and stood looking at the floor with a darkening face, one hand at her temple.

Her mother, darning stockings by the window, suddenly laid down her work and said: "Sylvia, how would you like to walk with me over to the Martins' to see if they have any eggs? Our hens have absolutely gone back on us."

Sylvia did not welcome this idea at all, feeling as overwhelming an aversion to companionship as to solitude, but she could think of no excuse, and in an ungracious silence put on her wraps and joined her mother, ready on the porch, the basket in her mittened hand.

Mrs. Marshall's pace was always swift, and on that crisp, cold, sunny day, with the wind sweeping free over the great open spaces of the plain about them, she walked even more rapidly than usual. Not a word was spoken. Sylvia, quite as tall as her mother now, and as vigorous, stepped beside her, not noticing their pace, nor the tingling of the swift blood in her feet and hands. Her fresh young face was set in desolate bitterness.

The Martins' house was about six miles from the Marshalls'. It was reached, the eggs procured, and the return begun. Still not a word had been exchanged between the two women. Mrs. Marshall would have been easily capable, under the most ordinary circumstances, of this long self-contained silence, but it had worked upon Sylvia like a sojourn in the dim recesses of a church. She felt moved, stirred, shaken. But it was not until the brief winter sun was beginning to set red across the open reaches of field and meadow that her poisoned heart overflowed. "Oh, Mother——!" she exclaimed in an unhappy tone, and said no more. She knew no words to phrase what was in her mind.

"Yes, dear," said her mother gently. She looked at her daughter anxiously, expectantly, with a passion of yearning in her eyes, but she said no more than those two words.

There was a silence. Sylvia was struggling for expression. They continued to walk swiftly through the cold, ruddy, sunset air, the hard-frozen road ringing beneath their rapid advance. Sylvia clasped her hands together hard in her muff. She felt that something in her heart was dying, was suffocating for lack of air, and yet that it would die if she brought it to light. She could find no words at all to ask for help, agonizing in a shy reticence impossible for an adult to conceive. Finally, beginning at random, very hurriedly, looking away, she brought out, faltering, " Mother, *is* it true that all men are—that when a girl marries she must expect to—aren't there *any* men who——" She stopped, burying her burning face in her muff.

Her words, her tone, the quaver of desperate sincerity in her accent, brought her mother up short. She stopped abruptly and faced the girl. " Sylvia, look at me! " she said in a commanding voice which rang loud in the frosty silences about them. Sylvia started and looked into her mother's face. It was moved so darkly and so deeply from its usual serene composure that she would have re-coiled in fear, had she not been seized upon and held motionless by the other's compelling eyes.

" Sylvia," said her mother, in a strong, clear voice, acutely contrasted to Sylvia's muffled tones, " Sylvia, it's a lie that men are nothing but sensual! There's nothing in marriage that a good girl honestly in love with a good man need fear."

" But—but——" began Sylvia, startled out of her shy-ness.

Her mother cut her short. " Anything that's felt by decent men in love is felt just as truly, though maybe not always so strongly, by women in love. And if a woman doesn't feel that answer in her heart to what he feels—why, he's no mate for her. Anything's better for her than going on. And, Sylvia, you mustn't get the wrong idea. Sensual feeling isn't bad in itself. It's in the world because we have bodies as well as minds—it's like the root of a plant. But it oughtn't to be a very big part of the plant. And it must be the root of the woman's feeling as well as the man's, or everything's all wrong."

" But how can you *tell!* " burst out Sylvia.

" You can tell by the way you feel, if you don't lie to yourself, or let things like money or social position count. If an honest girl shrinks from a man instinctively, there's something not right—sensuality is too big a part of what the man feels for her—and look here, Sylvia, that's not always the man's fault. Women don't realize as they ought how base it is to try to attract men by their bodies," she made her position clear with relentless precision, " when they wear very low-necked dresses, for instance——" At this chance thrust, a wave of scarlet burst up suddenly over Sylvia's face, but she could not withdraw her eyes from her mother's searching, honest gaze, which, even more than her words, spoke to the girl's soul. The strong, grave voice went on unhesitatingly. For once in her life Mrs. Marshall was speaking out. She was like one who welcomes the opportunity to make a confession of faith. " There's no healthy life possible without some sensual feeling between the husband and wife, but there's nothing in the world more awful than married life when it's the only common ground."

Sylvia gazed with wide eyes at the older woman's face, ardent, compelling, inspired, feeling too deeply, to realize it wholly, the vital and momentous character of the moment. She seemed to see nothing, to be aware of nothing but her mother's heroic eyes of truth; but the whole scene was printed on her mind for all her life—the hard, brown road they stood on, the grayed old rail-fence back of Mrs. Marshall, a field of brown stubble, a distant grove of beech-trees, and beyond and around them the immense sweeping circle of the horizon. The very breath of the pure, scentless winter air was to come back to her nostrils in after years.

" Sylvia," her mother went on, " it is one of the responsibilities of men and women to help each other to meet on a high plane and not on a low one. And on the whole— health's the rule of the world—on the whole, that's the way the larger number of husbands and wives, imperfect as they are, do live together. Family life wouldn't be possible a day if they didn't."

Like a strong and beneficent magician, she built up again and illuminated Sylvia's black and shattered world. " Your father is just as pure a man as I am a woman, and I

would be ashamed to look any child of mine in the face if
he were not. You know no men who are not decent—
except two—and those you did not meet in your parents'
home."

For the first time she moved from her commanding attitude of prophetic dignity. She came closer to Sylvia, but
although she looked at her with a sudden sweetness which
affected Sylvia like a caress, she but made one more impersonal statement: "Sylvia dear, don't let anything make
you believe that there are not as many decent men in the
world as women, and they're just as decent. Life isn't
worth living unless you know that—and it's true." Apparently she had said all she had to say, for she now
kissed Sylvia gently and began again to walk forward.

The sun had completely set, and the piled-up clouds on
the horizon flamed and blazed. Sylvia stood still, looking
at them fixedly. The great shining glory seemed reflected
from her heart, and cast its light upon a regenerated world
—a world which she seemed to see for the first time.
Strange, in that moment of intensely personal life, how
her memory was suddenly flooded with impersonal impressions of childhood, little regarded at the time and
long since forgotten, but now recurring to her with the
authentic and uncontrovertible brilliance which only first-
hand experiences in life can bring with them—all those
families of her public-school mates, the plain, ugly homes
in and out of which she had come and gone, with eyes
apparently oblivious of all but childish interests, but really
recording life-facts which now in her hour of need stretched
under her feet like a solid pathway across an oozing marsh.
All those men and women whom she had seen in a thousand
unpremeditated acts, those tired-faced, kind-eyed, unlettered
fathers and mothers were not breathing poisoned air, were
not harboring in their simple lives a ghastly devouring wild-
beast. She recalled with a great indrawn breath all the
farmer-neighbors, parents working together for the children, the people she knew so well from long observation
of their lives, whose mediocre, struggling existence had

filled her with scornful pity, but whom now she recalled with a great gratitude for the explicitness of the revelations made by their untutored plainness. For all she could ever know, the Drapers and the Fiskes and the others of their world might be anything, under the discreet reticence of their sophistication; but they did not make up all the world. She knew, from having breathed it herself, the wind of health which blew about those other lives, bare and open to the view, as less artless lives were not. There was some other answer to the riddle, beside Mrs. Draper's.

Sylvia was only eighteen years old and had the childish immaturity of her age, but her life had been so ordered that she was not, even at eighteen, entirely in the helpless position of a child who must depend on the word of others. She had accumulated, unknown to herself, quite apart from polished pebbles of book-information, a small treasury of living seeds of real knowledge of life, taken in at first-hand, knowledge of which no one could deprive her. The realization of this was a steadying ballast which righted the wildly rolling keel under her feet. She held up her head bravely against the first onslaught of the storm. She set her hand to the rudder!

Perceiving that her mother had passed on ahead of her she sprang forward in a run. She ran like a schoolboy, like a deer, like a man from whose limbs heavy shackles have been struck off. She felt so suddenly lightened of a great heaviness that she could have clapped her hands over her head and bounded into the air. She was, after all, but eighteen years old, and three years before had been a child.

She came up to her mother with a rush, radiating life. Mrs. Marshall looked at the glowing face and her own eyes, dry till then, filled with the tears so rare in her self-controlled life. She put out her hand, took Sylvia's, and they sped along through the quick-gathering dusk, hand-in-hand like sisters.

Judith and Lawrence had reached home before them, and the low brown house gleamed a cheerful welcome to them from shining windows. For the first time in her life,

Sylvia did not take for granted her home, with all that it meant. For an instant it looked strangely sweet to her. She had a passing glimpse, soon afterwards lost in other impressions, of how in after years she would look back on the roof which had sheltered and guarded her youth.

She lay awake that night a long time, staring up into the cold blackness, her mind very active and restless in the intense stillness about her. She thought confusedly but intensely of many things—the months behind her, of Jerry, of Mrs. Draper, of her yellow dress, of her mother—of herself. In the lucidity of those silent hours of wakefulness she experienced for a time the piercing, regenerating thrust of self-knowledge. For a moment the full-beating pulses of her youth slackened, and between their throbs there penetrated to her perplexed young heart the rarest of human emotions, a sincere humility. If she had not burned the yellow dress at Mercerton, she would have arisen and burned it that night. . . .

During the rest of the Christmas vacation she avoided being alone. She and Judith and Lawrence skated a great deal, and Sylvia learned at last to cut the grapevine pattern on the ice. She also mastered the first movement of the Sonata Pathétique, so that old Reinhardt was almost satisfied.

The day after the University opened for the winter term the Huberts announced the engagement of their daughter Eleanor to Jermain Fiske, Jr., the brilliant son of that distinguished warrior and statesman, Colonel Jermain Fiske. Sylvia read this announcement in the Society Column of the La Chance *Morning Herald,* with an enigmatic expression on her face, and betaking herself to the skating-pond, cut grapevines with greater assiduity than ever, and with a degree of taciturnity surprising in a person usually so talkative. That she had taken the first step away from the devouring egotism of childhood was proved by the fact that at least part of the time, this vigorous young creature, swooping about the icy pond like a swallow, was thinking pityingly of Eleanor Hubert's sweet face.

CHAPTER XXI

SOME YEARS DURING WHICH NOTHING HAPPENS

JUDITH had said to the family, taking no especial pains that her sister should not hear her, " Well, folks, now that Sylvia's got through with that horrid Fiske fellow, I do hope we'll all have some peace! " a remark which proved to be a prophecy. They all, including Sylvia herself, knew the tranquillity of an extended period of peace.

It began abruptly, like opening a door into a new room. Sylvia had dreaded the beginning of the winter term and the inevitable sight of Jerry, the enforced crossings of their paths. But Jerry never returned to his classes at all. The common talk was to the effect that the Colonel had " worked his pull " to have Jerry admitted to the bar without further preliminaries. After some weeks of relief, it occurred to Sylvia that perhaps Jerry had dreaded meeting her as much as she had seeing him. For whatever reason, the campus saw young Fiske no more, except on the day in May when he passed swiftly across it on his way to the Hubert house where Eleanor, very small and white-faced, waited for him under a crown of orange blossoms.

Sylvia did not go to the wedding, although an invitation had come, addressed economically and compendiously to " Professor and Mrs. Marshall and family." It was a glorious spring day and in her Greek history course they had just reached the battle of Salamis, at the magnificent recital of which Sylvia's sympathetic imagination leaped up rejoicing, as all sympathetic imaginations have for all these many centuries. She was thrilling to a remembered bit of " The Persians " as she passed by the Hubert house late that afternoon. She was chanting to herself, " The right wing, well marshaled, led on foremost in good order, and we heard a mighty shout—'Sons of the Greeks! On! Free your country!'" She did not notice that she trod swiftly across a trail of soiled rice in the Hubert driveway.

She was like a person recovered from a fever who finds mere health a condition of joy. She went back to her music, to her neglected books, with a singing heart. And in accordance with the curious ways of Providence, noted in the proverb relating the different fates of him who hath and him who hath not, there was at once added to her pleasure in the old elements of her life the very elements she had longed for unavailingly. Seeing her friendly and shining of face, friendliness went out to her. She had made many new acquaintances during her brief glittering flight and had innumerable more points of contact with the University life than before. She was invited to a quite sufficient number of hops and proms, had quite the normal number of masculine " callers," and was naïvely astonished and disillusioned to find that those factors in life were by no means as entirely desirable and amusing as her anguished yearning had fancied them. She joined one of the literary societies and took a leading part in their annual outdoor play. At the beginning of her Junior year, Judith entered as a Freshman and thereafter became a close companion. Sylvia devoured certain of her studies, history, and English, and Greek, with insatiable zest and cast aside certain others like political economy and physics, which bored her, mastering just enough of their elements to pass an examination and promptly forgetting them thereafter. She grew rapidly in intellectual agility and keenness, not at all in philosophical grasp, and emotionally remained as dormant as a potato in a cellar.

She continually looked forward with a bright, vague interest to "growing up," to the mastery of life which adolescents so trustfully associate with the arrival of adult years. She spent three more years in college, taking a Master's degree after her B.A., and during those three years, through the many-colored, shifting, kaleidoscopic, disorganized life of an immensely populous institution of learning, she fled with rapid feet, searching restlessly everywhere for that entity, as yet non-existent, her own soul.

She had, in short, a thoroughly usual experience of modern American education, emerging at the end with a vast amount of information, with very little notion of what it was all about, with Phi Beta Kappa and a great wonder what she was to do with herself.

Up to that moment almost every step of her life had been ordered and systematized, that she might the more quickly and surely arrive at the goal of her diploma. Rushing forward with the accumulated impetus of years of training in swiftly speeding effort, she flashed by the goal . . . and stopped short, finding herself in company with a majority of her feminine classmates in a blind alley. "*Now* what?" they asked each other with sinking hearts. Judith looked over their heads with steady eyes which saw but one straight and narrow path in life, and passed on by them into the hospital where she began her nurse's training. Sylvia began to teach music to a few children, to take on some of Reinhardt's work as he grew older. She practised assiduously, advanced greatly in skill in music, read much, thought acutely, rebelliously and not deeply, helped Lawrence with his studies . . . and watched the clock.

For there was no denying that the clock stood still. She was not going forward to any settled goal now, she was not going forward at all. She was as far from suspecting any ordered pattern in the facts of life as when she had been in college, surrounded by the conspiracy of silence about a pattern in facts which university professors so conscientiously keep up before their students. She was slowly revolving in an eddy. Sometimes she looked at the deep, glowing content of her father and mother with a fierce resentment. "How *can* they!" she cried to herself. At other times she tried to chide herself for not being as contented herself, ". . . but it's their life they're living," she said moodily, "and I haven't any to live. I can't live on their happiness any more than the beefsteaks somebody else has eaten can keep me from starving to death."

The tradition of her life was that work and plenty of it would keep off all uneasiness, that it was a foolishness, not to say a downright crime, to feel uneasiness. So she practised many hours a day, and took a post-graduate course in early Latin. But the clock stood still.

One of the assistants in her father's department proposed to her. She refused him automatically, with a wondering astonishment at his trembling hands and white lips. Decidedly the wheels of the clock would never begin to revolve.

And then it struck an hour, loudly. Aunt Victoria wrote inviting Sylvia to spend a few weeks with her during the summer at Lydford.

Sylvia read this letter aloud to her mother on the vine-covered porch where she had sat so many years before, and repeated " star-light, star-bright " until she had remembered Aunt Victoria. Mrs. Marshall watched her daughter's face as she read, and through the tones of the clear eager voice she heard the clock striking. It sounded to her remarkably like a tolling bell, but she gave no sign beyond a slight paling. She told herself instantly that the slowly ticking clock had counted her out several years of grace beyond what a mother may expect. When Sylvia finished and looked up, the dulled look of resignation swept from her face by the light of adventurous change, her mother achieved the final feat of nodding her head in prompt, cheerful assent.

But when Sylvia went away, light-hearted, fleeting forward to new scenes, there was in her mother's farewell kiss a solemnity which she could not hide. " Oh, Mother dear ! " protested Sylvia, preferring as always to skim over the depths which her mother so dauntlessly plumbed. " Oh, Mother darling ! How can you be so—when it's only for a few weeks ! "

BOOK III

IN CAPUA AT LAST

CHAPTER XXII

A GRATEFUL CARTHAGINIAN

ARNOLD SMITH put another lump of sugar on his saucer, poured out a very liberal allowance of rum into his tea, and reached for a sandwich, balancing the cup and saucer with a deftness out of keeping with his long, ungraceful loose-jointedness. He remarked in an indifferent tone to Sylvia, back of the exquisitely appointed tea-tray: " I don't say anything because I haven't the least idea what you are talking about. Who *was* Capua, anyhow? "

Sylvia broke into a peal of laughter which rang like a silver chime through the vine-shaded, airy spaces of the pergola. Old Mr. Sommerville, nosing about in his usual five-o'clock quest, heard her and came across the stretch of sunny lawn to investigate. " Oh, *here's* tea! " he remarked on seeing Arnold, lounging, white-flanneled, over his cup. He spoke earnestly, as was his custom when eating was in question, and Sylvia served him earnestly and carefully, with an instant harmonious response to his mood, putting in exactly the right amount of rum and sugar to suit his taste, and turning the slim-legged " curate's assistant " so that his favorite sandwiches were nearest him.

" You spoil the old gentlemen, Sylvia," commented Arnold, evidently caring very little whether she did or not.

" She spoils everybody," returned Mr. Sommerville, tasting his tea complacently; " ' *c'est son métier.*' She has an uncanny instinct for suiting everybody's taste."

Sylvia smiled brightly at him, exactly the brilliant smile

which suited her brilliant, frank face and clear, wide-open
eyes. Under her smile she was saying to herself, "If that's
so, I wonder—not that I care at all—but I really wonder
why you don't like me."

Sylvia was encountering for the first time this summer
a society guided by tradition and formula, but she was not
without excellent preparation for almost any contact with
her fellow-beings, a preparation which in some ways served
her better than that more conscious preparation of young
ladies bred up from childhood to sit behind tea-tables and
say the right things to tea-drinkers. Association with the
crude, outspoken youth at the State University had been an
education in human nature, especially masculine nature, for
her acute mind. Her unvarnished association with the
other sex in classroom and campus had taught her, by means
of certain rough knocks which more sheltered boarding-
school girls never get, an accuracy of estimate as to the
actual feeling of men towards the women they profess to
admire unreservedly which (had he been able to conceive
of it) old Mr. Sommerville would have thought nothing
less than cynical.

But he did not conceive of it, and now sat, mellowed by
the rightness of his tea, white-haired, smooth-shaven, pink-
gilled, white-waistcoated, the picture of old age at its best,
as he smiled gallantly at the extremely pretty girl behind the
table. Unlike Sylvia he knew exactly why he did not like
her and he wasted no time in thinking about it. "What
were you laughing about, so delightfully, as I came in, eh?"
he asked, after the irretrievable first moment of joy in
gratified appetite had gone.

Sylvia had not the slightest backwardness about explaining. In fact she always took the greatest pains to be ex-
plicit with old Mr. Sommerville about the pit from which
she had been digged. "Why, this visit to Aunt Victoria
is like stepping into another world for me. Everything is
so different from my home-life. I was just thinking, as I
sat there behind all this glorious clutter," she waved a slim
hand over the silver and porcelain of the tea-table, "what

a change it was from setting the table one's self and washing up the dishes afterwards. That's what we always do at home. I hated it and I said to Arnold, 'I've reached Capua at last!' and he said," she stopped to laugh again, heartily, full-throated, the not-to-be-imitated laugh of genuine amusement, " he said, 'Who is Capua, anyhow?'"

Mr. Sommerville laughed, but grudgingly, with an impatient shake of his white head and an uneasy look in his eyes. For several reasons he did not like to hear Sylvia laugh at Arnold. He distrusted a young lady with too keen a sense of humor, especially when it was directed towards the cultural deficiencies of a perfectly eligible young man. To an old inhabitant of the world, with Mr. Sommerville's views as to the ambitions of a moneyless young person, enjoying a single, brief fling in the world of young men with fortunes, it seemed certain that Sylvia's lack of tactful reticence about Arnold's ignorance could only be based on a feeling that Arnold's fortune was not big enough. She was simply, he thought with dismay, reserving her tact and reticence for a not-impossible bigger. His apprehensions about the fate of a bigger of his acquaintance if its owner ever fell into the hands of this altogether too well-informed young person rose to a degree which almost induced him to cry out, " Really, you rapacious young creature, Arnold's is all any girl need ask, ample, well-invested, solid. . . ." But instead he said, "Humph! Rather a derogatory remark about your surroundings, eh?"

Arnold did not understand, did not even hear, leaning back, long, relaxed, apathetic, in his great wicker-chair and rolling a cigarette with a detached air, as though his hands were not a part of him. But Sylvia heard, and understood, even to the hostility in the old gentleman's well-bred voice. " Being in Capua usually referring to the fact that the Carthaginians went to pieces that winter?" she asked. " Oh yes, of course I know that. Good gracious! I was brought up on the idea of the dangers of being in Capua. Perhaps that's why I always thought it would be such fun to get there." She spoke rebelliously.

"They got everlastingly beaten by the Romans," advanced Mr. Sommerville.

"Yes, but they had had one grand good time before! The Romans couldn't take *that* away from them! I think the Carthaginians got the best of it!" Provocative, light-hearted malice was in her sparkling face. She was thinking to herself with the reckless bravado of youth, "Well, since he insists, I'll *give* him some ground for distrusting my character!"

Arnold suddenly emitted a great puff of smoke and a great shout of "Help! help! Molly to the rescue!" and when a little white-clad creature flitting past the door turned and brought into that quiet spot of leafy shadow the dazzling quickness of her smile, her eyes, her golden hair, he said to her nonchalantly: "Just in time to head them off. Sylvia and your grandfather were being so high-brow I was beginning to feel faint."

Molly laughed flashingly. "Did Grandfather keep his end up? I bet he couldn't!"

Arnold professed an entire ignorance of the relative status. "Oh, I fell off so far back I don't know who got in first. Who *was* this man Capua, anyhow? I'm a graduate of Harvard University and I never heard of him."

"I'm a graduate of Miss Braddon's Mountain School for Girls," said Molly, "and *I* think it's a river."

Mr. Sommerville groaned out, exaggerating a real qualm, "What my mother would have said to such ignorance, prefaced by 'I bet!' from the lips of a young lady!"

"Your mother," said Molly, "would be my great-grand-mother!" She disposed of him conclusively by this statement and went on: "And I'm not a young lady. Nobody is nowadays."

"What *are* you, if a mere grandfather may venture to inquire?" asked Mr. Sommerville deferentially.

"I'm a *femme watt-man*," said Molly, biting a large piece from a sandwich.

Arnold explained to the others: "That's Parisian for a lady motor-driver; some name!"

"Well, you won't be that, or anything else alive, if you go on driving your car at the rate I saw it going past the house this morning," said her grandfather. He spoke with an assumption of grandfatherly severity, but his eyes rested on her with a grandfather's adoration.

"Oh, I'd die if I went under thirty-five," observed Miss Sommerville negligently.

"Why, Mr. Sommerville," Arnold backed up his generation. "You can't call thirty-five per hour dangerous, not for a girl who can drive like Molly."

"Oh, I'm as safe as if I were in a church," continued Molly. "I keep my mind on it. If I ever climb a telegraph-pole you can be sure it'll be because I wanted to. I never take my eye off the road, never once."

"How you must enjoy the landscape," commented her grandfather.

"Heavens! I don't drive a car to look at the landscape!" cried Molly, highly amused at the idea, apparently quite new to her.

"Will you gratify the curiosity of the older generation once more, and tell me what you *do* drive a car for?" inquired old Mr. Sommerville, looking fondly at the girl's lovely face, like a pink-flushed pearl.

"Why, I drive to see how fast I can go, of course," explained Molly. "The fun of it is to watch the road eaten up."

"It *is* fascinating," Sylvia gave the other girl an unexpected reinforcement. "I've driven with Molly, and I've been actually hypnotized seeing the road vanish under the wheels."

"Oh, children, children! When you reach my age," groaned Arnold, "and have eaten up as many thousand miles as I, you'll stay at home."

"I've driven for three years now," asserted Molly, "and every time I buy a new car I get the craze all over again. This one I have now is a peach of an eight. I never want to drive a six again,—never! I can bring it up from a creep to—to fast enough to scare Grandfather into a fit, without changing gears at all—just on the throttle——" She broke off to ask, as at a sudden recollection, " What was it about Capua, anyhow? " She went to sit beside Sylvia, and put her arm around her shoulder in a caressing gesture, evidently familiar to her.

" It wasn't about Capua at all," explained Sylvia indulgently, patting the lovely cheek, as though the other girl had been a child. " It was your grandfather finding out what a bad character I am, and how I wallow in luxury, now I have the chance."

" Luxury? " inquired Molly, looking about her rather blankly.

Sylvia laughed, this time with a little veiled, pensive note of melancholy, lost on the others but which she herself found very touching. " There, you see you're so used to it, you don't even know what I'm talking about! "

" Never mind, Molly," Arnold reassured her. " Neither do I! Don't try to follow; let it float by, the way I do! "

Miss Sommerville did not smile. She thrust out her red lips in a wistful pout, and looking down into the sugar-bowl intently, she remarked, her voice as pensive as Sylvia's own: " I wish I *did!* I wish I understood! I wish I were as clever as Sylvia! "

As if in answer to this remark, another searcher after tea announced himself from the door—a tall, distinguished, ugly, graceful man, who took a very fine Panama hat from a very fine head of brown hair, slightly graying, and said in a rich, cultivated voice: " Am I too late for tea? I don't mind at all if it's strong."

" Oh! " said Molly Sommerville, flushing and drawing away from Sylvia; *" Lord! "* muttered Arnold under his breath; and " Not at all. I'll make some fresh. I haven't had mine yet," said Sylvia, busying herself with the alcohol flame.

" How're you, Morrison? " said Mr. Sommerville with no enthusiasm, holding out a well-kept old hand for the other to shake.

Arnold stood up, reached under his chair, and pulled out

a tennis racquet. "Excuse me, Morrison, won't you, if I run along?" he said. "It's not because you've come. I want a set of tennis before dinner if I can find somebody to play with me. Here, Molly, you've got your tennis shoes on already. Come along."

The little beauty shook her head violently. "No . . . goodness no! It's too hot. And anyhow, I don't ever want to play again, since I've seen Sylvia's game." She turned to the other girl, breathing quickly. "*You* go, Sylvia dear. *I'll* make Mr. Morrison's tea for him."

Sylvia hesitated a barely perceptible instant, until she saw old Mr. Sommerville's eyes fixed speculatively on her. Then she stood up with an instant, cheerful alacrity. "That's *awfully* good of you, Molly darling! *You* won't mind, will you, Mr. Morrison!" She nodded brightly to the old gentleman, to the girl who had slipped into her place, to the other man, and was off.

The man she had left looked after her, as she trod with her long, light step beside the young man, and murmured, "*Et vera incessu patuit dea.*"

Molly moved a plate on the table with some vehemence. "I suppose Sylvia would understand that language."

"She would, my dear Molly, and what's more, she would scorn me for using such a hackneyed quotation." To Mr. Sommerville he added, laughing, "Isn't it the quaintest combination—such radiant girlhood and her absurd book-learning!"

Mr. Sommerville gave his assent to the quaintness by silence, as he rose and prepared to retreat.

"*Good*-bye, Grandfather," said Molly with enthusiasm.

As they walked along, Arnold was saying to Sylvia with a listless appreciation: "You certainly know the last word of the game, don't you, Sylvia? I bet Morrison hasn't had a jolt like that for years."

"What are you *talking* about?" asked Sylvia, perhaps slightly overdoing her ignorance of his meaning.

"Why, it's a new thing for *him*, let me tell you, to have

a girl jump up as soon as he comes in and delightedly leave him to another girl. And then to thank the other girl for being willing to take him off your hands,—that's more than knowing the rules,—that's art!" He laughed faintly at the recollection. "It's a new one for Morrison to meet a girl who doesn't kowtow. He's a very great personage in his line, and he can't help knowing it. The very last word on Lord-knows-what-all in the art business is what one Felix Morrison says about it. He's an eight-cylinder fascinator too, into the bargain. Mostly he makes me sore, but when I think about him straight, I wonder how he manages to keep on being as decent as he is—he's really a good enough sort!—with all the high-powered petti-coats in New York burning incense. It's enough to turn the head of a hydrant. That's the hold Madrina has on him. She doesn't burn any incense. She wants all the incense there is being burned, for herself; and it keeps old Felix down in his place—keeps him hanging around too. You stick to the same method if you want to make a go of it."

"I thought he wrote. I thought he did æsthetic criticisms and essays," said Sylvia, laughing aloud at Arnold's quaint advice.

"Oh, he does. I guess he's chief medicine-man in his tribe all right. It's not only women who kowtow; when old man Merriman wants to know for sure whether to pay a million for a cracked Chinese vase. he always calls in Felix Morrison. Chief adviser to the predatory rich, that's one of his jobs! So you see," he came back to his first point, " it must be some jolt for the sacred F. M. to have a young lady, *just a young lady,* refuse to bow at the shrine. You couldn't have done a smarter trick, by heck! I've been watching you all those weeks, just too tickled for words. And I've been watching Morrison. It's been as good as a play! He can't stick it out much longer, unless I miss my guess, and I've known him ever since I was a kid. He's just waiting for a good chance to turn on the faucet and hand you a full cup of his irresistible fascination." He

means admiringly. Her life in the State University had brought her into such incessant contact with young men that the mere fact of sitting beside one in the twilight left her unmoved to a degree which Mr. Sommerville's mother would have found impossible to imagine. When she spoke, it was with an impatient scorn of his weakness, which might have been felt by a fellow-athlete: "What in the world makes you do it, then?"

"Why not?" he said challengingly.

"You've just said why not—it spoils your tennis. It must spoil your polo. Was that what spoiled your baseball in college? You'd be twice the man if you wouldn't."

"Oh, what's the use?" he said, an immense weariness in his voice.

"What's the use of anything, if you are going to use *that* argument?" said Sylvia, putting him down conclusively.

He spoke with a sudden heartfelt simplicity, "Damn 'f I *know*, Sylvia." For the first time in all the afternoon, his voice lost its tonelessness, and rang out with the resonance of sincerity.

She showed an unflattering surprise. "Why, I didn't know you ever thought about such things."

He looked at her askance, dimly amused. "High opinion you have of me!"

She looked annoyed at herself and said with a genuine good-will in her voice, "Why, Arnold, you *know* I've always liked you."

"You like me, but you don't think much of me," he diagnosed her, "and you show your good sense." He looked up at the picturesque white house, spreading its well-proportioned bulk on the top of the terraced hillside before them. "I hope Madrina is looking out of a window and sees us here, our heads together in the twilight. You've guessed, I suppose, that she had you come on here for my benefit. She thinks she's tried everything else,—now it's her idea to get me safely married. She'd have one surprise, wouldn't she, if she could hear what we're saying!"

"Well, it *would* be a good thing for you," remarked Sylvia, as entirely without self-consciousness as though they were discussing the tennis game.

He was tickled by her coolness. "Well, Madrina sure made a mistake when she figured on *you!*" he commented ironically. And then, not having been subjected to the cool, hardy conditions which caused Sylvia's present clear-headedness, he felt his blood stirred to feel her there, so close, so alive, so young, so beautiful in the twilight. He leaned towards her and spoke in a husky voice, "See here, Sylvia, why *don't* you try it!"

"Oh, nonsense!" said the girl, not raising her voice at all, not stirring. "You don't care a bit for me."

"Yes, I do! I've *always* liked you!" he said, not perceiving till after the words were out of his mouth that he had repeated her own phrase.

She laughed to hear it, and he drew back, his faint stirring of warmth dashed, extinguished. "The fact is, Sylvia," he said, "you're too nice a girl to fall in love with."

"What a horrid thing to say!" she exclaimed.

"About *you?*" he defended himself. "I mean it as a compliment."

"About falling in love," she said.

"Oh!" he said blankly, evidently not at all following her meaning.

"What time is it?" she now inquired, and on hearing the hour, "Oh, we'll be late to dress for dinner," she said in concern, rising and ascending the marble steps to the terrace next above them.

He came after her, long, loose-jointed, ungraceful. He was laughing. "Do you realize that I've proposed marriage to you and you've turned me down?" he said.

"No such a thing!" she said, as lightly as he.

"It's the nearest *I* ever came to it!" he averred.

She continued to flit up the terraces before him, her

voice rippling with amusement dropping down on him through the dusk. " Well, you'll have to come nearer than that, if you ever want to make a go of it!" she called over her shoulder. Upon which note this very modern conversation ended.

CHAPTER XXIII

MORE TALK BETWEEN YOUNG MODERNS

WHEN they met at dinner, they laughed outright at the sight of one another, a merry and shadowless laugh. For an instant they looked like light-hearted children. The change of Arnold's long sallow face was indeed so noticeable that Mrs. Marshall-Smith glanced sharply at him, and then looked again with great satisfaction. She leaned to Sylvia and laid her charming white hand affectionately over the girl's slim, strong, tanned fingers. "It's just a joy to have you here, my dear. You're brightening us stupid, bored people like fresh west wind!" She went on addressing herself to the usual guest of the evening: "Isn't it always the most beautiful sight, Felix, how the mere presence of radiant youth can transform the whole atmosphere of life!"

"I hadn't noticed that my radiant youth had transformed much," commented Arnold dryly; "and Sylvia's only a year younger than I."

He was, as usual, disregarded by the course of the conversation. "Yes, sunshine in a shady place . . ." quoted Morrison, in his fine mellow tenor, looking at Sylvia. It was a wonderful voice, used with discretion, with a fine instinct for moderation which would have kept the haunting beauty of its intonations from seeming objectionable or florid to any but American ears. In spite of the invariable good taste with which it was used, American men, accustomed to the toneless speech of the race, and jealously suspicious of anything approaching art in everyday life, distrusted Morrison at the first sound of his voice. Men who were his friends (and they were many) were in the habit of rather apologizing for those rich and harmonious accents. The first time she had heard it, Sylvia had thought of the G string of old Reinhardt's violin.

"I never in my life saw anything that looked less like a shady place," observed Sylvia, indicating with an admiring gesture the table before them, gleaming and flashing its glass and silver and close-textured, glossy damask up into the light.

"It's *morally* that we're so shady!" said Arnold, admiring his own wit so much that he could not refrain from adding, "Not so bad, what?" The usual conversation at his stepmother's table was, as he would have said, so pestilentially high-brow that he seldom troubled himself to follow it enough to join in. Arnold was in the habit of dubbing "high-brow" anything bearing on æsthetics; and Mrs. Marshall-Smith's conversational range hardly extending at all outside of æsthetics of one kind or another, communication between these two house-mates of years' standing was for the most part reduced to a primitive simplicity for which a sign-language would have sufficed. Arnold's phrase for the situation was, "I let Madrina alone, and she don't bother me." But now, seeing that neither the façade of Rouen, nor the influence of Chardin on Whistler, had been mentioned, his unusual loquacity continued. "Well, if one west wind (I don't mean that as a slam on Sylvia for coming from west of the Mississippi) has done us so much good, why not have another?" he inquired. "Why couldn't Judith come on and make us a visit too? It would be fun to have a scrap with her again." He explained to Morrison: "She's Sylvia's younger sister, and we always quarreled so, as kids, that after we'd been together half an hour the referee had to shoulder in between and tell us, 'Nix on biting in clinches.' She was great, all right, Judith was! How *is* she now?" he asked Sylvia. "I've been meaning ever so many times to ask you about her, and something else has seemed to come up. I can't imagine Judy grown up. She hasn't pinned up that great long braid, has she, that used to be so handy to pull?"

Sylvia took the last of her soup, put the spoon on the

plate, and launched into a description of Judith, one of her favorite topics. "Oh, Judith's just *fine!* You ought to see her! She's worth ten of me: she has such lots of character! And handsome! You never saw anything like Judith's looks. Yes, she's put her hair up! She's twenty years old now, what do you *suppose* she does with her hair? She wears it in a great smooth braid all around her head. And she has *such* hair, Aunt Victoria!" She turned from Arnold to another woman, as from some one who would know nothing of the fine shades of the subject. "No short hairs at all, you know, like everybody else, that *will* hang down and look untidy!" She pulled with an explanatory petulance at the soft curls which framed her own face in an aureole of light. "Hers is all long and smooth, and the color like a fresh chestnut, just out of the burr; and her nose is like a Greek statue—she *is* a Greek statue!"

She had been carried by her affectionate enthusiasm out of her usual self-possession, her quick divination of how she was affecting everybody, and now, suddenly finding Morrison's eyes on her with an expression she did not recognize, she was brought up short. What had she said to make him look at her so oddly?

He answered her unspoken question at once, his voice making his every casual word of gold: "I am thinking that I am being present at a spectacle which cynics say is impossible, the spectacle of a woman delighting—and with the most obvious sincerity—in the beauty of another."

"Oh!" said Sylvia, relieved to know that the odd look concealed no criticism, "I didn't know that anybody nowadays made such silly Victorian generalizations about woman's cattiness,—anybody under old Mr. Sommerville's age, that is. And anyhow, Judith's my *sister.*"

"Cases of sisters, jealous of each other's good looks, have not been entirely unknown to history," said Morrison, smiling and beginning to eat his fish with a delicate relish.

"Well, if Judy's so all-fired good-looking, let's *have* her come on, Madrina," said Arnold. "With her and Sylvia together, we'd crush Lydford into a pulp." He attacked his plate with a straggling fork, eating negligently, as he did everything else.

"She has a standing invitation, of course," said Mrs. Marshall-Smith. "Indeed, I wrote the other day, asking her if she could come here instead of to La Chance for her vacation. It's far nearer for her."

"Oh, Judith couldn't waste time to go visiting," said Sylvia. "I've told you she is worth ten of me. She's on the home-stretch of her trained-nurse's course now. She has only two weeks' vacation."

"She's going to be a trained nurse?" asked Arnold in surprise, washing down a large mouthful of fish with a large mouthful of wine. "What the dickens does she do that for?"

"Why, she's crazy about it,—ever since she was a little girl, fifteen years old and first saw the inside of a hospital. That's just Judith,—so splendid and purposeful, and single-minded. I wish to goodness *I* knew what I want to do with myself half so clearly as she always has."

If she had, deep under her consciousness, a purpose to win more applause from Morrison, by more disinterested admiration of Judith's good points, she was quite rewarded by the quickness with which he championed her against her own depreciation. "I've always noticed," he said meditatively, slowly taking a sip from his wine-glass, "that nobody can be single-minded who isn't *narrow*-minded; and I think it likely that people who aren't so cocksure what they want to do with themselves, hesitate because they have a great deal more to do *with*. A nature rich in fine and complex possibilities takes more time to dispose of itself, but when it does, the world's beauty is the gainer." He pointed the reference frankly by a smile at Sylvia, who flushed with pleasure and looked down at her plate. She was surprised at the delight which his leisurely, whimsically philosophical little speech gave her. She forgot to make any answer, absorbed as she was in poring over it and making out new meanings in it. How he had understood at less than a word the secret uncertainty of herself which so troubled her; and with what astonishing sureness he had known what to say to reassure her, to make her see clear! And then, her quick mind leaped to another significance. . . . All during these past weeks when she had been falling more and more under the fascination of his personality, when she had been piqued at his disregard of her, when she had thought he found her "young," and had bracketed her carelessly with Arnold, he had been in reality watching her, he had found her interesting enough to observe her, to study her, to have a theory about her character; and having done all that, to admire her as she admired him. Never in her life had she been the recipient of flattery so precisely to her taste. Her glow of pleasure was so warm that she suddenly distrusted her own judgment, she looked up at him quickly to see if she had not mistaken his meaning, had not absurdly exaggerated the degree to which he . . . she found his eyes on hers, deep-set, shadowy eyes which did not, as she looked up, either smile or look away. Under cover of a rather wrangling discussion between Arnold and his stepmother as to having some champagne served, the older man continued to look steadily into Sylvia's eyes, with the effect of saying to her, gravely, kindly, intimately: "Yes, I am here. You did not know how closely you have drawn me to you, but here I am." Across the table, across the lights, the service, the idle talk of the other two, she felt him quietly, ever so gently but quite irresistibly, open an inner door of her nature . . . and she welcomed him in.

After dinner, when Mrs. Marshall-Smith lifted her eyebrows at Sylvia and rose to go, Arnold made no bones of his horror at the prospect of a tête-à-tête with the distinguished critic. "Oh, I'm going in with you girls!" he said, jumping up with his usual sprawling uncertainty of action. He reserved for athletic sports all his capacity for physical accuracy. "Morrison and I bore each other more than's legal!"

"I may bore *you,* my dear Arnold," said the other, rising, "but you never bored me in your life, and I've known you from childhood."

To which entirely benevolent speech, Arnold returned nothing but the uneasy shrug and resentful look of one baffled by a hostile demonstration too subtle for his powers of self-defense. He picked up the chair he had thrown over, and waited sulkily till the others were in the high-ceilinged living-room before he joined them. Then when Morrison, in answer to a request from his hostess and old friend, sat down to the piano and began to play a piece of modern, plaintive, very wandering and chromatic music, the younger man drew Sylvia out on the wide, moon-lighted veranda.

"Morrison is the very devil for making you want to punch his head, and yet not giving you a decent excuse. I declare, Sylvia, I don't know but that what I like best of all about you is the way you steer clear of him. He's opening up on you too. Maybe you didn't happen to notice . . . at the dinner-table? It wasn't much, but I spotted it for a beginning. I know old Felix, a few." Sylvia felt uneasy at the recurrence of this topic, and cast about for something to turn the conversation. "Oh, Arnold," she began, rather at random, "whatever became of Professor Saunders? I've thought about him several times since I've been here, but I've forgotten to ask you or Tantine. He was my little-girl admiration, you know."

Arnold smoked for a moment before answering. Then, "Well, I wouldn't ask Madrina about him, if I were you. He's not one of her successes. He wouldn't stay put."

Sylvia scented something uncomfortable, and regretted having introduced the subject.

Arnold added thoughtfully, looking hard at the ash of his cigarette, "I guess Madrina was pretty bad medicine for Saunders, all right."

Sylvia shivered a little and drew back, but she instantly put the matter out of her mind with a trained and definite action of her will. It was probably "horrid"; nothing could be done about it now; what else could they talk about that would be cheerful? This was a thought-sequence very familiar to Sylvia, through which she passed with rapid ease.

Arnold made a fresh start by offering her his cigarette box. "Have one," he invited her, sociably.

She shook her head.

"Oh, all the girls do," he urged her.

Sylvia laughed. "I may be a fresh breeze from beyond the Mississippi, but I'm not so fresh as to think it's wicked for a girl to smoke. In fact I like to, myself, but I can't stand the dirty taste in my mouth the next morning. Smoking's not worth it."

"*Well . . .*" commented Arnold. Apparently he found something very surprising in this speech. His surprise spread visibly from the particular to the general, like the rings widening from a thrown pebble, and he finally broke out: "You certainly do beat the band, Sylvia. You get *me!* You're a sample off a piece of goods that I never saw before!"

"What now?" asked Sylvia, amused.

"Why, for instance,—that reason for your not smoking. That's not a girl's reason. That's a man's . . . a man who's tried it!"

"No, it isn't!" she said, the flicker of amusement still on her lips. "A man wouldn't have sense enough to know that smoking isn't worth waking up with your mouth full of rancid fur."

"Oh gosh!" cried Arnold, tickled by the metaphor: "rancid fur!"

"The point about me, why I seem so queer to you," explained Sylvia, brightening, "is that I'm a State University girl. I'm used to you. I've seen hundreds of you! The fact that you wear trousers and have to shave and wear your hair cut short, and smell of tobacco, doesn't thrill me for a cent. I know that I could run circles around you if it came to a problem in calculus, not that I want to brag."

Arnold did not seem as much amused as she thought he would be. He smoked in a long, meditative silence, and when he spoke again it was with an unusual seriousness. "It's not what *you* feel or don't feel about me . . . it's what *I* feel and don't feel about you, that gets me," he explained, not very lucidly. "I mean liking you so, without . . . I never felt so about a girl. I like it. . . . I don't make it out. . . ." He looked at her with sincerely puzzled eyes.

She answered him as seriously. "I think," she said, speaking a little slowly, "I think the two go together, don't they?"

"How do you mean?" he asked.

"Why—it's hard to say——" she hesitated, but evidently not at all in embarrassment, looking at him with serious eyes, limpid and unafraid. "I've been with boys and men a lot, of course, in my classes and in the laboratories and everywhere, and I've found out that in most cases if the men and the girls really, really in their own hearts don't want to hurt each other, don't want to get something out of the other, but just want to be friends—why, they *can* be! Psychologists and all the big-wigs say they can't be, I know—but, believe me!—I've tried it—and it's awfully nice, and it's a shame that everybody shouldn't know that lots of the time you *can* do it—in spite of the folks who write the books! Maybe it wasn't so when the books were written, maybe it's only going to be so, later, if we all are as square as we can be now. But as a plain matter of fact, in one girl's experience, it's so, *now!* Of course," she modified by a sweeping qualification the audacity of her naïvely phrased, rashly innocent guess at a new possibility for humanity, "of course if the man's a *decent* man."

Arnold had not taken his gaze for an instant from her gravely thoughtful eyes. He was quite pale. He looked astonishingly moved, startled, arrested. When she stopped, he said, almost at once, in a very queer voice as though it were forced out of him, "I'm not a decent man."

And then, quite as though he could endure no longer her clear, steady gaze, he covered his eyes with his hand. An instant later he had sprung up and walked rapidly away out to the low marble parapet which topped the terrace. His gesture, his action had been so eloquent of surprised, intolerable pain, that Sylvia ran after him, all one quick impulse to console. " Yes, you are, Arnold; yes, you are!" she said in a low, energetic tone, " you *are!* "

He made a quavering attempt to be whimsical. " I'd like to know what *you* know about it! " he said.

" I know! I *know!* " she simply repeated.

He faced her in an exasperated shame. " Why, a girl like you can no more know what's done by a man like me . . ." his lips twitched in a moral nausea.

" Oh . . . what you've *done* . . ." said Sylvia . . . "it's what you are! "

" What I *am,*" repeated Arnold bitterly. " If I were worth my salt I'd hang myself before morning! " The heart-sick excitement of a man on the crest of some moral crisis looked out luridly from his eyes.

Sylvia rose desperately to meet that crisis. " Look here, Arnold. I'm going to tell you something I've never spoken of to anybody . . . not even Mother . . . and I'm going to do it, so you'll *believe* me when I say you're worth living. When I was eighteen years old I was a horrid, selfish, self-willed child. I suppose everybody's so at eighteen. I was just crazy for money and fine dresses and things like that, that we'd never had at home; and a man with a lot of money fell in love with me. It was my fault. I made him, though I didn't know then what I was doing, or at least I wouldn't let myself think what I was doing. And I got engaged to him. I got engaged at half-past four in the afternoon, and at seven o'clock that evening I was running away from him, and I've never seen him since." Her voice went on steadily, but a quick hot wave of scarlet flamed up over her face. " He was not a decent man," she said briefly, and went on: " It frightened me almost to death before I got my bearings: I was just a little girl and I hadn't understood anything—and I don't *understand* much now. But I did learn one thing from all that—I learned to know when a man isn't decent. I can't tell you how I know—it's all over him—it's all over me—it's his eyes, the way he stands, the expression of his mouth—I don't only see it—I feel it—I feel it the way a thermometer feels it when you put a match under the bulb . . . I *know!*" She brought her extravagant, her preposterous, her ignorant, her incredibly convincing claims to an abrupt end.

"And you 'feel' that I . . ." began Arnold, and could not go on.

"I'd like you for my brother," she said gently.

He tried to laugh at her, but the honest tears were in his eyes. "You don't know what you're talking about, you silly dear," he said unsteadily, "but I'm awfully glad you came to Lydford."

With her instinct for avoiding breaks, rough places, Sylvia quickly glided into a transition from this speech back into less personal talk. "Another queer thing about that experience I've never understood:—it cured me of being so crazy about clothes. You wouldn't think it would have anything to do with *that,* would you? And I don't see how it did. Oh, I don't mean I don't dearly love pretty dresses now. I *do.* And I spend altogether too much time thinking about them—but it's not the same. Somehow the poison is out. I used to be like a drunkard who can't get a drink, when I saw girls have things I didn't. I suppose," she speculated philosophically, "I suppose any great jolt that shakes you up a lot, shakes things into different proportions."

"Say, that fellow must have been just about the limit!" Arnold's rather torpid imagination suddenly opened to the story he had heard.

"No, no!" said Sylvia. "As I look back on it, I make a lot more sense out of it" (she might have been, by her accent, fifty instead of twenty-three), "and I can see that he wasn't nearly as bad as I thought him. When I said he wasn't decent, I meant that he belonged in the Stone Age, and I'm twentieth-century. We didn't fit together. I suppose that's what we all mean when we say somebody isn't decent . . . that he's stayed behind in the procession. I

don't mean that man was a degenerate or anything like that
. . . if he could have found a Stone Age woman he'd
have . . . they'd have made a good Stone Age marriage of
it. But he *didn't,* the girl he . . ."

"Do you know, Sylvia," Arnold broke in wonderingly,
"I never before in all my life had anybody speak to me of
anything that really mattered. And I never spoke this way
myself. I've wanted to, lots of times; but I didn't know
people ever did. And to think of its being a girl who does
it for me, a girl who . . ." His astonishment was immense.

"Look here, Arnold," said Sylvia, with a good-natured
peremptoriness. "Let a girl be something besides a girl,
can't you!"

But her attempt to change the tone to a light one failed.
Apparently, now that Arnold had broken his long silence, he
could not stop himself. He turned towards her with a
passionate gesture of bewilderment and cried: "Do you
remember, before dinner, you asked me as a joke what was
the use of anything, and I said I didn't know? Well, I
don't! I've been getting sicker and sicker over everything.
What the devil *am* I here for, anyhow!"

As he spoke, a girl's figure stepped from the house to the
veranda, from the veranda to the turf of the terrace, and
walked towards them. She was tall, and strongly, beautifully built; around her small head was bound a smooth braid
of dark hair. She walked with a long, free step and held
her head high. As she came towards them, the moonlight
full on her dark, proud, perfect face, she might have been
the youthful Diana.

But it was no antique spirit which looked out of those
frank, fearless eyes, and it was a very modern and col-
loquially American greeting which she now gave to the
astonished young people. "Well, Sylvia, don't you know
your own sister?" and "Hello there, Arnold."

"Why, Judith *Marshall!*" cried Sylvia, falling upon her
breathlessly. "However in the world did you get *here!*"

Arnold said nothing. He had fallen back a step and now
looked at the new-comer with a fixed, dazzled gaze.

CHAPTER XXIV

ANOTHER BRAND OF MODERN TALK

" WHERE's Judith? " said Arnold for sole greeting, as he saw Morrison at the piano and Sylvia sitting near it, cool and clear in a lacy white dress. Morrison lifted long fingers from the keys and said gravely, " She came through a moment ago, saying, ' *Where's* Arnold? ' and went out through that door." His fingers dropped and Chopin's voice once more rose plaintively.

The sound of Arnold's precipitate rush across the room and out of the door was followed by a tinkle of laughter from Sylvia. Morrison looked around at her over his shoulder, with a flashing smile of mutual understanding, but he finished the prelude before he spoke. Then, without turning around, as he pulled out another sheet from the music heaped on the piano, he remarked: " If that French philosopher was right when he said no disease is as contagious as love-making, we may expect soon to find the very chairs and tables in this house clasped in each other's arms. Old as I am, I feel it going to my head, like a bed of full-blooming valerian."

Sylvia made no answer. She felt herself flushing, and could not trust her voice to be casual. He continued for a moment to thumb over the music aimlessly, as though waiting for her to speak.

The beautiful room, darkened against the midsummer heat, shimmered dimly in a transparent half-light, the vivid life of its bright chintz, its occasional brass, its clean, daring spots of crimson and purple flowers, subdued into a fabulous, half-seen richness. There was not a sound. The splendid heat of the early August afternoon flamed, and paused, and held its breath.

Into this silence, like a bird murmuring a drowsy note over a still pool, there floated the beginning of *Am Meer*. Sylvia sat, passive to her finger-tips, a vase filled to the brim with melody. She stared with unseeing eyes at the back of the man at the piano. She was not thinking of him, she was not aware that she was conscious of him at all; but hours afterward wherever she looked, she saw for an instant again in miniature the slender, vigorous, swaying figure; the thick brown hair, streaked with white and curling slightly at the ends; the brooding head. . . .

When the last note was still, the man stood up and moved away from the piano. He dropped into an armchair near Sylvia, and leaning his fine, ugly head back against the brilliant chintz, he looked at her meditatively. His great bodily suavity gave his every action a curious significance and grace. Sylvia, still under the spell of his singing, did not stir, returning his look out of wide, dreaming eyes.

When he spoke, his voice blended with the silence almost as harmoniously as the music. . . . "Do you know what I wish you would do, Miss Sylvia Marshall? I wish you would tell me something about yourself. Now that I'm no longer forbidden to look at you, or think about you. . . ."

"Forbidden?" asked Sylvia, very much astonished.

"There!" he said, wilfully mistaking her meaning, and smiling faintly, "I am such an old gentleman that I'm perfectly negligible to a young lady. She doesn't even notice or not whether I look at her, and think about her."

A few years before this Sylvia would have burst out impetuously, "Oh yes, I have! I've wondered awfully what made you so indifferent," but now she kept this reflection to herself and merely said, "What in the world did you fancy was 'forbidding' you?"

"Honor!" said Morrison, with a note of mock solemnity. "*Honor!* Victoria was so evidently snatching at you as a last hope for Arnold. She gave me to understand that everybody else but Arnold was to be strictly non-existent. But now that Arnold has found a character beautifully and archaically simple to match his own primitive needs, I don't see why I shouldn't enjoy a little civilized talk with you. In any case, it was absurd to think of *you* for Arnold. It merely shows how driven poor Victoria was!"

Sylvia tried to speak lightly, although she was penetrated with pleasure at this explanation of his holding aloof. "Oh, *I* like Arnold very much. I always have. There's something . . . something sort of *touching* about Arnold, don't you think? Though I must say that I've heard enough about the difference between training quail dogs and partridge dogs to last me the rest of my life. But that's rather touching too, his not knowing what to do with himself but fiddle around with his guns and tennis-racquets. They're all he has to keep him from being bored to death, and they don't go nearly far enough. Some day he will just drop dead from ennui, poor Arnold! Wouldn't he have enjoyed being a civil engineer, and laying out railroads in wild country! He'd have been a good one too! The same amount of energy he puts into his polo playing would make him fight his way through darkest Thibet." She meditated over this hypothesis for a moment and then added with a nod of her head, "Oh yes, I like Arnold ever so much . . . one kind of ' liking.' "

"Of course you like him," assented the older man, who had been watching her as she talked, and whose manner now, as he took up the word himself, resembled that of an exquisitely adroit angler, casting out the lightest, the most feathery, the most perfectly controlled of dry-flies. "You're too intelligent not to like everybody who's not base—and Arnold's not base. And he ' likes ' you. If you had cared to waste one of your red-brown tresses on him, you could have drawn him by a single hair. But then, everybody ' likes ' you."

"Old Mr. Sommerville doesn't!" said Sylvia, on an impulse.

Morrison looked at her admiringly, and put the tips of his fingers together with exquisite precision. "So you add second sight to your other accomplishments! How in the world could a girl of your age have the experience and intuition to feel that? Old Sommerville passes for a great admirer of yours. You won't, I hope, go so uncannily far in your omniscience as to pretend to know *why* he doesn't like you?"

" No, I won't," said Sylvia, " because I haven't the very faintest idea. Have you?"

" I know exactly why. It's connected with one of the old gentleman's eccentricities. He's afraid of you on account of his precious nephew."

" I didn't know he *had* a nephew." Sylvia was immensely astonished.

" Well, he has, and he bows down and worships him, as he does his granddaughter. You see how he adores Molly. It's nice of the old fellow, the cult he has for his descendants, but occasionally inconvenient for innocent bystanders. He thinks everybody wants to make off with his young folks. You and I are fellow-suspects. Haven't you felt him wish he could strike me dead, when Molly makes tea for me, or turns over music as I play?" He laughed a little, a gentle, kind, indulgent laugh. " *Molly!*" he said, as if his point were more than elucidated by the mere mention of her name.

Sylvia intimated with a laugh that her point was clearer yet in that she had no name to mention. " But I never saw his nephew. I never even heard of him until this minute."

" No, and very probably never will see him. He's very seldom here. And if you did see him, you wouldn't like him—he's an eccentric of the worst brand," said Morrison tranquilly. " But monomanias need no foundation in fact——" He broke off abruptly to say: " Is this all another proof of your diabolical cleverness? I started in to hear something about yourself, and here I find myself talking about everything else in the world."

" I'm not clever," said Sylvia, hoping to be contradicted.

" Well, you're a great deal too nice to be *consciously* so," admitted Morrison. " See here," he went on, " it's

evident that you're more than a match for me at this game.
Suppose we strike a bargain. You introduce yourself to
me and I'll do the same by you. Isn't it quite the most
fantastic of all the bizarreries of human intercourse that
an ' introduction ' to a fellow-being consists in being informed of his name,—quite the most unimportant, fortuitous thing about him? "

Sylvia considered. " What do you want to know? " she
asked finally.

" Well, I'd *like* to know everything," said the man gaily.
" My curiosity has been aroused to an almost unappeasable
pitch. But of course I'll take any information you feel like
doling out. In the first place, *how*, coming from such
a . . ." He checked himself and changed the form of his
question: " I overheard you speaking to Victoria's maid,
and I've been lying awake nights ever since, wondering
how it happened that you speak French with so pure an
accent."

" Oh, that's simple! Professor and Madame La Rue
are old friends of the family and I've spent a lot of time
with them. And then, of course, French is another mother-
language for Father. He and Aunt Victoria were brought
up in Paris, you know."

Morrison sighed. " Isn't it strange how all the miracles
evaporate into mere chemical reactions when you once investigate! All the white-clad, ghostly spirits turn out to
be clothes on the line. I suppose there's some equally
natural explanation about your way on the piano—the
clear, limpid phrasing of that Bach the other day, and then
the color of the Bizet afterwards. It's astonishing to hear
anybody of your crude youth playing Bach at all—and then
to hear it played right—and afterwards to hear a modern
given *his* right note. . . ."

Sylvia was perfectly aware that she was being flattered,
and she was immensely enjoying it. She became more
animated, and the peculiar sparkle of her face more spirited.
" Oh, that's old Reinhardt, my music teacher. He would
take all the skin off my knuckles if I played a Bach gigue

the least bit like that Arlésienne Minuet. He doesn't approve of Bizet very much, anyhow. He's a tremendous classicist."

"Isn't it," inquired Morrison, phrasing his question carefully, "isn't it, with no disrespect to La Chance intended, isn't it rather unusually good fortune for a smallish Western city to own a real musician?"

"Well, La Chance bears up bravely under its good fortune," said Sylvia dryly. "Old Mr. Reinhardt isn't exactly a prime favorite there. He's a terribly beery old man, and he wipes his nose on his sleeve. Our house was the only respectable one in town that he could go into. But then, our house isn't so very respectable. It has its advantages, not being so very respectable, though it 'most killed me as a young girl to feel us so. But I certainly have a choice gallery of queer folks in my acquaintance, and I have the queerest hodge-podge of scraps of things learned from them. I know a little Swedish from Miss Lindström. She's a Swedish old maid who does uplift work among the negroes—isn't that a weird combination? You just ought to hear what she makes of negro dialect! And I know all the socialist arguments from hearing a socialist editor get them off every Sunday afternoon. And I even know how to manage planchette and write mediumistically—save the mark!—from Cousin Parnelia, a crazy old cousin of Mother's who hangs round the house more or less."

"I begin to gather," surmised Morrison, "that you must have a remarkable father and mother. What are *they* like?"

"Well," said Sylvia thoughtfully, "Mother's the bravest thing you ever saw. She's not afraid of *anything!* I don't mean cows, or the house-afire, or mice, or such foolishness. I mean life and death, and sickness and poverty and fear. . . ."

Morrison nodded his head understandingly, a fine light of appreciation in his eyes, "Not to be afraid of fear—that's splendid."

Sylvia went on to particularize. "When any of us **are**

sick—it's my little brother Lawrence who is mostly—
Judith and I are always well—Father just goes all to
pieces, he gets so frightened. But Mother stiffens her back
and *makes* everything in the house go on just as usual, very
quiet, very calm. She holds everything together *tight*. She
says it's sneaking and cowardly if you're going to accept
life at all, not to accept *all* of it—the sour with the sweet—
and not whimper."

"Very fine,—very fine! Possibly a very small bit . . .
grim?" commented Morrison, with a rising inflection.

"Oh, perhaps, a little!" agreed Sylvia, as if it did not
matter; "but I can't give you any idea of Mother. She's—
she's just *great!* And yet I couldn't live like her, without
wanting to smash everything up. She's somebody that
Seneca would have liked."

"And your father?" queried Morrison.

"Oh, he's great too—dear Father—but so different!
He and Mother between them have just about all the varieties of human nature that are worth while! Father's red-
headed (though it's mostly gray now), and quick, and blus-
tering, and awfully clever, and just adored by his students,
and talks every minute, and apparently does all the deciding,
and yet . . . he couldn't draw the breath of life without
Mother; and when it comes right down to *doing* anything,
what he always does is what he knows will come up to her
standard."

Morrison raised delightedly amused hands to heaven.
"The Recording Angel domiciled in the house!" he cried.
"It had never occurred to me before how appallingly discerning the eye of the modern offspring must be. Go on,
go on!"

Elated by the sensation of appearing clever, Sylvia continued with a fresh flow of eloquence. "And there never
was such a highly moral bringing-up as we children have
had. It's no fault of my family's if I've turned out a grasping materialist! I was brought up"—she flamed out suddenly as at some long-hoarded grievance—"I was brought
up in a moral hot-house, and I haven't yet recovered from

the shock of being transplanted into real earth in the real world."

Morrison paid instant tribute to her aroused and serious feeling by a grave look of attention. "Won't you explain?" he asked. "I'm so dull I don't follow you. But I haven't been so interested in years."

"Why, I mean," said Sylvia, trying hard to reduce to articulateness a complicated conception, "I mean that Father and Mother just deliberately represented values to me as different from what they really are, with real folks! And now I find that *I*'m real folks! I can't help it. You are as you *are,* you know. They kept representing to me always that the *best* pleasures are the ones that are the most important to folks—music, I mean, and Milton's poetry, and a fine novel—and, in Mother's case, a fine sunset, or a perfect rose, or things growing in the garden."

No old associate of Morrison's would have recognized the man's face, shocked as it was by surprise and interest out of his usual habit of conscious, acute, self-possessed observation. The angler had inadvertently stepped off a ledge into deep water, and a very swift current was tugging at him. He leaned forward, his eyes as eager with curiosity as a boy's. "Do I understand you to say that you repudiate those 'best pleasures'?"

"Of course you don't understand anything of the sort," said Sylvia very earnestly. "They've soaked me so in music that I'm a regular bond-slave to it. And a perfect rose is associated with so many lovely recollections of Mother's wonderful silent joy in it, that I could weep for pleasure. What I'm talking about—what I'm trying to tell you, is the shock it was to me, when I got out of that artificially unworldly atmosphere of home—for there's no use talking, it *is* artificial!—to find that *those* pleasures aren't the ones that are considered important and essential. How did I find things in the real world? Why, I find that people don't give a thought to those 'best pleasures' until they have a lot of other things first. Everything *I*'d been trained to value and treasure was negligible, not worth both-

ering about. But money—position—not having to work—
elegance—*those* are *vital*—prime! Real people can't enjoy
hearing a concert if they know they've got to wash up a
lot of dishes afterwards. Hiring a girl to do that work
is the *first* thing to do! There isn't another woman in the
world, except my mother, who'd take any pleasure in a
perfect rose if she thought her sleeves were so old-fashioned
that people would stare at her. Folks *talk* about liking to
look at a fine sunset, but what they give their blood and
bones for, is a fine house on the best street in town!"

"Well, but you're not 'people' in that vulgar sense!"
protested Morrison. He spoke now without the slightest
arrière-pensée of flattering her, and Sylvia in her sudden
burst for self-expression was unconscious of him, save as
an opponent in an argument.

"You just *say* that, in that superior way," she flashed at
him, "because *you* don't have to bother your head about
such matters, because you don't have to associate with
people who are fighting for those essentials. For they *are*
what everybody except Father and Mother—*every*body
feels to be the essentials—a pretty house, handsome clothes,
servants to do the unpleasant things, social life—oh, plenty
of money sums it all up, 'vulgar' as it sounds. And I
don't believe you are different. I don't believe anybody you
know is really a bit different! Let Aunt Victoria, let old
Mr. Sommerville, lose their money, and you'd see how unimportant Debussy and Masaccio would be to them, compared to having to black their own shoes!"

"Well, upon my word!" exclaimed Morrison. "Are
you at eighteen presuming to a greater knowledge of life
than I at forty?"

"I'm not eighteen, I'm twenty-three," said Sylvia. "The
difference is enormous. And if I don't know more about
plain unvarnished human nature than you, I miss my guess!
You haven't gone through five years at a State University,
rubbing shoulders with folks who haven't enough sophistication to pretend to be different from what they are. *You*
haven't taught music for three years in the middle-class

families of a small Western city!" She broke off to laugh an apologetic depreciation of her own heat. "You'd think I was addressing a meeting," she said in her usual tone. "I got rather carried away because this is the first time I ever really spoke out about it. There are so few who could understand. If I ever tried to explain it to Father and Mother, I'd be sure to find them so deep in a discussion of the relation between Socrates and Christ that they couldn't pay any attention! Professor Kennedy could understand—but he's such a fanatic on the other side."

Morrison looked a quick suspicion. "Who is Professor Kennedy?" he inquired; and was frankly relieved when Sylvia explained: "He's the head of the Mathematics Department, about seventy years old, and the crossest, cantankerousest old misanthrope you ever saw. And thinks himself immensely clever for being so! He just loathes people—the way they really are—and he dotes on Mother and Judith because they're not like anybody else. And he hates me because they couldn't all hypnotize me into looking through their eyes. He thinks it low of me to realize that if you're going to live at all, you've got to live *with people,* and you can't just calmly brush their values on one side. He said once that any sane person in this world was like a civilized man with plenty of gold coin, cast away on a desert island with a tribe of savages who only valued beads and calico, and buttons and junk. And I said (I knew perfectly well he was hitting at me) that if he was really cast away and couldn't get to another island, I thought the civilized man would be an idiot to starve to death, when he could buy food of the savages by selling them junk. And I thought he just wasted his breath by swearing at the savages for not knowing about the value of gold. There I was hitting at *him!* He's spoiled his digestion, hating the way people are made. And Professor Kennedy said something nasty and neat (he's awfully clever) about that being rather a low occupation for a civilized being—taking advantage of the idiocies of savages—he meant me, of course —and he's right, it *is* a mean business; I hate it. And that's why I've always wanted to get on another island—not an uninhabited island, like the one Father and Mother have—but one where—well, *this* is one!" she waved her hand about the lovely room, "this *is* just one! Where everything's beautiful—costly too—but not just costly; where all the horrid, necessary consequences of things are taken care of without one's bothering—where flowers are taken out of the vases when they wilt and fresh ones put in; and dishes get themselves washed invisibly, inaudibly—and litter just vanishes without our lifting a hand. Of course the people who live so always, can rejoice with a clear mind in sunsets and bright talk. That's what I meant the other day —the day Judith came—when I said I'd arrived in Capua at last; when old Mr. Sommerville thought me so materialistic and cynical. If *he* did that, on just that phrase—what must *you* think, after all this *confession intime d'un enfant du siècle?*" She stopped with a graceful pretense of dreading his judgment, although she knew that she had been talking well, and read nothing but admiration in his very expressive face.

"But all this means, you extraordinary young person, that you're not in the least an *enfant du siècle!*" he cried. "It means that you're dropped down in this groaning, heavy-spirited twentieth century, troubled about many things, from the exact year that was the golden climax of the Renaissance; that you're a perfect specimen of the high-hearted, glorious . . ." he qualified on a second thought, "unless your astonishing capacity to analyze it all, comes from the nineteenth century?"

"No, that comes from Father," explained Sylvia, laughing. "Isn't it funny, using the tool Father taught me to handle, against his ideas! He's just great on analysis. As soon as we were old enough to think at all, he was always practising us on analysis—especially of what made us want things, or not like them. It's one of his sayings—he's always getting it off to his University classes—that if you have once really called an emotion or an ambition by its right name, you have it by the tail, so to speak—that if you know, for instance, that it's your vanity and not your love that's wounded by something, you'll stop caring. But I never noticed that it really worked if you cared *hard* enough. Diagnosing a disease doesn't help you any, if you keep right on being sick with it."

"My dear! My dear!" cried the man, leaning towards her again, and looking—dazzled—into the beauty and intelligence of her eyes, "the idea that you are afflicted with any disease could only occur to the morbid mind of the bluest-nosed Puritan who ever cut down a May-pole! You're wonderfully, you're terrifyingly, you are superbly sound and vigorous!"

Breaking in upon this speech, there came the quick, smooth purr of an automobile with all its parts functioning perfectly, a streak of dark gray past the shutters, the sigh of an engine stopped suddenly— Molly Sommerville sprang from behind the steering wheel and ran into the house. She was exquisitely flushed and eager when she came in, but when she saw the two alone in the great, cool, dusky room, filled to its remotest corners with the ineffable aroma of long, intimate, and interrupted talk, she was brought up short. She faltered for an instant and then continued to advance, her eyes on Sylvia. "It's so hot," she said, at random, "and I thought I'd run over for tea——"

"Oh, of course," said Sylvia, jumping up in haste, "it's late! I'd forgotten it was time for tea! Blame *me!* Since I've been here, Aunt Victoria has left it to me— where shall I say to have it set?"

"The pergola's lovely," suggested Molly. She took her close motor-hat from the pure gold of her hair with a rather listless air.

"All right—the pergola!" agreed Sylvia, perhaps a little too anxiously. In spite of herself, she gave, and she knew she was giving, the effect of needing somehow to make something up to Molly. . . .

CHAPTER XXV

NOTHING IN THE LEAST MODERN

SYLVIA was sitting in the garden, an unread book on her knees, dreaming among red and yellow and orange gladioli. She looked with a fixed, bright, beatific stare at the flame-colored flowers and did not see them. She saw only Felix Morrison, she heard only his voice, she was brimming with the sense of him. In a few moments she would go into the house and find him in the darkened living-room, as he had been every afternoon for the last fortnight, ostensibly come in to lounge away the afternoon over a book, really waiting for her to join him. And when she came in, he would look up at her, that wonderful penetrating deep look of his . . . and she would welcome him with her eyes.

And then they would talk! Judith and Arnold would be playing tennis, oblivious of the heat, and Aunt Victoria would be annihilating the tedious center of the day by sleep. Nobody would interrupt them for hours. How they would talk! How they had talked! As she thought of it the golden fortnight hummed and sang about Sylvia's ears like a Liszt Liebes-Traum.

They had talked of everything in the world, and it all meant but one thing, that they had discovered each other, a discovery visibly as wonderful for Morrison as for the girl. They had discovered each other, and they had been intelligent enough to know at once what it meant. They knew! And in a moment she would go into the house to him. She half closed her eyes as before a too-great brilliance. . . .

Arnold appeared at the other end of the long row of gladioli. He was obviously looking for some one. Sylvia called to him, with the friendly tone she always had for him: "Here I am! I don't know where Judith is. Will I do?"

From a distance Arnold nodded, and continued to advance, the irregularity of his wavering gait more pronounced than usual. As soon as she could see the expression of his face, Sylvia's heart began to beat fast, with a divination of something momentous. He sat down beside her, took off his hat, and laid it on the bench. "Do you remember," he asked in a strange, high voice, "that you said you would like me for your brother?"

She nodded.

"Well, I'm going to be," he said, and covering his face with his hands, burst into sobs.

Sylvia was so touched by his emotion, so sympathetically moved by his news, that even through her happy ejaculations the tears rained down her own cheeks. She tried to wipe them away and discovered, absurdly enough, that she had lost her handkerchief. "Aren't we idiots!" she cried in a voice of joyful quavers. "I never understood before why everybody cries at a wedding. See here, Arnold, I've lost my handkerchief. Loan me yours." She pulled his handkerchief out of his pocket, she wiped her eyes, she put a sisterly kiss on his thin, sallow cheek, she cried: "You dears! Isn't it too good to be true! Arnold! So soon! Inside two weeks! How ever could you have the courage? Judith! My Judith! Why, she never looked at a man before. How did you dare?"

His overmastering fit of emotion was passed now. His look was of white, incredulous exaltation. "We saw each other and ran into each other's arms," he said; "I didn't have to 'dare.' It was like breathing."

"Oh, how perfect!" she cried, "how simply, simply perfect!" and now there was for an instant a note of wistful envy in her voice. "It's *all* perfect! She never so much as looked at a man before, and you said the other night you'd never been in love before."

Arnold looked at her wildly. "*I* said that!" he cried.

"Why, yes, don't you remember, after that funny, joking

talk with me, you said that was the nearest you'd ever come to proposing to any girl?"

"God Almighty!" cried the man, and did not apologize for the blasphemy. He looked at her fixedly, as though unguessed-at horizons of innocence widened illimitably before his horrified eyes. And then, following some line of association which escaped Sylvia, "I'm not fit to *look* at Judith!" he cried. The idea seemed to burst upon him like a thunder-clap.

Sylvia patted him on the shoulder reassuringly. "That's the proper thing for a lover to think!" she said with cheerful, commonplace inanity. She did not notice that he shrank from her hand, because she now sprang up, crying, "But where's Judy? Where *is* Judy?"

He nodded towards the house. "She sent me out to get you. She's in her room—she wants to tell you —but when I saw you, I couldn't keep it to myself." His exaltation swept back like a wave, from the crest of which he murmured palely, "Judith! Judith!" and Sylvia laughed at him, with the tears of sympathy in her eyes, and leaving him there on the bench staring before him at the living fire of the flame-colored flowers, she ran with all her speed into the house.

Morrison, lounging in a chair with a book, looked up, startled at her whirlwind entrance. "What's up?" he inquired.

At the sound of his voice, she checked herself and pirouetted with a thistle-down lightness to face him. Her face, always like a clear, transparent vase lighted from within, now gave out, deeply moved as she was, an almost visible brightness. "Judith!" she cried, her voice ringing like a silver trumpet, "Judith and Arnold!" She was poised like a butterfly, and as she spoke she burst into flight again, and was gone.

She had not been near him, but the man had the distinct impression that she had thrown herself on his neck and kissed him violently, in a transport of delight. In the silent room, still fragrant, still echoing with her passage, he closed his book, and later his eyes, and sat with the expression of a connoisseur savoring an exquisite, a perfect impression. . . .

Tea that afternoon was that strangest of phenomena, a formal ceremony of civilized life performed in the abashing and disconcerting presence of naked emotion. Arnold and Judith sat on opposite sides of the pergola, Judith shining and radiant as the dawn, her usually firmly set lips soft and tremulous; Arnold rather pale, impatient, oblivious to what was going on around him, his spirit prostrated before the miracle; and when their starry eyes met, there flowed from them and towards them from every one in the pergola, a thousand unseen waves of excitement.

The mistress of the house herself poured tea in honor of the great occasion, and she was very humorous and amusing about the mistakes caused by her sympathetic agitation. "There! I've put three lumps in yours, Mr. Sommerville. How *could* I! But I really don't know what I'm doing. This business of having love-at-first-sight in one's very family——! Give your cup to Molly; I'll make you a fresh one. Oh, Arnold! How *could* you look at Judith just then! You made me fill this cup so full I can't pass it!"

Mr. Sommerville, very gallant and full of compliments and whimsical allusions, did his best to help their hostess strike the decent note of easy pleasantry; but they were both battling with something too strong for them. Unseconded as they were by any of the others, they gave a little the effect of people bowing and smirking to each other at the foot of a volcano in full eruption. Morrison, picking up the finest and sharpest of his conversational tools, ventured the hazardous enterprise of expressing this idea to them. Mrs. Marshall-Smith, trying one topic after another, expressed an impatience with the slow progress of a Henry James novel she was reading, and Mr. Sommerville, remarking with a laugh, "Oh, you cannot hurry Henry," looked to see his mild witticism rewarded by a smile from the critic. But Morrison shook his head, "No, my dear old friend. *Il faut hurler avec les loups*—especially if you are so wrought up by their *hurlements* that you can't hear yourself think. I'm just giving myself up to the rareness, the richness of the impression."

The new fiancée herself talked rather more than usual, though this meant by no means loquacity, and presented more the appearance of composure than any one else there; although this was amusingly broken by a sudden shortness of breath whenever she met Arnold's eyes. She said in answer to a question that she would be going on to her hospital the day after tomorrow—her two weeks' vacation over—oh yes, she would finish her course at the hospital; she had only a few more months. And in answer to another question, Arnold replied, obviously impatient at having to speak to any one but Judith, that of course he didn't mind if she went on and got her nurse's diploma—didn't she *want* to? Anything she wanted. . . .

No—decidedly the thing was too big to make a successful fête of. Morrison was silent and appreciatively observant, his eyes sometimes on Sylvia, sometimes on Judith; Mr. Sommerville, continuing doggedly to make talk, descended to unheard-of trivialities in reporting the iniquities of his chauffeur; Molly stirred an untasted cup, did not raise her eyes at all, and spoke only once or twice, addressing to Sylvia a disconnected question or two, in the answers to which she had obviously no interest. Judith and Arnold had never been very malleable social material, and in their present formidable condition they were as little assistance in the manufacture of geniality as a couple of African lions.

The professional fête-makers were consequently enormously relieved when it was over and their unavailing efforts could be decently discontinued. Professing different reasons for escape, they moved in disjointed groups across the smooth perfection of the lawn towards the house, where Molly's car stood, gleaming in the sun. Sylvia found herself, as she expected, manœuvered to a place beside Morrison,

He arranged it with his unobtrusive deftness in getting what he wanted out of a group of his fellow-beings, and she admired his skill, and leaned on it confidently. They had had no opportunity that day for the long talk which had been a part of every afternoon for the last week; and she now looked with a buoyant certainty to have him arrange an hour together before dinner. Her anticipation of it on that burning day of reflected heat sent thrills of eager disquietude over her. It was not only for Judith and Arnold that the last week had been one of meeting eyes, long twilight evenings of breathless, quick-ripening intimacy. . . .

As they slackened their pace to drop behind Mr. Sommerville, who walked hand-in-hand with his granddaughter in front of them, Morrison said, looking at her with burning eyes, " . . . an instrument so finely strung that it vibrates at the mere sound of another wakened to melody—what mortal man lives who would not dream of its response if he could set his own hand to the bow? "

The afternoon had been saturated with emotional excitement and the moment had come for its inevitable crytallization into fateful words. The man spoke as though he were not wholly conscious of what he was saying. He stepped beside her like one in a dream. He could not take his eyes from her, from her flushed, grave, receptive face, from her downcast, listening eyes, her slow, trance-like step as she waited for him to go on. He went on: " It becomes, my dear, I assure you—the idea of that possibility becomes absolutely an obsession—even to a man usually quite his own master——"

They were almost at a standstill now, and the two in front of them had reached the house. Sylvia had a moment of what seemed to her the purest happiness she had ever known. . . .

From across the lawn they saw a violent gesture—Molly had thrown her grandfather's clinging hand from her, and flashed back upon the two, lingering there in the sunlight. She cast herself on Sylvia, panting and trying to laugh. Her little white teeth showed in what was almost a grimace. "Why in the world are you two poking along so?" she cried, passing her arm through Sylvia's. Her beautiful sunny head came no more than to Sylvia's shoulder. Without waiting for an answer she went on hurriedly, speaking in the tones of suppressed excitement which thrilled in every one's voice that day: "Come on, Sylvia—let's work it off together! Let me take you somewhere—let's go to Rutland and back."

"That's thirty miles away!" said Sylvia, "and it's past five now."

"I'll have you there and back long before seven," asserted Molly. "Come on . . . come on . . ." She pulled impatiently, petulantly at the other girl's arm.

"I'm not invited, I suppose," said Morrison, lighting a cigarette with care.

Molly looked at him a little wildly. "No, Felix, you're not invited!" she said, and laughed unsteadily.

She had hurried them along to the car, and now they stood by the swift gray machine, Molly's own, the one she claimed to love more than anything else in the world. She sprang in and motioned Sylvia to the seat beside her.

"Hats?" suggested Morrison, looking at their bare, shining heads. He was evidently fighting for time, manœuvering for an opening. His success was that of a man gesticulating against a gale. Molly's baldly unscrupulous determination beat down the beginnings of his carefully composed opposition before he could frame one of his well-balanced sentences. "No—no—it takes too long to go and get hats!" she cried peremptorily. "If you can't have what you want when you want it, it's no use having it at all!"

"I'm not sure," remarked Morrison, "that Miss Marshall wants this at all."

"Yes, she does; yes, she does!" Molly contradicted him heatedly. Sylvia, hanging undecided at the step, felt herself pulled into the car; the door banged, the engine started with a smooth sound of powerful machinery, the car leaped forward. Sylvia cast one backward glance at

Morrison, an annoyed, distinguished, futile presence, standing motionless, and almost instantly disappearing in the distance in which first he, and then the house and tall poplars over it, shrank to nothingness.

Their speed was dizzying. The blazing summer air blew hot and vital in their faces; their hair tugged at the pins and flew back in fluttering strands; their thin garments clung to their limbs, molded as closely by the compressing wind as by water. Molly did not turn her eyes from the road ahead, leaping up to meet them, and vanishing under the car. She tried to make a little casual talk: "Don't you love to let it out, give it all the gas there is?" "There's nothing like a quick spin for driving the nightmares out of your mind, is there?" But as Sylvia made no answer to these overtures (the plain fact was that Sylvia had no breath for speech,—for anything but a horrified fascinated glare at the road), she said suddenly, somberly, "If I were you, I certainly should despise me!" She took the car around a sharp curve on two wheels.

Sylvia clutched at the side and asked wonderingly, "*Why* in the world?" in a tone so permeated with sincerity that even Molly felt it.

"Don't you *know?*" she cried. "Do you mean to say you don't *know?*"

"Know *what?*" asked Sylvia. Hypnotized by the driver's intent and unwavering gaze on the road, she kept her own eyes as fiercely concentrated, her attention leaping from one quickly seen, instantly disappearing detail to another,—a pile of gravel here,—a half-buried rock there. —They both raised their voices to be heard above the sound of the engine and the rush of the car. "Know what?" repeated Sylvia loudly.

"Why do you *suppose* I made myself ridiculous by pulling you away from Felix that idiotic, humiliating way!" Molly threw this inquiry out, straight before her, angrily. The wind caught at her words and hurled them behind.

In a flash Sylvia understood something to which she had been resolutely closing her perceptions. She felt sick and scared. She clutched the side, watched a hill rise up steep before them and flatten out under the forward leap of the car. She thought hard. Something of her little-girl, over-mastering horror of things, rough, outspoken, disagreeable, swept over her. She violently wished that she could escape from the conversation before her. She would have paid almost any price to escape.

But Molly's nerves were not so sensitive. She evidently had no desire to escape or to let Sylvia. The grim little figure at the steering-wheel controlled with her small hands the fate of the two. She broke out now, impatient at Sylvia's silence: "Any fool could see that it was because I couldn't bear to see you with Felix another minute, and because I hadn't any other way to get you apart. Every-body else there knew why. I knew they knew. But I couldn't help it. I couldn't bear it another instant!"

She broke the glass of decent reticence with a great clat-tering blow. It shivered into fragments. There was noth-ing now between them but the real issue in all its uncomely bareness. This real issue, the mænad at the wheel now held up before them in a single brutal statement—"Are you in love with Felix? I am."

There was something eerie, terrifying, in her casting these words out, straight before her. Sylvia looked in awe at the pale, pinched profile, almost unrecognizable in its stern misery. "Because if you're not," Molly went on, her white lower lip twitching, "I wish you'd keep out. It was all right before you came with your horrible cleverness. It was all right. It was all right."

Through the iteration of this statement, through the tumult of her own thoughts, through the mad rush of the wind past her ears, Sylvia heard as clearly as though she sat again in the great, dim, quiet room, a melodious voice saying gently, indulgently, laughingly, "*Molly!*" Secure in her own safe place of favor she felt a great wave of generous pity for the helpless self-deception of her sister-woman. Fired by this and by the sudden perception of an opening for an act of spectacular magnanimity—would it be any the less magnanimous because it would cost her nothing in the end?—she reached for the mantle of the *beau rôle* and cast it about her shoulders. " Why, Molly dear ! " she cried, and her quick sympathies had never been more genuinely aroused, " Molly dear, of course I'll keep out, if you want me to. I'll leave the coast clear to you as long as you please."

She was almost thrown from the seat by the jarring grind of the car brought to a sudden standstill. Molly caught her hands, looked into her face, the first time their eyes had met. " Do you mean it . . . Sylvia ? "

Sylvia nodded, much agitated, touched by the other's pain, half ashamed of her own apparent generosity which was to mean no loss to her, no gain to Molly. In the sudden becalmed stillness of the hot afternoon their bright, blown hair fell about their faces in shining clouds.

" I didn't understand before," said Sylvia; and she was speaking the truth.

" And you'll let him alone? You won't talk to him—play his accompaniments—oh, those long talks of yours ! "

" We've been talking, you silly dear, of the Renaissance compared to the Twentieth Century, and of the passing of the leisure class, and all the beauty they always create," said Sylvia. Again she spoke the literal truth. But the true truth, burning on Molly's tongue, shriveled this to ashes. " You've been making him admire you, be interested in you, see how little *I* amount to ! " she cried. " But if you *don't* care about him yourself—if you'll—*two weeks, Sylvia*—just keep out for two weeks . . ." As if it were part of the leaping forward of her imagination, she suddenly started the car again, and with a whirling, reckless wrench at the steering-wheel she had turned the car about and was racing back over the road they had come.

" Where are you going? " cried Sylvia to her, above the noise of their progress.

" Back ! " she answered, laughing out. " What's the use of going on now? " She opened the throttle to its widest and pressing her lips together tightly, gave herself up to the intoxication of speed.

Once she said earnestly: " You're *fine,* Sylvia! I never knew a girl could be like you!" And once more she threw out casually: " Do you know what I was going to do if I found out you and Felix—if you hadn't . . .? I was going to jump the car over the turn there on Prospect Hill."

Remembering the terrible young face of pain and wrath which she had watched on the way out, Sylvia believed her; or at least believed that she believed her. In reality, her immortal youth was incapable of believing in the fact of death in any form. But the words put a stamp of tragic sincerity on their wild expedition, and on her companion's suffering. She thought of the two weeks which lay before Molly, and turned away her eyes in sympathy. . . .

Ten days after this, an announcement was made of the engagement of Mary Montgomery Sommerville, sole heiress of the great Montgomery fortune, to Felix Morrison, the well-known critic of æsthetics.

CHAPTER XXVI

MOLLY IN HER ELEMENT

SYLVIA faced her aunt's dictum with heartsick shrinking from its rigor; but she recognized it as an unexaggerated statement of the facts. "You can't go home now, Sylvia— everybody would say you couldn't stand seeing Molly's snatch at Felix successful. You really must stay on to let people see that you are another kind of girl from Molly, capable of impersonal interest in a man of Felix's brains."

Sylvia thought of making the obviously suitable remark that she cared nothing about what people thought, but such a claim was so preposterously untrue to her character that she could not bring the words past her lips. As a matter of fact, she did care what people thought. She always had! She always would! She remained silent, looking fixedly out of the great, plate-glass window, across the glorious sweep of blue mountain-slope and green valley commanded by Mrs. Marshall-Smith's bedroom. She did not resemble the romantic conception of a girl crossed in love. She looked very quiet, no paler than usual, quite self-possessed. The only change a keen eye could have noted was that now there was about her an atmosphere of slightly rigid dignity, which had not been there before. She seemed less girlish.

No eyes could have been more keenly analytical than those of Mrs. Marshall-Smith. She saw perfectly the new attribute, and realized perfectly what a resolute stiffening of the will it signified. She had never admired and loved Sylvia more, and being a person adept in self-expression, she saturated her next speech with her admiration and affection. "Of course, you know, my dear, that *I'm* not one of the herd. I know entirely that your feeling for Felix was just what mine is—immense admiration for his taste and accomplishments. As a matter of fact it was apparent to every one that, even in spite of all Molly's money, if you'd really cared to . . ."

Sylvia winced, actually and physically, at this speech, which brought back to her with a sharp flick the egregiousness of her absurd self-deception. What a simpleton she had been—what a little naïve, provincial simpleton! In spite of her high opinion of her own cleverness and knowledge of people, how stupidly steeped she had been in the childish, idiotic American tradition of entire disinterestedness in the relations of men and women. It was another instance of how betrayed she constantly was, in any manœuver in the actual world, by the fatuous idealism which had so colored her youth—she vented her emotion in despising that idealism and thinking of hard names to call it.

" . . . though of course you showed your intelligence by *not* really caring to," went on Mrs. Marshall-Smith; " it would have meant a crippled life for both of you. Felix hasn't a cent more than he needs for himself. If he was going to marry at all, he was forced to marry carefully. Indeed, it has occurred to me that he may have thrown himself into this, because he was in danger of losing his head over you, and knew how fatal it would be. For you, you lovely thing of great possibilities, you need a rich soil for *your* roots, too, if you're to bloom out as you ought to."

Sylvia, receiving this into a sore and raw consciousness, said to herself with an embittered instinct for cynicism that she had never heard more euphonious periphrases for selling yourself for money. For that was what it came down to, she had told herself fiercely a great many times during the night. Felix had sold himself for money as outright as ever a woman of the streets had done.

Mrs. Marshall-Smith, continuing steadily to talk (on the theory that talking prevents too great concentration of thought), and making the round of all the possible things to say, chanced at this moment upon a qualification to this theory of Morrison's conduct which for an instant caught Sylvia's attention, "——and then there's always the possibility that even if you *had* cared to—Molly might have been too much for you, for both of you. She always has had just what she wanted—and people who have, get the habit. I don't know if you've noticed it, in the little you've seen of her, but it's very apparent to me, knowing her from childhood up as I have, that there's a slight coarseness of grain in Molly, when it's a question of getting what she wants. I don't mean she's exactly horrid. Molly's a dear in her way, and I'm very fond of her, of course. If she can get what she wants *without* walking over anybody's prostrate body, she'll go round. But there's a directness, a brilliant lack of fine shades in Molly's grab. . . . It makes one remember that her Montgomery grandfather had firmness of purpose enough to raise himself from an ordinary Illinois farmer to arbiter of the wheat pit. Such impossible old aunts—such cousins—occasionally crop up still from the Montgomery connection. But all with the same crude force. It's almost impossible for a temperament like Felix's to contend with a nature like that."

Sylvia was struck by the reflection, but on turning it over she saw in it only another reason for anger at Morrison. "You make your old friend out as a very weak character," she said.

Mrs. Marshall-Smith's tolerant, clear view of the infirmities of humanity was grieved by this fling of youthful severity. "Oh, my dear! my dear! A young, beautiful, enormendously rich, tremendously enamored girl? That's a combination! I don't think we need consider Felix exactly weak for not having resisted!"

Sylvia thought she knew reasons for his not yielding, but she did not care to discuss them, and said nothing.

"But whether," continued Mrs. Marshall-Smith, attempting delicately to convey the only reflection supposed to be of comfort to a girl in Sylvia's situation, "whether or not Molly will find after marriage that even a very masterful and ruthless temperament may fail entirely to possess and hold the things it has grabbed and carried off . . ."

Sylvia repudiated the tacit conception that this would be a balm to her. "Oh, I'm sure I hope they'll manage!" she said earnestly.

"Of course! Of course!" agreed Mrs. Marshall-Smith. "Who doesn't hope so?" She paused, her loquacity run desperately thin. There was the sound of a car, driving up to the front door. Sylvia rose in apprehension. Her aunt motioned a reassurance. "I told Tojiko to tell every one that we are not in—to anybody."

Hélène came to the door on silent, felt-shod feet, a black-and-white picture of well-trained servility. "Pardon, Madame, Tojiko says that Mlle. Sommerville wishes to see Mlle. Sylvie."

Mrs. Marshall-Smith looked with considerable apprehension at her niece. "You must get it over with some time, Sylvia. It'll be easier here than with a lot of people staring at you both, and making nasty speculations." Neither she nor Sylvia noticed that for an instant, in her haste, she had quite dropped her careful pretension that Sylvia could, of course, if she had really cared to. . . .

Sylvia set her jaw, an action curiously visible under the smooth, subtle modeling of her young cheeks. She said to Hélène in a quiet voice: "*Mais bien sûr!* Tell her we're not yet dressed, but if she will give herself the trouble to come up. . . ."

Hélène nodded and retreated. Sylvia looked rather pale.

"You don't know what a joy your perfect French is to me, dear," said Mrs. Marshall-Smith, still rapidly turning every peg in sight in an endeavor to loosen tension; but no noticeable relaxation took place in Sylvia. It did not seem to her at just that moment of great importance that she could speak good French.

With desperate haste she was saying to herself, "At least Molly doesn't know about anything. I told her I didn't care. She believed me. I must go on pretending that I don't. But can I! But can I!"

Light, rapid steps came flying up the stairs and down the long hall. "Sylvia! Sylvia!" Molly was evidently hesitating between doors.

"Here—this way—last door—Aunt Victoria's room!" called Sylvia, and felt like a terror-stricken actor making a first public appearance, enormously surprised, relieved, and heartened to find her usual voice still with her. As Molly came flying into the room, she ran to meet her. They fell into each other's arms with incoherent ejaculations and, under the extremely appreciative eye of Mrs. Marshall-Smith, kissed each other repeatedly.

"Oh, isn't she the dear!" cried Molly, shaking out amply to the breeze a victor's easy generosity. "Isn't she the darlingest girl in the world! She *understands* so! When I saw how perfectly *sweet* she was the day Arnold and Judith announced their engagement, I said to myself I wanted her to be the first person I spoke to about mine."

The approach of the inexorable necessity for her first words roused Sylvia to an inspiration which struck out an almost visible spark of admiration from her aunt. "You just count too much on my being 'queer,' Molly," she said playfully, pulling the other girl down beside her, with an affectionate gesture. "How do *you* know that I'm not fearfully jealous of you? *Such* a charmer as your fiancé is!"

Molly laughed delightedly. "Isn't she wonderful—not to care a bit—really!" she appealed to Sylvia's aunt. "How anybody *could* resist Felix—but then she's so clever. She's wonderful!"

Sylvia, smiling, cordial, clear-eyed and bitter-hearted, thought that she really was.

"But I can't talk about it here!" cried Molly restlessly. "I came to carry Sylvia off. I can't sit still at home. I want to go ninety miles an hour! I can't think straight unless I'm behind the steering-wheel. Come along, Sylvia!"

Mrs. Marshall-Smith thereupon showed herself, for all her amenity and grace, more of a match of Molly's force and energy than either Sylvia or Morrison had been on a certain rather memorable occasion ten days before. She opposed the simple irresistible obstacle of a flat command. " Sylvia's *not* going out in a car dressed in a lace-trimmed négligée, with a boudoir cap on, whether you get what you want the minute you want it or not, Molly Sommerville," she said with the authoritative accent which had always quelled Arnold in his boyhood (as long as he was within earshot). The method was effective now. Molly laughed. Sylvia even made shift to laugh ; and Hélène was summoned to put on the trim shirt-waist, the short cloth skirt and close hat which Mrs. Marshall-Smith selected with care and the history of which she detailed at length, so copiously that there was no opportunity to speak of anything less innocuous. Her unusual interest in the matter even caused her to accompany the girls to the head of the stairs, still talking, and she called down to them finally as they went out of the front door, ". . . it's the only way with Briggs—he's simply incorrigible about delays—and yet no-body does skirts as he does! You just have to tell him you *will not take it,* if he doesn't get it done on time ! "

Sylvia cast an understanding, grateful upward look at her aunt and stepped into the car. So far it had gone better than she feared. But a tête-à-tête with Molly, overflowing with the confidences of the newly betrothed—she was not sure that she could get through with that with credit.

Molly, however, seemed as little inclined to overflow as Sylvia to have her. She talked of everything in the world except of Felix Morrison ; and it was not long before Sylvia's acuteness discovered that she was not thinking of what she was saying. There passed through her mind a wild, wretched notion that Molly might after all know— that Felix might have been base enough to talk about her to Molly, that Molly might be trying to " spare her." But this idea was instantly rejected : Molly was not subtle enough to conceive of such a course, and too headlong not to make a hundred blunders in carrying it out ; and besides, it would not explain her manner. She was abstracted obviously for the simple reason that she had something on her mind, something not altogether to her liking, judging from the uneasy color which came and went in her face, by her rattling, senseless flow of chatter, by her fidgeting, unnecessary adjustments of the mechanism of the car. . . .

Sylvia herself, in spite of her greater self-control, looked out upon the world with nothing of her usual eager welcome. The personality of the man they did not name hung between and around the two women like a cloud. As they swept along rapidly, young, fair, well-fed, beautifully dressed, in the costly, shining car, their clouded faces might to a country eye have been visible proofs of the country dictum that "rich city folks don't seem to get no good out'n their money and their automobiles: always layin' their ears back and lookin' 'bout as cheerful as a balky horse."

But the country eyes which at this moment fell on them were anything but conscious of class differences. It was a desperate need which reached out a gaunt claw and plucked at them when, high on the flank of the mountain, as they swung around the corner of a densely wooded road, they saw a wild-eyed man in overalls leap down from the bushes and yell at them.

Sylvia was startled and her first impression was the natural feminine one of fear—a lonely road, a strange man, excited, perhaps drunk— But Molly, without an instant's hesitation, ground the car to a stop in a cloud of dust. "What's the matter?" she shouted as the man sprang up on the running-board. He was gasping, purple, utterly spent, and for an instant could only beat the air with his hands. Then he broke out in a hoarse shout—the sound in that quiet sylvan spot was like a tocsin: "Fire! An awful fire! Hewitt's pine woods—up that road!" He waved a wild, bare arm—his shirt-sleeve was torn to the shoulder. "Go and git help. They need all the men they can git!"

He dropped from the running-board and ran back up the hill through the bushes. They saw him lurch from one side to the other; he was still exhausted from his dash down the mountain to the road; they heard the bushes crash, saw them close behind him. He was gone.

Sylvia's eyes were still on the spot where he had disappeared when she was thrown violently back against the seat in a great leap forward of the car. She caught at the side, at her hat, and saw Molly's face. It was transfigured. The brooding restlessness was gone as acrid smoke goes when the clear flame leaps up.

" What are you doing? " shouted Sylvia.

" To get help," answered Molly, opening the throttle another notch. The first staggering plunge over, the car settled down to a terrific speed, purring softly its puissant vibrant song of illimitable strength. " Hear her sing! Hear her sing! " cried Molly. In three minutes from the time the man had left them, they tore into the nearest village, two miles from the woods. It seemed that in those three minutes Molly had not only run the car like a demon, but had formed a plan. Slackening speed only long enough to waltz with the car on a street-corner while she shouted an inquiry to a passer-by, she followed the wave of his hand and flashed down a side-street to a big brick building which proclaimed itself in a great sign, " Peabody Brush-back Factory."

The car stopped. Molly sprang out and ran as though the car were a rifle and she the bullet emerging from it. She ran into a large, ugly, comfortable office, where several white-faced girls were lifting their thin little fingers from typewriter keys to stare at the young woman who burst through and in at a door marked " Manager."

" There's a fire on the mountain—a great fire in Hewitt's pine woods," she cried in a clear, peremptory voice that sounded like a young captain leading a charge. " I can take nine men on my car. Will you come with me and tell which men to go? "

A dignified, elderly man, with smooth, gray hair and a black alpaca office coat, sat perfectly motionless behind his desk and stared at her in a petrified silence. Molly stamped her foot. "There's not an instant to lose," she said; "they need every man they can get."

"Who's the fire-warden of this township?" said the elderly man foolishly, trying to assemble his wits.

Molly appeared visibly to propel him from his chair by her fury. "Oh, they need help *NOW!*" she cried. "Come on! Come on!"

Then they stood together on the steps of the office. "Those men unloading lumber over there could go," said the manager, "and I'll get three more from the packing-rooms."

"Don't go yourself! Send somebody to get them!" commanded Molly. "You go and telephone anybody in town who has a car. There'll be sure to be one or two at the garage."

Sylvia gasped at the prodigy taking place before her eyes, the masterful, keen-witted captain of men who emerged like a thunderbolt from their Molly—Molly, the pretty little beauty of the summer colony!

She had galvanized the elderly New Englander beside her out of his first momentary apathy of stupefaction. He now put his own competent hand to the helm and took command.

"Yes," he said, and with the word it was evident that he was aroused. Over his shoulder, in a quiet voice that carried like the crack of a gun: "Henderson, go get three men from the packing-room to go to a forest-fire. Shut down the machinery. Get all the able-bodied men ready in gangs of seven. Perkins, you 'phone Tim O'Keefe to bring my car here at once. And get Pat's and Tom's and the two at the hotel."

"Tools?" said Molly.

He nodded and called out to the men advancing with a rush on the car: "There are hoes and shovels inside the power-house door. Better take some axes too."

In four minutes from the time they had entered the village (Sylvia had her watch in her hand) they were flying back, the car packed with men in overalls and clustered thick with others on the running-board. Back of them the whistle of the factory shrieked a strident announcement of disaster. Women and children ran to the doors to stare up and down, to cry out, to look and with dismayed faces to see the great cloud of gray smoke pouring up from the side of the mountain. There was no soul in that village who did not know what a forest-fire meant.

Then in a flash the car had left the village and was rushing along the dusty highroad, the huge, ominous pillar of smoke growing nearer. The men stared up at it with sober faces. " Pretty hot fire! " said one uneasily.

They reached the place where the man had yelled to them—ten minutes exactly since they had left it. Molly turned the car into the steep sandy side-road which led up the mountain. The men shouted out in remonstrance, " Hey, lady! You can't git a car up there. We'll have to walk the rest of the way. They don't never take cars there."

" This one is going up," sang out Molly gallantly, almost gaily, opening the throttle to its fullest and going into second speed.

The sound of the laboring engine jarred loudly through all the still, hot woods; the car shook and trembled under the strain on it. Molly dropped into low. A cloud of evil-smelling blue gasoline smoke rose up from the exhaust behind, but the car continued to advance. Rising steadily, coughing and choking, up the cruelly steep grades, bump-ing heavily down over the great water-bars, smoking, rat-tling, quivering—the car continued to advance. A trickle of perspiration ran down Molly's cheeks. The floor was hot under their feet, the smell of hot oil pungent in their nostrils.

They were eight minutes from the main road now, and near the fire. Over the trail hung a cloud of smoke, and, as they turned a corner and came through this, they saw that they had arrived. Sylvia drew back and crooked her arm over her eyes. She had never seen a forest fire before. She came from the plain-country, where trees are almost sacred, and her first feeling was of terror. But then she dropped her arm and looked, and looked again at the glorious, awful sight which was to furnish her with nightmares for months to come.

The fire was roaring down one side of the road towards them, and away to the right was eating its furious, sulphurous way into the heart of the forest. They stopped a hundred feet short, but the blare of heat struck on their faces like a blow. Through the dense masses of smoke, terrifying glimpses of fierce, clean flame; a resinous dead stump burning like a torch; a great tree standing helpless like a martyr at the stake, suddenly transformed into a frenzied pillar of fire. . . . Along the front of this whirlpool of flame toiled, with despairing fury, four lean, powerful men. As they raised their blackened, desperate faces and saw the car there, actually there, incredibly there, black with its load of men, they gave a deep-throated shout of relief, though they did not for an instant stop the frantic plying of their picks and hoes. The nine men sprang out, their implements in their hands, and dispersed along the fighting-line.

Molly backed the car around, the rear wheels churning up the sand, and plunged down the hill into the smoke. Through the choking fumes of this, Sylvia shouted at her, " Molly! Molly! You're *great!* " She felt that she would always hear ringing in her ears that thrilling, hoarse shout of relief.

Molly shouted in answer, " I could scream, I'm so happy! " And as they plunged madly down the mountain road, she said: " Oh, Sylvia, you don't know—I never was any use before—never once—never! I got the first load of help there! How they shouted! "

At the junction of the side-road with the highway, a car was discharging a load of men with rakes and picks. " *I* took my car up! " screamed Molly, leaning from the steering wheel but not slackening speed as she tore past them.

The driver of the other car, a young man with the face

" I thought you were going to stick in Colorado all summer," said Molly.

" Well, I heard they were short of help at Austin Farm and I came on to help get in the hay," said the man. Both he and Molly seemed to consider this a humorous speech. Then, remembering Sylvia, Molly went through a casual introduction. " This is my cousin—Austin Page— my *favorite* cousin! He's really awfully nice, though so plain to look at." She went on, still astonished, " But how'd you get *here?* "

" Why, how does anybody in Vermont get to a forest fire? " he answered. " We were out in the hayfield, saw the smoke, left the horses, grabbed what tools we could find, and beat it through the woods. That's the technique of the game up here."

" I didn't know your farm ran anywhere near here," said Molly.

" It isn't so terribly near. We came across lots tolerable fast. But there's a little field, back up on the edge of the woods that isn't so far. Grandfather used to raise potatoes there. I've got it into hay now," he explained.

As they talked, the fire beyond them gave definite signs of yielding. It had evidently been stopped on the far side and now advanced nowhere, showed no longer a malign yellow crest, but only rolling sullenly heavenward a diminishing cloud of smoke. The fire-fighters began to straggle back across the burned tract towards the road, their eyeballs gleaming white in their dark faces.

" Oh, they mustn't walk! I'll take them back—the darlings! " said Molly, starting for her car. She was quite her usual brisk, free-and-easy self now. " Cracky! I hope I've got gas enough. I've certainly been going *some!* "

" Why don't you leave me here? " suggested Sylvia. " I'll walk home. That'll leave room for one more."

" Oh, you can't do that! " protested Molly faintly, though she was evidently at once struck with the plan. " How'd you find your way home? " She turned to her cousin. " See here, Austin, why don't *you* take Sylvia home? You

ought to go anyhow and see Grandfather. He'll be awfully
hurt to think you're here and haven't been to see him."
She threw instantly into this just conceived idea the force
which always carried through her plans. "Do go! I feel
so grateful to these men I don't want one of them to walk
a step!"

Sylvia had thought of a solitary walk, longing intensely
for isolation, and she did not at all welcome the suggestion
of adapting herself to a stranger. The stranger, on his
part, looked a very unchivalrous hesitation; but this proved
to be only a doubt of Sylvia's capacity as a walker.

"If you don't mind climbing a bit, I can take you over
the gap between Hemlock and Windward Mountain and
make a bee-line for Lydford. It's not an hour from here,
that way, but it's ten miles around by the road—and hot
and dusty too."

"Can she *climb!*" ejaculated Molly scornfully, impatient
to be off with her men. "She went up to Prospect Rock
in forty minutes."

She high-handedly assumed that everything was settled
as she wished it, and running towards the car, called with
an easy geniality to the group of men, starting down the
road on foot, "Here, wait a minute, folks, I'll take you
back!"

She mounted the car, started the engine, waved her hand
to the two behind her, and was off.

The lean, stooping man looked dubiously at Sylvia.
"You're sure you don't mind a little climb?" he said.

"Oh no, I like it," she said listlessly. The moment for
her was of stale, wearied return to real life, to the actual
world which she was continually finding uglier than she
hoped. The recollection of Felix Morrison came back to
her in a bitter tide.

"All ready?" asked her companion, mopping his forehead with a very dirty handkerchief.

"All ready," she said and turned, with a hanging head,
to follow him.

CHAPTER XXVII

BETWEEN WINDWARD AND HEMLOCK MOUNTAINS

FOR a time as they plodded up the steep wood-road, over-grown with ferns and rank grass, with dense green walls of beech and oak saplings on either side, what few desultory remarks they exchanged related to Molly, she being literally the only topic of common knowledge between them. Sylvia, automatically responding to her deep-lying impulse to give pleasure, to be pleasing, made an effort to overcome her somber lassitude and spoke of Molly's miraculous competence in dealing with the fire. Her companion said that of course Molly hadn't made all that up out of her head on the spur of the moment. "After spending every summer of her life in Lydford, it would be surprising if so energetic a child as Molly hadn't assimilated the Vermont formula for fighting fire. "They always put for the nearest factory and get all hands out," he explained, adding meditatively, as he chewed on a twig: "All the same, the incident shows what I've always maintained about Molly: that she is, like 'most everybody, lamentably miscast. Molly's spirit oughtn't to have taken up its abiding place in that highly ornamental blond shell, condemned after a fashionable girl's education to pendulum swings between Paris and New York and Lydford. It doesn't fit for a cent. It ought to have for habitation a big, gaunt, powerful man's body, and for occupation the running of a big factory." He seemed to be philosophizing more to himself than to Sylvia, and beyond a surprised look into his extremely grimy face, she made no comment. She had taken for granted from the talk between him and Molly that he was one of the "forceful, impossible Montgomery cousins," and had cast her own first remarks in a tone calculated to fit in with the supposititious dialect of such a person. But his voice, his intonations, and his whimsical idea about Molly fitted in with the conception of an "impossible" as little as with the actual visible facts of his ragged shirt-sleeves and faded, earth-stained overalls. They toiled upwards in silence for some moments, the man still chewing on his birch-twig. He noticed her sidelong half-satirical glance at it. "Don't you want one?" he asked, and gravely cut a long, slim rod from one of the saplings in the green wall shutting them into the road. As he gave it to her he explained, "It's the kind they make birch beer of. You nip off the bark with your teeth. You'll like it."

Still more at sea as to what sort of person he might be, and now fearing perhaps to wound him if he should turn out to be a very unsophisticated one, Sylvia obediently set her teeth to the lustrous, dark bark and tore off a bit, which gave out in her mouth a mild, pleasant aromatic tang, woodsy and penetrating, unlike any other taste she knew. "Good, isn't it?" said her companion simply.

She nodded, slowly awakening to a tepid curiosity about the individual who strode beside her, lanky and powerful in his blue jeans. What an odd circumstance, her trudging off through the woods thus with a guide of whom she knew nothing except that he was Molly Sommerville's cousin and worked a Vermont farm—and had certainly the dirtiest face she had ever seen, with the exception of the coal-blackened stokers in the power-house of the University. He spoke again, as though in answer to what might naturally be in her mind: "At the top of the road it crosses a brook, and I think a wash would be possible. I've a bit of soap in my pocket that'll help—though it takes quite a lot of scrubbing to get off fire-fighting grime." He looked pointedly down at her as he talked.

Sylvia was so astonished that she dropped back through years of carefully acquired self-consciousness into a moment of the stark simplicity of childhood. "Why—is *my* face dirty?" she cried out.

The man beside her apparently found the contrast between her looks and the heartfelt sincerity of her question too much for him. He burst into helpless laughter, though he was adroit enough to thrust forward as a pretext, " The picture of my *own* grime that I get from your accent is tremendous! " But it was evidently not at his own joke that he was laughing.

For an instant Sylvia hung poised very near to extreme annoyance. Never since she had been grown up, had she appeared at such an absurd disadvantage. But at once the mental picture of herself, making inaudible carping strictures on her companion's sootiness and, all unconscious, lifting to observe it a critical countenance as swart as his own— the incongruity smote her deliciously, irresistibly! Sore heart or not, black depression notwithstanding, she needs must laugh, and having laughed, laugh again, laugh louder and longer, and finally, like a child, laugh for the sake of laughing, till out through this unexpected channel she discharged much of the stagnant bitterness around her heart.

Her companion laughed with her. The still, sultry summer woods echoed with the sound. " How human, how lusciously *human!* " he exclaimed. " Neither of us thought that *he* might be the blackened one! "

" Oh, mine *can't* be as bad as yours! " gasped out Sylvia, but when she rubbed a testing handkerchief on her cheek, she went off in fresh peals at the sight of the resultant black smears.

" Don't, for Heaven's sake, waste that handkerchief," cautioned her companion. " It's the only towel between us. Mine's impossible! " He showed her the murky rag which was his own; and as they spoke, they reached the top of the road, heard the sound of water, and stood beside the brook.

He stepped across it, in one stride of his long legs, rolled up his shirt-sleeves, took a book out of his pocket, laid it on a stone, and knelt down. " I choose this for *my* washbasin," he said, indicating a limpid pool paved with clean gray pebbles.

Sylvia answered in the same note of play, "This'll be mine." It lay at the foot of a tiny waterfall, plashing with a tinkling note into transparent shallows. She cast an idle glance on the book he had laid down and read its title, "A History of the Institution of Property," and reflected that she had been right in thinking it had a familiar-looking cover. She had dusted books with that sort of cover all her life.

Molly's cousin produced from his overalls a small piece of yellow kitchen-soap, which he broke into scrupulously exact halves and presented with a grave flourish to Sylvia. "Now, go to it," he exhorted her; "I bet I get a better wash than you."

Sylvia took off her hat, rolled up her sleeves, and began on vigorous ablutions. She had laughed, yes, and heartily, but in her complicated many-roomed heart a lively pique rubbed shoulders with her mirth, and her merriment was tinctured with a liberal amount of the traditional feminine horrified disgust at having been uncomely, at having unconsciously been subjected to an indignity. She was determined that no slightest stain should remain on her smooth, fine-textured skin. She felt, as a pretty woman always feels, that her personality was indissolubly connected with her looks, and it was a symbolic act which she performed as she fiercely scrubbed her face with the yellow soap till its acrid pungency blotted out for her the woodland aroma of moist earth and green leaves. She dashed the cold water up on her cheeks till the spattering drops gleamed like crystals on the crisp waviness of her ruddy brown hair. She washed her hands and arms in the icy mountain water till they were red with the cold, hot though the day was. She was chilled, and raw with the crude astringency of the soap, but she felt cleansed to the marrow of her bones, as though there had been some mystic quality in this lustration in running water, performed under the open sky. The racy, black-birch tang still lingering on her tongue was a flavor quite in harmony with this severely washed feeling. It was a taste notably clean.

She looked across the brook at her companion, now sitting back on his heels, and saw that there had emerged from his grime a thin, tanned, high-nosed face, topped by drab-colored hair of no great abundance and lighted by a pair of extraordinarily clear, gray eyes. She perceived no more in the face at that moment, because the man, as he looked up at her, became nothing but a dazzled mirror from which was reflected back to her the most flattering image of her own appearance. Almost actually she saw herself as she appeared to him, a wood-nymph, kneeling by the flowing water, vital, exquisite, strong, radiant in a cool flush, her uncovered hair gleaming in a thousand loosened waves. Like most comely women of intelligence Sylvia was intimately familiar with every phase of her own looks, and she knew down to the last blood-corpuscle that she had never looked better. But almost at once came the stab that Felix Morrison was not the man who was looking at her, and the heartsick recollection that he would never again be there to see her. Her moment of honest joy in being lovely passed. She stood up with a clouded face, soberly pulled down her sleeves, and picked up her hat.

"Oh, why don't you leave it off?" said the man across the brook. "You'd be so much more comfortable!" She knew that he meant her hair was too pretty to cover, and did not care what he meant. "All right, I'll carry it," she assented indifferently.

He did not stir, gazing up at her frankly admiring. Sylvia made out, from the impression he evidently now had of her, that her face had really been very, very dirty; and at the recollection of that absurd ascent of the mountain by those two black-faced, twig-chewing individuals, a return of irrepressible laughter quivered on her lips. Before his eyes, as swiftly, as unaccountably, as utterly as an April day shifts its moods, she had changed from radiant, rosy wood-goddess to saddened mortal and thence on into tricksy, laughing elf. He burst out on her, "Who *are* you, anyhow?"

She remembered with a start. "Why, that's so, Molly

didn't mention my name—isn't that like Molly! Why, I'm Sylvia Marshall."

"You may be *named* Sylvia Marshall!" he said, leaving an inference in the air like incense.

"Well, yes, to be sure," rejoined Sylvia; "I heard somebody only the other day say that an introduction was the quaintest of grotesques, since people's names are the most——"

He applied a label with precision. "Oh, you know Morrison?"

She was startled at this abrupt emergence of the name which secretly filled her mind and was aware with exasperation that she was blushing. Her companion appeared not to notice this. He was attempting the difficult feat of wiping his face on the upper part of his sleeve, and said in the intervals of effort: "Well, you know *my* name. Molly didn't forget that."

"But *I* did," Sylvia confessed. "I was so excited by the fire I never noticed at all. I've been racking my brains to remember, all the way up here."

For some reason the man seemed quite struck with this statement and eyed her with keenness as he said: "Oh—really? Well, my name is Austin Page." At the candid blankness of her face he showed a boyish flash of white teeth in a tanned face. "Do you mean to say you've never heard of me?"

"*Should* I?" said Sylvia, with a graceful pretense of alarm. "Do you write, or something? Lay it to my ignorance. It's immense."

He shook his head. He smiled down on her. She noticed now that his eyes were very kind as well as clear and keen. "No, I don't write, or anything. There's no reason why you should ever have heard of me. I only thought—I thought possibly Molly or Uncle George might have happened to mention me."

"I'm only on from the West for a visit," explained Sylvia. "I never was in Lydford before. I don't know the people there."

" Well then, to avoid Morrison's strictures on introductions I'll add to my name the information that I am thirty-two years old; a graduate of Columbia University; that I have some property in Colorado which gives me a great deal of trouble; and a farm with a wood lot in Vermont which is the joy of my heart. I cannot endure politics; I play the flute, like my eggs boiled three minutes, and admire George Meredith."

His manœuvers with his sleeve were so preposterous that Sylvia now cried to him: " Oh, don't twist around that way. You'll give yourself a crick in the neck. Here's my handkerchief. We were going to share that, anyhow."

" And you," he went on gravely, wiping his face with the bit of cambric, " are Sylvia Marshall, presumably Miss; you can laugh at a joke on yourself; are not afraid to wash your face with kitchen soap; and apparently are the only girl in the twentieth century who has not a mirror and a powder-puff concealed about her person."

All approbation was sweet to Sylvia. She basked in this. ' Oh, I'm a Hottentot, a savage from the West, as I told you," she said complacently.

" You've been in Lydford long enough to hear Morrison hold forth on the idiocies of social convention, the while he neatly manipulates them to his own advantage."

Sylvia had dreaded having to speak of Morrison, but she was now greatly encouraged by the entire success of her casual tone, as she explained, " Oh, he's an old friend of my aunt's, and he's been at the house a good deal." She ventured to try herself further, and inquired with a bright look of interest, " What do you think of his engagement to your cousin Molly? "

He was petrified with astonishment. " *Molly* engaged to *Morrison!* " he cried. " We can't be talking about the same people. I mean *Felix* Morrison the critic."

She felt vindicated by his stupefaction and liked him for it. " Why, yes, hadn't you heard? " she asked, with an assumption of herself seeing nothing surprising in the news.

" No, I hadn't, and I can't believe it now! " he said,

blinking his eyes. " I never heard such an insane combination of names in my life." He went on, " What under
the *sun* does Molly want of Morrison!"

Sylvia was vexed with him for this unexpected view.
He was not so discerning as she had thought. She turned
away and picked up her hat. " We ought to be going on,"
she said, and as they walked she answered, " You don't
seem to have a very high opinion of Mr. Morrison."

He protested with energy. " Oh yes, I have. Quite the
contrary, I think him one of the most remarkable men
I know, and one of the finest. I admire him immensely.
I'd trust his taste sooner than I would my own."

To this handsome tribute Sylvia returned, smiling, " The
inference is that you don't think much of Molly."

" I *know* Molly!" he said simply. " I've known her
and loved her ever since she was a hot-tempered, imperious
little girl—which is all she is now. Engaged . . . and
engaged to Morrison! It's a plain case of schoolgirl in-
fatuation!" He was lost in wonder, uneasy wonder it
seemed, for after a period of musing he brought out:
" They'll cut each other's throats inside six months. Or
Molly'll cut her own. What under the sun was her
grandfather thinking of?"

Sylvia said gravely, " Girls' grandfathers have such an
influence in their marriages."

He smiled a rueful recognition of the justice of her
thrust and then fell into silence.

The road did not climb up now, but led along the side
of the mountain. Through the dense woods the sky-line,
first guessed at, then clearly seen between the thick-
standing tree-trunks, sank lower and lower. " We are
approaching," said Page, motioning in front of them,
" the jumping-off place." They passed from the tempered
green light of the wood and emerged upon a great windy
plateau, carpeted thickly with deep green moss, flanked
right and left with two mountain peaks and roofed over
with an expanse of brilliant summer sky. Before them the
plateau stretched a mile or more, wind-swept, sun-drenched,

with an indescribable bold look of great altitude; but close to them at one side ran a parapet-like line of tumbled rock and beyond this a sheer descent. The eye leaped down abrupt slopes of forest to the valley they had left, now a thousand feet below them, jewel-like with mystic blues and greens, tremulous with heat. On the noble height where they stood, the wind blew cool from the sea of mist-blue peaks beyond the valley.

Sylvia was greatly moved. "Oh, what a wonderful spot!" she said under her breath. "I never dreamed that anything could be——" She burst out suddenly, scarcely knowing what she said, "Oh, I wish my *mother* could be here!" She had not thought of her mother for days, and now hardly knew that she had spoken her name. Standing there, poised above the dark richness of the valley, her heart responding to those vast airy spaces by an upward-soaring sweep, the quick tears of ecstasy were in her eyes. She had entirely forgotten herself and her companion. He did not speak. His eyes were on her face.

She moved to the parapet of rock and leaned against it. The action brought her to herself and she flashed around on Page a grateful smile. "It's a very beautiful spot you've brought me to," she said.

He came up beside her now. "It's a favorite of mine," he said quietly. "If I come straight through the woods it's not more than a mile from my farm. I come up here for the sunsets sometimes—or for dawn."

Sylvia found the idea almost too much for her. "*Oh!*" she cried—"dawn here!"

"Yes," said the man, smiling faintly. "It's all of that!"

In her life of plains and prairies Sylvia had never been upon a great height, had never looked down and away upon such reaches of far valley, such glorious masses of sunlit mountain; and beyond them, giving wings to the imagination, were mountains, more mountains, distant, incalculably distant, with unseen hollow valleys between; and finally, mountains again, half cloud, melting indistinguishably into the vaporous haze of the sky. Above her, sheer and vast, lay Hemlock Mountain, all its huge bulk a sleeping, passionless calm. Beyond was the solemnity of Windward Mountain's concave shell, full to the brim with brooding blue shadows, a well of mystery in that day of wind-blown sunshine. Beneath her, above her, before her, seemingly the element in which she was poised, was space, illimitable space. She had never been conscious of such vastness, she was abashed by it, she was exalted by it, she knew a moment of acute shame for the pettiness of her personal grievances. For a time her spirit was disembarrassed of the sorry burden of egotism, and she drank deep from the cup of healing which Nature holds up in such instants of beatitude. Her eyes were shining pools of peace. . . .

They went on in a profound silence across the plateau, the deep, soft moss bearing them up with a tough elasticity, the sun hot and lusty on their heads, the sweet, strong summer wind swift and loud in their ears, the only sound in all that enchanted upland spot. Often Sylvia lifted her face to the sky, so close above her, to the clouds moving with a soundless rhythm across the sky; once or twice she turned her head suddenly from one side to the other, to take in all the beauty at one glance, and smiled on it all, a vague, sunny, tender smile. But she did not speak.

As she trod on the thick moss upspringing under her long, light step, her advance seemed as buoyant as though she stepped from cloud to cloud. . . .

When they reached the other side, and were about to begin the descent into Lydford valley, she lingered still. She looked down into the valley before her, across to the mountains, and, smiling, with half-shut eyes of supreme satisfaction, she said under her breath: " It's Beethoven—just the blessedness of Beethoven! The valley is a legato passage, quiet and flowing; those far, up-pricking hills, staccato; and the mountains here, the solemn chords."

Her companion did not answer. She looked up at him, inquiringly, thinking that he had not heard her, and found him evidently too deeply moved to speak. She was startled, almost frightened, almost shocked by the profundity of his gaze upon her. Her heart stood still and gave a great leap. Chiefly she was aware of an immense astonishment and incredulity. An hour before he had never seen her, had never heard of her—and during that hour she had been barely aware of him, absorbed in herself, indifferent. How could he in that hour have . . .

He looked away and said steadily, "—and the river is the melody that binds it all together."

Sylvia drew a great breath of relief. She had been the victim of some extraordinary hallucination: "—with the little brooks for variations on the theme," she added hastily.

He held aside an encroaching briar, stretching its thorny arm across the path. "Here's the beginning of the trail down to Lydford," he said. "We will be there in twenty minutes. It's almost a straight drop down."

CHAPTER XXVIII

SYLVIA ASKS HERSELF "WHY NOT?"

IF Sylvia wondered, as she dropped down the heights to the valley, what her reception might be at her aunt's ceremonious household when she entered escorted by a strange hatless man in blue overalls, her fancy fell immeasurably short of the actual ensuing sensation. Mrs. Marshall-Smith, her stepson, Felix Morrison, and old Mr. Sommerville were all sitting together on the wide north veranda, evidently waiting to be called to luncheon when, at half-past one, the two pedestrians emerged through a side wicket in the thick green hedge of spruce, and advanced up the path, with the free, swinging step of people who have walked far and well. The effect on the veranda was unimaginable. Sheer, open-mouthed stupefaction blurred for an instant the composed, carefully arranged masks of those four exponents of decorum. They gaped and stared, unable to credit their eyes.

And then, according to their natures, they acted. Mrs. Marshall-Smith rose quickly, smiled brilliantly, and stepped forward with welcoming outstretched hands. "Why, Sylvia dear, how delightful! What an unexpected pleasure, Mr. Page!"

Old Mr. Sommerville fairly bounded past Sylvia, caught the man's arm, and said in an anxious, affectionate, startled voice, "Why, Austin! Austin! Austin!"

Morrison rose, but stood quietly by his chair, his face entirely expressionless, palpably and correctly "at attention." He had not seen Sylvia since the announcement of his engagement the day before. He gave her now a graceful, silent, friendly salute from a distance as she stood by her aunt, he called out to her companion a richly cordial greeting of " Well, Page. This is luck indeed! " but he indicated by his immobility that as a stranger he would not presume to go further until the first interchange between blood-kin was over.

As for Arnold, he neither stirred from his chair, nor opened his mouth to speak. A slow smile widened on his lips: it expanded. He grinned delightedly down at his cigarette, and up at the ceiling, and finally broke into an open laugh of exquisite enjoyment of the scene before him.

Four people were talking at once; Mr. Sommerville, a dismayed old hand still clutching at the new-comer, was protesting with extreme vigor, and being entirely drowned out by the others. " Of course he can't stay—as he *is!* I'll go home with him at once! His room at my house is always ready for him!—fresh clothes!—No, no—impossible to stay! " Mrs. Marshall-Smith was holding firm with her loveliest manner of warm friendliness concentrated on Page. " Oh, no ceremony, Mr. Page, not between old friends. Luncheon is just ready—who cares how you look? " She did not physically dispute with Mr. Sommerville the possession of the new-comer, but she gave entirely that effect.

Sylvia, unable to meet Morrison's eyes, absorbed in the difficulty of the moment for her, unillumined by the byplay between her aunt and old Mr. Sommerville, strove for an appearance of vivacious loquacity, and cast into the conversation entirely disregarded bits of description of the fire. " Oh, Tantine, such an excitement!—we took nine men with hoes up such a steep——! " And finally Page, resisting old Mr. Sommerville's pull on his arm, was saying: " If luncheon is ready, and I'm invited, no more needs to be said. I've been haying and fire-fighting since seven this morning. A wolf is nothing compared with me." He looked across the heads of the three nearest him and called to Arnold: " Smith, you'll lend me some flannels, won't you? We must be much of the same build."

Mrs. Marshall-Smith turned, taking no pains to hide her satisfaction. She positively gloated over the crestfallen

Mr. Sommerville. " Sylvia, run quick and have Hélène smooth your hair. And call to Tojiko to put on an extra place for luncheon. Arnold, take Mr. Page up to your room, won't you, so that he——"

Sylvia, running up the stairs, heard her late companion protesting: " Oh, just for a change of clothes, only a minute—you needn't expect me to do any washing. I'm clean. I'm washed within an inch of my life—yellow soap—kitchen soap! "

" And our little scented toilet futilities," Morrison's cameo of small-talk carried to the upper hall. " What could they add to such a Spartan lustration? "

" Hurry, Hélène," said Sylvia. " It is late, and Mr. Page is dying of hunger."

In spite of the exhortation to haste, Hélène stopped short, uplifted brush in hand. " Mr. Page, the million-aire! " she exclaimed.

Sylvia blinked at her in the glass, amazed conjectures racing through her mind. But she had sufficient self-possession to say, carelessly as though his identity was nothing to her: " I don't know. It is the first time I have seen him. He certainly is not handsome."

Hélène thrust in the hairpins with impassioned haste and deftness, and excitedly snatched a lace jacket from a drawer. To the maid's despair Sylvia refused this adorn-ment, refused the smallest touch of rouge, refused an orna-ment in her hair. Hélène wrung her hands. " But see, Mademoiselle is not wise! For what good is it to be so savage! He is more rich than all! They say he owns all the State of Colorado! "

Sylvia, already in full retreat towards the dining-room, caught this last geographic extravagance of Gallic fancy, and laughed, and with this mirth still in her face made her re-entry on the veranda. She had not been away three minutes from the group there, and she was to the eye as merely flushed and gay when she came back as when she went away; but a revolution had taken place. Closely shut in her hand, she held, held fast, the key Hélène had thrust there. Behind her smile, her clear, bright look of valiant youth, a great many considerations were being revolved with extreme rapidity 1 y an extremely swift and active brain.

Swift and active as was the brain, it fairly staggered under the task of instantly rearranging the world according to the new pattern: for the first certainty to leap into sight was that the pattern was utterly changed by the events of the morning. She had left the house, betrayed, defenseless save for a barren dignity, and she had re-entered it in triumph, or at least with a valid appearance of triumph, an appearance which had already tided her over the aching difficulty of the first meeting with Morrison and might carry her . . . she had no time now to think how far.

Page and Arnold were still invisible when she emerged again on the veranda, and Mrs. Marshall-Smith pounced on her with the frankest curiosity. "Sylvia, do tell us— how in the world——"

Sylvia was in the midst of a description of the race to the fire, as vivid as she could make it, when Arnold saun- tered back and after him, in a moment, Page, astonishingly transformed by clothes. His height meant distinction now. Sylvia noted again his long, strong hands, his aquiline, tanned face and clear eyes, his thoughtful, observant eyes. There was a whimsical quirk of his rather thin but gentle lips which reminded her of the big bust of Emerson in her father's study. She liked all this; but her suspicious- ness, alert for affront, since the experience with Morrison, took offense at his great ease of manner. It had seemed quite natural and unaffected to her, in fact she had not at all noticed it before; but now that she knew of his great wealth, she instantly conceived a resentful idea that possibly it might come from the self-assurance of a man who knows himself much courted. She held her head high, gave to him as to Arnold a nod of careless recognition, and con- tinued talking: "Such a road—so steep—sand half-way to the hubs, such water-bars!" She turned to Morrison with her first overt recognition of the new status between them. "You ought to have seen your fiancée! She was wonderful! I was proud of her!"

Morrison nodded a thoughtful assent. "Yes, Molly's energy is irresistible," he commented, casting his remark in the form of a generalization the significance of which did not pass unnoticed by Sylvia's sharp ears. They were the first words he had spoken to her since his engagement.

"Luncheon is ready," said Mrs. Marshall-Smith. "Do come in." Every one by this time being genuinely hungry, and for various reasons extremely curious about the happenings back of Sylvia's appearance, the meal was dedicated frankly to eating, varied only by Sylvia's running account of the fire. "And then Molly wanted to take the fire-fighters home, and I offered to walk to have more room for them, and Mr. Page brought me up the other side of Hemlock and over the pass between Hemlock and Windward and down past Deer Cliff, home," she wound up, compressing into tantalizing brevity what was patently for her listeners by far the most important part of the expedition.

"Well, whatever route he took, it is astonishing that he knew the way to Lydford at all," commented Mrs. Marshall-Smith. "I don't believe you've been here before for years!" she said to Page.

"It's my confounded shyness," he explained, turning to Sylvia with a twinkle. "The grand, sophisticated ways of Lydford are too much for the nerves of a plain-living rustic like me. When I farm in Vermont the spirit of the place takes hold of me. I'm quite apt to eat my pie with my knife, and Lydford wouldn't like that."

Sylvia was aware, through the laughter which followed this joking remark, that there was an indefinable stir around the table. His turning to her had been pronounced. She took a sore pleasure in Morrison's eclipse. For the first time he was not the undisputed center of that circle. He accepted it gravely, a little preoccupied, a little absent, a wonderfully fine and dignified figure. Under her misanthropic exultation, Sylvia felt again and again the stab of her immense admiration for him, her deep affinity for his way of conducting life. Whatever place he might take in the circle around the luncheon table, she found him inevitably at the center of all her own thoughts. However it might seem to those evidently greatly struck with her extraordinary good luck, her triumph was in reality only the most pitiful of pretenses. But such as it was, and it gleamed richly enough on the eyes of the onlookers, she shook it out with a flourish and gave no sign of heartsick qualms. She gave a brilliantly undivided attention to the bit of local history Page was telling her, of a regiment of Green Mountain Boys who had gone down to the Battle of Bennington over the pass between Windward and Hemlock Mountain, and she was able to stir Page to enthusiasm by an appreciative comparison of their march with the splendid and affecting incident before Marathon, when the thousand hoplites from the little town of Platæa crossed the Cithæron range and went down to the plain to join the Athenians in their desperate stand.

"How do you *happen* to come East just now, anyhow?" inquired old Mr. Sommerville, resolutely shouldering his way into the conversation.

"My yellow streak!" affirmed his nephew. "Colorado got too much for me. And besides, I was overcome by an atavistic longing to do chores." He turned to Sylvia again, the gesture as unconscious and simple as a boy's. "My great-grandfather was a native of these parts, and about once in so often I revert to type."

"All my mother's people came from this region too," Sylvia said. She added meditatively, "And I think I must have reverted to type—up there on the mountain, this morning."

He looked at her silently, with softening eyes.

"You'll be going back soon, I suppose, as usual!" said old Mr. Sommerville with determination.

"To Colorado?" inquired Page. "No, I think—I've a notion I'll stay on this summer for some time. There is an experiment I want to try with alfalfa in Vermont."

Over his wineglass Arnold caught Sylvia's eye, and winked.

"Still reading as much as ever, I suppose." Mr. Sommerville was not to be put down. "When I last saw you, it was some fool socialistic poppycock about the iniquity of private exploitation of natural resources. How'd they ever have been exploited any other way I'd like to know! What's socialism? Organized robbery! Nothing else! 'Down with success! Down with initiative! Down with brains!' Stuff!"

"It's not socialism this time: it's Professor Merritt's theories on property," said Sylvia to the old gentleman, blandly ignoring his ignoring of her.

Page stared at her in astonishment. "Are you a clairvoyant?" he cried.

"No, no," she explained, laughing. "You took it out of your pocket up there by the brook."

"But you saw only the title. Merritt's name isn't on the cover."

"Oh, it's a pretty well-known book," said Sylvia easily. "And my father's a professor of Economics. When I was little I used to have books like that to build houses with, instead of blocks. And I've had to keep them in order and dusted ever since. I'm not saying that I know much about their insides."

"Just look there!" broke in Arnold. "Did I ever see a young lady pass up such a perfectly good chance to bluff!"

As usual nobody paid the least attention to his remark. The conversation shifted to a radical play which had been on the boards in Paris, the winter before.

After luncheon, they adjourned into the living-room. As the company straggled across the wide, dimly shining, deeply shaded hall, Sylvia felt her arm seized and held, and turning her head, looked into the laughing face of Arnold. "What kind of flowers does Judy like the best?" he inquired, the question evidently the merest pretext to detain her, for as the others moved out of earshot he said in a delighted whisper, his eyes gleaming in the dusk with amused malice: "Go it, Sylvia! Hit 'em out! It's worth enduring oceans of Greek history to see old Sommerville squirm. Molly gone—Morrison as poor as a church mouse; and now Page going fast before his very eyes——"

She shook off his hand with genuine annoyance. "I don't know what you're talking about, Arnold. You're horrid! Judith doesn't like cut flowers at all,—any kind. She likes them alive, on plants."

"She *would!*" Arnold was rapt in his habitual certainty that every peculiarity of Judith's was another reason for prostrate adoration. "I'll send her a window-box for every window in the hospital." His admiration overflowed to Judith's sister. He patted her on the shoulder. "You're all right too, Sylvia. You're batting about three-sixty, right now. I've always told the girls when they said Page was offish that if they could only get in under his guard once— and somehow you've done it. I bet on *you*——" He began to laugh at her stern face of reproof. "Oh, yes, yes, I agree! You don't know what I'm talking about! It's just alfalfa in Vermont! Only my low vulgarity to think anything else!" He moved away down the hall. "Beat it! I slope!"

"Where are you going?" she asked.

"Away! Away!" he answered. "Anywhere that's away. The air is rank with Oscar Wilde and the Renaissance. I feel them coming." Still laughing, he bounded upstairs, three steps at a time.

Sylvia stepped forward, crossed the threshold of the living-room, and paused by the piano, penetrated by bittersweet associations. If Morrison felt them also, he gave no sign. He had chosen a chair by a distant window and was devoting himself to Molly's grandfather, who accepted this delicate and entirely suitable attention with a rather glum face. Mrs. Marshall-Smith and Page still stood in the center of the room, and turned as Sylvia came in. "Do give us some music, Sylvia," said her aunt, sinking into a chair while Page came forward to sit near the piano.

Sylvia's fingers rested on the keys for a moment, her face very grave, almost somber, and then, as though taking a sudden determination, she began to play a Liszt Liebes-Traum. It was the last music Morrison had played to her before the beginning of the change. Into its fevered cadences she poured the quivering, astonished hurt of her young heart.

No one stirred during the music nor for the moment afterward, in which she turned about to face the room. She looked squarely at Morrison, who was rolling a cigarette with meticulous care, and as she looked, he raised his eyes and gave her across the room one deep, flashing glance of profound significance. That was all. That was enough. That was everything. Sylvia turned back to the piano shivering, hot and cold with secret joy. His look said, " Yes, of course, a thousand times of course, you are the one in my heart." What the facts said for him was, " But I am going to marry Molly because she has money."

Sylvia was horrified that she did not despise him, that she did not resent his entering her heart again with the intimacy of that look. Her heart ran out to welcome him back; but from the sense of furtiveness she shrank back with her lifetime habit and experience of probity, with the instinctive distaste for stealth engendered only by long and unbroken acquaintance with candor. With a mental action as definite as the physical one of freeing her feet from a quicksand she turned away from the alluring, dim possibility opened to her by that look. No, no! No stains, no smears, no shufflings! She was conscious of no moral impulse, in the usual sense of the word. Her imagination took in no possibility of actual wrong. But when, with a fastidious impulse of good taste, she turned her back on something ugly, she turned her back unwittingly on something worse than ugly.

But it was not easy! Oh, not at all easy! She quailed with a sense of her own weakness, so unexpected, so frightening. Would she resist it the next time? How pierced with helpless ecstasy she had been by that interchange of glances! What was there, in that world, by which she could steady herself?

"How astonishingly well you play," said Page, rousing himself from the dreamy silence of appreciation.

"I ought to," she said with conscious bitterness. "I earn my living by teaching music."

She was aware from across the room of an electric message from Aunt Victoria protesting against her perversity; and she reflected with a morose amusement that however delicately phrased Aunt Victoria's protests might be, its substance was the same as that of Hélène, crying out on her for not adding the soupçon of rouge. She took a sudden resolution. Well, why not? Everything conspired to push her in that direction. The few factors which did not were mere imbecile idealism, or downright hypocrisy. She drew a long breath. She smiled at Page, a smile of reference to something in common between them. "Shan't I play you some Beethoven?" she asked, "something with a legato passage and great solemn chords, and a silver melody binding the whole together?"

"Oh yes, do!" he said softly. And in a moment she was putting all of her intelligence, her training, and her capacity to charm into the tones of the E-flat Minuet.

CHAPTER XXIX

A HYPOTHETICAL LIVELIHOOD

THE millionaire proprietor had asked them all over o
the Austin Farm, and as they drew near the end of the
very expensive and delicately served meal which Page had
spoken of as a " picnic-lunch," various plans for the disposition of the afternoon were suggested. These suggestions were prefaced by the frank statement of the owner
of the place that whatever else the others did, it was his
own intention to take Miss Marshall through a part of
his pine plantations and explain his recent forestry operations to her. The assumption that Miss Marshall would
of course be interested in his pine plantations and lumbering operations struck nobody but Miss Marshall as queer.
With the most hearty and simple unconsciousness, they
unanimously felt that of course Miss Marshall *would* be
interested in the pine plantations and the lumbering operations of any man who was worth nobody knew how many
millions in coal, and who was so obviously interested in her.

Sylvia had been for some weeks observing the life about
her with very much disillusioned eyes and she now labeled
the feeling on the part of her friends with great accuracy,
saying to herself cynically, " If it were prize guinea-pigs or
collecting beer-steins, they would all be just as sure that I
would jump up and say, ' Oh yes, *do* show me, Mr.
Page!'" Following this moody reflection she immediately
jumped up and said enthusiastically, " Oh yes, *do* show
me, Mr. Page!" The brilliance in her eyes during these
weeks came partly from a relieved sense of escape from
a humiliating position, and partly from an amusement at
the quality of human nature which was as dubiously enjoy-
able as the grim amusement of biting on a sore tooth.

She now took her place by the side of their host, and thought, looking at his outdoor aspect, that her guess at what to wear had been better than Aunt Victoria's or Molly's. For the question of what to wear had been a burning one. Pressure had been put on her to don just a lacy, garden-party toilette of lawn and net as now automatically barred both Aunt Victoria and Molly from the proposed expedition to the woods. Nobody had had the least idea what was to be the color of the entertainment offered them, for the great significance of the affair was that it was the first time that Page had ever invited any one to the spot for which he evidently felt such an unaccountable affection. Aunt Victoria had explained to Sylvia, " It's always at the big Page estate in Lenox that he entertains, or rather that he gets his mother to do the absolutely indispensable entertaining for him." Morrison said laughingly : " Isn't it the very quintessence of quaintness to visit him there ! To watch his detached, whimsical air of not being in the least a part of all the magnificence which bears his name. He insists, you know, that he doesn't begin to know his way around that huge house ! " " It was his father who built the Lenox place," commented Mrs. Marshall-Smith. " It suited *his* taste to perfection. Austin seems to have a sort of Marie-Antoinette reaction towards a somewhat painfully achieved simplicity. He's not the man to take any sort of pose. If he were, it would be impossible not to suspect him of a little pose in his fondness for going back to his farmer great-grandfather's setting." Guided by this conversation, and by shrewd observations of her own, Sylvia had insisted, even to the point of strenuousness, upon wearing to this first housewarming a cloth skirt and coat, tempering the severity of this costume with a sufficiently feminine and beruffled blouse of silk. As their car had swung up before the plain, square, big-chimneyed old house, and Page had come to meet them, dressed in khaki-colored forester's garb, with puttees, Aunt Victoria had been generous enough to admit by an eye-flash to Sylvia

that the girl knew her business very well. There was not,
of course, Sylvia reflected, the slightest pretense of obscur-
ity between them as to what, under the circumstances, her
business was.

All this lay back of the fact that, as Sylvia, her face
bright with spontaneous interest in pine plantations and
lumbering operations, stepped to the side of the man in
puttees, her costume exactly suited his own.

From the midst of a daring and extremely becoming
arrangement of black and white striped chiffon and emerald-
green velvet, Molly's beautiful face smiled on them ap-
provingly. For various reasons, the spectacle afforded her
as much pleasure as it did extreme discomfort to her
grandfather, and with her usual masterful grasp on a situation she began to arrange matters so that the investigation
of pine plantations and lumber operations should be conducted *en tête-à-tête.* " Mrs. Marshall-Smith, you're going
to stay here, of course, to look at Austin's lovely view!
Think of his having hidden that view away from us all till
now! I want to go through the house later on, and without
Austin, so I can linger and pry if I like! I want to look
at every single thing. It's lovely—the completest Yankee
setting! It looks as though we all ought to have on clean
gingham aprons and wear steel-rimmed spectacles. No,
Austin, don't frown! I don't mean that for a knock. I
love it, honestly I do! I always thought I'd like to wear
clean gingham aprons myself. The only things that are
out of keeping are those shelves and shelves and shelves of
solemn books with such terrible titles!"

" That's a fact, Page," said Morrison, laughing. " Molly's
hit the nail squarely. Your modern, economic spasms over
the organization of industrialism are out of place in that
delightful, eighteenth century, plain old interior. They
threw *their* fits over theology!"

The owner of the house nodded. " Yes, you know your
period! A great-great-grandfather of mine, a ministerial
person, had left a lot of books on the nature of the Trinity
and Free Will and such. They had to be moved up to the

attic to make room for mine. What books will be on those shelves a hundred years from now, I wonder?"

"Treatises on psychic analysis, on how to transfer thought without words, unless I read the signs of the times wrong," Morrison hazarded a guess.

Molly was bored by this talk and anxious to get the walkers off. "You'd better be starting if you're going far up on the mountain, Austin. We have to be back for a tea at Mrs. Neville's, where Sylvia's to pour. Mrs. Neville would have a thing or two to say to us, if we made her lose her main drawing card."

"Are you coming, Morrison?" asked Page.

"No, he isn't," said Molly decidedly. "He's going to stay to play to me on that delicious tin-panny old harpsichordy thing in your 'best room.' You do call it the 'best room,' don't you? They always do in New England dialect stories. Grandfather, you have your cards with you, haven't you? You always have. If you'll get them out, Felix and Arnold and I'll play whist with you."

Only one of those thus laid hold of, slipped out from her strong little fingers. Arnold raised himself, joint by joint, from his chair, and announced that he was a perfect nuthead when it came to whist. "And, anyhow," he went on insistently, raising his voice as Molly began to order him back into the ranks—"And, anyhow, I don't want to play whist! And I do want to see what Page has been up to all this time he's kept so dark about his goings-on over here. No, Molly, you needn't waste any more perfectly good language on me. You can boss everybody else if you like, but I'm the original, hairy wild-man who gets what he wants."

He strolled off across the old-fashioned garden and out of the gate with the other two, his attention given as usual to lighting a cigarette. It was an undertaking of some difficulty on that day of stiff September wind which blew Sylvia's hair about her ears in bright, dancing flutters.

They were no more than out of earshot of the group left on the porch, than Sylvia, as so often happened in her growing acquaintanceship with Page, found herself obliged entirely to reconstruct an impression of him. It was with anything but a rich man's arrogant certainty of her interest that he said, very simply as he said everything: " I appreciate very much, Miss Marshall, your being willing to come along and see all this. It's a part of your general kindness to everybody. I hope it won't bore you to extremity. I'm so heart and soul in it myself, I shan't know when to stop talking about it In fact I shan't want to stop, even if I know I should. I've never said much about it to any one before, and I very much want your opinion on it."

Sylvia felt a decent pinch of shame, and her eyes were not brilliant with sardonic irony but rather dimmed with self-distrust as she answered with a wholesome effort for honesty: " I really don't know a single thing about forestry, Mr. Page. You'll have to start in at the very beginning, and explain everything. I hope I've sense enough to take an intelligent interest." Very different, this, from the meretricious sparkle of her, " Oh yes, do show me, Mr. Page." She felt that to be rather cheap, as she remembered it. She wondered if he had seen its significance, had seen through her. From a three weeks' intensive acquaintance with him, she rather thought he had. His eyes were clear, formidably so. He put her on her mettle.

Arnold had lighted his cigarette by this time, offered one to Page with his incurable incapacity to remember that not every sane man smokes, and on being refused, put his hands deep in his pockets. The three tall young people were making short work of the stretch of sunny, windy, upland pasture, and were already almost in the edge of the woods which covered the slope of the mountain above them up to the very crest, jewel-green against the great, piled, cumulus clouds.

" Well, I will begin at the beginning, then," said Page. " I'll begin back in 1762, when this valley was settled and my ever-so-many-greats-grandfather took possession of a big slice of this side of Hemlock Mountain, with the sole idea that trees were men's enemies. The American colo-

nists thought of forests, you know, as places for Indians
to lurk, spots that couldn't be used for corn, growths to
be exterminated as fast as possible."

They entered the woods now, walking at a good pace up
the steeply rising, grass-grown wood-road. Sylvia quite
consciously summoned all her powers of attention and concentration for the hour before her, determined to make a
good impression to counteract whatever too great insight
her host might have shown in the matter of ner first interest. She bent her fine brows with the attention she
had so often summoned to face a difficult final examination, to read at the correct tempo a complicated piece of
music, to grasp the essentials of a new subject. Her
trained interest in understanding things, which of late had
been feeding on rather moldy scraps of cynical psychology,
seized with energy and delight on a change of diet. She
not only tried to be interested. Very shortly she was interested, absorbed, intent. What Page had to say fascinated her. She even forgot who he was, and that he was
immensely rich. Though this forgetfulness was only momentary it was an unspeakable relief and refreshment to
her.

She listened intently; at times she asked a pertinent
question; as she walked she gave the man an occasional
direct survey, as impersonal as though he were a book
from which she was reading. And exactly as an intelligent reader, in a first perusal of a new subject, snatches
the heart out of paragraph after paragraph, ignoring the
details until later, she took to herself only the gist of her
host's recital. Yes, yes, she saw perfectly the generations
of Vermont farmers who had hated trees because they
meant the wilderness, and whose destruction of forests was
only limited by the puniness of the forces they matched
against the great wooded slopes of the mountains they
pre-empted. And she saw later, the long years of utter
neglect of those hacked-at and half-destroyed forests while
Page's grandfather and father descended on the city and on
financial operations with the fierce, fresh energy of fron-

tiersmen. She was struck by the fact that those ruthless victors of Wall Street had not sold the hundreds of worthless acres, which they never took the trouble to visit; and by the still more significant fact that as the older ones of the family died, the Austins, the Pages, the Woolsons, the Hawkers, and as legacy after legacy of more worthless mountain acres came by inheritance to the financiers, those tracts too were never sold. They never thought of them, Page told her, except grumblingly to pay the taxes on them; they considered them of ridiculously minute proportions compared to their own titanic manipulations, but they had never sold them. Sylvia saw them vividly, those self-made exiles from the mountains, and felt in them some unacknowledged loyalty to the soil, the barren soil which had borne them, some inarticulate affection which had lived through the heat and rage of their embattled lives. The taproot had been too deep for them to break off, and now from it there was springing up this unexpected stem, this sole survivor of their race who turned away from what had been the flaming breath of life in their brazen nostrils, back to the green fragrance of their mutilated and forgotten forests.

Not the least of the charm of this conception for Sylvia came from the fact that she quarried it out for herself from the bare narration presented to her, that she read it not at all in the words, but in the voice, the face, the manner of the raconteur. She was amused, she was touched, she was impressed by his studiously matter-of-fact version of his enterprise. He put forward with the shy, prudish shamefacedness of the New Englander the sound financial basis of his undertaking, as its main claim on his interest, as its main value. " I heard so much about forestry being nothing but a rich man's plaything," he said. " I just got my back up, and wanted to see if it couldn't be made a paying thing. And I've proved it can be. I've had the closest account kept of income and outgo, and so far from being a drain on a man to reforest his woodland and administer it as he should, there's an actual profit in it, enough to make a business of it, enough to occupy a man for his lifetime and his son after him, if he gives it his personal care."

At this plain statement of a comprehensible fact, Arnold's inattention gave place to a momentary interest. "Is there?" he asked with surprise. "How much?"

"Well," said Page, "my system, as I've gradually worked it out, is to clear off a certain amount each year of our mediocre woodland, such as for the most part grows up where the bad cutting was done a couple of generations ago—maple and oak and beech it is, mostly, with little stands of white birch, where fires have been. I work that up in my own sawmill so as to sell as little of a raw product as possible; and dispose of it to the wood-working factories in the region." (Sylvia remembered the great "brush-back factory" whence Molly had recruited her fire-fighters.) "Then I replant that area to white pine. That's the best tree for this valley. I put about a thousand trees to the acre. Or if there seems to be a good prospect of natural reproduction, I try for that. There's a region over there, about a hundred acres," he waved his hand to the north of them, "that's thick with seedling ash. I'm leaving that alone. But for the most part, white pine's our best lay. Pine thrives on soil that stunts oak and twists beech. Our oak isn't good quality, and maple is such an interminably slow grower. In about twenty years from planting, you can make your first, box-board cutting of pine, and every ten years thereafter——"

Arnold had received this avalanche of figures and species with an astonished blink, and now protested energetically that he had had not the slightest intention of precipitating any such flood. "Great Scott, Page, catch your breath! If you're talking to me, you'll have to use English, anyhow. I've no more idea what you're talking about! Who do you take me for? *I* don't know an ash-tree from an ash-cart. You started in to tell me what the profit of the thing is."

Page looked pained but patient, like a reasonable man

who knows his hobby is running away with him, but who cannot bring himself to use the curb. "Oh yes," he said apologetically. "Why, we cleared last year (exclusive of the farm, which yields a fair profit)—we cleared about two thousand dollars." Arnold seemed to regard this statement as quite the most ridiculous mouse which ever issued from a mountain. He burst into an open laugh. "Almost enough to buy you a new car a year, isn't it?" he commented.

Page looked extremely nettled. An annoyed flush showed through the tan of his clear skin. He was evidently very touchy about his pet lumbering operations. "A great many American families consider that a sufficient income," he said stiffly.

Sylvia had another inspiration, such as had been the genesis of her present walking-costume. "You're too silly, Arnold. The important thing isn't what the proportion with Mr. Page's own income is! What he was trying to do, and what he *has* done, only you don't know enough to see it, is to prove that sane forestry is possible for forest-owners of small means. I know, if you don't, that two thousand is plenty to live on. My father's salary is only twenty-four hundred now, and we were all brought up when it was two thousand."

She had had an intuitive certainty that this frank revelation would please Page, and she was rewarded by an openly ardent flash from his clear eyes. There was in his look at her an element of enchanted, relieved recognition, as though he had nodded and said: "Oh, you *are* my kind of a woman after all! I was right about you."

Arnold showed by a lifted eyebrow that he was conscious of being put down, but he survived the process with his usual negligent obliviousness of reproof. "Well, if two thousand a year produced Judith, go ahead, Page, and my blessing on you!" He added in a half-apology for his offensive laughter, "It just tickled me to hear a man who owns most of several counties of coal-mines so set up over finding a nickel on the street!"

Page had regained his geniality. " Well, Smith, maybe I
needn't have jumped so when you stepped on my toe. But
it's my pet toe, you see. You're quite right—I'm everlastingly set up over my nickel. But it's not because I
found it. It's because I earned it. It happens to be the
only nickel I ever earned. It's natural I should want it
treated with respect."

Arnold did not trouble to make any sense out of this
remark, and Sylvia was thinking bitterly to herself : " But
that's pure bluff ! I'm *not* his kind of a woman. I'm
Felix Morrison's kind ! " No comment, therefore, was
made on the quaintness of the rich man's interest in earning capacity.

They were now in one of the recent pine plantations,
treading a wood-road open to the sky, running between
acres and acres of thrifty young pines. Page's eyes glist-
ened with affection as he looked at them, and with the un-
wearied zest of the enthusiast he continued expanding on
his theme. Sylvia knew the main outline of her new
subject now, felt that she had walked all around it, and was
agreeably surprised at her sympathy with it. She continued with a genuine curiosity to extract more details ;
and like any man who talks of a process which he knows
thoroughly, Page was wholly at the mercy of a sympathetic
listener. His tongue tripped itself in his readiness to answer, to expound, to tell his experiences, to pour out a
confidently accurate and precise flood of information. Sylvia began to take a playful interest in trying to find a weak
place in his armor, to ask a question he could not answer.
But he knew all the answers. He knew the relative weight
per cubic foot of oak and pine and maple ; he knew the
railroad rates per ton on carload lots ; he knew why it is
cheaper in the long run to set transplants in sod-land
instead of seeding it ; he knew what per cent to write off
for damage done by the pine weevil, he reveled in complicated statistics as to the actual cost per thousand for chop-
ping, skidding, drawing, sawing logs. He laughed at
Sylvia's attempts to best him, and in return beat about her

ears with statistics for timber cruising, explained the variations of the Vermont and the scribner's decimal log rule, and recited log-scaling tables as fluently as the multiplication table. They were in the midst of this lively give-and-take, listened to with a mild amusement on Arnold's part, when they emerged on a look-out ledge of gray slate, and were struck into silence by the grave loveliness of the immense prospect below them.

"—and of course," murmured Page finally, on another note, " of course it's rather a satisfaction to feel that you are making waste land of use to the world, and helping to protect the living waters of all that——" He waved his hand over the noble expanse of sunlit valley. " It seems "—he drew a long breath—" it seems something quite worth doing."

Sylvia was moved to a disinterested admiration for him; and it was a not unworthy motive which kept her from looking up to meet his eyes on her. She felt a petulant distaste for the calculating speculations which filled the minds of all her world about his intentions towards her. He was really too fine for that. At least, she owed it to her own dignity not to abuse this moment of fine, impersonal emotion to advance another step into intimacy with him.

But as she stood, looking fixedly down at the valley, she was quite aware that a sympathetic silence and a thoughtful pose might make, on the whole, an impression quite as favorable as the most successfully managed meeting of eyes.

CHAPTER XXX

ARNOLD CONTINUES TO DODGE THE RENAISSANCE

A CAUNT roaming figure of ennui and restlessness, Arnold appeared at the door of the pergola and with a petulant movement tore a brilliant autumn leaf to pieces as he lingered for a moment, listening moodily to the talk within. He refused with a grimace the chair to which Sylvia motioned him. "Lord, no! Hear 'em go it!" he said quite audibly and turned away to lounge back towards the house. Sylvia had had time to notice, somewhat absently, that he looked ill, as though he had a headache.

Mrs. Marshall-Smith glanced after him with misgiving, and, under cover of a brilliantly resounding passage at arms between Morrison and Page, murmured anxiously to Sylvia, "I wish Judith would give up her nonsense and *marry* Arnold!"

"Oh, they've only been engaged a couple of months," said Sylvia. "What's the hurry! She'll get her diploma in January. It'd be a pity to have her miss!"

Arnold's stepmother broke in rather impatiently, "If I were a girl engaged to Arnold, I'd *marry* him!"

"—the trouble with all you connoisseurs, Morrison, is that you're barking up the wrong tree. You take for granted, from your own tastes, when people begin to buy jade Buddhas and Zuloaga bull-fighters that they're wanting to surround themselves with beauty. Not much! It's the consciousness of money they want to surround themselves with!"

Morrison conceded part of this. "Oh, I grant you, there's a disheartening deal of imitation in this matter. But

America's new to æsthetics. Don't despise beginnings because they're small!"

"A nettle leaf is small. But that's not the reason why it won't ever grow into an oak. Look here! A sheaf of winter grasses, rightly arranged in clear glass, has as much of the essence of beauty as a bronze vase of the Ming dynasty. I ask you just one question, How many people do you know who are capable of——"

The art-critic broke in: "Oh come! You're setting up an impossibly high standard of æsthetic feeling."

"I'm not presuming to do any such thing as setting up a standard! I'm just insisting that people who can't extract joy from the shadow pattern of a leafy branch on a gray wall, are liars if they claim to enjoy a fine Japanese print. What they enjoy in the print is the sense that they've paid a lot for it. In my opinion, there's no use trying to advance a step towards any sound æsthetic feeling till *some* step is taken away from the idea of cost as the criterion of value about anything." He drew a long breath and went on, rather more rapidly than was his usual habit of speech: "I've a real conviction on that point. It's come to me of late years that one reason we haven't any national art is because we have too much magnificence. All our capacity for admiration is used up on the splendor of palace-like railway stations and hotels. Our national tympanum is so deafened by that blare of sumptuousness that we have no ears for the still, small voice of beauty. And perhaps," he paused, looking down absently at a crumb he rolled between his thumb and finger on the table, "it's possible that the time is ripening for a wider appreciation of another kind of beauty . . . that has little to do even with such miracles as the shadow of a branch on a wall."

Morrison showed no interest in this vaguely phrased hypothesis, and returned to an earlier contention: "You underestimate," he said, "the amount of education and taste and time it takes to arrange that simple-looking vase of grasses, to appreciate your leaf-shadows."

"All I'm saying is that your campaign of æsthetic education hasn't made the matter vital enough to people, to any people, not even to people who call themselves vastly æsthetic, so that they *give* time and effort and self-schooling to the acquisition of beauty. They not only want their money to do their dirty work for them, they try to make it do their fine living for them too, with a minimum of effort on their part. They want to *buy* beauty, outright, with cash, and have it stay put, where they can get their fingers on it at any time, without bothering about it in the meantime. That's the way a Turk likes his women—same impulse exactly."

"I've known a few Caucasians too . . .," Mrs. Marshall-Smith contributed a barbed point of malice to the talk.

Page laughed, appreciating her hit. "Oh, I mean Turk as a generic term." Sylvia, circling warily about the contestants, looking for a chance to make her presence felt, without impairing the masculine gusto with which they were monopolizing the center of the stage, tossed in a suggestion, "Was it Hawthorne's—it's a queer fancy like Hawthorne's—the idea of the miser, don't you remember, whose joy was to roll naked in his gold pieces?"

Page snatched up with a delighted laugh the metaphor she had laid in his hand. "Capital! Precisely! There's the thing in a nutshell. We twentieth century Midases have got beyond the simple taste of that founder of the family for the shining yellow qualities of money, but we love to wallow in it none the less. We like to put our feet on it, in the shape of rugs valued according to their cost, we like to eat it in insipid, out-of-season fruit and vegetables."

"Doesn't it occur to you," broke in Morrison, "that you may be attacking something that's a mere phase, an incident of transition?"

"Is anything ever anything else!" Page broke in to say.

Morrison continued, with a slight frown at the interruption, "America is simply emerging from the frontier condition of bareness, and it is only natural that one, or per-

haps two generations must be sacrificed in order to attain
a smooth mastery of an existence charged and enriched
with possession." He gave the effect of quoting a paragraph from one of his lectures.

"Isn't the end of that 'transition,'" inquired Page,
"usually simply that after one or two generations people
grow dulled to everything *but* possession and fancy themselves worthily occupied when they spend their lives regu-
lating and caring for their possessions. I hate," he cried
with sudden intensity, "I hate the very sound of the
word!"

"Does you great credit, I'm sure," said Morrison, with a
faint irony, a hidden acrimony, pricking, for an instant, an
ugly ear through his genial manner.

Ever since the day of the fire, since Page had become a
more and more frequent visitor in Lydford and had seen
more and more of Sylvia, she had derived a certain
amount of decidedly bad-tasting amusement from the fact
of Morrison's animosity to the other man. But this was
going too far. She said instantly, "Do you know, I've just
thought what it is you all remind me of—I mean Lydford
and the beautiful clothes, and nobody bothering about anything but tea and ideas and knowing the right people. I
knew it made me think of something else, and now I know—
it's a Henry James novel!"

Page took up her lead instantly, and said gravely, putting himself beside her as another outsider: "Well, of
course, that's their ideal. That's what they *try* to be like
—at least to talk like James people. But it's not always
easy. The vocabulary is so limited."

"Limited!" cried Mrs. Marshall-Smith. "There are
more words in a Henry James novel than in any dic-
tionary!"

"Oh yes, *words* enough!" admitted Page, "but all about
the same sort of thing. It reminds me of the seminarist
in Rome, who have to use Latin for everything. They can
manage predestination and vicarious atonement like a shot,
but when it comes to ordering somebody to call them for

the six-twenty train to Naples they're lost. Now, you can talk about your bric-à-brac in Henry-Jamesese, you can take away your neighbor's reputation by subtle suggestion, you can appreciate a fine deed of self-abnegation, if it's not too definite! I suppose a man could even make an attenuated sort of love in the lingo, but I'll be hanged if I see how anybody could order a loaf of bread."

"One might do without bread, possibly?" suggested Morrison, pressing the tips of his beautiful fingers together.

"By Jove," cried Page, in hearty assent, "I've a notion that lots of times they do!"

This was getting nowhere. Mrs. Marshall-Smith put her hand to the helm, and addressed herself to Morrison with a plain reminder of the reason for the grotesqueness of his irritability. "Where's *Molly* keeping herself nowadays?" she inquired. "She hasn't come over with you, to tea, for ever so long. The pergola isn't itself without her sunny head."

"Molly is a grain of sand in a hurricane, nowadays," said Morrison seriously. "It seems that the exigencies of divine convention decree that a girl who is soon to be married belongs neither to herself, to her family, to her fiancé—oh, least of all to her fiancé—but heart and soul and body to a devouring horde of dressmakers and tailors and milliners and hairdressers and corsetières and petticoat specialists and jewelers and hosiery experts and——"

They were all laughing at the interminable defile of words proceeding with a Spanish gravity, and Mrs. Marshall-Smith broke in, "I don't hear anything about house-furnishers."

"No," said Morrison, "the house-furnisher's name is F. Morrison, and he has no show until after the wedding."

"What *are* your plans?" asked Mrs. Marshall-Smith.

"Nothing very definite except the great Date. That's fixed for the twenty-first."

"Oh, so soon . . . less than three weeks from now!"

Morrison affected to feel a note of disapproval in her

voice, and said with his faint smile, " You can hardly blame me for not wishing to delay."

" Oh, no *blame!* " she denied his inference. " After all it's over a month since the engagement was announced, and who knows how much longer before that you and Molly knew about it. No. I'm not one who believes in long engagements. The shorter the better."

Sylvia saw an opportunity to emerge with an appearance of ease from a silence that might seem ungracious. It was an enforced manœuver with which the past weeks had made her wearily familiar. " Aunt Victoria's hitting at Arnold and Judith over your head," she said to Morrison. " It's delicious, the way Tantine shows herself, for all her veneer of modernity, entirely nineteen century in her impatience of Judith's work. Now that there's a chance to escape from it into the blessed haven of idle matrimony, she can't see why Judith doesn't give up her lifetime dream and marry Arnold tomorrow."

Somewhat to her surprise, her attempt at playfulness had no notable success. The intent of her remarks received from her aunt and Morrison the merest formal recognition of a hasty, dim smile, and with one accord they looked at once in another direction. " And after the wedding? " Mrs. Marshall-Smith inquired—" or is that a secret? "

" Oh no, when one belongs to Molly's exalted class or is about to be elevated into it, nothing is secret. I'm quite sure that the society editor of the *Herald* knows far better than I the names of the hotels in Jamaica we're to frequent."

" Oh! Jamaica! How . . . how . . . original! " Mrs. Marshall-Smith cast about her rather desperately for a commendatory adjective.

" Yes, quite so, isn't it? " agreed Morrison. " It's Molly's idea. She *is* original, you know. It's one of her greatest charms. She didn't want to go to Europe because there is so much to see there, to do. She said she wanted a honeymoon and not a personally conducted trip."

They all laughed again, and Sylvia said: " How *like*

Molly! How clever! Nobody does her thinking for
her!"

"The roads in Jamaica are excellent for motoring, too,
I hear," added Morrison. "That's another reason, of
course."

Page gave a great laugh. "Well, as Molly's cousin, let
me warn you! Molly driving a car in Jamaica will be like
Pavlova doing a bacchante on the point of a needle! You'll
have to keep a close watch on her to see that she doesn't
absentmindedly dash across the island and jump off the
bank right on into the ocean."

"Where does F. Morrison, house-furnishing-expert, come
in?" asked Mrs. Marshall-Smith.

"After the wedding, after Jamaica," said Morrison.
"We're to come back to New York and for a few months
impose on the good nature of Molly's grandfather's household, while we struggle with workmen *et al.* The Montgomery house on Fifth Avenue, that's shut up for so many
years,—ever since the death of Molly's parents,—is the one
we've settled on. It's very large, you know. It has possibilities. I have a plan for remodeling it and enlarging it
with a large inner court, glass-roofed—something slightly
Saracenic about the arches—and what is now a suite of
old-fashioned parlors on the north side is to be made into
a long gallery. There'll be an excellent light for paintings.
I've secured from Duveen a promise for some tapestries I've
admired for a long time--Beauvais, not very old, Louis
XVII—but excellent in color. Those for the staircase . . ."

He spoke with no more animation than was his custom,
with no more relish than was seemly; his carefully chosen
words succeeded each other in their usual exquisite precision, no complacency showed above the surface; his attitude
was, as always, composed of precisely the right proportion
of dignity and ease; but as he talked, some untarnished instinct in Sylvia shrank away in momentary distaste, the
first she had ever felt for him.

Mrs. Marshall-Smith evidently did not at all share this
feeling. "Oh, what a house that will be!" she cried, lost

in forecasting admiration. "*You!* with a free hand! A second house of Jacques Cœur!" Sylvia stood up, rather abruptly. "I think I'll go for a walk beside the river," she said, reaching for her parasol.

"May I tag along?" said Page, strolling off beside her with the ease of familiarity.

Sylvia turned to wave a careless farewell to the two thus left somewhat unceremoniously in the pergola. She was in brown corduroy with suède leather sailor collar and broad belt, a costume which brought out vividly the pure, clear coloring of her face. "Good-bye," she called to them with a pointedly casual accent, nodding her gleaming head.

"She's a *very* pretty girl, isn't she?" commented Mrs. Marshall-Smith. Morrison, looking after the retreating figures, agreed with her briefly. "Yes, very. Extraordinarily perfect specimen of her type." His tone was dry.

Mrs. Marshall-Smith looked with annoyance across the stretch of lawn to the house. "I think I would better go to see where Arnold is," she said. Her tone seemed to signify more to the man than her colorless words. He frowned and said, "Oh, is Arnold . . .?"

She gave a fatigued gesture. "No—not yet—but for the last two or three days . . ."

He began impatiently, "Why can't you get him off this time before he . . ."

"An excellent idea," she broke in, with some impatience of her own. "But slightly difficult of execution."

CHAPTER XXXI

SYLVIA MEETS WITH PITY

UNDER the scarlet glory of frost-touched maples, beside
the river strolled Sylvia, conscious of looking very well and
being admired; but contrary to the age-old belief about her
sex and age, the sensation of looking very well and being
admired by no means filled the entire field of her consciousness. In fact, the corner occupied by the sensation was so
small that occasional efforts on her part to escape to it from
the less agreeable contents of her mind were lamentable
failures. Aloud, in terms as felicitous as she could make
them, she was commenting on the beauty of the glass-smooth
river, with the sumptuously colored autumn trees casting
down into it the imperial gold and crimson of their reflections. Silently she was struggling to master and dominate
and suppress a confusion of contradictory mental processes.
At almost regular intervals, like a hollow stroke on a brazen
gong, her brain resounded to the reverberations of " The
wedding is on the twenty-first." And each time that she
thrust that away, there sprang up with a faint hissing note
of doubt and suspicion, " Why does Aunt Victoria want
Arnold married? " A murmur, always drowned out but incessantly recurring, ran: " What about Father and Mother?
What about their absurd, impossible, cruel, unreal, and
beautiful standards? " Contemptible little echoes from the
silly self-consciousness of the adolescence so recently left
behind her . . . " I must think of something clever to say.
I must try to seem different and original and independent
and yet must attract," mingled with an occasional fine sincerity of appreciation and respect for the humanity of the
man beside her. Like a perfume borne in gusts came reaction to the glorious color about her. Quickly recurring

and quickly gone, a sharp cymbal-clap of alarm . . .
"What shall I do if Austin Page now . . . today . . . or
tomorrow . . . tells me . . . !" And grotesquely, the companion cymbal on which this smote, gave forth an antiph-
onal alarm of, "What shall I do if he does not!" While,
unheard of her conscious ear, but coloring everything with
its fundamental note of sincerity, rose solemnly from the
depths of her heart the old cry of desperate youth, "What
am I to do with my life?"

No, the eminently successful brown corduroy, present
though it was to the mind of the handsome girl wearing it,
was hardly the sure and sufficient rock of refuge which tradition would have had it.

With an effort she turned her attention from this confused tumult in her ears, and put out her hand, rather at
random, for an introduction to talk. "You spoke, back there
in the pergola, of another kind of beauty—I didn't know
what you meant." He answered at once, with his usual
direct simplicity, which continued to have for Sylvia at this
period something suspiciously like the calmness of a reigning sovereign who is above being embarrassed, who may
speak, without shamefacedness, of anything, even of moral
values, that subject tabu in sophisticated conversation.
"Ah, just a notion of mine that perhaps all this modern
ferment of what's known as 'social conscience' or 'civic
responsibility,' isn't a result of the sense of duty, but of the
old, old craving for beauty."

Sylvia looked at him, astonished. "Beauty?"

"Why yes, beauty isn't only a matter of line and color, is
it? There's the desire for harmony, for true proportions,
for grace and suavity, for nobility of movement. Perhaps
the lack of those qualities is felt in human lives as much
as on canvases . . . at least perhaps it may be felt in the
future."

"It's an interesting idea," murmured Sylvia, "but I don't
quite see what it means, concretely, as applied to our actual
America."

He meditated, looking, as was his habit when walking, up

at the trees above them. " Well, let's see. I think I mean
that perhaps our race, not especially inspired in its instinct
for color and external form, may possibly be fumbling
toward an art of living. Why wouldn't it be an art to keep
your life in drawing as well as a mural decoration?" He
broke off to say, laughing, " I bet you the technique would
be quite as difficult to acquire," and went on again, thoughtfully: " In this modern maze of terrible closeness of inter-
relation, to achieve a life that's happy and useful and causes
no undeserved suffering to the untold numbers of other
lives which touch it—isn't there an undertaking which needs
the passion for harmony and proportion? Isn't there a
beauty as a possible ideal of aspiration for a race that probably never could achieve a Florentine or Japanese beauty
of line?" He cast this out casually, as an idea which had
by chance been brought up to the top by the current of the
talk, and showed no indication to pursue it further when
Sylvia only nodded her head. It was one of the moments
when she heard nothing but the brazen clangor of " the
wedding is on the twenty-first," and until the savage con-
striction around her heart had relaxed she had not breath
to speak. But that passed again, and the two sauntered
onward, in the peaceable silence which was one of the great
new pleasures which Page was able to give her. It now
seemed like a part of the mellow ripeness of the day.

They had come to a bend in the slowly flowing river,
where, instead of torch-bright maples and poplars, rank upon
rank of somber pines marched away to the summit of a
steeply ascending foothill. The river was clouded dark with
their melancholy reflections. On their edge, overhanging
the water, stood a single sumac, a standard-bearer with a
thousand little down-drooping flags of crimson.

"Oh," said Sylvia, smitten with admiration. She sat
down on a rock partly because she wanted to admire at her
leisure, partly because she was the kind of a girl who looks
well sitting on a rock; and as she was aware of this latter
motive, she felt a qualm of self-scorn. What a cheap vein
of commonness was revealed in her—in every one—by the

temptation of a great fortune! Morrison had succumbed entirely. She was nowadays continually detecting in herself motives which made her sick.

Page stretched his great length on the dry leaves at her feet. Any other man would have rolled a cigarette. It was one of his oddities that he never smoked. Sylvia looked down at his thoughtful, clean face and reflected wonderingly that he seemed the only person not warped by money. Was it because he had it, or was it because he was a very unusual person?

He was looking partly at the river, at the pines, at the flaming tree, and partly at the human embodiment of the richness and color of autumn before him. After a time Sylvia said: " There's Cassandra. She's the only one who knows of the impending doom. She's trying to warn the pines." It had taken her some moments to think of this.

Page accepted it with no sign that he considered it anything remarkable, with the habit of a man for whom people produced their best: " She's using some very fine language for her warning, but like some other fine language it's a trifle misapplied. She forgets that no doom hangs over the pines. *She's* the fated one. They're safe enough."

Sylvia clasped her hands about her knees and looked across the dark water at the somber trees. " And yet they don't seem to be very cheerful about it." It was her opinion that they were talking very cleverly.

" Perhaps," suggested Page, rolling over to face the river—" perhaps she's not prophesying doom at all, but blowing a trumpet-peal of exultation over her own good fortune. The pines may be black with envy of her."

Sylvia enjoyed this rather macabre fancy with all the zest of healthful youth, secure in the conviction of its own immortality. " Yes, yes, life's ever so much harder than death."

Page dissented with a grave irony from the romantic exaggeration of this generalization. " I don't suppose the statistics as to the relative difficulty of life and death are really very reliable."

Sylvia perceived that she was being, ever so delicately, laughed at, and tried to turn her remark so that she could carry it off. " Oh, I don't mean for those who die, but those who are left know something about it, I imagine. My mother always said that the encounter with death is the great turning-point in the lives of those who live on. She said you might miss everything else irrevocable and vital—falling in love, having children, accomplishing anything—but that sooner or later you have to reckon with losing somebody dear to you." She spoke with an academic interest in the question.

" I should think," meditated Page, taking the matter into serious consideration, " that the vitalness of even that experience would depend somewhat on the character undergoing it. I've known some temperaments of a proved frivolity which seemed to have passed through it without any great modifications. But then I know nothing about it personally. I lost my father before I could remember him, and since then I haven't happened to have any close encounter with such loss. My mother, you know, is very much alive."

" Well, I haven't any personal experience with death in my immediate circle either," said Sylvia. " But I wasn't brought up with the usual cult of the awfulness of it. Father was always anxious that we children should feel it something as natural as breathing—you are dipped up from the great river of consciousness, and death only pours you back. If you've been worth living, there are more elements of fineness in humanity."

Page nodded. " Yes, that's what they all say nowadays. Personal immortality is as out of fashion as big sleeves."

" Do you believe it?" asked Sylvia, seeing the talk take an intimate turn, " or are you like me, and don't know at all what you do believe?" If she had under this pseudo-philosophical question a veiled purpose analogous to that of the less subtle charmer whose avowed expedient is to get " a man to talk about himself " the manœuver was eminently successful.

"I've never had the least chance to think about it," he said, sitting up, "because I've always been so damnably beset by the facts of living. I know I am not the first of my race to feel convinced that his own problems are the most complicated, but . . ."

"*Yours!*" cried Sylvia, genuinely astonished.

"And one of the hardships of my position," he told her at once with a playful bitterness, "is that everybody refuses to believe in the seriousness of it. Because my father, after making a great many bad guesses as to the possible value of mining stock in Nevada, happened to make a series of good guesses about the value of mining stock in Colorado, it is assumed that all questions are settled for me, that I can joyously cultivate my garden, securely intrenched in the certainty that this is the best possible of all possible worlds."

"Oh yes—labor unions—socialism—I. W. W.," Sylvia murmured vaguely, unable, in spite of her intelligence, to refrain from marking, by a subsidence of interest, her instinctive feeling that those distant questions could not in the nature of things be compared to present, personal complications.

"No—no—!" he protested. "That's no go! I've tried for five years now to shove it out of sight on some one of those shelves. I've learned all the arguments on both sides. I can discuss on both sides of those names as glibly as any other modern quibbler. I can prove the rights of all those labels or I can prove the wrongs of them, according to the way my dinner is digesting. What stays right there, what I never can digest (if you'll pardon an inelegant simile that's just occurred to me), a lump I never can either swallow entirely down or get up out of my throat, is the fact that there are men, hundreds of men, thousands of men, working with picks underground all day, every day, all their lives, and that part of their labor goes to provide me with the wherewithal to cultivate my taste, to pose as a patron of the arts, to endow promising pianists—to go through all the motions suitable to that position to which it has pleased 'rovidence to call me. It sticks in my crop that my only connection with the entire business was to give myself the trouble to be born my father's son."

" But you *do* work!" protested Sylvia. " You work on your farm here. You run all sorts of lumbering operations in this region. The first time I saw you, you certainly looked less like the traditional idea of a predatory coal-operator." She laughed at the recollection.

" Oh yes, I work. When my undigested lump gets too painful I try to work it off—but what I do bears the same relation to real sure-enough work that playing tennis does to laying brick. But such as it is, it's real satisfaction I get out of my minute Vermont holdings. They come down to me from my farmer great-grandfather who held the land by working it himself. There's no sore spot there. But speak of Colorado or coal—and you see me jump with the same shooting twinge you feel when the dentist's probe reaches a nerve. An intelligent conscience is a luxury a man in my position can't afford to have." He began with great accuracy to toss small stones at a log showing above the surface of the water.

Sylvia, reverting to a chance remark, now said: " I never happened to hear you speak of your mother before. Does she ever come to Lydford?"

He shook his head. " No, she vibrates between the Madison Avenue house and the Newport one. She's very happy in those two places. She's Mr. Sommerville's sister, you know. She's one of Morrison's devotees too. She collects under his guidance."

" Collects?" asked Sylvia, a little vaguely.

" Oh, it doesn't matter much what—the instinct, the resultant satisfaction are the same. As a child, it's stamps, or buttons, or corks, later on—— As a matter of fact, it's lace that my mother collects. She specializes in Venetian lace—the older the better, of course. The connection with coal-mines is obvious. But after all, her own fortune, coming mostly from the Sommerville side, is derived from oil. The difference is great!"

"Do you live with her?" asked Sylvia.

"My washing is said to be done in New York," he said seriously. "I believe that settles the question of residence for a man."

"Oh, how quaint!" said Sylvia, laughing. Then with her trained instinct for contriving a creditable exit before being driven to an enforced one by flagging of masculine interest, she rose and looked at her watch.

"Oh, don't go!" he implored her. "It's so beautiful here—we never were so—who knows when we'll ever again be in so . . ."

Sylvia divined with one of her cymbal-claps that he had meant, perhaps, that very afternoon to— She felt a dissonant clashing of triumph and misgiving. She thought she decided quite coolly, quite dryly, that pursuit always lent luster to the object pursued; but in reality she did not at all recognize the instinct which bade her say, turning her watch around on her wrist: "It's quite late. I don't think I'd better stay longer. Aunt Victoria likes dinner promptly." She turned to go.

He took his small defeat with his usual imperturbable good nature, in which Sylvia not infrequently thought she detected a flavor of the unconscious self-assurance of the very rich and much-courted man. He scrambled to his feet now promptly, and fell into step with her quick-treading advance. "You're right, of course. There's no need to be grasping. There's tomorrow—and the day after—and the day after that—and if it rains we can wear rubbers and carry umbrellas."

"Oh, I don't carry an umbrella for a walk in the rain," she told him. "It's one of our queer Marshall ways. We only own one umbrella for the whole family at home, and that's to lend. I wear a rubber coat and put on a sou'wester and *let* it rain."

"You would!" he said in an unconscious imitation of Arnold's accent.

She laughed up at him. "Shall I confess why I do? Because my hair is naturally curly."

" Confession has to be prompter than that to save souls,"
he answered. " I knew it was, five weeks ago, when you
splashed the water up on it so recklessly there by the
brook."

She was astonished by this revelation of depths behind
that well-remembered clear gaze of admiration, and dismayed by such unnatural accuracy of observation.

" How cynical of you to make such a mental comment! "

He apologized. " It was automatic—unconscious. I've
had a good deal of opportunity to observe young ladies."
And then, as though aware that the ice was thin over an
unpleasant subject, he shifted the talk. " Upon my word,
I wonder how Molly and Morrison *will* manage? "

" Oh, Molly's wonderful. She'd manage anything," said
Sylvia with conviction.

" Morrison is rather wonderful himself," advanced Page.
" And that's a magnanimous concession for me to make
when I'm now so deep in his bad books. Do you know, by
the way," he asked, looking with a quick interrogation at
the girl, " *why* I'm so out of favor with him? "

Sylvia's eyes opened wide. She gazed at him, startled,
fascinated. Could " it " be coming so suddenly, in this
casual, abrupt manner? " No, I don't know," she managed
to say; and braced herself.

" I don't blame him in the least. It was very vexing. I
went back on him—so to speak; dissolved an æsthetic
partnership, in which he furnished the brains, and my coal-
mines the sinews of art. *I* was one of his devotees, you
know. For some years after I got out of college I col-
lected under his guidance, as my mother does, as so many
people do. I even specialized. I don't like to boast, but I
dare affirm that no man knows more than I about sixteenth
century mezza-majolica. It is a branch of human knowledge which you must admit is singularly appropriate for a
dweller in the twentieth century. And of great value to
the world. My collection was one of Morrison's triumphs."

Sylvia felt foolish and discomfited. With an effort she

showed a proper interest in his remarks. " Was? " she asked. " What happened to it?"

" I went back on it. In one of the first of those fits of moral indigestion. One day, I'd been reading a report in one of the newspapers on the status of the coal-miner, and the connection between my bright-colored pots and platters, and my father's lucky guess, became a little too dramatic for my taste. I gave the collection to the Metropolitan, and I've never bought a piece since. Morrison was immensely put out. He'd been to great trouble to find some fine Fontana specimens for me. And then not to have me look at them—— He was right too. It was a silly, pettish thing to do. I didn't know any better then. I don't know any better now."

It began to dawn on Sylvia that, under his air of whimsical self-mockery he was talking to her seriously. She tried to adjust herself to this, to be sympathetic, earnest; though she was still smarting with the sense of having appeared to herself as undignified and ridiculous.

" And besides that," he went on, looking away, down the dusty highroad they were then crossing on their way back to the house—" besides that, I went back on a great scheme of Morrison's for a National Academy of Æsthetic Instruction, which I was to finance and he to organize. He had gone into all the details. He had shown wonderful capacity. It's really very magnanimous of him not to bear me more of a grudge. He thought that giving it up was one of my half-baked ideas. And it was. As far as anything I've accomplished since, I might as well have been furthering the appreciation of Etruscan vases in the Middle West. But then, I don't think he'll miss it now. If he still has a fancy for it, he can do it with Molly's money. She has plenty. But I don't believe he will. It has occurred to me lately (it's an idea that's been growing on me about everybody) that Morrison, like most of us, has been miscast. He doesn't really care a continental about the æsthetic salvation of the country. It's only the contagion of the American craze for connecting everything with social betterment, tagging everything with that label, that ever made him think he did. He's far too thoroughgoing an æsthete himself. What he was brought into the world for, was to appreciate, as nobody else can, all sorts of esoterically fine things. Now that he'll be able to gratify that taste, he'll find his occupation in it. Why shouldn't he? It'd be a hideously leveled world if everybody was trying to be a reformer. Besides, who'd be left to reform? I love to contemplate a genuine, whole-souled appreciator like Morrison, without any qualms about the way society is put together. And I envy him! I envy him as blackly as your pines envied the sumac. He's got out of the wrong rôle into the right one. I wish to the Lord I could!"

They were close to the house now, in the avenue of poplars, yellow as gold above them in the quick-falling autumn twilight. Sylvia spoke with a quick, spirited sincerity, her momentary pique forgotten, her feeling rushing out generously to meet the man's simple openness. "Oh, that's the problem for all of us! To know what rôle to play! If you think it hard for you who have only to choose—how about the rest of us who must——?" She broke off. "What's that? What's that?"

She had almost stumbled over a man's body, lying prone, half in the driveway, half on the close-clipped grass on the side; a well-dressed man, tall, thin, his limbs sprawled about broken-jointedly. He lay on his back, his face glimmering white in the clear, dim dusk. Sylvia recognized him with a cry. "Oh, it's Arnold! He's been struck by a car! He's dead!"

She sprang forward, and stopped short, at gaze, frozen.

The man sat up, propping himself on his hands and looked at her, a wavering smile on his lips. He began to speak, a thick, unmodulated voice, as though his throat were stiff. "Comingtomeetyou," he articulated very rapidly and quite unintelligibly, "an 'countered hill in driveway . . . no hill *in* driveway, and climbed and climbed"—he lost himself in repetition and brought up short to begin again, "—labor so 'cessive had to rest——"

Sylvia turned a paper-white face on her companion. "What's the matter with him?" she tried to say, but Page only saw her lips move. He made no answer. That she would know in an instant what was the matter flickered from her eyes, from her trembling white lips; that she did know, even as she spoke, was apparent from the scorn and indignation which like sheet-lightning leaped out on him. "Arnold! For *shame!* Arnold! Think of Judith!"

At the name he frowned vaguely as though it suggested something extremely distressing to him, though he evidently did not recognize it. "Judish? Judish?" he repeated, drawing his brows together and making a grimace of great pain. "What's Judish?"

And then, quite suddenly the pain and distress were wiped from his face by sodden vacuity. He had hitched himself to one of the poplars, and now leaned against this, his head bent on his shoulder at the sickening angle of a man hanged, his eyes glassy, his mouth open, a trickle of saliva flowing from one corner. He breathed hard and loudly. There was nothing there but a lump of uncomely flesh.

Sylvia shrank back from the sight with such disgust that she felt her flesh creep. She turned a hard, angry face on Page. "Oh, the beast! The beast!" she cried, under her breath. She felt defiled. She hated Arnold. She hated life.

Page said quietly: "You'll excuse my not going with you to the house? I'll have my car and chauffeur here in a moment." He stepped away quickly and Sylvia turned to flee into the house.

But something halted her flying feet. She hesitated, stopped, and pressed her hands together hard. He could not be left alone there in the driveway. A car might run over him in the dusk. She turned back.

She stood there, alone with the horror under the tree. She turned her back on it, but she could see nothing but the abject, strengthless body, the dreadful ignominy of the face. They filled the world.

And then quickly—everything came quickly to Sylvia—
there stood before her the little boy who had come to see
them in La Chance so long ago, the little honest-eyed boy
who had so loved her mother and Judith, who had loved
Pauline the maid and suffered with her pain; and then the
bigger boy who out of his weakness had begged for a share
of her mother's strength and been refused; and then the
man, still honest-eyed, who, aimless, wavering, had cried
out to her in misery upon the emptiness of his life; and
who later had wept those pure tears of joy that he had
found love. She had a moment of insight, of vision, of
terrible understanding. She did not know what was taking place within her, something racking—spasmodic throes
of sudden growth, the emergence for the first time in all her
life of the capacity for pity . . .

When, only a moment or two later, Page's car came
swiftly down the driveway, and he sprang out, he found
Sylvia sitting by the drunkard, the quiet tears streaming
down her face. She had wiped his mouth with her handkerchief, she held his limp hand in hers, his foolish staring
face was hidden on her shoulder. . . .

The two men lifted him bodily, an ignoble, sagging weight,
into the car. She stood beside him and, without a word,
stooped and gently disposed his slackly hanging arms beside him.

Dark had quite fallen by this time. They were all silent,
shadowy forms. She felt that Page was at her side. He
leaned to her. Her hand was taken and kissed.

CHAPTER XXXII

MUCH ADO . . .

THE rest of October was a period never clear in Sylvia's head. Everything that happened was confusing and almost everything was painful; and a great deal happened. She had thought at the time that nothing would ever blur in her mind the shock of finding Aunt Victoria opposed to what seemed to her the first obvious necessity: writing to Judith about Arnold. She had been trying for a long time now with desperate sincerity to take the world as she found it, to see people as they were with no fanatic intolerance, to realize her own inexperience of life, to be broad, to take in without too much of a wrench another point of view; but to Aunt Victoria's idea, held quite simply and naturally by that lady, that Judith be kept in ignorance of Arnold's habits until after marriage, Sylvia's mind closed as automatically, as hermetically as an oyster-shell snaps shut. She could not discuss it, she could not even attend with hearing ears to Mrs. Marshall-Smith's very reasonable presentation of her case; the long tradition as to the justifiability of such ignorance on a bride's part; the impossibility that any woman should ever know all of any man's character before marriage; the strong presumption that marriage with a woman he adored would cure habits contracted only through the inevitable aimlessness of too much wealth; the fact that, once married, a woman like Judith would accept, and for the most part deal competently with, facts which would frighten her in her raw girlish state of ignorance and crudeness. Sylvia did not even hear these arguments and many more like them, dignified with the sanction of generations of women trying their best to deal with life. She had never thought of the question before.

It was the sort of thing from which she had always averted
her moral eyes with extreme distaste; but now that it was
forced on her, her reaction to it was instantaneous. From
the depths of her there rose up fresh in its original vigor,
never having been dulled by a single enforced compliance
with a convention running counter to a principle, the most
irresistible instinct against concealment. She did not argue;
she could not. She could only say with a breathless certainty against which there was no holding out: " Judith
must know! Judith must know!"

Mrs. Marshall-Smith, alarmed by the prospect of a
passage-at-arms, decreed quietly that they should both
sleep on the question and take it up the next morning. Sylvia had not slept. She had lain in her bed, wide-eyed; a
series of pictures passing before her eyes with the unnatural vividness of hallucinations. These pictures were
not only of Arnold, of Arnold again, of Arnold and Judith.
There were all sorts of odd bits of memories—a conversation overheard years before, between her father and Lawrence, when Lawrence was a little, little boy. He had
asked—it was like Lawrence's eerie ways—apropos of nothing at all, " What sort of a man was Aunt Victoria's husband?"

His father had said, " A rich man, very rich." This
prompt appearance of readiness to answer had silenced the
child for a moment: and then (Sylvia could see his thin
little hands patting down the sand-cake he was making)
he had persisted, " What kind of a rich man?" His father
had said, " Well, he was bald—quite bald—Lawrence, come
run a race with me to the woodshed." Sylvia now, ten
years later, wondered why her father had evaded. What
kind of a man _had_ Arnold's father been?

But chiefly she braced herself for the struggle with Aunt
Victoria in the morning. It came to her in fleeting glimpses
that Aunt Victoria would be only human if she resented
with some heat this entire disregard of her wishes; that the
discussion might very well end in a quarrel, and that a
quarrel would mean the end of Lydford with all that Lyd-

ford meant now and potentially. But this perception was swept out of sight, like everything else, in the single-ness of her conviction: " Judith must know! Judith must know! "

There was, however, no struggle with Aunt Victoria in the morning. Mrs. Marshall-Smith, encountering the same passionate outcry, recognized an irresistible force when she encountered it; recognized it, in fact, soon enough to avoid the long-drawn-out acrimony of discussion into which a less intelligent woman would inevitably have plunged; recognized it almost, but not quite, in time to shut off from Sylvia's later meditations certain startling vistas down which she had now only fleeting glimpses. " Very well, my dear," said Mrs. Marshall-Smith, her cherished clarity always unclouded by small resentments,—"very well, we will trust in your judgment rather than my own. I don't pre-tend to understand present-day girls, though I manage to be very fond of one of them. Judith is your sister. You will do, of course, what you think is right. It means, of course, Judith being what she is, that she will instantly cast him off; and Arnold being what he is, that means that he will drink himself into delirium tremens in six months. His father . . ." She stopped short, closing with some haste the door to a vista, and poured herself another cup of coffee. They were having breakfast in her room, both in négligée and lacy caps, two singularly handsome rep-resentatives of differing generations. Mrs. Marshall-Smith looked calm, Sylvia extremely agitated. She had been awake at the early hour of deadly pale dawn when a swift, long-barreled car had drawn up under the porte-cochère and Arnold had been taken away under the guard of a short, broad, brawny man with disproportionately long arms. She was not able to swallow a mouthful of breakfast.

During the night, she had not looked an inch beyond her blind passion of insistence. Now that Aunt Victoria yielded with so disconcerting a suddenness, she faced with a pang what lay beyond. " Oh, Judith wouldn't cast him off! She loves him so! She'll give him a chance. You

don't know Judith. She doesn't care about many things,
but she gives herself up absolutely to those that do matter to
her. She adores Arnold! It fairly frightened me to see
how she was burning up when he was near. She'll insist
on his reforming, of course—she ought to—but——"

" Suppose he doesn't reform to suit her," suggested Mrs.
Marshall-Smith, stirring her coffee. " He's been reformed
at intervals ever since he was fifteen. He never could stay
through a whole term in any decent boys' school." Here
was a vista, ruthlessly opened. Sylvia's eyes looked down
it and shuddered. " Poor Arnold!" she said under her
breath, pushing away her untasted cup.

" I'm dull enough to find you take an odd way to show
your sympathy for him," murmured Mrs. Marshall-Smith,
with none of the acidity the words themselves seemed to
indicate. She seemed indeed genuinely perplexed. " It's
not been exactly a hilarious element in *my* life either. But
I've always tried to hold on to Arnold. I thought it my
duty. And now, since Felix Morrison has found this excellent specialist for me, it's much easier. I telegraph to him
and he comes at once and takes Arnold back to his sanitarium, till he's himself again." For the first time in weeks
Morrison's name brought up between them no insistently
present, persistently ignored shadow. The deeper shadow
now blotted him out.

" But Aunt Victoria, it's for Judith to decide. *She*'ll do
the right thing."

" Sometimes people are thrown by circumstances into a
situation where they wouldn't have dreamed of putting
themselves—and yet they rise to it and conquer it," philos-
ophized Aunt Victoria. " Life takes hold of us with strong
hands and makes us greater than we thought. Judith will
mean to do the right thing. If she were married, she'd
have to do it! It seems to me a great responsibility you
take, Sylvia—you may, with the best of intentions in the
world, be ruining the happiness of two lives."

Sylvia got up, her eyes red with unshed tears. It was
not the first time that morning. " It's all too horrible," she

murmured. " But I haven't any right to conceal it from Judith."

Her eyes were still red when, an hour later, she stepped into the room again and said, " I've mailed it."

Her aunt, still in lavender silk négligée, so far progressed towards the day's toilet as to have her hair carefully dressed, looked up from the *Revue Bleue,* and nodded. Her expression was one of quiet self-possession.

Sylvia came closer to her and sat down on a straight-backed chair. She was dressed for the street, and hatted, as though she herself had gone out to mail the letter. " And now, Tantine," she said, with the resolute air of one broaching a difficult subject, " I think I ought to be planning to go home very soon." It was a momentous speech, and a momentous pause followed it. It had occurred to Sylvia, still shaken with the struggle over the question of secrecy, that she could, in decency, only offer to take herself away, after so violently antagonizing her hostess. She realized with what crude intolerance she had attacked the other woman's position, how absolutely with claw and talon she had demolished it. She smarted with the sense that she had seemed oblivious of an " obligation." She detested the sense of obligation. And having become aware of a debt due her dignity, she had paid it hastily, on the impulse of the moment. But as the words still echoed in the air, she was struck to see how absolutely her immediate future, all her future, perhaps, depended on the outcome of that conversation she herself had begun. She looked fixedly at her aunt, trying to prepare herself for anything. But she was not prepared for what Mrs. Marshall-Smith did.

She swept the magazine from her lap to the floor and held out her arms to Sylvia. " I had hoped—I had hoped you were happy—with me," she said, and in her voice was that change of quality, that tremor of sincerity which Sylvia had always found profoundly moving. The girl was overcome with astonishment and remorse—and immense relief. She ran to her. " Oh, I am! I am! I was only thinking— I've gone against your judgment." Her nerves, stretched with the sleepless night and the strain of writing the dreadful letter to Judith, gave way. She broke into sobs. She put her arms tightly around her aunt's beautiful neck and laid her head on her shoulder, weeping, her heart swelling, her mind in a whirling mass of disconnected impressions. Arnold—Judith . . . how strange it was that Aunt Victoria really cared for her—did she really care for Aunt Victoria or only admire her?—did she really care for anybody, since she was agreeing to stay longer away from her father and mother?—how good it would be not to have to give up Hélène's services—what a heartless, materialistic girl she was—she cared for nothing but luxury and money —she would be going abroad now to Paris—Austin Page— he had kissed her hand . . . and yet she felt that he saw through her, saw through her mean little devices and stratagems—how astonishing that he should be so very, very rich—it seemed that a very, very rich man ought to be different from other men—his powers were so unnaturally great—girls could not feel naturally about him . . . And all the while that these varying reflections passed at lightning speed through her mind, her nervous sobs were continuing.

Aunt Victoria taking them, naturally enough, as signs of continued remorse, lifted her out of this supposed slough of despond with affectionate peremptoriness. "Don't feel so badly about it, darling. We won't have any more talk for the present about differing judgments, or of going away, or of anything uncomfortable"; and in this way, with nothing clearly understood, on a foundation indeed of misunderstanding, the decision was made, in the haphazard fashion which characterizes most human decisions.

The rest of the month was no more consecutive or logical. Into the midst of the going-away confusion of a household about to remove itself half around the world, into a house distracted with packing, cheerless with linen-covers, desolate with rolled-up rugs and cold lunches and half-packed trunks, came, in a matter-of-fact manner characteristic of its writer, Judith's answer to Sylvia's letter. Sylvia opened it, shrinking and fearful of what she would read. She had, in the days since hers had been sent, imagined Judith's answer in every possible form; but never in any form remotely resembling what Judith wrote. The letter stated in Judith's concise style that of course she agreed with Sylvia that there should be no secrets between betrothed lovers, nor, in this case, were there any. Arnold had told her, the evening before she left Lydford, that he had inherited an alcoholic tendency from his father. She had been in communication with a great specialist in Wisconsin about the case. She knew of the sanitarium to which Arnold had been taken and did not like it. The medical treatment there was not serious. She hoped soon to have him transferred to the care of Dr. Rivedal. If Arnold's general constitution were still sound, there was every probability of a cure. Doctors knew so much more about that sort of thing than they used to. Had Sylvia heard that Madame La Rue was not a bit well, that old trouble with her heart, only worse? They'd been obliged to hire a maid—how in the world were the La Rues going to exist on American cooking? Cousin Parnelia said she could cure Madame with some Sanopractic nonsense, a new fad that Cousin Parnelia had taken up lately. Professor Kennedy had been elected vice-president of the American Mathematical Association, and it was funny to see him try to pretend that he wasn't pleased. Mother's garden this autumn was . . .

"*Well!*" ejaculated Sylvia, stopping short. Mrs. Marshall-Smith had stopped to listen in the midst of the exhausting toil of telling Hélène which dresses to pack and which to leave hanging in the Lydford house. She now resumed her labors unflaggingly, waving away to the closet a mauve satin, and beckoning into a trunk a favorite black-and-white chiffon. To Sylvia she said, " Now I know exactly how a balloon feels when it is pricked."

Sylvia agreed ruefully. " I might have known Judith would manage to make me feel flat if I got wrought up about it. She hates a fuss made over anything, and she can always take you down if you make one." She remembered with a singular feeling of discomfiture the throbbing phrases of her letter, written under the high pressure of the quarrel with Aunt Victoria. She could almost see the expression of austere distaste in the stern young beauty of Judith's face. Judith was always making her appear foolish!

" We were both of us," commented Mrs. Marshall-Smith dryly, " somewhat mistaken about the degree of seriousness with which Judith would take the information."

Sylvia forgot her vexation and sprang loyally to Judith's defense. " Why, of course she takes it like a trained nurse, like a doctor—feels it a purely medical affair—as I suppose it is. We might have known she'd feel that way. But as to how she really feels inside, personally, you can't tel anything by her letter! You probably couldn't tell anything by her manner if she were here. You never can. She may be simply wild about a thing inside, but you'd never guess."

Mrs. Marshall-Smith ventured to express some skepticism as to the existence of volcanic feelings always so sedulously concealed. " After all, can you be so very sure that she is ever ' simply wild ' if she never shows anything? "

" Oh, you're *sure,* all right, if you've lived with her—you feel it. And then, after about so long a time of keeping it down, she breaks loose and *does* something awful, that I'd never have the nerve to do, and tears into flinders anything she doesn't think is right. Why, when we were little girls and went to the public schools together, two of our little playmates, who turned out to have a little negro blood, we . . ." Sylvia stopped, suddenly warned by some instinct that Aunt Victoria would not be a sympathetic listener to that unforgotten episode of her childhood, that episode which had seemed to have no consequences, no sequel, but which ever since that day had insensibly affected the course of her growth, like a great rock fallen into the current of her life.

Mrs. Marshall-Smith, deliberating with bated breath between broadcloth and blue panama, did not notice the pause. She did, however, add a final comment on the matter, some moments later, when she observed, " How any girl in her senses can go on studying, when she's engaged to a man who needs her as much as Arnold needs Judith!" To which Sylvia answered irrelevantly with a thought which had just struck her thrillingly, "But how perfectly fine of Arnold to tell her himself!"

"She must have hypnotized him," said Mrs. Marshall-Smith with conviction, "but then I don't pretend to understand the ways of young people nowadays." She was now forty-five, in the full bloom of a rarely preserved beauty, and could afford to make remarks about the younger generation. "At any rate," she went on, "it is a comfort to know that Judith has set her hand to the wheel. I have not in years crossed the ocean with so much peace of mind about Arnold as I shall have this time," said his stepmother. "No, leave that blue voile, Hélène, the collar never fitted."

"Oh, he doesn't spend the winters in Paris with you?" asked Sylvia.

"He's been staying here in Lydford of late—crazy as it sounds. He was simply so bored that he couldn't think of anything else to do. He has, besides, an absurd theory that he enjoys it more in winter than in summer. He says the natives are to be seen then. He's been here from his childhood. He knows a good many of them, I suppose. Now, Hélène, let's see the gloves and hats."

It came over Sylvia with a passing sense of great strangeness that she had been in this spot for four months and, with the exception of the men at the fire, she had not met, had not spoken to, had not even consciously seen a single inhabitant of the place.

And in the end, she went away in precisely the same state of ignorance. On the day they drove to the station she did, indeed, give one fleeting glimpse over the edge of her narrow prison-house of self-centered interest. Surrounded by a great many strapped and buckled pieces of baggage, with Hélène, fascinatingly ugly in her serf's uniform, holding the black leather bag containing Aunt Victoria's jewels, they passed along the street for the last time, under the great elms already almost wintry with their bare boughs. Now that it was too late, Sylvia felt a momentary curiosity about the unseen humanity which had been so near her all the summer. She looked out curiously at the shabby vehicles (it seemed to her that there were more of them than in the height of the season), at the straight-standing, plainly dressed, briskly walking women and children (there seemed to be a new air of life and animation about the street now that most of the summer cottages were empty), and at the lounging, indifferent, powerfully built men. She wondered, for a moment, what they were like, with what fortitude their eager human hearts bore the annual display of splendor they might never share. They looked, in that last glimpse, somehow quite strong, as though they would care less than she would in their places. Perhaps they were only hostile, not envious.

"I dare say," said Aunt Victoria, glancing out at a buckboard, very muddy as to wheels, crowded with children, "that it's very forlorn for the natives to have the life all go out of the village when the summer people leave. They must feel desolate enough!"

Sylvia wondered.

The last thing she saw as the train left the valley was the upland pass between Windward and Hemlock mountains. It brought up to her the taste of black birch, the formidably clean smell of yellow soap, and the rush of summer wind past her ears.

CHAPTER XXXIII

"WHOM GOD HATH JOINED . . ."

They were to sail on the 23d, and ever since the big square invitation had come it had been a foregone conclusion, conceded with no need for wounding words, that there was no way out of attending the Sommerville-Morrison wedding on the 21st. They kept, of course, no constrained silence about it. Aunt Victoria detested the awkwardness of not mentioning difficult subjects as heartily as she did the mention of them; and as the tree toad evolves a skin to answer his needs, she had evolved a method all her own of turning her back squarely on both horns of a dilemma. No, there was no silence about the wedding, only about the possibility that it might be an ordeal, or that the ordeal might be avoided. It could not be avoided. There was nothing to be said on that point. But there was much talk, during the few days of their stay in New York, about the elaborate preparations for the ceremony. Morrison, who came to see them in their temporary quarters, kept up a somewhat satirical report as to the magnificence of the performance, and on the one occasion when they went to see Molly they found her flushed, excited, utterly inconsecutive, distracted by a million details, and accepting the situation as the normal one for a bride-to-be. There were heart-searchings as to toilets to match the grandeur of the occasion; and later satisfaction with the moss-green chiffon for Sylvia and violet-colored velvet for her aunt. There were consultations about the present Aunt Victoria was to send from them both, a wonderfully expensive, newly patented, leather traveling-case for a car, guaranteed to hold less to the square inch and pound than any other similar, heavy, gold-mounted contrivance. Mrs. Marshall-Smith told Morrison frankly, in

364

this connection, that she had tried to select a present which Molly herself would enjoy.

" Am I not to have a present myself? " asked Morrison. " Something that you selected expressly for me? "

" No," said Sylvia, dropping the sugar into his tea with deliberation. " You are not to have any present for yourself."

She was guiltily conscious that she was thinking of a certain scene in " The Golden Bowl," a scene in which a wedding present figures largely; and when, a moment later, he said, " I have a new volume of Henry James I'd like to loan you," she knew that the same scene had been in his head. She would not look at him lest she read in his eyes that he had meant her to know. As she frequently did in those days, she rose, and making an excuse of a walk in the park, took herself off.

She was quite calm during this period, her mind full of trivial things. She had the firm conviction that she was living in a dream, that nothing of what was happening was irrevocable. And besides, as at Lydford, for much of the day, she was absorbed in the material details of her life, being rubbed and dressed and undressed, and adorned and fed and catered to. They were spending the few days before sailing in a very grand hotel, overlooking Central Park. Sylvia had almost every day the thought that she herself was now in the center of exactly the same picture in which, as a child, she had enviously watched Aunt Victoria. She adored every detail of it. It was an opening-out, even from the Lydford life. She felt herself expanding like a dried sponge placed in water, to fill every crack and crevice of the luxurious habits of life. The traveling along that road is always swift; and Sylvia's feet were never slow. During the first days in Vermont, it had seemed a magnificence to her that she need never think of dish-washing or bed-making. By this time it seemed quite natural to her that Hélène drew and tempered the water for her bath, and put on her stockings. Occasionally she noticed with a little surprise that she seemed to have no more free time than in the laborious life of La Chance; but for the most part she threw out, in all haste, innumerable greedy root-tendrils into the surcharged richness of her new soil and sent up a rank growth of easeful acquiescence in redundance.

The wedding was quite as grand as the Sommervilles had tried to make it. The street was crowded with staring, curious, uninvited people on either side of the church, and when the carriage containing the bride drove up, the surge forward to see her was as fierce as though she had been a defaulting bank-president being taken to prison. The police had to intervene. The interior, fern and orchid swathed, very dimly lighted by rich purple stained glass and aristocratic dripping wax candles instead of the more convenient electric imitations, was murmurous with the wonderful throbbing notes of a great organ and with the discreet low tones of the invited guests as they speculated about the relative ages and fortunes of the bride and bridegroom. The chancel was filled with a vested choir which, singing and carrying a cross, advanced down the aisle to meet the bridal party. Molly, who had not been in a church since her childhood, had needed to be coached over and over again in the ins and outs of the complicated service.

Sylvia, seated several guests away from the aisle, saw little of the procession as it went up into the chancel. She caught a glimpse of a misty mass of white and, beside it, old Mr. Sommerville's profile, very white and nervous and determined. She did not at that time see the bridegroom at all. The ceremony, which took place far within the chancel, was long and interspersed with music from the choir. Sylvia, feeling very queer and callous, as though, under an anæsthetic, she were watching with entire unconcern the amputation of one of her limbs, fell to observing the people about her. The woman in front of her leaned against the pew and brought her broad, well-fed back close under Sylvia's eyes. It was covered with as many layers as a worm in a cocoon. There were beads on lace, the lace incrusted on other lace, chiffon, fish-net, a dimly seen filmy satin, cut in points, and, lower down, an invisible foundation of taffeta. Through the interstices there gleamed a revelation of the back itself, fat, white, again like a worm in a cocoon.

Sylvia began to plan out a comparison of dress with architecture, bringing out the insistent tendency in both to the rococo, to the burying of structural lines in ornamentation. The cuff, for instance, originally intended to protect the skin from contact with unwashable fabrics, degenerated into a mere bit of " trimming," which has lost all its meaning, which may be set anywhere on the sleeve. Like a strong hand about her throat came the knowledge that she was planning to say all this to please Felix Morrison, who was now within fifty feet of her, being married to another woman.

She flamed to fever and chilled again to her queer absence of spirit. . . . There was a chorister at the end of the line near her, a pale young man with a spiritual face who chanted his part with shining rapt eyes. While he sang he slipped his hand under his white surplice and took out his watch. Still singing " Glory be to the Father, the Son, and the Holy Ghost," he cast a hasty eye on the watch and frowned impatiently. He was evidently afraid the business in hand would drag along and make him late to another appointment, "——is now and ever shall be, world without end. Amen ! " he sang fervently. Sylvia repressed an hysterical desire to laugh.

The ceremony was over; the air in the building beat wildly against the walls, the stained-glass windows, and the ears of the worshipers in the excited tumult of the wedding-march; the procession began to leave the chancel. This time Sylvia caught one clear glimpse of the principals, but it meant nothing to her. They looked like wax effigies of themselves, self-conscious, posed, emptied of their personalities by the noise, the crowds, the congestion of ceremony. The idea occurred to Sylvia that they looked as though they had taken in as little as she the significance of what had happened. The people about her were moving in relieved restlessness after the long immobility of the wedding. The woman next her went down on her knees for a devout period, her face in her white gloves. When she rose, she said earnestly to her companion, " Do you know if I had to choose one hat-trimming for all the rest of my life, I should make it small pink roses in clusters. It's perfectly miraculous how, with black chiffon, they *never* go out! " She settled in place the great cluster of costly violets at her breast which she seemed to have exuded like some natural secretion of her plump and expensive person. " Why don't they let us out! " she said complainingly.

A young man, one of those born to be a wedding usher, now came swiftly up the aisle on patent leather feet and untied with pearl-gray fingers the great white satin ribbon which restrained them in the pew. Sylvia caught her aunt's eye on her, its anxiety rather less well hidden than usual. With no effort at all the girl achieved a flashing smile. It was not hard. She felt quite numb. She had been present only during one or two painful, quickly passed moments.

But the reception at the house, the big, old-fashioned, very rich Sommerville house, was more of an ordeal. There was the sight of the bride and groom in the receiving-line, now no longer badly executed graven images, but quite themselves—Molly starry-eyed, triumphant, astonishingly beautiful, her husband distinguished, ugly, self-possessed, easily the most interesting personality in the room; there was the difficult moment of the presentation, the handclasp with Felix, the rapturous vague kiss from Molly, evidently too uplifted to have any idea as to the individualities of the people defiling before her; then the passing on into the throng, the eating and drinking and talking with acquaintances from the Lydford summer colony, of whom there were naturally a large assortment. Sylvia had a growing sense of pain, which was becoming acute when across the room she saw Molly, in a lull of arrivals, look up to her husband and receive from him a smiling, intimate look of possession. Why, they were *married!* It was done!

The delicate food in Sylvia's mouth turned to ashes.

Mrs. Marshall-Smith's voice, almost fluttered, almost (for her) excited, came to her ears: " Sylvia—here is Mr. Page! And he's just told me the most delightful news, that he's decided to run over to Paris for a time this fall."

" I hope Miss Marshall will think that Paris will be big enough for all of us?" asked Austin Page, fixing his remarkably clear eyes on the girl.

She made a great effort for self-possession. She turned her back on the receiving-line. She held out her hand cordially. " I hope Paris will be quite, quite small, so that we shall all see a great deal of each other," she said warmly.

CHAPTER XXXIV

SYLVIA TELLS THE TRUTH

THEY left Mrs. Marshall-Smith with a book, seated on a little yellow-painted iron chair, the fifteen-centime kind, at the top of the great flight of steps leading down to the wide green expanse of the Tapis Vert. She was alternately reading Huysmans' highly imaginative ideas on Gothic cathedrals, and letting her eyes stray up and down the long façade of the great Louis. Her powers of æsthetic assimilation seemed to be proof against this extraordinary mixture of impressions. She had insisted that she would be entirely happy there in the sun, for an hour at least, especially if she were left in solitude with her book. On which intimation Sylvia and Page had strolled off to do some exploring. It was a situation which a month of similar arrangements had made very familiar to them.

" No, I don't know Versailles very well," he said in answer to her question, " but I believe the gardens back of the Grand and Petit Trianon are more interesting than these near the Château itself. The conscientiousness with which they're kept up is not quite so formidable."

So they walked down the side of the Grand Canal, admiring the rather pensive beauty of the late November woods, and talking, as was the proper thing, about the great Louis and his court, and how they both detested his style of gilded, carved wall ornamentation, although his chairs weren't as bad as some others. They turned off at the cross-arm of the Canal towards the Great Trianon; they talked, again dutifully in the spirit of the place, about Madame de Maintenon. They differed on this subject just enough to enjoy discussing it. Page averred that the whole affair had always passed his comprehension, "—what that

370

ease-loving, vain, indulgent, trivial-minded grandson of Henri Quatre could ever have seen for all those years in that stiff, prim, cold old school-ma'am——"

But Sylvia shook her head. " I know how he felt. He *had* to have her, once he'd found her. She was the only person in all his world he could depend on."

" Why not depend on himself ? " Page asked.

" Oh, he couldn't! He couldn't! She had character and he hadn't."

" What do you mean by character? " he challenged her.

" It's what I haven't! " she said.

He attempted a chivalrous exculpation. " Oh, if you mean by character such hard, insensitive lack of imagination as Madame de Maintenon's——"

" No, not that," said Sylvia. " *You* know what I mean by character as well as I."

By the time they were back of the Little Trianon, this beginning had led them naturally enough away from the frivolities of historical conversation to serious considerations, namely themselves. The start had been a reminiscence of Sylvia's, induced by the slow fall of golden leaves from the last of the birches into the still water of the lake in the midst of Marie Antoinette's hamlet. They stopped on an outrageously rustic bridge, constructed quite in the artificially rural style of the place, and, leaning on the railing, watched in a fascinated silence the quiet, eddying descent of the leaves. There was not a breath of wind. The leaves detached themselves from the tree with no wrench. They loosened their hold gradually, gradually, and finally out of sheer fullness of maturity floated down to their graves with a dreamy content.

" I never happened to see that effect before," said Page. " I supposed leaves were detached only by wind. It's astonishingly peaceful, isn't it ? "

" I saw it once before," said Sylvia, her eyes fixed on the noiseless arabesques traced by the leaves in their fall—" at home in La Chance. I'll never forget it." She spoke in a low tone as though not to break the charmed silence about them, and, upon his asking her for the incident, she went on, almost in a murmur: " It isn't a story you could possibly understand. You've never been poor. But I'll tell you if you like. I've talked to you such a lot about home and the queer people we know—did I ever mention Cousin Parnelia? She's a distant cousin of my mother's, a queer woman who lost her husband and three children in a train-wreck years ago, and has been a little bit crazy ever since. She has always worn, for instance, exactly the same kind of clothes, hat and everything, that she had on, the day the news was brought to her. The Spiritualists got hold of her then, and she's been one herself for ever so long—table-rapping—planchette-writing—all the horrid rest of it, and she makes a little money by being a " medium " for ignorant people. But she hardly earns enough that way to keep her from starving, and Mother has for ever so long helped her out.

" Well, there was a chance to buy a tiny house and lot for her—two hundred and twenty dollars. It was just a two-roomed cottage, but it would be a roof over her head at least. She is getting old and ought to have something to fall back on. Mother called us all together and said this would be a way to help provide for Cousin Parnelia's old age. Father never could bear her (he's so hard on ignorant, superstitious people), but he always does what Mother thinks best, so he said he'd give up the new typewriter he'd been hoping to buy. Mother gave up her chicken money she'd been putting by for some new rose-bushes, and she loves her roses too! Judith gave what she'd earned picking raspberries, and I—oh, how I hated to do it! but I was ashamed not to—I gave what I'd saved up for my autumn suit. Lawrence just stuck it out that he hated Cousin Parnelia and he wouldn't give a bit. But he was so little that he only had thirty cents or something like that in a tin bank, so it didn't matter. When we put it all together it wasn't nearly enough of course, and we took the rest out of our own little family savings-bank rainy-day savings and bought the tiny house and lot. Father wanted to 'surprise'

Cousin Parnelia with the deed. He wanted to lay it under some flowers in a basket, or slip it into her pocket, or send it to her with some eggs or something. But Mother—it was so like her!—the first time Cousin Parnelia happened to come to the house, Mother picked up the deed from her desk and said offhand, ' Oh, Parnelia, we bought the little Garens house for you,' and handed her the paper, and went to talking about cutworms or Bordeaux mixture."

Page smiled, appreciative of the picture. " I see her. I see your mother—Vermont to the core."

" Well, it was only about two weeks after that, I was practising and Mother was rubbing down a table she was fixing over. Nobody else happened to be at home. Cousin Parnelia came in, her old battered black straw hat on one ear as usual. She was all stirred up and pleased about a new ' method' of using planchette. You know what planchette is, don't you? The little heart-shaped piece of wood spiritualists use, with a pencil fast to it, to take down their silly ' messages.' Some spiritualistic fake was visiting town conducting séances and he claimed he'd discovered some sort of method for inducing greater receptivity—or something like that. I don't know anything about spiritualism but little tags I've picked up from hearing Cousin Parnelia talk. Anyway, he was ' teaching' other mediums for a big price. And it came out that Cousin Parnelia had mortgaged the house for more than it was worth, and had used the money to take those ' lessons.' I couldn't believe it for a minute. When I really understood what she'd done, I was so angry I felt like smashing both fists down on the piano keys and howling! I thought of my blue corduroy I'd given up—I was only fourteen and just crazy about clothes. Mother was sitting on the floor, scraping away at the table-leg. She got up, laid down her sandpaper, and asked Cousin Parnelia if she'd excuse us for a few minutes. Then she took me by the hand, as though I was a little girl. I felt like one too, I felt almost frightened by Mother's face, and we both marched out of the house. She didn't say a word. She took me down to our swimming-hole

in the river. There is a big maple-tree leaning over that.
It was a perfectly breathless autumn day like this, and the
tree was shedding its leaves like that birch, just gently,
slowly, steadily letting them go down into the still water.
We sat down on the bank and watched them. The air was
full of them, yet all so quiet, without any hurry. The water
was red with them, they floated down on our shoulders, on
our heads, in our laps—not a sound—so peaceful—so calm—
so perfect. It was like the andante of the Kreutzer.

"I knew what Mother wanted, to get over being angry
with Cousin Parnelia. And she was. I could see it in her
face, like somebody in church. I felt it myself—all over, like
an E string that's been pulled too high, slipping down into
tune when you turn the peg. But I didn't *want* to feel it. I
wanted to hate Cousin Parnelia. I thought it was awfully
hard in Mother not to want us to have even the satisfaction
of hating Cousin Parnelia! I tried to go on doing it. I
remember I cried a little. But Mother never said a word—
just sat there in that quiet autumn sunshine, watching the
leaves falling—falling—and I had to do as she did. And
by and by I felt, just as she did, that Cousin Parnelia was
only a very small part of something very big.

"When we went in, Mother's face was just as it always
was, and we got Cousin Parnelia a cup of tea and gave her
part of a boiled ham to take home and a dozen eggs and
a loaf of graham bread, just as though nothing had happened."

She stopped speaking. There was no sound at all but the
delicate, forlorn whisper of the leaves.

"That is a very fine story!" said Page finally. He spoke
with a measured, emphatic, almost solemn accent.

"Yes, it's a very fine story," murmured Sylvia a little
wistfully. "It's finer as a story than it was as real life. It
was years before I could look at blue corduroy without feeling stirred up. I really cared more about my clothes than I
did about that stupid, ignorant old woman. If it's only a
cheerful giver the Lord loves, He didn't feel much affection
for me."

They began to retrace their steps. "You gave up the blue corduroy," he commented as they walked on, "and you didn't scold your silly old kinswoman."

"That's only because Mother hypnotized me. *She* has character. I did it as Louis signed the revocation of the Edict of Nantes, because Madame de Maintenon thought he ought to."

"But she couldn't hypnotize your brother Lawrence, al-thought he was so much younger. He didn't give up his thirty-seven cents. I think you're bragging without cause if you claim any engaging and picturesque absence of char-acter."

"Oh, Lawrence—he's different! He's extraordinary! Sometimes I think he is a genius. And it's Judith who hypnotizes him. *She* supplies his character."

They emerged into an opening and walked in silence for some moments towards the Grand Trianon.

"You're lucky, very lucky," commented Page, "to have such an ample supply of character in the family. I'm an only child. There's nobody to give me the necessary hypo-dermic supply of it at the crucial moments." He went on, turning his head to look at the Great Trianon, very mel-low in the sunshine. "It's my belief, however, that at the crucial moments you have plenty of it of your own."

"That's a safe guess!" said Sylvia ironically, "since there never have *been* any crucial moments in a life so uninter-estingly eventless as mine. I wonder what I *would* do," she mused. "My own conviction is that—suppose I'd lived in the days of the Reformation—in the days of Christ —in the early Abolition days——" She had an instant cer-tainty: "Oh, I have been entirely on the side of whatever was smooth, and elegant, and had amenity—I'd have hated the righteous side!"

Page did not look very deeply moved by this revelation of depravity. Indeed, he smiled rather amusedly at her, and changed the subject. "You said a moment ago that I couldn't understand, because I'd always had money. Isn't it a bit paradoxical to say that the people who haven't a thing are the only ones who know anything about it?"

"But you couldn't realize what *losing* the money meant to us. You can't know what the absence of money can do to a life."

"I can know," said Page, "what the presence of it cannot do for a life." His accent implied rather sadly that the omissions were considerable.

"Oh, of course, of course," Sylvia agreed. "There's any amount it can't do. After you have it, you must get the other things too."

He brought his eyes down to her from a roving quest among the tops of the trees. "It seems to me you want a great deal," he said quizzically.

"Yes, I do," she admitted. "But I don't see that you have any call to object to my wanting it. You don't have to wish for everything at once. You have it already."

He received this into one of his thoughtful silences, but presently it brought him to a standstill. They were within sight of the Grand Canal again, looking down from the terrace of the Trianon. He leaned against the marble balustrade and thrust his hands deep into his pockets. His clear eyes were clouded. He looked profoundly grave. "I am thirty-two years old," he said, "and never for a moment of that time have I made any sense out of my position in life. If you call that 'having everything'——"

It occurred to Sylvia fleetingly that she had never made any sense out of her position in life either, and had been obliged to do a great many disagreeable things into the bargain, but she kept this thought to herself, and looked conspicuously what she genuinely felt, a sympathetic interest. The note of plain direct sincerity which was Page's hallmark never failed to arrest her attention, a little to arouse her wonder, and occasionally, for a reason that she did not like to dwell upon, somewhat to abash her. The reason was that he never spoke for effect, and she often did. He was not speaking for effect now: he seemed scarcely even to be speaking to her, rather to be musingly formulating something for his own enlightenment. He went on. " The fact is that there *is* no sense to be made out of my situation in life. I am like a man with a fine voice, who has no ear."

He showed surprise that Sylvia failed to follow this, and explained. " I mean the voice is no good to that kind of a man, it's no good to anybody. It's the craziest, accidental affair anyhow, haven't you ever noticed it?—who draws the fine voices. Half the time—more than half the time, *most* of the time it seems to me when I've been recently to a lot of concerts, the people who have the voices haven't any other qualifications for being singers. And it's so with coal-mines, with everything else that's inherited. For five years now I've given up what I'd like to do, and I've tried, under the best *maestri* I could find, to make something out of my voice, so to speak. And it's no go. It's in the nature of things that I can't make a go of it. Over everything I do lies the taint that I'm the ' owner '! They are suspicious of me, always will be—and rightly so. Anybody else not connected with the mediæval idea of ' possession ' could do better than I. The whole relation's artificial. I'm in it for the preposterous reason that my father, operating on Wall Street, made a lucky guess,—as though I should be called upon to run a locomotive because my middle initial is L!"

Sylvia still felt the same slight sense of flatness when this recurring topic thrust itself into a personal talk; but during the last month she had adjusted herself to Page so that this no longer showed on the surface. She was indeed quite capable of taking an interest in the subject, as soon as she could modulate herself into the new key. " Yes, of course," she agreed, " it's like so many other things that are perfectly necessary to go on with, perfectly absurd when you look closely at them. My father nearly lost his position once for saying that all inheritance was wrong. But even he never had the slightest suggestion as to what to do about it, how to get an inheritance into the hands of the people who might make the best use of it." She was used from her childhood to this sort of academic doubt of everything, conducted side by side with a practical acceptance of everything. Professor and Madame La Rue, in actual life devotedly faithful married lovers, staid, stout, habit-ridden elderly people, professed a theoretical belief in the flexibility of relationships sanctioned by the practice of free love. It was perhaps with this recollection in her mind that she suggested, "Don't you suppose it will be like the institution of marriage, very, very gradually altered till it fits conditions better?"

"In the meantime, how about the cases of those who are unhappily married?"

"I don't see anything for them but just to get along the best they can," she told him.

"You think I'd better give up trying to do anything with my Colorado——?" he asked her, as though genuinely seeking advice.

"I should certainly think that five years was plenty long enough for a fair trial! You'd make a better ambassador than an active captain of industry, anyhow," she said with conviction. Whereupon he bestowed on her a long, thoughtful stare, as though he were profoundly pondering her suggestion.

They moved forward towards the Grand Canal in silence. Privately she was considering his case hardly one of extreme hardship. Privately also, as they advanced nearer and nearer the spot where they had left Mrs. Marshall-Smith, she was a little dreading the return to the perfect breeding with which Aunt Victoria did not ask, or intimate, or look, the question which was in her mind after each of these strolling tête-à-têtes which consistently led nowhere. There were instants when Sylvia would positively have preferred the vulgar openness of a direct question to which she might have answered, with the refreshing effect to her of a little honest blood-letting: "Dear Aunt Victoria, I haven't the least idea myself what's happening! I'm simply letting myself go because I don't see anything else to do. I have even no very clear idea as to what is going on inside my own head. I only know that I like Austin Page so much (in spite of a certain quite unforgotten episode) there would be nothing at all unpleasant about marrying him; but I also know that I didn't feel the least interest in him until Hélène told me about his barrels of money: I also know that I feel the strongest aversion to returning to the Spartan life of La Chance; and it occurs to me that these two things may throw considerable light on my 'liking' for Austin. As for what's in *his* mind, there is no subject on which I'm in blacker ignorance. And after being so tremendously fooled, in the case of Felix, about the degree of interest a man was feeling, I do not propose to take anything for granted which is not on the surface. It is quite possible that this singularly sincere and simple-mannered man may not have the slightest intention of doing anything more than enjoy a pleasant vacation from certain rather hair-splitting cares which seem to trouble him from time to time." As they walked side by side along the stagnant waters, she was sending inaudible messages of this sort towards her aunt· she had even selected the particular mauve speck at the top of the steps which might be Mrs. Marshall-Smith.

In the glowing yellow gold of the sky, a faintly whirring dark-gray spot appeared: an airman made his way above the Grand Canal, passed above the Château, and disappeared. They had sat down on a bench, the better to crane their heads to watch him out of sight. Sylvia was penetrated with the strangeness of that apparition in that spot and thrilled out: "Isn't it wonderful! Isn't it wonderful! *Here!*"

"There's something *more* wonderful!" he said, indicating with his cane the canal before them, where a group of neat, poorly dressed, lower middle-class people looked proudly out from their triumphal progress in the ugly, gasping little motor-boat which operates at twenty-five centimes a trip.

She had not walked and talked a month with him for nothing. She knew that he did not refer to motor-boats as against aëroplanes. "You mean," she said appreciatively, "you mean those common people going freely around the royal canal where two hundred years ago——"

He nodded, pleased by her quickness. "Two hundred years from now," he conjectured, "the stubs of my checkbook will be exhibited in an historical museum along with the regalia of the last hereditary monarch."

Here she did not follow, and she was too intelligent to pretend she did.

He lifted his eyebrows. " Relic of a quaint old social structure inexplicably tolerated so late as the beginning of the twentieth century."

" Oh, coal-mines forever!" she said, smiling, her eyes brilliant with friendly mockery.

" Aye! *Toujours perdrix!* " he admitted. He continued to look steadily and seriously into her smiling, sparkling face, until, with a sudden pulse of premonition, she was stricken into a frightened gravity. And then, with no prelude, no approach, quite simply and directly, he spoke. " I wonder how much you care for me? " he said musingly, as he had said everything else that afternoon: and as she positively paled at the eeriness of this echo from her own thought, he went on, his voice vibrating in the deep organ note of a great moment, " You must know, of course, by this time that I care everything possible for you."

Compressed into an instant of acute feeling Sylvia felt the pangs which had racked her as a little girl when she had stood in the schoolyard with Camilla Fingál before her, and the terrifying hostile eyes about her. Her two selves rose up against each other fiercely, murderously, as they had then. The little girl sprang forward to help the woman who for an instant hesitated. The fever and the struggle vanished as instantly as they had come. Sylvia felt very still, very hushed. Page had told her that she always rose to crucial moments. She rose to this one. " I don't know," she said as quietly as he, with as utter a bravery of bare sincerity, " I don't know how much I care for you—but I think it is a great deal." She rose upon a solemn wing of courage to a greater height of honesty. Her eyes were on his, as clear as his. The mere beauty of her face had gone like a lifted veil. For a instant he saw her as Sylvia herself did not dream she could be. " It is very hard," said Sylvia Marshall, with clear eyes and trembling lips of honest humility, " for a girl with no money to know how much she cares for a very rich man."

She had never been able to imagine what she would say if the moment should come. She had certainly not intended to say this. But an unsuspected vein of granite in her rang an instant echo to his truth. She was bewildered to see his ardent gaze upon her deepen to reverence. He took her hand in his and kissed it. He tried to speak, but his voice broke.

She was immensely moved to see him so moved. She was also entirely at a loss. How strangely different things always were from forecasts of them! They had suddenly taken the long-expected stride away from their former relation, but she did not know where they had arrived. What was the new status between them? What did Austin think she meant? It came to her with a shock that the new status between them was, on the surface, exactly what it was in reality; that the avowed relation between them was, as far as it went, precisely in accord with the facts of the case. The utter strangeness of this in any human relationship filled her with astonishment, with awe, almost with uneasiness. It seemed unnatural not to have to pretend anything!

Apparently it did not seem unnatural to the man beside her. " You are a very wonderful woman," he now said, his voice still but partly under his control. " I had not thought that you could exist." He took her hand again and continued more steadily: " Will you let me, for a little while longer, go on living near you? Perhaps things may seem clearer to us both, later——"

Sylvia was swept by a wave of gratitude as for some act of magnanimity. " *You* are the wonderful one! " she cried. Not since the day Hélène had told her who he was, had she felt so whole, so sound, so clean, as now. The word came rushing on the heels of the thought: " You make one feel so *clean!* " she said, unaware that he could scarcely understand her, and then she smiled, passing with her free, natural grace from the memorable pause, and the concentration of a great moment forward into the even-stepping advance of life. "That first day—even then you made me feel clean— that soap! that cold, clean water—it is your aroma!"

Their walk along the silent water, over the great lawn, and up the steps was golden with the level rays of the sun setting back of them, at the end of the canal, between the distant, sentinel poplars. Their mood was as golden as the light. Sometimes they spoke, sometimes they were silent. Truth walked between them.

Sylvia's mind, released from the tension of that great moment, began making its usual, sweeping, circling explorations of its own depths. Not all that it found was of an equal good report. Once she thought fleetingly: "This is only a very, very pretty way of saying that it is all really settled. With his great wealth, he is like a reigning monarch —let him be as delicate-minded as he pleases, when he indicates a wish——" More than once—many, many times— Felix Morrison's compelling dark eyes looked at her penetratingly, but she resolutely turned away her head from them, and from the impulse to answer their reproach even with an indignant, well-founded reproach of her own. Again and again she felt a sweet strangeness in her new position. The aroma of utter sincerity was like the scent of a wildflower growing in the sun, spicy, free. She wondered at a heart like his that could be at once ardent and subtle, that could desire so profoundly (the deep vibrations of that voice of yearning were in her ears still) and yet pause, and stand back, and wait, rather than force a hair's breadth of pretense. How he had liberated her! And once she found herself thinking, "I shall have sables myself, and diamonds, and a house as great as Molly's, and I shall learn how to entertain ambassadors, as she will never know." She was ashamed of this, she knew it to be shockingly out of key with the grand passage behind them. But she had thought it.

And, as these thoughts, and many more, passed through her mind, as she spoke with a quiet peace, or was silent, she was transfigured into a beauty almost startling, by the accident of the level golden beams of light back of her.

Her aureole of bright hair glowed like a saint's halo. The curiously placed lights and unexpected shadows brought out new subtleties in the modeling of her face. Her lightened heart gleamed through her eyes, like a lighted lamp. After a time, the man fell into a complete silence, glancing at her frequently as though storing away a priceless memory. . . .

CHAPTER XXXV

'A MILESTONE PASSED, THE ROAD SEEMS CLEAR"

As the " season " heightened, the beautiful paneled walls of Mrs. Marshall-Smith's salon were frequently the background for chance gatherings of extremely appropriate callers. They seemed a visible emanation of the room, so entirely did they represent what that sort of a room was meant to contain. They were not only beautifully but severely dressed, with few ornaments, and those few a result of the same concentrated search for the rare which had brought together the few bibelots in the room, which had laid the single great dull Persian rug on the unobtrusively polished oaken floor, which had set in the high, south windows the boxes of feathery green plants with delicate star-like flowers.

And it was not only in externals that these carefully brushed and combed people harmonized with the mellow beauty of their background. They sat, or stood, moved about, took their tea, and talked with an extraordinary perfection of manner. There was not a voice there, save perhaps Austin Page's unstudied tones, which was not carefully modulated in a variety of rhythm and pitch which made each sentence a work of art. They used, for the most part, low tones and few gestures, but those well chosen. There was an earnest effort apparent to achieve true conversational give-and-take, and if one of the older men found himself yielding to the national passion for lengthy monologues on a favorite theme, or to the mediocre habit of anecdote, there was an instant closing in on him of carefully casual team-work on the part of the others which soon reduced him to the tasteful short comment and answer which formed the framework of the afternoon's social activities.

The topics of the conversation were as explicitly in harmony with the group-ideal as the perfectly fitting gloves of the men, or the smooth, burnished waves of the women's hair. They talked of the last play at the Français, of the exhibitions then on view at the Petit Palais, of a new tenor in the choir of the Madeleine, of the condition of the automobile roads in the Loire country, of the restoration of the stained glass at Bourges.

On such occasions, a good deal of Sylvia's attention being given to modulating her voice and holding her hands and managing her skirts as did the guests of the hour, she usually had an impression that the conversation was clever. Once or twice, looking back, she had been somewhat surprised to find that she could remember nothing of what had been said. It occurred to her, fleetingly, that of so much talk, some word ought to stick in her usually retentive memory; but she gave the matter no more thought. She had also been aware, somewhat dimly, that Austin Page was more or less out of drawing in the carefully composed picture presented on those social afternoons. He had the inveterate habit of being at his ease under all circumstances, but she had felt that he took these great people with a really exaggerated lack of seriousness, answering their chat at random, and showing no chagrin when he was detected in the grossest ignorance about the latest move of the French Royalist party, or the probabilities as to the winner of the Grand Prix. She had seen in the corners of his mouth an inexplicable hidden imp of laughter as he gravely listened, cup in hand, to the remarks of the beautiful Mrs. William Winterton Perth about the inevitable promiscuity of democracy, and he continually displayed a tendency to gravitate into the background, away from the center of the stage where their deference for his name, fortune, and personality would have placed him. Sylvia's impression of him was far from being one of social brilliance, but rather of an almost wilful negligence. She quite grew used to seeing him, a tall, distinguished figure, sitting at ease in a far corner, and giving to the scene a pleasant though not remarkably respectful attention.

On such an afternoon in January, the usual routine had been preserved. The last of the callers, carrying off Mrs. Marshall-Smith with her, had taken an urbane, fair-spoken departure. Sylvia turned back from the door of the salon, feeling a fine glow of conscious amenity, and found that Austin Page's mood differed notably from her own. He had lingered for a tête-à-tête, as was so frequently his habit, and now stood before the fire, his face all one sparkle of fun. "Don't they do it with true American fervor!" he remarked. "It would take a microscope to tell the difference between them and a well-rehearsed society scene on the stage of the Français! That's their model, of course. It is positively touching to see old Colonel Patterson subduing his twang and shutting the lid down on his box of comic stories. I should think Mrs. Patterson might allow him at least that one about the cowboy and the tenderfoot who wanted to take a bath!"

The impression made on Sylvia had not in the least corresponded to this one; but with a cat-like twist of her flexible mind, she fell on her feet, took up his lead, and deftly produced the only suitable material she had at command. "They *seem* to talk well, about such interesting things, and yet I can never remember anything they say. It's odd," she sat down near the fireplace with a great air of pondering the strange phenomenon.

"No, it isn't odd," he explained, dropping into the chair opposite her and stretching out his long legs to the blaze. "It's only people who do something, who have anything to say. These folks don't do anything except get up and sit down the right way, and run their voices up and down the scale so that their great-aunts would faint away to hear them! They haven't any energy left over. If some one would only write out suitable parts for them to memorize, the performance would be perfect!" He threw back his head and laughed aloud, the sound ringing through the

room. Sylvia had seldom seen him so lightheartedly
amused. He explained: " I haven't seen this sort of solemn,
genteel posturing for several years now, and I find it too
delicious! To see the sweet, invincible American naïveté
welling up in their intense satisfaction in being so sophisticated,—oh, the harmless dears!" He cried out upon them
gaily, with the indulgence of an adult who looks on at children's play.

Sylvia was a trifle breathless, seeing him disappear so
rapidly down this unexpected path, but she was for the
moment spared the effort to overtake him by the arrival of
Tojiko with a tray of fresh mail. " Oh, letters from
home!" Sylvia rejoiced, taking a bulky one and a thin one
from the pile. " The fat one is from Father," she said, holding it up. " He is like me, terribly given to loquaciousness.
We always write each other reams when we're apart. The
little flat one is from Judith. She never can think of anything to say except that she is still alive and hopes I am,
and that her esteem for me is undiminished. Dear Spartan
Judy!"

"Do you know," said the man opposite her, " if I hadn't
met you, I should have been tempted to believe that the
institution of the family had disappeared. I never saw
anything like you Marshalls! You positively seem to have
a real regard for each other in spite of what Bernard Shaw
says about the relations of blood-kin. You even, incredible
as it seems, appear to feel a mutual respect!"

" That's a very pretty compliment indeed," said Sylvia,
smiling at him flashingly, " and I'm going to reward you
by reading some of Judith's letter aloud. Letters do paint
personalities so, don't they?"

He settled himself to listen.

" Oh, it won't take long!" she reassured him laughingly.
She read:

" ' DEAR SYLVIE: Your last letter about the palaces at
Versailles was very interesting. Mother looked you up on
the plan of the grounds in Father's old Baedeker. I'm glad

to know you like Paris so much. Our chief operating surgeon says he thinks the opportunities at the School of Medicine in Paris are fully as good as in Vienna, and chances for individual diagnoses greater. Have you visited that yet?'" Over the letter Sylvia raised a humorous eyebrow at Page, who smiled, appreciative of the point.

She went on: "'Lawrence is making me a visit of a few days. Isn't he a queer boy! I got Dr. Wilkinson to agree, as a great favor, to let Lawrence see a very interesting operation. Right in the middle of it, Lawrence fainted dead away and had to be carried out. But when he came to, he said he wouldn't have missed it for anything, and before he could really sit up he was beginning a poem about the "cruel mercy of the shining knives."'" Sylvia shook her head. "Isn't that Lawrence! Isn't that Judith!"

Page agreed thoughtfully, their eyes meeting in a trustful intimacy. They themselves might have been bound together by a family tie, so wholly natural seemed their sociable sitting together over the fire. Sylvia thought with an instant's surprise, "Isn't it odd how close he has come to seem—as though I'd always, always known him; as though I could speak to him of anything—nobody else ever seemed that way to me, nobody!"

She read on from the letter: "'All of us at St. Mary's are feeling very sore about lawyers. Old Mr. Winthrop had left the hospital fifteen thousand dollars in his will, and we'd been counting on that to make some changes in the operating-room and the men's accident ward that are awfully needed. And now comes along a miserable lawyer who finds something the matter with the will, and everything goes to that worthless Charlie Winthrop, who'll probably blow it all in on one grand poker-playing spree. It makes me tired! We can't begin to keep up with the latest X-ray developments without the new apparatus, and only the other day we lost a case, a man hurt in a railroad wreck, that I know we could have pulled through if we'd been better equipped! Well, hard luck! But I try to remember Mother's old uncle's motto, "Whatever else you do, *don't*

make a fuss!'" Father has been off for a few days, speaking
before Alumni reunions. He looks very well. Mother has
got her new fruit cellar fixed up, and it certainly is great.
She's going to keep the carrots and parsnips there too. I've
just heard that I'm going to graduate first in my class—
thought you might like to know. Have a good time, Sylvia.
And don't let your imagination get away with you.

"'Your loving sister,
"'JUDITH.'"

"Of all the perfect characterizations!" murmured Page,
as Sylvia finished. "I can actually see her and hear her!"
"Oh, there's nobody like Judith!" agreed Sylvia, falling
into a reverie, her eyes on the fire.

The peaceful silence which ensued spoke vividly of the
intimacy between them.

After a time Sylvia glanced up, and finding her companion's eyes abstractedly fixed on the floor, she continued
to look into his face, noting its fine, somewhat gaunt modeling, the level line of his brown eyebrows, the humor and
kindness of his mouth. The winter twilight cast its first
faint web of blue shadow into the room. The fire burned
with a steady blaze.

As minute after minute of this hushed, wordless calm
continued, Sylvia was aware that something new was happening to her, that something in her stirred which had
never before made its presence known. She felt very queer,
a little startled, very much bewildered. What was that half-
thought fluttering a dusky wing in the back of her mind?
It came out into the twilight and she saw it for what it was.
She had been wondering what she would feel if that silent
figure opposite her should rise and take her in his arms. As
she looked at that tender, humorous mouth, she had been
wondering what she would feel to press her lips upon it?

She was twenty-three years old, but so occupied with
mental effort and physical activity had been her life, that
not till now had she known one of those half-daring, half-
frightened excursions of the fancy which fill the hours of

any full-blooded idle girl of eighteen. It was a woman grown with a girl's freshness of impression, who knew that ravished, scared, exquisite moment of the first dim awakening of the senses. But because it was a woman grown with a woman's capacity for emotion, the moment had a solemnity, a significance, which no girl could have felt. This was no wandering, flitting, wingèd excursion. It was a grave step upon a path from which there was no turning back. Sylvia had passed a milestone. But she did not know this. She sat very still in her chair as the twilight deepened, only knowing that she could not take her eyes from those tender, humorous lips. That was the moment when if the man had spoken, if he had but looked at her . . .

But he was following out some thought of his own, and now rose, went to Mrs. Marshall-Smith's fine, small desk, snapped on an electric light, and began to write.

When he finished, he handed a bit of paper to Sylvia. "Do you suppose your sister would be willing to let me make up for the objectionable Charlie Winthrop's deficiencies?" he asked with a deprecatory air as though he feared a refusal.

Sylvia looked at the piece of paper. It was a check for fifteen thousand dollars. She held there in her hand seven years of her father's life, as much money as they all had lived on from the years she was sixteen until now. And this man had but to dip pen into ink to produce it. There was something stupefying about the thought to her. She no longer saw the humor and tenderness of his mouth. She looked up at him and thought, "What an immensely rich man he is!" She said to him wonderingly, "You can't imagine how strange it is—like magic—not to be believed—to have money like that!"

His face clouded. He looked down uncertainly at his feet and away at the lighted electric bulb. "I thought it might please your sister," he said and turned away.

Sylvia was aghast to think that she had perhaps wounded him. He seemed to fear that he had flaunted his fortune in her face. He looked acutely uncomfortable. She found that, as she had thought, she could say anything, anything to him, and say it easily. She went to him quickly and laid her hand on his arm. " It's splendid," she said, looking deeply and frankly into his eyes. " Judith will be too rejoiced! It *is* like magic. And nobody but you could have done it so that the money seems the least part of the deed! "

He looked down at her, touched, moved, his eyes very tender, but sad as though with a divination of the barrier his fortune eternally raised between them.

The door opened suddenly and Mrs. Marshall-Smith came in quickly, not looking at them at all. From the pale agitation of her face they recoiled, startled and alarmed. She sat down abruptly as though her knees had given way under her. Her gloved hands were perceptibly trembling in her lap. She looked straight at Sylvia, and for an instant did not speak. If she had rushed in screaming wildly, her aspect to Sylvia's eyes would scarcely have been more eloquent of portentous news to come. It was a fitting introduction to what she now said to them in an unsteady voice: " I've just heard—a despatch from Jamiaca—something terrible has happened. The news came to the American Express office when I was there. It is awful. Molly Sommerville driving her car alone—an appalling accident to the steering-gear, they think. Molly found dead under the ca

CHAPTER XXXVI

THE ROAD IS NOT SO CLEAR

It shocked Sylvia that Molly's death should make so little difference. After one sober evening with the stunning words fresh before their eyes, the three friends quickly returned to their ordinary routine of life. It was not that they did not care, she reflected—she *did* care. She had cried and cried at the thought of that quivering, vital spirit broken by the inert crushing mass of steel—she could not bring herself to think of the soft body, mangled, bloody. Austin cared too: she was sure of it; but when they had expressed their pity, what more could they do? The cabled statement was so bald, they hardly could believe it—they failed altogether to realize what it meant—they had no details on which to base any commentary. She who had lived so intensely, was dead. They were sorry for her. That was all.

As an apology for their seeming callousness they reiterated Aunt Victoria's dictum: " We can know nothing about it until Felix comes. Let us hold our minds in suspense until we know what to think." That Morrison would be in Paris soon, none of them doubted. Indeed, they united in insisting on the number of natural—oh, perfectly natural—reasons for his coming. He had always spent a part of every winter there, had in fact a tiny apartment on the Rue St. Honoré which dated from his bachelor life; and now he had a double reason for coming, since much of Molly's fortune chanced to be in French bonds. Her father had been (among other things) American agent for the Comptoir National des Escomptes, and he had taken advantage of his unusual opportunities for acquiring solid French and remunerative Algerian securities. Page had said at once that Morrison would need to go through a good many formalities, under the French laws. So pending fuller information, they did not discuss the tragedy. Their lives ran on, and Molly, dead, was in their minds almost as little as Molly, living but absent, had been.

It was only two months before Felix Morrison arrived in Paris. They had expected him. They had spoken of the chance of his arrival on this or that day. Sylvia had rehearsed all the possible forms of self-possession for their first meeting; but on the rainy February afternoon when she came in from representing Aunt Victoria at a reception and saw him sitting by the fire, her heart sank down and stopped for an instant, and when it went on beating she could hear no sound but the drumming of her pulse. The back of his chair was towards her. All she could see as she stood for a moment in the doorway was his head, the thick, graying dark hair, and one long-fingered, sensitive, beautiful hand lying on the arm of the chair. At the sight, she felt in her own palm the soft firmness of those fingers as palpably as ever she had in reality.

The instant's pause before Aunt Victoria saw her standing there, gave her back her self-control. When Mrs. Marshall-Smith turned and gravely held out her hand, Sylvia came forward with a sober self-possession. The man turned too, sprang up with an exclamation apparently of surprise, "Miss Marshall, you *here!*" and extended his hand. Sylvia, searching his face earnestly, found it so worn, saw in it such dark traces of suffering and sorrow, that the quick tears of sympathy stood in her eyes.

Her dread of the meeting, a morbid dread that had in it an acknowledged element of horror, vanished. Before that moment she had seen only Molly's face as it had looked the day of their desperate talk, white and despairing, and resolutely bent over the steering-wheel. She had not been able to imagine Felix' face at all, had instinctively put it out of her mind; but as she looked into it now, her fear of it disappeared. It was the fine, sensitive face of a fine, sensitive man who has known a great shock. What had she feared she would see there? He was still holding her hand, very much affected at seeing her, evidently still in a super-sensitive condition when everything affected him strongly. "She loved you—she admired you so!" he said, his wonderful voice wavering and uncertain. Sylvia's tears fell openly at this. She sat down on a low stool near her aunt's knees. "I can't believe it—I haven't been able to believe it!" she told him; "Molly was—she was more alive than anybody I ever saw!"

"If you had seen her that morning," he told them both,—"like a flame of vitality—almost frightening—so vivid. She waved good-bye, and then that was not enough; she got out of the car and ran back up the hotel-step to say good-bye for just those few moments—and was off—such youth! such youth in all her——"

Sylvia cried out, "Oh, no! no! it's too dreadful!" She felt the horror sweep down on her again; but now it did not bear Felix' face among its baneful images. He stood there, shocked, stricken, but utterly bewildered, utterly ignorant—for the moment in her relief she had called his ignorance utter innocence . . .

They did not see him again for many days, and when he came, very briefly, speaking of business technicalities which absorbed him, he was noticeably absent and careworn. He looked much older. The gray in his thick hair had increased. He looked very beautiful and austere to Sylvia. They exchanged no more than the salutations of arrival and farewell.

Then one day, as she and Aunt Victoria and Austin Page strolled down the long gallery of the Louvre, they came upon him, looking at the Ribera Entombment. He joined them, walking with them through the Salon Carré and out to the Winged Victory, calling Sylvia's attention to the Botticelli frescoes beyond on the landing. "It's the first time I've been here," he told them, his only allusion to what lay back of him. "It is like coming back to true friends. Blessed be all true friends." He shook hands with them, and went away down the great stairway, a splendid figure of dignity and grace.

After this he came once and again to the apartment of the Rue de Presbourg, generally it would appear to use the piano. He had none in his own tiny *pied-à-terre* and he missed it. Sylvia immensely liked his continuing to cling for a time to the simple arrangements of his frugal bachelor days. He could now of course have bought a thousand pianos. They understood how he would miss his music, and stole in quietly when, upon opening the door, Tojiko told them that Mr. Morrison had come in, and they heard from the salon his delicately firm touch on the keys. Sometimes they listened from their rooms, sometimes the two women took possession of the little octagonal room off the salon, all white paneling and gilt chairs, and listened there; sometimes, as the weeks went on and an especially early spring began to envelop Paris in a haze of sunshine and budding leaves, they stepped out to listen on the wrought-iron balcony which looked down the long, shining vista of the tree-framed avenue. For the most part he played Bach, grave, courageous, formal, great-hearted music.

Sometimes he went away with no more than a nod and a smile to them, but more and more, when he had finished, he came out where they were, and stood or sat to exchange brief impressions on the enchanting season, or on some social or æsthetic treat which *" ces dames "* had been enjoying. Austin Page was frequently with them, as in the earlier part of the winter, and it was finally he himself who one day took the step of asking Morrison if he would not go with them to the Louvre. " No one could appreciate more than Miss Marshall what has always been such a delight to us all."

They went, and not only once. That was the beginning of another phase; a period when, as he began to take up life again, he turned to his old friends to help him do it. He saw almost no one else, certainly no one else there, for he was sure to disappear upon the arrival of a caller, or the announcement of an expedition in which other people were included. But he returned again and again to the Louvre with them, his theory of galleries necessitating frequent visits. Nothing could be more idiotic, he held, than to try to see on one occasion all, or even half, or even a tenth part, of a great collection of works of art. " It is exactly as reasonable," he contended, " as to read through on the same day every poem in a great anthology. Who could have anything but nausea for poetry after such a gorge? And they *must* hate pictures or else be literally blind to them, the people who look at five hundred in a morning! If I had looked at every picture in the Long Gallery in one walk through it, I should thrust my cane through the Titian Francis-First itself when I came to the Salon Carré."

So he took them to see only a few, five or six, carefully selected things—there was one wonderful day when he showed them nothing but the Da Vinci Saint Anne, and the Venus of Melos, comparing the dissimilar beauty of those two divine faces so vitally, that Sylvia for days afterwards, when she closed her eyes and saw them, felt that she looked on two living women. She told them this and, " Which one do you see most?" he asked her. " Oh, the Saint Anne," she told him.

He seemed dissatisfied. But she did not venture to ask him why. They lived in an atmosphere where omissions were vital.

Sylvia often wondered in those days if there ever had been a situation so precariously balanced which continued to hang poised and stable, minute after minute, hour after hour, day after day. There were moments when her head was swimming with moral dizziness. She wondered if such moments ever came to the two quiet, self-controlled men who came and went, with cordial, easy friendliness, in and out of the appartement on the Rue de Presbourg. They gave no sign of it, they gave no sign of anything beyond the most achieved appearance of a natural desire to be obliging and indulgent to the niece of an old friend. This appearance was kept up with such unflagging perseverance that it almost seemed consciously concerted between them. They so elaborately avoided the slightest appearance of rivalry that their good taste, like a cloth thrown over an unknown object, inevitably excited curiosity as to what was concealed beneath it.

And Sylvia was not to be outdone. She turned her own eyes away from it as sedulously as they. She never let a conscious thought dwell on it—and like all other repressed and strangled currents of thought, it grew swollen and restive, filling her subconsciousness with monstrous, unformulated speculations. She was extremely absorbed in the luxury, the amenity, the smooth-working perfection of the life about her. She consciously concentrated all her faculties on her prodigious opportunity for æsthetic growth, for appreciation of the fine and marvelous things about her. She let go the last scruple which had held her back from accepting from Aunt Victoria the shower of beautiful things to wear which that connoisseur in wearing apparel delighted to bestow upon an object so deserving. She gave a brilliant outward effect of enjoying life as it came which was as impersonal as that of the two men who looked at her so frequently, and this effect went as deep as her will-power had command. But beneath—unacknowledged waves beating on the shore of her life and roughly, irresistibly, rudely fashioning it—rolled a ground-swell of imperious questionings. . . .

Was Felix' perfect manner of impersonal interest solely due to the delicacy of his situation? Did he feel now that he was as rich as Austin . . .? But, on the other hand, why did he come now and put himself in a situation which required the utmost efforts for unconsciousness on everybody's part if not because Austin's being there had meant he dared not wait? And Austin's change of manner since the arrival of the other man, the film of ceremony which had slid imperceptibly over the tender friendliness of his manner, did that mean that he would not take advantage of Morrison's temporarily tied hands, but, with a scrupulousness all his own, would wait until the race was even and they stood foot to foot on the same level? Or had he noticed at once, with those formidably clear eyes of his, some shade of her manner to Felix which she had not been able to command, and was he waiting for some move from her? And how could she move until she had some sign from Felix and how could he give a sign? There was nothing to do but to wait, to hope that the thin ice which now bent perilously under the pleasant ceremonies of their life in common, would hold them until . . . Even the wildest up-leaping wave of that tossing tide never went beyond the blank wall which came after the " until. . . ."

There were other moments when all that surge swung back and forth to the rhythm of the poisoned recollection of her unacknowledged humiliation in Lydford; when, in-flamed with determination to avoid another such blow in the face, Sylvia almost consciously asked herself, self-con-temptuously, " Who am I, an obscure, poverty-stricken music-teacher out of the West, to fancy that I have but to choose between two such men, two such fortunes? " but against this counted strongly the constantly recurring revelations of the obscure pasts of many of the women whom she met during those days, women who were now shining, acknowledged firsts in the procession of success. The serene, stately, much-admired Princesse de Chevrille had been a Miss Sommers from Cleveland, Ohio, and she had come to Paris first as a governess. The beautiful Mrs. William Winterton Perth, now Aunt Victoria's favorite friend, who entertained lesser royalty and greater men of letters with equal quiet dignity, had in her youth, so she chanced casually one day to mention, known what it was to be thrifty about car-fares. There was nothing in-trinsically impossible in any of the glittering vistas down which Sylvia's quick eye cast involuntary glances.

But inevitably, when the heaving dark tide rose as high as this, there came a swift and deadly ebbing away of it all, and into Sylvia's consciousness (always it seemed to her with the most entire irrelevance) there flared up the picture of Molly as she had seen her last, shimmering like a jewel in her white veil—then the other picture, the over-turned car, the golden head bruised and bloody and forever stilled—and always, always beyond that, the gaunt, monstrous possibility, too awful ever to be put into words, too impossible for credence . . .

From that shapeless, looming, black mass, Sylvia fled away actually and physically, springing to her feet wherever she was, entering another room, taking up some other occupation.

Just once she had the faintest sign from beyond the wall that she was not alone in her fear of this horror. She was sitting near Austin Page at a tea, one of the frequent, small, richly chosen assemblages which Mrs. Marshall-Smith gathered about her. Part of the ensuing chatter on one of these occasions turned, as modern chatter frequently does, on automobiles. The husband of Mrs. William Winterton Perth was an expert on such matters, having for some years diverted by an interest in mechanics the immense enforced leisure of a transplanted male American. He was talking incessantly that day of the wonderful improvement in steering mechanism the last few years had brought about. " I tell you what, Miss Marshall! " he insisted, as though she had disputed the point with him, " I tell you *what,* there used to be some excuse for piling your car up by the side of the road, but nowadays any one who doesn't keep in the road and right side up must be just plain *looking* for a chance to use his car like a dose of cold poison." For a moment Sylvia could not conceive why she felt so sickening a thrust at her heart. She turned her eyes from the speaker. They fell on a man's hand, on the arm of the chair next hers. It was Austin's hand and it was shaking uncontrollably. As she gazed at it, fascinated, he thrust it deep into his pocket. She did not look at him. In a moment he rose and crossed the room. The husband of Mrs. William Winterton Perth asked for another *petit four,* confessing his fondness for chocolate éclairs.—and embarked upon demountable rims.

CHAPTER XXXVII

. . His wife and children perceiving it, began to cry after him to return; but the man put his fingers in his ears and ran on, crying, ' Life! Life Eternal!' "

THEY had been in the Louvre, had spent an hour with Felix in that glowing embodiment of the pomp and majesty of human flesh known as the Rubens Medici-Room, and now, for the sheer pleasure of it, had decided to walk home. Mrs. Marshall-Smith, endowed with a figure which showed as yet no need for exercise, and having passed youth's restless liking for it, had vetoed the plan as far as she went, and entering her waiting car, had been borne smoothly off, an opulent Juno without her peacocks.

The three who were left, lingered for a moment in the quiet sunny square of the Louvre, looking up at the statue of Lafayette, around at the blossoming early shrubs. Sylvia was still under the spell of the riotous, full-blown splendor of the paintings she had seen. Wherever she looked, she saw again the rainbow brilliance of those glossy satins, that rippling flooding golden hair, those ample, heaving bosoms, those liquid gleaming eyes, the soft abundance of that white and ruddy flesh, with the patina of time like a golden haze over it. The spectacle had been magnificent and the scene they now entered was a worthy successor to it. They walked down through the garden of the Tuileries and emerged upon the Place de la Concorde at five o'clock of a perfect April afternoon, when the great square hummed and sang with the gleaming traffic of luxury. Countless automobiles, like glistening beetles, darted about, each one with its load of carefully dressed and coiffed women, looking out on the weaving glitter of the street with the proprietary, complacent stare of those who feel themselves in the midst of a civilization with which they are in perfect accord. Up the avenue, beyond, streamed an incessant parade of more costly cars, more carriages, shining, caparisoned horses, every outfit sumptuous to its last detail, every one different from all the others, and hundreds and hundreds and hundreds of them, till in the distance they dwindled to a black stream dominated by the upward sweep of the Arc de Triomphe, magnified to fabulous proportions by the filmy haze of the spring day. To their left flowed the Seine, blue and flashing. A little breeze stirred the new leaves on the innumerable trees.

Sylvia stopped for an instant to take in the marvel of this pageant, enacted every day of every season against that magnificent background. She made a gesture to call her companions' attention to it—" Isn't it in the key of Rubens—bloom, radiance, life expansive!"

" And Chabrier should set it to music," said Morrison.

" What does it make you think of?" she asked. " It makes me think of a beautiful young Greek, in a purple chiton, with a wreath of roses in his hair."

" It makes me think of a beautiful young woman, all fire and spirit, and fineness, who drinks life like a perfumed wine," said Morrison, his eyes on hers. She felt a little shiver of frightened pleasure, and turned to Page to carry it off, " What does it make you think of?" she asked.

" It makes me think," he answered her at once, his eyes on the haze caught like a dream in the tender green of the budding trees,—" it makes me think of a half-naked, sweating man, far underground in black night, striking at a rock with a pick."

If he had burst into loud profanity, the effect could not have been more shocking. " Oh!" said Sylvia, vexed and put out. She began to walk forward. Morrison in his turn gave an exclamation which seemed the vent of long-stored exasperation, and said with heat: " Look here, Page, you're getting to be a perfect monomaniac on the subject! What earthly good does it do your man with a pick to ruin a fine moment by lugging him in!"

They were all advancing up the avenue now, Sylvia between the two men. They talked at each other across her. She listened intently, with the feeling that Morrison was voicing for her the question she had been all her life wishing once for all to let fly at her parents' standards: " What good *did* it do anybody to go without things you might have? Conditions were too vast for one person to influence."

" No earthly good," said Page peaceably; " I didn't say it did him any good. Miss Marshall asked me what all this made me think of, and I told her."

" It is simply becoming an obsession with you! " urged Morrison. Sylvia remembered what Page had said about his irritation years ago when Austin had withdrawn from the collector's field.

" Yes, it's becoming an obsession with me," agreed Page thoughtfully. He spoke as he always did, with the simplest manner of direct sincerity.

" You ought to make an effort against it, really, my dear fellow. It's simply spoiling your life for you! "

" Worse than that, it's making me bad company! " said Page whimsically. " I either ought to reform or get out."

Morrison set his enemy squarely before him and proceeded to do battle. " I believe I know just what's in your mind, Page: I've been watching it grow in you, ever since you gave up majolica."

" I never claimed that was anything but the blindest of impulses! " protested Page mildly.

" But it wasn't. I knew! It was a sign you had been infected by the spirit of the times and had ' caught it ' so hard that it would be likely to make an end of you. It's all right for the collective mind. That's dense, obtuse; it resists enough to keep its balance. But it's not all right for you. Now you just let me talk for a few minutes, will you? I've an accumulated lot to say! We are all of us living through the end of an epoch, just as much as the people of the old régime lived through the last of an epoch in the years before the French Revolution. I don't believe it's going to come with guillotines or any of those picturesque trimmings. We don't do things that way any more. In my opinion it will come gradually, and finally arrive about two or three generations from now. And it oughtn't to come any sooner! Sudden changes never save time. There's always the reaction to be gotten over with, if they're sudden. Gradual growths are what last. Now anybody who knows about the changes of society knows that there's little enough any one person can do to hasten them or to put them off. They're actuated by a law of their own, like the law which makes typhoid fever come to a crisis in seven days. Now then, if you admit that the process ought not to be hastened, and in the second place that you couldn't hasten it if you tried, what earthly use *is* there in bothering your head about it! There are lots of people, countless people, made expressly to do whatever is necessary, blunt chisels fit for nothing but shaping grindstones. *Let them do it!* You'll only get in their way if you try to interfere. It's not your job. For the few people capable of it, there is nothing more necessary to do for the world than to show how splendid and orderly and harmonious a thing life can be. While the blunt chisels hack out the redemption of the overworked (and Heaven knows I don't deny their existence), let those who can, preserve the almost-lost art of living, so that when the millennium comes (you see I don't deny that this time it's on the way!) it won't find humanity solely made up of newly freed serfs who don't know what use to make of their liberty. How is beauty to be preserved by those who know and love and serve her, and how can they guard beauty if they insist on going down to help clean out the sewers? Miss Marshall, don't you see how I am right? Don't you see how no one can do more for the common weal than just to live, as finely, as beautifully, as intelligently as possible? And people who are capable of this noblest service to the world only waste themselves and serve nobody if they try to do the work of dray-horses."

Sylvia had found this wonderfully eloquent and convincing. She now broke in. " When I was a young girl in college, I used to have a pretentious, jejune sort of idea that what I wanted out of life was to find Athens and live in it—and your idea sounds like that. The best Athens, you know, not sensuous and selfish, but full of lovely and leisurely sensations and fine thoughts and great emotions."

"It wasn't pretentious and jejune at all!" said Morrison warmly, "but simply the most perfect metaphor of what must have been—of course, I can see it from here—the instinctive sane effort of a nature like yours. Let's all try to live in Athens so that there will be some one there to welcome in humanity."

Page volunteered his first contribution to the talk. "Oh, I wouldn't mind a bit if I thought we were really doing what Morrison thinks is our excuse for living, creating fine and beautiful lives and keeping alive the tradition of beauty and fineness. But our lives aren't beautiful, they're only easeful. They're not fine, they're only well-upholstered. You've got to have fitly squared and substantial foundations before you can build enduring beauty. And all this," he waved his hand around him at the resplendent, modern city, "this isn't Athens; it's—it's Corinth, if you want to go on being classic. As near as I can make out from what Sylvia lets fall, the nearest approach to Athenian life that I ever heard of, was the life she left behind her, her parents' life. That has all the elements of the best Athenian color, except physical ease. And ease is no Athenian quality! It's Persian! Socrates was a stone-cutter, you know. And even in the real Athens, even that best Athens, the one in Plato's mind—there was a whole class given over to doing the dirty work for the others. That never seemed to bother Plato—happy Plato! but—I'm sure I don't pretend to say if it ultimately means more or less greatness for the human race—but somehow since Christianity, people find it harder and harder to get back to Plato's serenity on that point. I'm not arguing the case against men like you, Morrison—except that there's only one of you. You've always seemed to me more like Plato than anybody alive, and I've regarded you as the most

enviable personality going. I'd emulate you in a minute—
if I could; but if mine is a case of mania, it's a genuine
case. I'm sane on everything else, but when it comes to
that—it's being money that I don't earn, but they, those
men off there underground, do earn and are forced to
give to me—when it comes to that, I'm as fixed in my
opinion as the man who thought he was a hard-boiled egg.
I don't blame you for being out of patience with me. As
you say I only spoil fine minutes by thinking of it, and as
you charitably refrained from saying, I spoil other people's
fine moments by speaking of it."

" What would you *have* us do!" Morrison challenged
him—" all turn in and clean sewers for a living? And
wouldn't it be a lovely world, if we did!"

Page did not answer for a moment. " I wonder," he
finally suggested mildly, " if it were all divided up, the
dirty work, and each of us did our share——"

" Oh, impractical! impractical! Wholly a back-eddy in
the forward-moving current. You can't go back of a
world-wide movement. Things are too complicated now
for everybody to do his share of anything. It's as reasonable, as to suggest that everybody do his share of watch-
making, or fancy juggling. Every man to his trade! And
if the man who makes watches, or cleans sewers, or even
mines coal—your especial sore spot—does his work well,
and is suited to it in temperament, who knows that he does
not find it a satisfaction as complete as mine in telling a bit
of genuine Palissy ware from an imitation. You, for instance, you'd make a *pretty* coal-miner, wouldn't you?
You're about as suited to it as Miss Marshall here for being
a college settlement worker!"

Sylvia broke out into an exclamation of wonder. " Oh,
how you do put your finger on the spot! If you knew
how I've struggled to justify myself for not going into
' social work' of some kind! Every girl nowadays who
doesn't marry at twenty, is slated for ' social betterment'
whether she has the least capacity for it or not. Public
opinion pushes us into it as mediæval girls were shoved

into convents, because it doesn't know what else to do with us. It's all right for Judith,—it's fine for her. She's made for it. I envy her. I always have. But me—I never could bear the idea of interfering in people's lives to tell them what to do about their children and their husbands just because they were poor. It always seemed to me it was bad enough to be poor without having other people with a little more money messing around in your life. I'm different from that kind of people. If I'm sincere I can't pretend I'm not different. And I'm not a bit sure I know what's any better for them to do than what they're doing!" She had spoken impetuously, hotly, addressing not the men beside her but a specter of her past life.

"How true that is—how unerring the instinct which feels it!" said Morrison appreciatively.

Page looked at Sylvia quickly, his clear eyes very tender. "Yes, yes; it's her very own life that Sylvia needs to live," he said in unexpected concurrence of opinion. Sylvia felt that the honors of the discussion so far were certainly with Felix. And Austin seemed oddly little concerned by this. He made no further effort to retrieve his cause, but fell into a silence which seemed rather preoccupied than defeated.

They were close to the Arc de Triomphe now. A brilliant sunset was firing a salvo of scarlet and gold behind it, and they stood for a moment to admire. "Oh, Paris! Paris!" murmured Morrison. "Paris in April! There's only one thing better, and that we have before us—Paris in May!"

They turned in past the loge of the concierge, and mounted in the languidly moving elevator to the appartement. Felix went at once to the piano and began playing something Sylvia did not recognize, something brilliantly colored, vivid, resonant, sonorous, perhaps Chabrier, she thought, remembering his remark on the avenue. Without taking off her hat she stepped to her favorite post of observation, the balcony, and sat down in the twilight with a sigh of exquisitely complete satisfaction, facing the sunset, the great arch lifting his huge, harmonious bulk up

out of the dim, encircling trees, the resplendent long stretch
of the lighted boulevard.   The music seemed to rise up
from the scene like its natural aroma.

Austin Page came out after her and leaned silently on
the railing, looking over the city.   Morrison finished the
Chabrier and began on something else before the two on
the balcony spoke.   Sylvia was asking no questions of fate
or the future, accepting the present with wilful blindness to
its impermanence.

Austin said: " I have been trying to say good-bye all
afternoon.   I am going back to America tomorrow."

Sylvia was so startled and shocked that she could not believe her ears.   Her heart beat hard.   To an incoherent,
stammered inquiry of hers, he answered, " It's my Colorado
property—always that.   It spoils everything.   I must go
back, and make a decision that's needed there.   I've been
trying to tell you.   But I can't.   Every time I have tried,
I have not dared.   If I told you, and you should beckon
me back, I should not be strong enough to go on.   I could
not leave you, Sylvia, if you lifted your hand.   And that
would be the end of the best of us both."   He had turned
and faced her, his hands back of him, gripping the railing.
The deep vibrations of his voice transported her to that
never-forgotten moment at Versailles.   He went on: " When
it is—when the decision is made, I'll write you.   I'll write
you, and then—I shall wait to hear your answer!"   From
inside the room Felix poured a dashing spray of diamond-
like trills upon them.

She murmured something, she did not know what; her
breathing oppressed by her emotion.   " Won't you—shan't
we see you—here——? "   She put her hand to her side,
feeling an almost intolerable pain.

He moved near her, and, to bring himself to her level,
knelt down on one knee, putting his elbows on the arm
of her chair.   The dusk had fallen so thickly that she had
not seen his face before.   She now saw that his lips were
quivering, that he was shaking from head to foot.   " It
will be for you to say, Sylvia," his voice was rough and

harsh with feeling, " whether you see me again." He took her hands in his and covered them with kisses—no grave tokens of reverence these, as on the day at Versailles, but human, hungry, yearning kisses that burned, that burned—

And then he was gone. Sylvia was there alone in the enchanted twilight, the Triumphal Arch before her, the swept and garnished and spangled city beneath her. She lifted her hand and saw that he had left on it not only kisses but tears. If he had been there then, she would have thrown herself into his arms.

CHAPTER XXXVIII

SYLVIA COMES TO THE WICKET-GATE

THREE weeks passed before his letter came. The slow, thrilling crescendo of May had lifted the heart up to a devout certainty of June. The leaves were fully out, casting a light, new shadow on the sprinkled streets. Every woman was in a bright-colored, thin summer dress, and every young woman looked alluring. The young men wore their hats tilted to one side, swung jaunty canes as they walked, and peered hopefully under the brim of every flowered feminine headdress. The days were like golden horns of plenty, spilling out sunshine, wandering perfumed airs, and the heart-quickening aroma of the new season. The nights were cool and starry. Every one in Paris spent as much as possible of every hour out of doors. The pale-blue sky flecked with creamy clouds seemed the dome, and the city the many-colored pavement of some vast building, so grandly spacious that the sauntering, leisurely crowds thronging the thoroughfares seemed no crowds at all, but only denoted a delightful sociability.

All the spring vegetables were at their crispest, most melting perfection, and the cherries from Anjou were like miniature apples of Hesperides. Up and down the smaller streets went white-capped little old women, with baskets on their arms, covered with snowy linen, and they chanted musically on the first three notes of the scale, so that the sunny vault above them resounded to the cry, " De la crème, fromage à la crème! " The three Americans had enchanted expeditions to Chantilly, to Versailles again, called back from the past and the dead by the miracle of spring ; to more distant formidable Coucy, grimly looking out over the smiling country at its foot, to Fontainebleau, even a two days' dash into Touraine, to Blois, Amboise, Loches, jewels set in the green enamels of May . . . and all the time Sylvia's attempt to take the present and to let the future bring what it would, was pitched perforce in a higher and higher key,—took a more violent effort to achieve.

She fell deeper than ever under Morrison's spell, and yet the lack of Austin was like an ache to her. She had said to herself, "I will not let myself think of him until his letter comes," and she woke up in the night suddenly, seeing the fire and tenderness and yearning of his eyes, and stretching out her arms to him before she was awake. And yet she had never tried so hard to divine every shade of Morrison's fastidiousness and had never felt so supreme a satisfaction in knowing that she did. There were strange, brief moments in her life now, when out of the warring complexity in her heart there rose the simple longing of a little girl to go to her mother, to feel those strong, unfailing arms about her. She began to guess dimly, without thinking about it at all, that her mother knew some secret of life, of balance, that she did not. And yet if her mother were at hand, she knew she could never explain to her—how could she, when she did not know herself?—what she was living through. How long she had waited the moment when she *would* know!

One day towards the end of May, Morrison had come in for lunch, a delicately chosen, deceptively simple meal for which Yoshida had outdone himself. There had been a savory mixture of sweetbreads and mushrooms in a smooth, rich, creamy sauce; green peas that had been on the vines at three o'clock that morning, and which still had the aroma of life in their delectable little balls; sparkling Saumur; butter with the fragrance of dew and clover in it; crisp, crusty rolls; artichokes in oil—such a meal as no money can buy anywhere but in Paris in the spring, such a simple, simple meal as takes a great deal of money to buy even in Paris.

"It is an art to eat like this," said Morrison, more than half seriously, after he had taken the first mouthful of the

golden soufflé which ended the meal. "What a May we
have had! I have been thinking so often of Talleyrand's
saying that no one who had not lived before the French
Revolution, under the old régime, could know how sweet
life could be; and I've been thinking that we may live to say
that about the end of this régime. Such perfect, golden
hours as it has for those who are able to seize them. It
is a debt we own the Spirit of Things to be grateful and to
appreciate our opportunity."

"As far as the luncheon goes, it's rather a joke, isn't
it," said his hostess, "that it should be an Oriental cook
who has so caught the true Gallic accent? I'll tell Tojiko
to tell Yoshido that his efforts weren't lost on you. He
adores cooking for you. No, you speak about it yourself.
Here comes Tojiko with the mail."

She reached for the *Herald* with one hand, and with the
other gave Sylvia a letter with the American postmark.
"Oh, Tojiko," said Morrison with the familiarity of an
habitué of the house, "will you tell your brother for me
that I never tasted anything like his . . ."

Mrs. Marshall-Smith broke in with an exclamation of
extreme astonishment. "Oh—what *do* you think—! Sylvia,
did you know anything about this? Of all the crazy—why,
what under the sun——? I always knew there was a vein
of the fanatic—any man who won't smoke—you may be
sure there's something unbalanced——!" She now turned
the paper as she spoke and held it so that the headlines
leaped out across the table:

MILLIONAIRE COAL OPERATOR TURNS VAST HOLDINGS OVER TO THE STATE

Son of Old Peter Page Converted to Socialism

"What!" cried Morrison. Even in the blankness of her
stupefaction, Sylvia was aware of a rising note in his voice
that was by no means dismay.

"Yes," continued Mrs. Marshall-Smith, reading rapidly

and disconnectedly from the paper, beginning an item and dropping it, as she saw it was not the one she was searching for, " ' Mr. Page is said to have contemplated some such step for a long . . .'—m-m-m, not that . . . ' well-known collector of ceramics—Metropolitan Museum—member of the Racquet, the Yacht, the Century, the Yale—thirty-two— Mother Miss Allida Sommerville of Baltimore, formerly a great beauty '—*here* it is," she stopped skimming and read consecutively : " ' Mr. Page's plan has been worked out in all detail with experts. A highly paid, self-perpetuating commission of labor experts, sociologists, and men of practical experience in coal-operating has been appointed to administer Mr. Page's extremely extensive holdings. The profits form a fund which, under the stipulations of Mr. Page's agreement with the State, is to be used to finance a program of advanced social activities; to furnish money for mothers' pensions, even perhaps for fathers' pensions in the case of families too numerous to be adequately cared for on workingmen's wages; to change the public school system of the locality into open-air schools with spacious grounds for manual activities of all kinds; greatly to raise wages; to lengthen the period of schooling before children go into remunerative occupations. . . .'" Mrs. Marshall-Smith looked up, said, "Oh, *you* know, the kind of thing such people are always talking about," and began to skip again, " '—extensive plans for garden cities—public libraries—books of the business to be open to employés— educational future—no philanthropy—and so forth and so forth.' " She glanced hurriedly down the page, caught the beginning of another sentence, and read : " ' The news has created an immense sensation all over the country. It is prophesied that Mr. Page's unexpected action will throw the coal business into great confusion. Other operators will find it extremely difficult to go on with the old conditions. Already it is rumored that the Chilton Coal and Coke Company . . .' "

" Well, I should think so indeed ! " cried Morrison emphatically, breaking in. " With modern industrial condi-

tions hung on a hair trigger as they are, it's as though a
boy had exploded a fire-cracker in the works of a watch.
That means his whole fortune gone. Old Peter put everything into coal. Austin will not have a cent—nothing but
those Vermont scrub forests of his. What a mad thing to
do! But it's been growing on him for a long time. I've
seen—I've felt it!"

Sylvia gave a dazed, mechanical look at the letter she
held and recognized the handwriting. She turned very
white.

Aunt Victoria said instantly: "I see you have a letter to
read, my dear, and I want Felix to play that D'Indy Inter-
lude for me and explain it—Bauer is going to play it tonight
for the Princess de Chevrille. We'll bother you with our
chatter. Don't you want to take it to your room to read?"

Sylvia stood up, holding the unopened letter in her hand.
She looked about her a little wildly and said: "Oh no, no!
I think I'd rather be out of doors. I'll go out on the
balcony."

"It's raining," said Mrs. Marshall-Smith.

"No, not yet," said Morrison, making a great effort to
speak in an ordinary tone. "It's only going to." He sat
down at the piano. Sylvia passed him and went out to
the balcony. She opened the letter and read it through
very carefully. It was a long one and this took some time.
She did not hear a note of the music which poured its plaintive, eerie cadences around her. When she had finished the
letter she instantly started to read it again, with the sensation that she had not yet begun to understand it. She
was now deeply flushed. She continually put back a floating
strand of hair, which recurrently fell across her forehead
and cheek.

After a time, Mrs. Marshall-Smith said from the open
door: "Felix and I are going to Madeleine Perth's. Would
you rather stay here?" Sylvia nodded without looking up.

She sat motionless, looking at the letter long after she had
finished it. An hour passed thus. Then she was aware
that it was beginning to rain. The drops falling on the open

letter dissolved the ink into blurred smears. She sprang up hastily and went into the salon, where she stood irreso-lute for a moment, and then, without calling Hélène, went to her room and dressed for the street. She moved very quickly as though there were some need for extreme haste, and when she stepped into the street she fell at once automatically into the swinging step of the practised walker who sees long miles before him.

Half an hour later she was looking up at the façade of Notre Dame through the rain, and seeing there these words: " I shall be waiting at Austin Farm to hear if you are at all able to sympathize with me in what I have done. The memory of our last words together may help you to imagine with what anxiety I shall be waiting."

She pushed open the greasy, shining leather door, passed into the interior, and stood for a moment in the incense-laden gloom of the nave. A mass was being said. The rapidly murmured Latin words came to her in a dim drone, in which she heard quite clearly, quite distinctly: " There is another kind of beauty I faintly glimpse—that isn't just sweet smells and lovely sights and harmonious lines—it's the beauty that can't endure disharmony in conduct, the fine, true ear for the loveliness of life lived at its best—Syl-via, finest, truest Sylvia, it's what you could, if you would— you more than any other woman in the world—if we were together to try——"

Sylvia sank to her knees on a prie-Dieu and hid her face in her hands, trying to shut out the words, and yet listening to them so intently that her breath was suspended. . . . " What Morrison said is true—for him, since he feels it to be true. No man can judge for another. But other things are true too, things that concern me. It's true that an honest man cannot accept an ease founded, even remotely, on the misery of others. And my life has been just that. I don't know what success I shall have with the life that's beginning, but I know at least it will begin straight. There seems a chance for real shapeliness if the foundations are all honest—doesn't there? Oh, Sylvia—oh, my dearest love,

if I could think you would begin it with me, Sylvia!
Sylvia!"

The girl sprang up and went hastily out of the church.
The nun kneeling at the door, holding out the silent prayer
for alms for the poor, looked up in her face as she passed
and then after her with calm, understanding eyes. Kneeling
there, day after day, she had seen many another young,
troubled soul fleeing from its own thoughts.

Sylvia crossed the parvis of Notre Dame, glistening wet,
and passed over the gray Seine, slate under the gray mist
of the rain. Under her feet the impalpable dust of a city
turned to gray slime which clung to her shoes. She walked
on through a narrow, mean street of mediæval aspect where
rag-pickers, drearily oblivious of the rain, quarreled weakly
over their filthy piles of trash. She looked at them in
astonishment, in dismay, in horror. Since leaving La
Chance, save for that one glimpse over the edge back in
the Vermont mountains, she had been so consistently surrounded by the padded satin of possessions that she had
forgotten how actual poverty looked. In fact, she had
never had more than the briefest fleeting glances at it.
This was so extravagant, so extreme, that it seemed impossible to her. And yet—and yet— She looked fleetingly
into those pale, dingy, underfed, repulsive faces and wondered if coal-miners' families looked like that.

But she said aloud at once, almost as though she had
crooked an arm to shield herself: " But he *said* he did not
want me to answer at once! He *said* he wanted me to take
time—to take time—to take time . . ." She hastened her
steps to this refrain, until she was almost running; and
emerged upon the broad, well-kept expanse of the Boulevard St. Germain with a long-drawn breath of relief.

Ahead of her to the right, the Rue St. Jacques climbed the
hill to the Pantheon. She took it because it was broad
and clean and differed from the musty darkness from which
she had come out; she fled up the steep grade with a swift,
light step as though she were on a country walk. She
might indeed have been upon some flat road near La

Chance for all she saw of the buildings, the people around her.

How like Austin's fine courage that was, his saying that he did not want her to decide in haste, but to take time to know what she was doing! What other man would not have stayed to urge her, to hurry her, to impose his will on hers, masterfully to use his personality to confuse her, to carry her off? For an instant, through all her wretched bewilderment, she thrilled to a high, impersonal appreciation of his saying: "If I had stayed with you, I should have tried to take you by force—but you are too fine for that, Sylvia! What you could be to the man you loved if you went to him freely—that is too splendid to risk losing. I want all of you—heart, soul, mind—or nothing!" Sylvia looked up through this clear white light to Austin's yearning eyes, and back through the ages with a wondering pity at the dark figure of Jerry Fiske, emerging from his cave. She had come a long way since then.

And then all this, everything fine, everything generous, ebbed away from her with deadly swiftness, and in a cold disgust with herself she knew that she had been repeating over and over Morrison's "Austin will not have a cent left . . . nothing but those Vermont scrub forests." So that was the kind of a woman she was. Well, if that was the kind of woman she was, let her live her life accordingly. She was sick with indecision as she fled onward through the rain.

Few pedestrians were abroad in the rain, and those who were, sheltered themselves slant-wise with their umbrellas against the wind, and scudded with the storm. Sylvia had an umbrella, but she did not open it. She held her face up once, to feel the rain fall on it, and this reminded her of home, and long rainy walks with her father. She winced at this, and put him hastily out of her mind. And she had been unconsciously wishing to see her mother! At the very recollection of her mother she lengthened her stride. There was another thought to run away from!

She swung around the corner near the Pantheon and

rapidly approached the door of the great Library of Ste. Geneviève. A thin, draggled, middle-aged woman-student, entering hastily, slipped on the wet stones and knocked from under his arm the leather portfolio of a thin, draggled, middle-aged man who was just coming out. The woman did not stop to help repair the damage she had done, but hastened desperately on into the shelter of the building. Sylvia's eyes, absent as they were, were caught and held by the strange, blank look of the man, who stood motionless, his shabby hat knocked to one side of his thin, gray hair, his curiously filmed eyes fixed stupidly on the litter of papers scattered at his feet. The rain was beginning to convert them into sodden pulp, but he did not stir. The idea occurred to Sylvia that he might be ill, and she advanced to help him. As he saw her stoop to pick them up, he said in French, in a toneless voice, very indifferently : " Don't give yourself the trouble. They are of no value. I carry them only to make the Library attendants think I am a bona-fide reader. I go there to sleep because I have no other roof."

His French was entirely fluent, but the accent was American. Sylvia looked up at him surprised. He returned her gaze dully, and without another look at the papers, scuffled off through the rain, across the street towards the Pantheon. His boots were lamentable.

Sylvia had an instantly vanishing memory of a pool of quiet sunshine, of a ripely beautiful woman and a radiant young man. Before she knew she was speaking, an impulsive cry had burst from her : " Why, Professor Saunders ! Professor Saunders ! Don't you know me ? I am Sylvia Marshall ! "

CHAPTER XXXIX

SYLVIA DRIFTS WITH THE MAJORITY

" No, they don't let you sit down in here if you're as shabby as I am," said the man, continuing his slow, feeble, shuffling progress. " They know you're only a vagrant, here to get out of the rain. They won't even let you stand still long."

Sylvia had not been inside the Pantheon before, had never been inside a building with so great a dome. They stood under it now. She sent her glance up to its vast, dim, noble heights and brought it down to the saturnine, unsavory wreck at her side. She was regretting the impulse which had made her call out to him. What could she say to him now they were together? What word, what breath could be gentle enough, light enough not to be poison to that open sore?

On his part he seemed entirely unconcerned about the impression he made on her. His eyes, his sick, filmed eyes, looked at her with no shrinking, with no bravado, with an entire indifference which gave, through all the desolation of his appearance, the strangest, careless dignity to the man. He did not care what she thought of him. He did not care what any one thought of him. He gave the impression of a man whose accounts are all reckoned and the balance struck, long ago.

" So this is Sylvia," he said, with the slightest appearance of interest, glancing at her casually. " I always said you would make a beautiful woman. But since I knew Victoria, I've seen that you must be quite what she was at your age." It might have been a voice speaking from beyond the grave, so listless, so dragging was its rhythm. " How do you happen to be in Paris? " he asked. " Are your parents still alive? "

" Oh *yes!*" said Sylvia, half startled by the preposterousness of the idea that they might not be. " They're very well too. I had such a good letter from Mother the other day. Do you remember Professor Kennedy? He has just given up his position to be professor emeritus. I suppose now he'll write that book on the idiocy of the human race he's been planning so long. And old Mr. Reinhardt, he's still the same, they say . . . wonderful, isn't it, at his age? " She was running on, not knowing what to say, and chattering rather foolishly in her embarrassment. " Judith is a trained nurse; isn't that just the right thing for her? I'm visiting Aunt Victoria here for a while. Lawrence is a Freshman at . . ."

He broke in, his hollow voice resounding in the immense, vault-like spaces around them. " You'd better go home," he said. " I'd leave tonight, if I were you." She looked at him startled, half-scared, thinking that she had been right to fancy him out of his mind. She saw with relief a burly attendant in a blue uniform lounging near a group of statuary. She could call to him, if it became necessary.

" You'd better go away from her at once," went on the man, advancing aimlessly from one bay of the frescoes to another.

Sylvia knew now of whom he was speaking, and as he continued talking with a slow, dreary monotony, her mind raced back over the years, picking up a scrap here, a half-forgotten phrase there, an intercepted look between her father and mother, a recollection of her own, a half-finished sentence of Arnold's . . .

" She can't be fatal for you in the same way she has been for the others, of course," the man was saying. " What she'll do for you is to turn you into a woman like herself. I remember now, I have thought many times, that you *were* like her . . . of the same clay. But you have something else too, you have something that she'll take away from you if you stay. You can't keep her from doing it. No one can get the better of her. She doesn't fight. But she always takes life. She has taken mine. She must have taken her bogie-husband's, she took young Gilbert's, she took Gilbert's wife's, she took Arnold's in another way. . . . God! think of leaving a young, growing, weak soul in the care of a woman like Victoria! She took that poet's, I forget his name; I suppose by this time Felix Morrison is . . ."

At this name, a terrible contraction of the heart told Sylvia that she was listening to what he said. "Felix Morrison!" she cried in stern, angry protest. "I don't know what you're talking about—but if you think that Aunt Victoria—if you think Felix Morrison——" She was inarticulate in her indignation. "He was married last autumn to a beautiful girl—and Aunt Victoria—what an idea!—no one was more pleased than she—why—you are *crazy!*" She flung out at him the word, which two moments before she would not have been so cruel as to think.

It gave him no discomfort. "Oh no, I'm not," he said with a spectral laugh, which had in it, to Sylvia's dismay, the very essence of sanity. She did not know why she now shrank away from him, far more frightened than before. "I'm about everything else you might mention, but I'm not crazy. And you take my word for it and get out while you still can . . . *if* you still can?" He faintly indicated an inquiry, looking at her sideways, his dirty hand stroking the dishonoring gray stubble of his unshaven face. "As for Morrison's wife . . . let her get out too. Gilbert tried marrying, tried it in all unconsciousness. It's only when they try to get away from her that they know she's in the marrow of their bones. She lets them try. She doesn't even care. She knows they'll come back. Gilbert did. And his wife . . . well, I'm sorry for Morrison's wife."

"She's dead," said Sylvia abruptly.

He took this in with a nod of the head. "So much the better for her. How did it happen that *you* didn't fall for Morrison's . . ." he looked at her sharply at a change in her face she could not control. "Oh, you did," he commented slackly. "Well, you'd better start home for La Chance tonight," he said again.

They were circling around and around the shadowy interior, making no pretense of looking at the frescoed walls, to examine which had been their ostensible purpose in entering. Sylvia was indeed aware of great pictured spaces, crowded dimly with thronging figures, men, horses, women —they reached no more than the outer retina of her eye. She remembered fleetingly that they had something to do with the story of Ste. Geneviève. She wanted intensely to escape from this phantom whom she herself had called up from the void to stalk at her side. But she felt she ought not to let pass, even coming from such a source, such utterly frenzied imaginings against one to whom she owed loyalty. She spoke coldly, with extreme distaste for the subject: " You're entirely wrong about Aunt Victoria. She's not in the least that kind of a woman."

He shook his head slowly. " No, no; you misunderstand me. Your Aunt Victoria is quite irreproachable, she always has been, she always will be. She is always in the right. She always will be. She did nothing to me but hire me to teach her stepson, and when my habits became too bad, discharge me, as any one would have done. She did nothing to Arnold except to leave him to the best schools and the best tutors money could buy. What more could any one have done? She had not the slightest idea that Horace Gilbert would try to poison his wife, had not the slightest connection with their quarrel. The young poet,—Adams was his name, now I remember—did not consult her before he took to cocaine. Morphine is my own specialty. Victoria of course deplored it as much as any one could. No, I'm not for a minute intimating that Victoria is a Messalina. We'd all be better off if she were. It's only our grossness that finds fault with her. Your aunt is one of the most respectable women who ever lived, as ' chaste as unsunned snow—the very ice of chastity is in her ! ' Indeed, I've often wondered if the redoubtable Ephraim Smith himself, for all that he succeeded in marrying her, fared any better than the rest of us. Victoria would be quite capable of cheating him out of his pay. She parches, yes, she dries up the blood—but it's not by her passion, not even by ours. Honest passion never kills. It's the Sahara sands of her egotism into which we've all emptied our veins."

Sylvia was frozen to the spot by her outraged indignation that any one should dare speak to her thus. She found herself facing a fresco of a tall, austere figure in an enveloping white garment, an elderly woman with a thin, worn, noble face, who laid one fine old hand on a stone parapet and with divine compassion and tenderness looked out over a sleeping city. The man followed the direction of her eyes. " It's Puvis de Chavannes' Ste. Geneviève as an old woman, guarding and praying for the city. Very good, isn't it? I especially admire the suggestion of the plain bare cell she has stepped out from. I often come here to look at it when I've nothing to eat." He seemed as flaccidly willing to speak on this as on any other topic; to find it no more interesting than the subject of his former speech.

Sylvia was overcome with horror of him. She walked rapidly away, towards the door, hoping he would not follow her. He did not. When she glanced back fearfully over her shoulder, she saw him still standing there, looking up at the gaunt gray figure of beneficent old age. His dreadful broken felt hat was in his hand, the water dripped from his frayed trousers over the rotting leather of his shoes. As she looked, he began to cough, loudly, terribly, so that the echoing reaches of the great nave resounded to the sound. Sylvia ran back to him and thrust her purse into his hand. At first he could not speak, for coughing, but in a moment he found breath to ask, " Is it Victoria's money? "

She did not answer.

He held it for a moment, and then opening his hand let it drop. As she turned away Sylvia heard it fall clinking on the stone floor. At the door she turned for one last look. and saw him weakly stooping to pick it up again. She fairly burst out of the door.

It was almost dusk when she was on the street again, looking down the steep incline to the Luxembourg Gar-

dens. In the rainy twilight the fierce tension of the Rodin
" Thinker" in front of the Pantheon loomed huge and
tragic. She gave it a glance of startled sympathy. She had
never understood the statue before. Now she was a prey
to those same ravaging throes. There was for the moment
no escaping them. She felt none of her former wild impulse to run away. What she had been running away from
had overtaken her. She faced it now, looked at it squarely,
gave it her ear for the first time ; the grinding, dissonant note
under the rich harmony of the life she had known for all
these past months, the obscure vaults underlying the shining
temple in which she had been living.

What beauty could there be which was founded on such
an action as Felix' marriage to Molly—Molly, whose passionate directness had known the only way out of the im-
passe into which Felix should never have let her go ? . . . .
An echo from what she had heard in the mass at Notre
Dame rang in her ears, and now the sound was louder—
Austin's voice, Austin's words : " A beauty that can't endure
disharmony in conduct, the fine true ear for the deeper
values, the foundations——" It was Austin, asking himself what beauty could be in any life founded, even remotely
as his was, on any one's misery ?

For a long time she stood there, silent, motionless, her
hands clenched at her sides, looking straight before her in
the rain. Above her on his pedestal, the great, bronze,
naked, tortured man ground his teeth as he glared out from
under the inexorable limitations of his ape-like forehead,
and strove wildly against the barriers of his flesh . . .

Wildly and vainly, against inexorable limitations ! Sylvia was aware that an insolent young man, with moist pro-
tuberant eyes, had come up where she stood there, alone,
motionless on the public street. He put his arm in hers,
clasped her hand in a fat, soft palm, and, " *Allons, ma
belle !*" he said with a revolting gayety.

Sylvia pulled away from him, cried out fiercely in
English, " Don't you dare to touch me ! " and darted
away.

He made no attempt at pursuit, acknowledging his mistake with an easy shrug and turning off to roam, a dim, predatory figure, along the dusky street. He had startled and frightened the girl so that she was trembling when she ventured to slow down to a walk under the glaring lights of the Boulevard St. Michel. She was also shivering with wet and cold, and without knowing it, she was extremely hungry. As she fled along the boulevard in the direction of her own quarter of the city, her eye caught the lighted clock at the kiosk near Cluny. She was astonished to see that it was after seven o'clock. How long could she have stood there, under the shadow of that terrific Thinker, consumed quite as much as he by the pain of trying to rise above mere nature? An hour—more than an hour, she must have been there. The Pantheon must have closed during that time, and the dreadful, sick man must have passed close by her. Where was he now? What makeshift shelter harbored that cough, those dirty, skeleton hands, those awful eyes which had outlived endurance and come to know peace before death . . .

She shivered and tried to shrink away from her wet, clinging clothing. She had never, in all her life before, been wet and cold and hungry and frightened, she had never known from what she had been protected. And now the absence of money meant that she must walk miles in the rain before she could reach safety and food. For three cents she could ride. But she had not three cents. How idiotic she had been not to keep a few sous from her purse. What a sickening thing it had been to see him stoop to pick it up after he had tried to have the pride not to touch it. That was what morphine had done for him. And he would buy more morphine with that money, that was the reason he had not been able to let it lie . . . the man who had been to her little girlhood the radiant embodiment of strength and fineness!

Her teeth were chattering, her feet soaked and cold. She tried to walk faster to warm her blood, and discovered that she was exhausted, tired to the marrow of her bones. Her feet dragged on the pavement, her arms hung heavily by her side, but she dared not stop a moment lest some other man with abhorrent eyes should approach her.

She set her teeth and walked; walked across the Seine without a glance at its misted lights blinking through the rain, walked on past the prison of Marie Antoinette, without a thought of that other harmless woman who had loved bright and lovely things while others suffered: walked on upon the bridge across the Seine again. This bewildered her, making her think that she was so dazed she had doubled on her tracks. She saw, a long way off, a solitary hooded sergent de ville, and dragged herself across an endless expanse of wet asphalt to ask him her way. But just before she reached him, she remembered suddenly that of course she was on the island and was obliged to cross the Seine again before reaching the right bank. She returned weary and disheartened to her path, crossed the bridge, and then endlessly, endlessly, set one heavy foot before the other under the glare of innumerable electric lights staring down on her and on the dismal, wet, and deserted streets. The clocks she passed told her that it was nearly eight o'clock. Then it was past eight. What must they be thinking of her on the Rue de Presbourg? She tried again to hurry, but could force her aching muscles to no more than the plod, plod, plod of her dogged advance over those interminable miles of pavement. There was little of her then that was not cold, weary, wet flesh, suffering all the discomforts that an animal can know. She counted her steps for a long time, and became so stupidly absorbed in this that she made a wrong turning and was blocks out of her way before she noticed her mistake. This mishap reduced her almost to tears, and it was when she was choking them weakly back and setting herself again to the cruel long vista of the Champs-Elysées that an automobile passed her at top speed with a man's face pressed palely to the panes. Almost at once the car stopped in answer to a shouted command; it whirled about and bore down on her. Felix Morrison sprang out and ran to her with outstretched arms, his rich voice ringing through the desolation of the rain and the night—" Sylvia! Sylvia! Are you safe?"

He almost carried her back to the car, lifted her in. There were wraps there, great soft, furry, velvet wraps which he cast about her, murmuring broken ejaculations of emotion, of pity, of relief—" Oh, your hands, how cold! Sylvia, how *could* you? Here, drink this! I've been insane,—absolutely out of my mind! Let me take off your hat—Oh, your poor feet—I was on my way to—I was afraid you might have—— Oh, Sylvia, Sylvia, to have you safe!" She tried to bring to mind something she had intended to remember; she even repeated the phrase over to herself, " It was an ugly, ugly thing to have married Molly," but she knew only that he was tenderness and sheltering care and warmth and food and safety. She drew long quivering breaths like a child coming out of a sobbing fit.

Then before there was time for more thought, the car had whirled them back to the door, where Aunt Victoria, outwardly calm, but very pale, stood between the concierge and his wife, looking out into the rainy deserted street.

At the touch of those warm embracing arms, at that radiant presence, at the sound of that relieved, welcoming voice, the nightmare of the Pantheon faded away to blackness. . . .

Half an hour later, she sat, fresh from a hot bath, breathing out delicately a reminiscence of recent violet water and perfumed powder; fresh, fine under-linen next her glowing skin; shining and refreshed, in a gown of chiffon and satin; eating her first mouthful of Yoshido's ambrosial soup.

" Why, I'm so sorry," she was saying. " I went out for a walk, and then went further than I meant to. I've been over on the left bank part of the time, in Notre Dame and the Pantheon. And then when I started to come home it took longer than I thought. It's so apt to, you know."

" Why in the world, my dear, did you *walk* home?" cried Aunt Victoria, still brooding over her in pitying sympathy.

" I'd—I'd lost my purse. I didn't have any money."

" But you don't pay for a cab till you come to the end

of your journey! You could have stepped into a taxi and borrowed the money of the concierge here."

Sylvia was immensely disconcerted by her rustic naïveté in not thinking of this obvious device. "Oh, of course! How could I have been so—but I was tired when I came to start home—I was very tired—too tired to think clearly!"

This brought them all back to the recollection of what had set her off on her walk. There was for a time rather a strained silence; but they were all very hungry—dinner was two hours late—and the discussion of Yoshido's roast duckling was anything but favorable for the consideration of painful topics. They had champagne to celebrate her safe escape from the adventure. To the sensation of perfect ease induced by the well-chosen dinner this added a little tingling through all Sylvia's nerves, a pleasant, light, bright titillation.

All might have gone well if, after the dinner, Felix had not stepped, as was his wont, to the piano. Sylvia had been, up to that moment, almost wholly young animal, given over to bodily ecstasy, of which not the least was the agreeable warmth on her silk-clad ankle as she held her slippered foot to the fire.

But at the first chords something else in her, slowly, with extreme pain, awoke to activity. All her life music had spoken a language to which she could not shut her ears, and now—her face clouded, she shifted her position, she held up a little painted screen to shield her face from the fire, she finally rose and walked restlessly about the room. Every grave and haunting cadence from the piano brought to her mind, flickering and quick, like fire, a darting question, and every one she stamped out midway, with an effort of the will.

The intimacy between Felix and Aunt Victoria, it was strange she had never before thought——of course not— what a hideous idea! That book, back in Lydford, with Horace Gilbert's name on the fly-leaf, and Aunt Victoria's cool, casual voice as she explained, "Oh, just a young architect who used to——" Oh, the man in the Pantheon was simply brutalized by drugs; he did not know what he was saying. His cool, spectral laugh of sanity sounded faintly in her ears again.

And then, out of a mounting foam of arpeggios, there bloomed for her a new idea, solid enough, broad enough, high enough, for a refuge against all these wolfish fangs. She sat down to think it out, hot on the trail of an answer, the longed-for answer.

It had just occurred to her that there was no possible logical connection between any of those skulking phantoms and the golden lovely things they tried to defile. Even if some people of wealth and ease and leisure were not as careful about moral values as about colors, and æsthetic harmonies—that meant nothing. The connection was purely fortuitous. How silly she had been not to see that. Grant, for purposes of argument, that Aunt Victoria was self-centered and had lived her life with too little regard for its effect on other people,—grant even that Felix had, under an almost overpowering temptation, not kept in a matter of conduct the same rigid nicety of fastidiousness which characterized his judgment of marbles—what of it? That did not mean that one could only be fine and true in conduct by giving up all lovely things and wearing hair-shirts. What an outgrown, mediæval idea! How could she have been for a moment under its domination! It was just that old Puritanism, Spartanism of her childhood, which was continually reaching up its bony hand from the grave where she had interred it.

The only danger came, she saw it now, read it plainly and clear-headedly in the lives of the two people with her, the only danger came from a lack of proportion. It certainly did seem to be possible to allow the amenities and æsthetic pleasures to become so important that moral fineness must stand aside till they were safe. But anybody who had enough intelligence could keep his head, even if the temptation was alluring. And simply because there was that possible danger, why not enjoy delightful things as long as they did not run counter to moral fineness! How absurd to think there was any reason why they should; quite the contrary, as a thousand philosophers attested. They would not in her case, at least! Of course, if a decision had to be taken between the two, she would never hesitate—never! As she phrased this conviction to herself, she turned a ring on her white slim finger and had a throb of pleasure in the color of the gem. What harmless, impersonal pleasures they were! How little they hurt any one! And as to this business of morbidly probing into healthy flesh, of insisting on going back of everything, farther than any one could possibly go, and scrutinizing the origin of every dollar that came into your hand . . . why, that way lay madness! As soon try to investigate all the past occupants of a seat in a railway before using it for a journey. Modern life was not organized that way. It was too complicated.

Her mind rushed on excitedly, catching up more certainty, more and more reinforcements to her argument as it advanced. There was, therefore, nothing inherent in the manner of life she had known these last months to account for what seemed ugly underneath. There was no reason why some one more keenly on his guard could not live as they did and escape sounding that dissonant note!

The music stopped. Morrison turned on the stool and seeing her bent head and moody stare at the fire, sent an imploring glance for help to Mrs. Marshall-Smith.

Just let her have the wealth and leisure and let her show how worthily she could use it! There would be an achievement! Sylvia came around to another phase of her new idea, there would be something worth doing, to show that one could be as fine and true in a palace as in a hut,— even as in a Vermont farmhouse! At this, suddenly all thought left her. Austin Page stood before her, fixing on her his clear and passionate and tender eyes. At that dear and well-remembered gaze, her lip began to quiver like a child's, and her eyes filled.

Mrs. Marshall-Smith stirred herself with the effect of a splendid ship going into action with all flags flying. " Syl-

via dear," she said, " this rain tonight makes me think of
a new plan. It will very likely rain for a week or more
now. Paris is abominable in the rain. What do you say
to a change? Madeleine Perth was telling ne this afternoon that the White Star people are runni ; a few ships
from Portsmouth by way of Cherbourg arour. i by Gibraltar,
through the Mediterranean to Naples. That's one trip your
rolling-stone of an aunt has never taken, and I'd rather
like to add it to my collection. We could be in Naples in
four days from Cherbourg and spend a month in Italy,
going north as the heat arrived. Felix—why don't you
come along? You've been wanti.ng to see the new low
reliefs in the Terme, in Rome?"

Sylvia's heart, like all young hearts, was dazzled almost
to blinking by the radiance shed from the magic word
Italy. She turned, looking very much taken aback and
bewildered, but with light in her eyes, color in her face.

Morrison burst out: " Oh, a dream realized! Something
to live on all one's days, the pines of the Borghese—the
cypresses of the Villa Medici—roses cascading over the
walls in Rome, the view across the Campagna from the
terraces at Rocca di Papa——"

Sylvia thought rapidly to herself: " Austin *said* he did
not want me to answer at once. He *said* he wanted me to
take time—to take time! I can decide better, make more
sense out of everything, if I—after I have thought more,
have taken more time. No, I am not turning my back on
him. Only I must have more time to think——"

Aloud she said, after a moment's silence, " Oh, nothing
could be lovelier!"

She lay in her warm, clean white bed that night, sleeping the sound sleep of the healthy young animal which has
been wet and cold and hungry, and is now dry and warmed
and fed.

Outside, across the city, on his bronze pedestal, the tortured Thinker, loyal to his destiny, still strove terribly
against the limitations of his ape-like forehead.

BOOK IV

THE STRAIT PATH

CHAPTER XL

A CALL FROM HOME

It was quite dark when they arrived in the harbor at Naples; and they were too late to go through the necessary formalities of harbor entering. In company with several other in- and outward-bound steamers, the *Carnatic* lay to for the night. Some one pointed out a big liner which would sail for New York the next morning, lying like a huge, gaily lighted island, the blare of her band floating over the still water.

Sylvia slept little that night, missing the rolling swing of the ship, and feeling breathless in the stifling immobility of the cabin. She tossed about restlessly, dozing off at intervals and waking with a start to get up on her knees and look out through the port-hole at the lights of Naples blazing steadily in their semicircle. She tried to think several times, about her relations to Felix, to Austin—but nothing came to her mind except a series of scenes in which they had figured, scenes quite disconnected, which brought no enlightenment to her.

As she lay awake thus, staring at the ceiling, feeling in the intense silence and blackness that the fluttering of her eyelids was almost audible, her heart beating irregularly, now slow, now fast, it occurred to her that she was beginning to know something of the intensity of real life—real grown-up life. She was astonished to enjoy it so little.

She fell at last, suddenly, fathoms deep into youthful slumber, and at once passed out from tormented darkness

into some strange, sunny, wind-swept place on a height
And she was all one anguish of longing for Austin. And
he came swiftly to her and took her in his arms and kissed
her on the lips. And it was as it had been when she was a
child and heard music, she was carried away by a great
swelling tide of joy . . . But dusk began to fall again:
Austin faded; through the darkness something called and
called to her, imperatively. With great pain she struggled
up through endless stages of half-consciousness, until she
was herself again, Sylvia Marshall, heavy-eyed, sitting up
in her berth and saying aloud, " Yes, what is it? " in answer
to a knocking on the door.

The steward's voice answered, announcing that the first
boat for shore would leave in an hour. Sylvia sprang out
of bed, the dream already nothing more than confused
brightness in her mind. By the time she was dressed, it
had altogether gone, and she only knew that she had had a
restless night. She went out on the deck, longing for the
tonic of pure air. The morning was misty—it had rained
during the night—and clouds hung heavy and low over the
city. Out from this gray smother the city gleamed like a
veiled opal. Neither Felix nor her aunt was to be seen.
When she went down to breakfast, after a brisk tramp back
and forth across the deck, she was rosy and dewy, her triumphant youth showing no sign of her vigils. She was saying
to herself: " Now I've come, it's too idiotic not to enjoy it.
I *shall* let myself go! "

Hélène attended to the ladies' packing and to the labeling
and care of the baggage. Empty-handed, care-free, feeling
like a traveling princess, Sylvia climbed down from the
great steamer into a dirty, small harbor-boat. Aunt Victoria sat down at once on the folding camp-chair which
Hélène always carried for her. Sylvia and Felix stood
together at the blunt prow, watching the spectacle before
them. The clouds were lifting from the city and from
Vesuvius, and from Sylvia's mind. Her spirits rose as the
boat went forward into the strange, foreign, glowing scene.

The oily water shimmered in smooth heavings as the

clumsy boat advanced upon it. The white houses on the hills gleamed out from their palms. As the boat came closer to the wharf, the travelers could see the crowds of foreign-looking people, with swarthy faces and cheap, ungraceful clothes, looking out at the boat with alert, speculative, unwelcoming eyes. The noise of the city streets, strange to their ears after the days of sea silence, rose clattering, like a part of the brilliance, the sparkle. The sun broke through the clouds, poured a flood of glory on the refulgent city, and shone hotly on the pools of dirty water caught in the sunken spots of the uneven stone pavement.

Aunt Victoria made her way up the gang-plank to the landing dock, achieving dignity even there. Felix sprang after her, to hand her her chair, and Hélène and Sylvia followed. Mrs. Marshall-Smith sat down at once, opening her dark-purple parasol, the tense silk of which was changed by the hot Southern sun into an iridescent bubble. " We will wait here till the steward gets our trunks out," she announced. " It will be amusing to watch the people." The four made an oasis of aristocracy in the seething, shouting, frowzy, gaudy, Southern crowd, running about with the scrambling, undignified haste of ants, sweating, gesticulating, their faces contorted with care over their poor belongings. Sylvia was acutely conscious of her significance in the scene. She was also fully aware that Felix missed none of the contrast she made with the other women. She felt at once enhanced and protected by the ignobly dressed crowd about her. Felix was right—in America there could be no distinction, there was no background for it.

The scene about them was theatrically magnificent. In the distance Vesuvius towered, cloud-veiled and threatening, the harbor shone and sparkled in the sun, the vivid, out-reaching arms of Naples clasped the jewel-like water. From it all Sylvia extracted the most perfect distillation of traveler's joy. She felt the well-to-do tourist's care-free detachment from the fundamentals of life, the tourist's sense that everything exists for the purpose of being a sight for him to see. She knew, and knew with delight, the wan-

derer's lightened, emancipated sense of being at a distance
from obligations, that cheerful sense of an escape from the
emprisoning solidarity of humanity which furnishes the zest
of life for the tourist and the tramp, enabling the one lightheartedly to offend proprieties and the other casually to
commit murder. She was embarked upon a moral vacation. She was out of the Bastile of right and wrong. She
had a vision of what freedom from entangling responsibilities is secured by traveling. She understood her aunt's
classing it as among the positive goods of life.

A man in a shabby blue uniform, with a bundle of letters
in his hand, walked past them towards the boat.

"Oh, the mail," said Mrs. Marshall-Smith. "There may
be some for us." She beckoned the man to her, and said,
"Marshall-Smith? Marshall? Morrison?"

The man sorted over his pile. "Cable for Miss Marshall," he said, presenting it to the younger lady with a
bold, familiar look of admiration. "Letter for F. Morrison: two letters for Mrs. Marshall-Smith." Sylvia
opened her envelope, spread out the folded sheet of paper,
and read what was scrawled on it, with no realization of
the meaning. She knew only that the paper, Felix, her
aunt, the crowd, vanished in thick blackness, through which,
much later, with a great roaring in her ears, she read, as
though by jagged flashes of lightning: "Mother very ill.
Come home at once. Judith."

It seemed to her an incalculably long time between
her first glance at the words and her understanding of
them, but when she emerged from the blackness and
void, into the flaunting sunlight, the roaring still in her
ears, the paper still in her hands, the scrawled words still
venomous upon it, she saw that not a moment could have
passed, for Felix and her aunt were unfolding letters of
their own, their eyes beginning to run quickly over the
pages.

Sylvia stood quite still, feeling immeasurably and bitterly
alone. She said to herself: "Mother is very sick. I must

go home at once. Judith." But she did not know what she said. She felt only an impulse to run wildly away from something that gave her intolerable pain.

Mrs. Marshall-Smith turned over a page of her letter, smiling to herself, and glanced up at her niece. Her smile was smitten from her lips. Sylvia had a fantastic vision of her own aspect from the gaping face of horror with which her aunt for an instant reflected it. She had never before seen Aunt Victoria with an unprepared and discom posed countenance. It was another feature of the nightmare.

For suddenly everything resolved itself into a bad dream, —her aunt crying out, Hélène screaming and running to her, Felix snatching the telegram from her and reading it aloud —it seemed to Sylvia that she had heard nothing for years but those words, " Mother very sick. Come home at once. Judith." She heard them over and over after his voice was silent. Through their constant echoing roar in her ears she heard but dimly the babel of talk that arose— Aunt Victoria saying that she could not of course leave at once because no passage had been engaged, Hélène foolishly offering smelling-salts, Felix darting off to get a carriage to take them to the hotel where she could be out of the crowd and they could lay their plans—" Oh, my poor dear ! —but you may have more reassuring news tomorrow, you know," said Mrs. Marshall-Smith soothingly.

The girl faced her aunt outraged. She thought she cried out angrily, " tomorrow ! " but she did not break her silence. She was so torn by the storm within her that she had no breath for recriminations. She turned and ran rapidly some distance away to the edge of the wharf, where some small rowboats hung bobbing, their owners sprawled on the seats, smoking cigarettes and chattering. Sylvia addressed the one nearest her in a strong, imperious voice. " I want you to take me out to that steamer," she said, pointing out to the liner in the harbor.

The man looked up at her blankly, his laughing, impertinent brown face sobered at once by the sight of her own. He made a reply in Italian, raising his shoulders. Some ill-dressed, loafing stragglers on the wharf drew near Sylvia with an indolent curiosity. She turned to them and asked, " Do any of you speak English? " although it was manifestly inconceivable that any of those typical Neapolitans should. One of them stepped forward, running his hand through greasy black curls. " I kin, lady," he said with a fluent, vulgar New York accent. " What ye want? "

" Tell that man," said Sylvia, her lips moving stiffly, " to take me out to the ship that is to leave for America this morning—and now—this minute, I may be late now! "

After a short impassioned colloquy, the loafer turned to her and reported : " He says if he took you out, you couldn't git on board. Them big ships ain't got no way for folks in little boats to git on. And he'd ask you thirty lire, anyhow. That's a fierce price. Say, if you'll wait a minute, I can get you a man that'll do it for——" Mrs. Marshall-Smith and Hélène had followed, and now broke through the line of ill-smelling loungers. Mrs. Marshall-Smith took hold of her niece's arm firmly, and began to draw her away with a dignified gesture. " You don't know what you are doing, child," she said with a peremptory accent of authority. " You are beside yourself. Come with me at once. This is no——"

Sylvia did not resist her. She ignored her. In fact, she did not understand a word that her aunt said. She shook off the older woman's hand with one thrust of her powerful young arm, and gathering her skirts about her, leaped down into the boat. She took out her purse and showed the man a fifty-lire bill. " Row fast! Fast! " she motioned to him, sitting down in the stern and fixing her eyes on the huge bulk of the liner, black upon the brilliance of the sunlit water. She heard her name called from the wharf and turned her face backward, as the light craft began to move jerkily away.

Felix had come up and now stood between Mrs. Marshall-Smith and her maid, both of whom were passionately appealing to him! He looked over their heads, saw the girl already a boat-length from the wharf, and gave a gesture of utter consternation. He ran headlong to the edge of the dock and again called her name loudly, "Sylvia! *Sylvia!*" There was no mistaking the quality of that cry. It was the voice of a man who sees the woman he loves departing from him, and who wildly, imperiously calls her back to him. But she did not return. The boat was still so close that she could look deeply into his eyes. Through all her tumult of horror, there struck cold to Sylvia's heart the knowledge that they were the eyes of a stranger. The blow that had pierced her had struck into a quivering center of life, so deep within her, that only something as deep as its terrible suffering could seem real. The man who stood there, so impotently calling to her, belonged to another order of things—things which a moment ago had been important to her, and which now no longer existed. He had become for her as remote, as immaterial as the gaudy picturesqueness of the scene in which he stood. She gave him a long strange look, and made a strange gesture, a gesture of irrevocable leave-taking. She turned her face again to the sea, and did not look back.

They approached the liner, and Sylvia saw some dark heads looking over the railing at her. Her boatman rowed around the stern to the other side, where the slanting stairs used in boarding the harbor-boats still hung over the side. The landing was far above their heads. Sylvia stood up and cried loudly to the dull faces, staring down at her from the steerage deck. "Send somebody down on the stairs to speak to me." There was a stir; a man in a blue uniform came and looked over the edge, and went away. After a moment, an officer in white ran down the stairs to the hanging landing with the swift, sure footing of a seaman. Sylvia stood up again, turning her white face up to him, her eyes blazing in the shadow of her hat. "I've just heard that my mother is very sick, and I must get back to America at once. If you will let down the rope ladder, I can climb up. I must go! I have plenty of money. I *must!*"

The officer stared, shook his head, and ran back up the stairs, disappearing into the black hole in the ship's side. The dark, heavy faces continued to hang over the railing, staring fixedly down at the boat with a steady, incurious gaze. Sylvia's boatman balanced his oar-handles on his knees, rolled a cigarette and lighted it. The boat swayed up and down on the shimmering, heaving roll of the water, although the ponderous ship beside it loomed motionless as a rock. The sun beat down on Sylvia's head and up in her face from the molten water till she felt sick, but when another officer in white, an elderly man with an impassive, bearded face, came down the stairs, she rose up, instantly forgetful of everything but her demand. She called out her message again, straining her voice until it broke, poised so impatiently in the little boat, swinging under her feet, that she seemed almost about to spring up towards the two men leaning over to catch her words. When she finished, the older man nodded, the younger one ran back up the stairs, and returned with a rope ladder.

Sylvia's boatman stirred himself with an ugly face of misgiving He clutched at her arm, and made close before her face the hungry, Mediterranean gesture of fingering money. She took out her purse, gave him the fifty-lire note, and catching at the ladder as it was flung down, disregarding the shouted commands of the men above her to " wait! " she swung herself upon it, climbing strongly and surely in spite of her hampering skirts.

The two men helped her up, alarmed and vexed at the risk she had taken. They said something about great crowds on the boat, and that only in the second cabin was there a possibility for accommodations. If she answered them, she did not know what she said. She followed the younger man down a long corridor, at first dark and smelling of hemp, later white, bright with electric light, smelling strongly of fresh paint, stagnant air, and machine-oil. They emerged in a round hallway at the foot of a staircase. The officer went to a window for a conference with the official behind it, and returned to Sylvia to say that there was no room, not even a single berth vacant. Some shabby woman-passengers with untidy hair and crumpled clothes drew near, looking at her with curiosity. Sylvia appealed to them, crying out again, " My mother is very sick and I must go back to America at once. Can't any of you—can't you——? " she stopped, catching at the banisters. Her knees were giving way under her. A woman with a flabby pale face and disordered gray hair sprang towards her and took her in her arms with a divine charity. " You can have half my bed! " she cried, drawing Sylvia's head down on her shoulder. " Poor girl! Poor girl! I lost my only son last year! "

Her accent, her look, the tones of her voice, some emanation of deep humanity from her whole person, reached Sylvia's inner self, the first message that had penetrated to that core of her being since the deadly, echoing news of the telegram. Upon her icy tension poured a flood of dissolving warmth. Her hideous isolation was an illusion. This plain old woman, whom she had never seen before, was her sister, her blood-kin,—they were both human beings. She gave a cry and flung her arms about the other's neck, clinging to her like a person falling from a great height, the tears at last streaming down her face.

CHAPTER XLI

HOME AGAIN

THE trip home passed like a long shuddering bad dream in which one waits eternally, bound hand and foot, for a blow which does not fall. Somehow, before the first day was over, an unoccupied berth was found for Sylvia, in a tiny corner usually taken by one of the ship's servants. Sylvia accepted this dully. She was but half alive, all her vital forces suspended until the journey should be over. The throbbing of the engines came to seem like the beating of her own heart, and she lay tensely in her berth for hours at a time, feeling that it was partly her energy which was driving the ship through the waters. She only thought of accomplishing the journey, covering the miles which lay before her. From what lay at the end she shrank back, returning again to her hypnotic absorption in the throbbing of the engines. The old woman who had offered to share her berth had disappeared at the first rough water and had been invisible all the trip. Sylvia did not think of her again. That was a recollection which with all its sacred significance was to come back later to Sylvia's maturer mind.

The ship reached New York late in the afternoon, and docked that night. Sylvia stood alone, in her soiled wrinkled suit, shapeless from constant wear, her empty hands clutching at the railing, and was the first passenger to dart down the second-class gang-plank. She ran to see if there were letters or a telegram for her.

"Yes, there is a telegram for you," said the steward, holding out a sealed envelope to her. "It came on with the pilot and ought to have been given you before."

She took the envelope, but was unable to open it. The

arc lights flared and winked above her in the high roof
of the wharf; the crowds of keen-faced, hard-eyed men
and women in costly, neat-fitting clothing were as oblivious
of her and as ferociously intent on their own affairs as the
shabby, noisy crowd she had left in Naples, brushing by
her as though she were a part of the wharf as they bent over
their trunks anxiously, and locked them up with determination. It seemed to Sylvia that she could never break the
spell of fear which bound her fast. Minute after minute
dragged by, and she still stood, very white, very sick.

She was aware that some one stood in front of her,
looking into her face, and she recognized one of the ship's
officials whom she had noticed from a distance on the ship,
an under-officer, somehow connected with the engines, who
had sat at table with the second-class passengers. He was
a burly, red-faced man, with huge strong hands and a
bald head.

He looked at her now for a moment with an intent kindness, and taking her arm led her a step to a packing-case on
which he made her sit down. At the break in her immobility, a faintness came over Sylvia. The man bent over her
and began to fan her with his cap. A strong smell of stale
and cheap tobacco reached Sylvia from all of his obese
person, but his vulgar, ugly face expressed a profoundly
self-forgetful concern. "There, feelin' better?" he asked,
his eyes anxiously on hers. The man looked at the envelope comprehendingly: "Oh—bad news——" he murmured. Sylvia opened her hand and showed him that it
had not been opened. "I haven't looked at it yet," she said
pitifully.

The man made an inarticulate murmur of pity—put out
his thick red fingers, took the message gently from her hand,
and opened it. As he read she searched his face with an
impassioned scrutiny.

When he raised his eyes from the paper, she saw in
them, in that grossly fleshy countenance, such infinite pity
that even her swift intuition of its meaning was not so
swift as to reach her heart first. The blow did not reach

her naked and unprotected in the solitude of her egotism, as it had at Naples. Confusedly, half-resentfully, but irresistibly she knew that she did not—could not—stand alone, was not the first thus to be struck down. This knowledge brought the tonic summons to courage. She held out her hand unflinchingly, and stood up as she read the message, "Mother died this morning at dawn." The telegram was dated three days before. She was now two days from home.

She looked up at the man before her and twice tried to speak before she could command her voice. Then she said quite steadily: "I live in the West. Can you tell me anything about trains to Chicago?"

"I'm going with ye, to th' train," he said, taking her arm and moving forward. Two hours later his vulgar, ugly, compassionate face was the last she saw as the train moved out of the station. He did not seem a stranger to Sylvia. She saw that he was more than middle-aged, he must have lost *his* mother, there must have been many deaths in his past. He seemed more familiar to her than her dearest friends had seemed before; but from now on she was to feel closer to every human being than before to her most loved. A great breach had been made in the wall of her life—the wall which had hidden her fellows from her. She saw them face the enigma as uncomprehendingly, as helplessly as she, and she felt the instinct of terror to huddle close to others, even though they feel—*because* they feel—a terror as unrelieved. It was not that she loved her fellow-beings more from this hour, rather that she felt, to the root of her being, her inevitable fellowship with them.

The journey home was almost as wholly a period of suspended animation for Sylvia as the days on the ocean had been. She had read the telegram at last; now she knew what had happened, but she did not yet know what it meant. She felt that she would not know what it meant until she reached home. How could her mother be dead? What did it mean to have her mother dead?

She said the grim words over and over, handling them with heartsick recklessness as a desperate man might

handle the black, ugly objects with smoking fuses which he
knows carry death. But for Sylvia no explosion came.
No ravaging perception of the meaning of the words reached
her strained inner ear. She said them over and over, the
sound of them was horrifying to her, but in her heart she
did not believe them. Her mother, *her* mother could not
die!

There was no one, of course, at the La Chance station to
meet her, and she walked out through the crowd and took
the street-car without having seen a familiar face. It was
five o'clock in the afternoon then, and six when she walked
up the dusty country road and turned in through the gate
in the hedge. There was home—intimately a part of her
in every detail of its unforgotten appearance. The pines
stood up strong in their immortal verdure, the thick golden
hush of the summer afternoon lay like an enchantment about
the low brown house. And something horrible, unspeakably horrible had happened there. Under the forgotten
dust and grime of her long railway journey, she was deadly
pale as she stepped up on the porch. Judith came to the
door, saw her sister, opened her arms with a noble gesture,
and clasped Sylvia to her in a strong and close embrace.
Not a word was spoken. The two clung to each other
silently, Sylvia weeping incessantly, holding fast to the
dear human body in her arms, feeling herself dissolved in
a very anguish of love and pain. Her wet cheek was pressed
against Judith's lips, the tears rained down in a torrent. All
the rich, untapped strength of her invincible youth was in
that healthful flood of tears.

There were none such in the eyes of Professor Marshall
as he came down the stairs to greet his daughter. Sylvia
was immeasurably shocked by his aspect. He did not look
like her father. She sought in vain in that gray countenance for any trace of her father's expression. He came
forward with a slow, dragging step, and kissed his daughter, taking her hand—his, she noticed, felt like a sick man's,
parched, the skin like a dry husk. He spoke, in a voice
which had no resonance, the first words that had been

uttered: "You must be very tired, Sylvia. You would better go and lie down. Your sister will go with you." He himself turned away and walked slowly towards the open door. Sylvia noticed that he shuffled his feet as he walked.

Judith drew Sylvia away up the stairs to her own slant-ceilinged room, and the two sat down on the bed, side by side, with clasped hands. Judith now told briefly the out-line of what had happened. Sylvia listened, straining her swollen eyes to see her sister's face, wiping away the tears which ran incessantly down her pale, grimy cheeks, re-pressing her sobs to listen, although they broke out in one burst after another. Her mother had gone down very suddenly and they had cabled at once—then she grew better—she had been unspeakably brave—fighting the disease by sheer will-power—she had conquered it—she was gaining—they were sorry they had cabled Sylvia—she had not known she was going to die—none of them had dreamed she was going to die—suddenly as the worst of her disease had spent itself and the lungs were beginning to clear—sud-denly her heart had given way, and before the nurse could call her husband and children to her, she was gone. They had been there under the same roof, and had not been with her at the last. The last time they had seen her, she was alive and smiling at them—such a brave, wan shadow of her usual smile—for a few moments they went about their affairs, full of hope—and when they entered the sick-room again——

Sylvia could bear no more, screaming out, motioning Judith imperiously to stop;—she began to understand what had happened to her; the words she had repeated so dully were like thunder in her ears. Her mother was dead.

Judith took her sister again in her arms, holding her close, as though she were the older. Sylvia was weeping again, the furious, healing, inexhaustible tears of youth. To both the sisters it seemed that they were passing an hour of supreme bitterness; but their strong young hearts, clinging with unconscious tenacity to their right to joy, were at that moment painfully opening and expanding beyond the narrow bounds of childhood. Henceforth they were to be great enough to harbor joy—a greater joy—and sorrow, side by side.

Moreover, as though their action-loving mother were still watching over them, they found themselves confronted at once with an inexorable demand for their strength and courage.

Judith detached herself, and said in a firm voice: " Sylvia, you mustn't cry any more. We must think what to do."

As Sylvia looked at her blankly, she went on: " Somehow Lawrence must be taken away for a while—until Father's —either you or I must go with him and stay, and the other one be here with Father until he's—he's more like himself."

Sylvia, fresh from the desolation of solitude in sorrow, cried out: " Oh, Judith, how can you! Now's the time for us all to stay together! Why should we——?"

Judith went to the door and closed it before answering, a precaution so extraordinary in that house of frank openness that Sylvia was struck into silence by it. Standing by the door, Judith said in a low tone, " You didn't notice— anything—about Father?"

" Oh yes, he looks ill. He is so pale—he frightened me!"

Judith looked down at the floor and was silent a moment. Sylvia's heart began to beat fast with a new foreboding. " Why, what *is* the matter with——" she began.

Judith covered her face with her hands. " I don't know what to *do!*" she said despairingly.

No phrase coming from Judith could have struck a more piercing alarm into her sister's heart. She ran to Judith, pulled her hands down, and looked into her face anxiously. " What do you mean, Judy—what do you mean?"

" Why—it's five days now since Mother died, three days since the funeral—and Father has hardly eaten a mouthful —and I don't think he's slept at all. I know he hasn't taken his clothes off. And—and—" she drew Sylvia again to the bed, and sat down beside her, " he says such things . . .

the night after Mother died Lawrence had cried so I was afraid he would be sick, and I got him to bed and gave him some hot milk,"—the thought flashed from one to the other almost palpably, " That is what Mother would have done "—" and he went to sleep—he was perfectly worn out. I went downstairs to find Father. It was after midnight. He was walking around the house into one room after another and out on the porch and even out in the garden, as fast as he could walk. He looked so——" She shuddered. " I went up to him and said, ' Father, Father, what are you doing?' He never stopped walking an instant, but he said, as though I was a total stranger and we were in a railway station or somewhere like that, ' I am looking for my wife. I expect to come across her any moment, but I can't seem to remember the exact place I was to meet her. She must be somewhere about, and I suppose——' and then, Sylvia, before I could help it, he opened the door to Mother's room quick—and the men were there, and the coffin——" She stopped short, pressing her hand tightly over her mouth to stop its quivering. Sylvia gazed at her in horrified silence.

After a pause, Judith went on : " He turned around and ran as fast as he could up the stairs to his study and locked the door. He locked me out—the night after Mother died. I called and called to him—he didn't answer. I was afraid to call very loud for fear of waking Lawrence. I've had to think of Lawrence too." She stopped again to draw a long breath. She stopped and suddenly reached out imploring hands to hold fast to Sylvia. " I'm so *glad* you have come!" she murmured.

This from Judith ran like a galvanic shock through Sylvia's sorrow-sodden heart. She sat up, aroused as she had never been before to a stern impulse to resist her emotion, to fight it down. She clasped Judith's hand hard, and felt the tears dry in her eyes. Judith went on : " If it hadn't been for Lawrence—he's sick as it is. I've kept him in his room—twice when he's been asleep I've managed to get Father to eat something and lie down—there seem to be

times when he's so worn out that he doesn't know what
he's doing. But it comes back to him. One night I had
just persuaded him to lie down, when he sat up again
with that dreadful face and said very loud: 'Where is
my wife? Where is Barbara?' That was on the night
after the funeral. And the next day he came to me, out
in the garden, and said,—he never seems to know who
I am: 'I don't mind the separation from my wife, you
understand—it's not that—I'm not a child, I can endure
that—but I *must* know where she is. I *must* know where
she is!' He said it over and over, until his voice got
so loud he seemed to hear it himself and looked around—
and then he went back into the house and began walking
all around, opening and shutting all the doors. What
I'm afraid of is his meeting Lawrence and saying something like that. Lawrence would go crazy. I thought,
as soon as you came, you could take him away to the
Helman farm—the Helmans have been so good—and Mrs.
Helman offered to take Lawrence—only he oughtn't to
be alone—he needs one of us——"

Judith was quiet now, and though very pale, spoke with
her usual firmness. Sylvia too felt herself iron under the
pressure of her responsibilities. She said: " Yes, I see. All
right—I'll go," and the two went together into Lawrence's
room. He was lying on the bed, his face in the pillows. At
the sound of their steps he turned over and showed a pitiful
white face. He got up and moved uncertainly towards
Sylvia, sinking into her arms and burying his face on her
shoulder.

But a little later when their plan was told him, he turned
to Judith with a cry: " No, *you* go with me, Judy! I want
you! You ' know'—about it."

Over his head the sisters looked at each other with
questioning eyes; and Sylvia nodded her consent. Lawrence
had always belonged to Judith.

CHAPTER XLII

"Strange that we creatures of the petty ways,
Poor prisoners behind these fleshly bars,
Can sometimes think us thoughts with God ablaze,
Touching the fringes of the outer stars."

AND so they went away, Lawrence very white, stooping with the weight of his suitcase, his young eyes, blurred and red, turned upon Judith with an infinite confidence in her strength. Judith herself was pale, but her eyes were dry and her lips firm in her grave, steadfast face, so like her mother's, except for the absence of the glint of humor. Sylvia kissed her good-bye, feeling almost a little fear of her resolute sister; but as she watched them go down the path, and noted the appealing drooping of the boy towards Judith, Sylvia was swept with a great wave of love and admiration—and courage.

She turned to face the difficult days and nights before her and forced herself to speak cheerfully to her father, who sat in a chair on the porch, watching the departing travelers and not seeing them. "How splendid Judith is!" she cried, and went on with a break in the voice she tried to control: "She will take Mother's place for us all!"

Her father frowned slightly, as though she had interrupted him in some effort where concentration was necessary, but otherwise gave no sign that he heard her.

Sylvia watched him anxiously through the window. Presently she saw him relax from his position of strained attention with a great sigh, almost a groan, and lean back in his chair, covering his eyes with his hands. When he took them down, his face had the aged, ravaged expression of exhaustion which had so startled her on her arrival. Now she felt none of her frightened revulsion, but only an aching pity which sent her out to him in a rush, her arms outstretched, crying to him brokenly that he still had his children who loved him more than anything in the world.

For the first time in her life, her father repelled her, shrinking away from her with a brusque, involuntary recoil that shocked her, thrusting her arms roughly to one side, and rising up hastily to retreat into the house. He said in a bitter, recriminating tone, " You don't know what you are talking about," and left her standing there, the tears frozen in her eyes. He went heavily upstairs to his study on the top floor and locked the door. Sylvia heard the key turn. It shut her into an intolerable solitude. She had not thought before that anything could seem worse than the desolation of her mother's absence.

She felt a deathlike sinking of her heart. She was afraid of her father, who no longer seemed her father, created to protect and cherish her, but some maniac stranger. She felt an impulse like that of a terrified child to run away, far away to some one who should stand before her and bear the brunt. She started up from her chair with panic haste, but the familiar room, saturated with recollections of her mother's gallant spirit, stood about her like a wall, shutting her in to the battle with her heart. Who was there to summon whom she could endure as a spectator of her father's condition? Her mother's empty chair stood opposite her, against the wall. She looked at it fixedly; and drawing a long breath sat down quietly.

This act of courage brought a reward in the shape of a relaxation of the clutch on her throat and about her heart. Her mother's wise materialism came to her mind now and she made a heartsick resolve that she would lead as physically normal a life as possible, working out of doors, forcing herself to eat, and that, above all things, she would henceforth deny herself the weakening luxury of tears. And yet but an hour later, as she bent over her mother's flower-beds blazing in the sun, she found the tears again streaming from her eyes.

She tried to wipe them away, but they continued to rain

down on her cheeks. Her tongue knew their saltness. She was profoundly alarmed and cowed by this irresistible weakness, and stood helplessly at bay among the languid roses The sensation of her own utter weakness, prostrate before her dire need for strength, was as bitter as the taste of her tears.

She stood there, among the sun-warmed flowers, looking like a symbolic figure of youth triumphant . . . and she felt herself to be in a black and windowless prison, where the very earth under her feet was treacherous, where everything betrayed her.

Then, out of her need, her very great need, out of the wide and empty spaces of her inculcated unbelief, something rose up and overwhelmed her. The force stronger than herself which she had longed to feel, blew upon her like a wind out of eternity.

She found herself on her knees, her face hidden in her hands, sending out a passionate cry which transcended words. The child of the twentieth century, who had been taught not to pray, was praying.

She did not know how long she knelt there before the world emerged from the white glory which had whirled down upon it, and hidden it from her. But when she came to herself, her eyes were dry, and the weakening impulse to tears had gone. She stretched out her hands before her, and they did not tremble. The force stronger than herself was now in her own heart. From her mother's garden there rose a strong, fragrant exhalation, as sweet as honey.

For more than an hour Sylvia worked steadily among the flowers, consciously wrought upon by the healing emanations from the crushed, spicy leaves, the warm earth, and the hot, pure breath of the summer wind on her face.

Once she had a passing fancy that her mother stood near her . . . smiling.

CHAPTER XLIII

" Call now; is there any that will answer thee? "—Job.

When she went back to the silent, echoing house, she felt calmer than at any time since she had read the telegram in Naples. She did not stop to wash her earth-stained hands, but went directly up the stairs to the locked door at the top. She did not knock this time. She stood outside and said authoritatively in a clear, strong voice, the sound of which surprised her, " Father dear, please open the door and let me in."

There was a pause, and then a shuffle of feet. The door opened and Professor Marshall appeared, his face very white under the thick stubble of his gray, unshaven beard, his shoulders bowed, his head hanging. Sylvia went to his side, took his hand firmly in hers, and said quietly : " Father, you must eat something. You haven't taken a bit of food in two days. And then you must lie down and rest." She poured all of her new strength into these quietly issued commands, and permitted herself no moment's doubt of his obedience to them. He lifted his head, looked at her, and allowed her to lead him down the stairs and again into the dining-room. Here he sat, quite spent, staring before him until Sylvia returned from the kitchen with a plate of cold meat and some bread. She sat down beside him, putting out again consciously all her strength, and set the knife and fork in his nerveless hands. In the gentle monologue with which she accompanied his meal she did not mention her mother, or anything but slight, casual matters about the house and garden. She found herself speaking in a hushed tone, as though not to awake a sleeping person. Although she sat quite quietly, her hands loosely folded on the table, her heart was thrilling and burning to a high resolve. " Now it is my turn to help my father."

After he had eaten a few mouthfuls and laid down the knife and fork, she did not insist further, but rose to lead him to the couch in the living-room. She dared not risk his own room, the bed on which her mother had died.

"Now you must lie down and rest, Father," she said, loosening his clothes and unlacing his shoes as though he had been a sick child. He let her do what she would, and as she pushed him gently back, he yielded and lay down at full length. Sylvia sat down beside him, feeling her strength ebbing. Her father lay on his back, his eyes wide open. On the ceiling above him a circular flicker of light danced and shimmered, reflected from a glass of water on the table. His eyes fastened upon this, at first unwinkingly, with a fixed intensity, and later with dropped lids and half-upturned eyeballs. He was quite quiet, and finally seemed asleep, although the line of white between his eyelids made Sylvia shudder.

With the disappearance of the instant need for self-control and firmness, she felt an immense fatigue. It had cost her dearly, this victory, slight as it was. She drooped in her chair, exhausted and undone. She looked down at the ash-gray, haggard face on the pillow, trying to find in those ravaged features her splendidly life-loving father. It was so quiet that she could hear the big clock in the dining-room ticking loudly, and half-consciously she began to count the swings of the pendulum: One—two—three—four—five—six—seven—eight—nine—ten—eleven—twelve—thirteen—fourteen——

She awoke to darkness and the sound of her mother's name loudly screamed. She started up, not remembering where she was, astonished to find herself sitting in a chair. As she stood bewildered in the dark, the clock in the dining-room struck two. At once from a little distance, outside the window apparently, she heard the same wild cry ringing in her ears—"*Bar-ba-ra!*" All the blood in her body congealed and the hair on her head seemed to stir itself, in the instant before she recognized her father's voice.

The great impulse of devotion which had entered her

heart in the garden still governed her. Now she was not afraid. She did not think of running away. She only knew that she must find her father quickly and take care of him. Outside on the porch, the glimmering light from the stars showed her his figure, standing by one of the pillars, leaning forward, one hand to his ear. As she came out of the door, he dropped his hand, threw back his head, and again sent out an agonizing cry—" *Bar-ba-ra!* Where are you?" It was not the broken wail of despair; it was the strong, searching cry of a lost child who thinks trustingly that if he but screams loudly enough his mother must hear him and come—and yet who is horribly frightened because she does not answer. But this was a man in his full strength who called! It seemed the sound must reach beyond the stars. Sylvia felt her very bones ringing with it. She went along the porch to her father, and laid her hand on his arm. Through his sleeve she could feel how tense and knotted were the muscles. " Oh, Father, *don't!* " she said in a low tone. He shook her off roughly, but did not turn his head or look at her. Sylvia hesitated, not daring to leave him and not daring to try to draw him away; and again was shaken by that terrible cry.

The intensity of his listening attitude seemed to hush into breathlessness the very night about him, as it did Sylvia. There was not a sound from the trees. They stood motionless, as though carved in wood; not a bird fluttered a wing; not a night-insect shrilled; the brook, dried by the summer heat to a thread, crept by noiselessly. As once more the frantic cry resounded, it seemed to pierce this opaque silence like a palpable missile, and to wing its way without hindrance up to the stars. Not the faintest murmur came in answer. The silence shut down again, stifling. Sylvia and her father stood as though in the vacuum of a great bell-glass which shut them away from the rustling, breathing, living world. Sylvia said again, imploringly, " Oh, *Father!* " He looked at her angrily, sprang from the porch, and walked rapidly towards the road, stumbling and tripping over the laces of his shoes, which Sylvia had loosened when she had persuaded him to lie down. Sylvia ran after him, her long bounds bringing her up to his side in a moment. The motion sent the blood racing through her stiffened limbs again. She drew a long breath of liberation. As she stepped along beside her father, peering in the starlight at his dreadful face, half expecting him to turn and strike her at any moment, she felt an immense relief. The noise of their feet on the path was like a sane voice of reality. Anything was more endurable than to stand silent and motionless and hear that screaming call lose itself in the grimly unanswering distance.

They were on the main road now, walking so swiftly that, in the hot summer night, Sylvia felt her forehead beaded and her light dress cling to her moist body. She took her father's hand. It was parched like a sick man's, the skin like a dry husk. After this, they walked hand-in-hand. Professor Marshall continued to walk rapidly, scuffling in his loose, unlaced shoes. They passed barns and farmhouses, the latter sleeping, black in the starlight, with darkened windows. In one, a poor little shack of two rooms, there was a lighted pane, and as they passed, Sylvia heard the sick wail of a little child. The sound pierced her heart. She longed to go in and put her arms about the mother. Now she understood. She tightened her hold on her father's hand and lifted it to her lips.

He suffered this with no appearance of his former anger, and soon after Sylvia was aware that his gait was slackening. She looked at him searchingly, and saw that he had swung from unnatural tension to spent exhaustion. His head was hanging and as he walked he wavered. She put her hand under his elbow and turned him about on the road. " Now we will go home," she said, drawing his arm through hers. He made no resistance, not seeming to know what she had done, and shuffled along wearily, leaning all his weight on her arm. She braced herself against this drag, and led him slowly back, wiping her face from time to time with her sleeve. There were moments when she thought she must let him sink on the road, but she fought through these, and as the sky was turning faintly gray over their heads, and the implacably silent stars were disappearing in this pale light, the two stumbled up the walk to the porch.

Professor Marshall let himself be lowered into the steamer chair. Sylvia stood by him until she was sure he would not stir, and then hurried into the kitchen. In a few moments she brought him a cup of hot coffee and a piece of bread. He drank the one and ate the other without protest. She set the tray down and put a pillow under her father's head, raising the foot-rest. He did not resist her. His head fell back on the pillow, but his eyes did not close. They were fixed on a distant point in the sky.

Sylvia tiptoed away into the house and sank down shivering into a chair. A great fit of trembling and nausea came over her. She rose, walked into the kitchen, her footsteps sounding in her ears like her mother's. There was some coffee left, which she drank resolutely, and she cooked an egg and forced it down, her mother's precepts loud in her ears. Whatever else happened, she must have her body in condition to be of use.

After this she went out to the porch again and lay down in the hammock near her father. The dawn had brightened into gold, and the sun was showing on the distant, level, green horizon-line.

It was almost the first moment of physical relaxation she had known, and to her immense, her awed astonishment it was instantly filled with a pure, clear brilliance, the knowledge that Austin Page lived and loved her. It was the first, it was the only time she thought of anything but her father, and this was not a thought, it was a vision. In the chaos about her, a great sunlit rock had emerged. She laid hold on it and knew that she would not sink.

But now, *now* she must think of nothing but her father! There was no one else who could help her father. Could she? Could any one?

She herself, since her prayer among the roses, cherished in her darkened heart a hope of dawn. But how could she tell her father of that? Even if she had been able to force him to listen to her, she had nothing that words could say, nothing but the recollection of that burning hour in the garden to set against the teachings of a lifetime. That had changed life for her . . . but what could it mean to her father? How could she tell him of what was only a wordless radiance? Her father had taught her that death meant the return of the spirit to the great, impersonal river of life. If the spirit had been superb and splendid, like her mother's, the river of life was the brighter for it, but that was all. Her mother had lived, and now lived no more. That was what they had tried to teach her to believe. That was what her father had taught her—without, it now appeared, believing it himself.

And yet she divined that it was not that he would not, but that he could not now believe it. He was like a man set in a vacuum fighting for the air without which life is impossible. And she knew no way to break the imprisoning wall and let in air for him. *Was* there, indeed, any air outside? There must be, or the race could not live from one generation to the next. Every one whose love had encountered death must have found an air to breathe or have died.

Constantly through all these thoughts, that day and for many days and months to come, there rang the sound of her mother's name, screamed aloud. She heard it as though she were again standing by her father under the stars. And there had been no answer.

She felt the tears stinging at her eyelids and sat up, terrified at the idea that her weakness was about to overtake her. She would go again out to the garden where she had found strength before. The morning sun was now hot and glaring in the eastern sky.

CHAPTER XLIV

*"A bruised reed will He not break, and a dimly burning wick will He not quench." —*ISAIAH.

As she stepped down the path, she saw a battered black straw hat on the other side of the hedge. Cousin Parnelia's worn old face and dim eyes looked at her through the gate. Under her arm she held planchette. Sylvia stepped through the gate and drew it inhospitably shut back of her. "What is it, Cousin Parnelia?" she said challengingly, determined to protect her father.

The older woman's face was all aglow. "Oh, my dear; I've had such a wonderful message from your dear mother. Last night——"

Sylvia recoiled from the mad old creature. She could not bear to have her sane, calm, strong mother's name on those lips. Cousin Parnelia went on, full of confidence: "I was sound asleep last night when I was awakened by the clock's striking two. It sounded so loud that I thought somebody had called to me. I sat up in bed and said, 'What is it?' and then I felt a great longing to have planchette write. I got out of bed in my nightgown and sat down in the dark at the table. Planchette wrote so fast that I could hardly keep up with it. And when it stopped, I lighted a match and see . . . here . . . in your mother's very handwriting"—fervently she held the bit of paper up for Sylvia to see. The girl cast a hostile look at the paper and saw that the writing on it was the usual scrawl produced by Cousin Parnelia, hardly legible, and resembling anything rather than her mother's handwriting.

"Read it—read it—it is too beautiful!" quivered the other, "and then let me show it to your father. It was meant for him——"

Sylvia shook like a roughly plucked fiddle-string. She seized the wrinkled old hand fiercely. " Cousin Parnelia, I forbid you going anywhere near my father! You know as well as I do how intensely he has always detested spiritualism. To see you might be the thing that would——"

The old woman broke in, protesting, her hat falling to one side, her brown false front sliding with it and showing the thin, gray hairs beneath. " But, Sylvia, this is the very thing that would save him—such a beautiful, beautiful message from your mother,—*see!* In her own handwriting!"

Sylvia snatched the sheet of yellow paper. "*That's* not my mother's handwriting! Do you think I am as crazy as *you* are!" She tore the paper into shreds and scattered them from her, feeling a relief in the violence of her action. The next moment she remembered how patient her mother had always been with her daft kinswoman and seeing tears in the blurred old eyes, went to put placating arms about the other's neck. " Never mind, Cousin Parnelia," she said with a vague kindness, " I know you mean to do what's right—only we don't believe as you do, and Father *must* not be excited!" She turned sick as she spoke and shrank away from the hedge, carrying her small old cousin with her. Above the hedge appeared her father's gray face and burning eyes.

He was not looking at her, but at Cousin Parnelia, who now sprang forward, crying that she had had a beautiful, beautiful message from Cousin Barbara. " It came last night at two o'clock . . . just after the clock struck two——"

Professor Marshall looked quickly at his daughter, and she saw that he too had heard the clock striking in the dreadful night, and that he noted the coincidence.

" Just after the clock struck two she wrote the loveliest message for you with planchette. Sylvia tore it up. But I'm sure that if we try with faith, she will repeat it . . ."

Professor Marshall's eyes were fixed on his wife's old

cousin. " Come in," he said in a hoarse voice. They were almost the first words Sylvia had heard him say.

Cousin Parnelia hastened up the path to the house. Sylvia followed with her father, at the last extremity of agitation and perplexity.

When Cousin Parnelia reached the dining-room table, she sat down by it, pushed the cloth to one side, and produced a fresh sheet of yellow paper from her shabby bag. " Put yourselves in a receptive frame of mind," she said in a glib, professional manner. Sylvia stiffened and tried to draw her father away, but he continued to stand by the table, staring at the blank sheet of paper with a strange, wild expression on his white face. He did not take his eyes from the paper. In a moment, he sat down suddenly, as though his knees had failed him.

There was a long silence, in which Sylvia could hear the roaring of the blood in her arteries. Cousin Parnelia put one deeply veined, shrunken old hand on planchette and the other over her eyes and waited, her wrinkled, commonplace old face assuming a solemn expression of importance. The clock ticked loudly.

Planchette began to write—at first in meaningless flourishes, then with occasional words, and finally Sylvia saw streaming away from the pencil the usual loose, scrawling handwriting. Several lines were written and then the pencil stopped abruptly. Sylvia standing near her father heard his breathing grow loud and saw in a panic that the veins on his temples were swollen.

Cousin Parnelia took her hand off planchette, put on her spectacles, read over what had been written, and gave it to Professor Marshall. Sylvia was in such a state of bewilderment that nothing her father could have done would have surprised her. She half expected to see him dash the paper in the old woman's face, half thought that any moment he would fall, choking with apoplexy.

What he did was to take the paper and try to hold it steadily enough to read. But his hand shook terribly.

" I will read it to you," said Cousin Parnelia, and she

read aloud in her monotonous, illiterate voice: "'I am well and happy, dearest Elliott, and never far from you. When you call to me, I hear you. All is not yet clear, but I wish I could tell you more of the whole meaning. I am near you this moment. I wish that——' The message stopped there," explained Cousin Parnelia, laying down the paper.

Professor Marshall leaned over it, straining his eyes to the rude scrawls, passing his hand over his forehead as though to brush away a web. He broke out in a loud, high voice. "That is her handwriting. . . . Good God, her very handwriting—the way she writes Elliott—it is from *her!*" He snatched the paper up and took it to the window, stumbling over the chairs blindly as he went. As he held it up to the light, poring over it again, he began to weep, crying out his wife's name softly, the tears streaming down his unshaven cheeks. He came back to the table, and sank down before it, still sobbing, still murmuring incessantly, "Oh, Barbara—Barbara!" and laid his head on his outstretched arms.

"Let him cry!" whispered Cousin Parnelia sentimentally to Sylvia, drawing her away into the hall. A few moments later when they looked in, he had fallen asleep, his head turned to one side so that Sylvia saw his face, tear-stained and exhausted, but utterly relaxed and at peace, like that of a little child in sleep. Crushed in one hand was the yellow sheet of paper covered with coarse, wavering marks.

CHAPTER XLV

" That our soul may swim
We sink our heart down, bubbling, under wave."

THE two sisters, their pale faces grave in the shadow of
their wide hats, were on their knees with trowels in a
border of their mother's garden. Judith had been giving
a report of Lawrence's condition, and Sylvia was just finishing an account of what had happened at home, when the
gate in the osage-orange hedge clicked, and a blue-uniformed boy came whistling up the path. He made an
inquiry as to names, and handed Sylvia an envelope. She
opened it, read silently, " Am starting for America and
you at once. Felix." She stood looking at the paper for
a moment, her face quite unmoved from its quiet sadness.
The boy asked, " Any answer? "

" No," she said decisively, shaking her head. " No
answer."

As he lingered, lighting a cigarette, she put a question in
her turn, " Anything to pay? "

" No," said the boy, putting the cigarette-box back in
his pocket, " Nothing to pay." He produced a worn and
greasy book, " Sign on this line," he said, and after she had
signed, he went away down the path, whistling. The
transaction was complete.

Sylvia looked after the retreating figure and then turned
to Judith as though there had been no interruption.
" . . . and you can see for yourself how little use I am to
him now. Since he got Cousin Parnelia in the house, there's
nothing anybody else could do for him. Even you couldn't,
if you could leave Lawrence. Not for a while, anyhow. I
suppose he'll come slowly out of this to be himself again
. . but I'm not sure that he will. And for now, I actually

believe that he'd be easier in his mind if we were both away. I never breathe a word of criticism about planchette, of course. But he knows. There's that much left of his old self. He knows how I must feel. He's really ever so much better too, you know. He's taken up his classes in the Summer School again. He said he had 'a message' from Mother that he was to go back to his work bravely; and the very next day he went over to the campus, and taught all his classes as though nothing had happened. Isn't it awfully, terribly touching to see how even such a poor, incoherent make-believe of a 'message' from Mother has more power to calm him than anything we could do with our whole hearts? But how *can* he! I can't understand it! I can't bear it, to come in on him and Cousin Parnelia, in their evenings, and see them bent over that grotesque planchette and have him look up at me so defiantly, as though he were just setting his teeth and saying he wouldn't care what I thought of him. He doesn't really care either. He doesn't think of anything but of having evening come when he can get another 'message' from Mother . . . from Mother! Mother!"

"Well, perhaps it would be as well for us not to be here for a while," murmured Judith. There were deep dark rings under her eyes, as though she had slept badly for a long time. "Perhaps it may be better later on. I can take Lawrence back with me when I go to the hospital. I want to keep him near me of course, dear little Lawrence. My little boy! He'll be my life now. He'll be what I have to live for."

Something in the quality of her quiet voice sent a chill to Sylvia's heart. "Why, Judy dear, after you are married of course you and Arnold can keep Lawrence with you. That'll be the best for him, a real home, with you. Oh, Judy dear," she laid down her trowel, fighting hard against a curious sickness which rose within her. She tried to speak lightly. "Oh, Judy dear, when *are* you going to be married? Or don't you want to speak about it now, for a while? You never write long letters, I know—but your late ones haven't had *any* news in them! You positively haven't so much as mentioned Arnold's name lately."

As she spoke, she knew that she was voicing an uneasiness which had been an unacknowledged occupant of her mind for a long time. But she looked confidently to see one of Judith's concise, comprehensive statements make her dim apprehensions seem fantastic and far-fetched, as Judith always made any flight of the imagination appear. But nothing which Sylvia's imagination might have been able to conceive would have struck her such a blow as the fact which Judith now produced, in a dry, curt phrase: " I'm not going to be married."

Sylvia did not believe her ears. She looked up wildly as Judith rose from the ground, and advanced upon her sister with a stern, white face. Before she had finished speaking, she had said more than Sylvia had ever heard her say about a matter personal to her; but even so, her iron words were few. " Sylvia, I want to tell you about it, of course. I've got to. But I won't say a word, unless you can keep quiet, and not make a fuss. I couldn't stand that. I've got all I can stand as it is."

She stood by an apple-tree and now broke from it a small, leafy branch, which she held as she spoke. There was something shocking in the contrast between the steady rigor of her voice and the fury of her fingers as they tore and stripped and shredded the leaves. " Arnold is an incurable alcoholic," she said; " Dr. Rivedal has pronounced him hopeless. Dr. Charton and Dr. Pansard (they're the best specialists in that line) have had him under observation and they say the same thing. He's had three dreadful attacks lately. We . . . none of their treatment does any good. It's been going on too long—from the time he was first sent away to school, at fourteen, alone! There was an inherited tendency, anyhow. Nobody took it seriously, that and—and the other things boys with too much money do. Apparently everybody thought it was just the way boys are—if anybody thought anything about it, except that it was a bother. He never had anybody, you know—*never,*

never anybody who . . ." her voice rose, threatened to break. She stopped, swallowed hard, and began again: "The trouble is he has no constitution left—nothing for a doctor to work with. It's not Arnold's fault. If he had come out to us, that time in Chicago when he wanted to— we—he could—with Mother to——" Her steady voice gave way abruptly. She cast the ravaged, leafless branch violently to the ground and stood looking down at it. There was not a fleck of color in her beautiful, stony face.

Sylvia concentrated all her will-power on an effort to speak as Judith would have her, quietly, without heroics; but when she broke her silence she found that she had no control of her voice. She tried to say, "But, Judith dear, if Arnold is like that—doesn't he need you more than ever? You are a nurse. How can you abandon him now!" But she could produce only a few, broken, inarticulate words in a choking voice before she was obliged to stop short, lest she burst out in the flood of horror which Judith had forbidden.

Broken and inarticulate as they were, Judith knew what was the meaning of those words. The corners of her mouth twitched uncontrollably. She bit her marble lower lip repeatedly before she could bring out the few short phrases which fell like clods on a coffin. "If I—if we—— Arnold and I are in love with each other." She stopped, drew a painful breath, and said again: "Arnold and I are in love with each other. Do you know what that means? He is the only man I could not take care of—Arnold! If I should try, we would soon be married, or lovers. If we were married or lovers, we would soon have——" She had overestimated her strength. Even she was not strong enough to go on.

She sat down on the ground, put her long arms around her knees, and buried her face in them. She was not weeping. She sat as still as though carved in stone.

Sylvia herself was beyond tears. She sat looking down at the moist earth on the trowel she held, drying visibly in the hot sun, turning to dust, and falling away in a crumbling, impalpable powder. It was like seeing a picture of her heart. She thought of Arnold with an indignant, passionate pity—how could Judith——? But she was so close to Judith's suffering that she felt the dreadful rigidity of her body. The flat, dead tones of the man in the Pantheon were in her ears. It seemed to her that Life was an adventure perilous and awful beyond imagination. There was no force to cope with it, save absolute integrity. Everything else was a vain and foolish delusion, a two-edged sword which wounded the wielding hand.

She did not move closer to Judith, she did not put out her hand. Judith would not like that. She sat quite motionless, looking into black abysses of pain, of responsibilities not met, feeling press upon her the terrifying closeness of all human beings to all other human beings—there in the sun of June a cold sweat stood on her forehead. . . .

But then she drew a long breath. Why, there was Austin! The anguished contraction of her heart relaxed. The warm blood flowed again through her veins. There was Austin!

She was rewarded for her effort to bring herself to Judith's ways, when presently her sister moved and reached out blindly for her hand. At this she opened her arms and took Judith in. No word was spoken. Their mother was there with them.

Sylvia looked out over the proud, dark head, now heavy on her bosom, and felt herself years older. She did not try to speak. She had nothing to say. There was nothing she could do, except to hold Judith and love her.

There was nothing, *nothing* left but love.

CHAPTER XLVI

A LONG TALK WITH ARNOLD

THE tall, lean young man, sitting his galloping horse very slackly, riding fast with a recklessly loose rein, and staring with bloodshot eyes down at the dust of the road, gave an exclamation, brought the mare upon her haunches, and sprang down from the saddle. A woman, young, tall, grave, set like a pearl in her black mourning dress, stood up from the roadside brook and advanced to meet him. They looked at each other as people do who meet after death has passed by. They stammered vague words, their eyes brimming.

" I—she was always so good to me," said Arnold, his voice breaking and quavering as he wrung Sylvia's hand again and again. " I never knew—saw much of her, I know—but when I was a little boy, I used—I used to dream about her at night." His thin, sallow face flushed with his earnestness. " I don't believe—honestly, Sylvia, I don't believe her own children loved her any more than I did. I've thought so many times how different everything would have been if I'd—I don't suppose you remember, but years ago when you and she were in Chicago, I ran away from school to go out there, and ask if——"

Sylvia remembered, had thought of nothing else from the moment she had seen far down the road the horseman vainly fleeing the black beast on his crupper. She shook her head now, her hand at her throat, and motioned him to silence. " Don't! Don't! " she said urgently. " Yes, I remember. I remember."

There was a moment's silence, filled by the murmur of the little brook at their feet. The mare, which had been drinking deeply, now lifted her head, the water running from the corners of her mouth. She gave a deep breath of satisfaction, and began cropping the dense green grass which grew between the water and the road. Her master tossed the reins over the pommel and let her go. He began speaking again on a different note. " But, Sylvia, what in the world—here, can't we go up under those trees a few minutes and have a talk? I can keep my eye on the mare." As they took the few steps he asked again, " How ever does it happen that you're here at Lydford Junction of all awful holes? "

Sylvia took an abrupt resolution, sat down on the pine-needles, and said, very directly, " I am on my way to Austin Farm to see if Austin Page still wants to marry me." Her manner had the austere simplicity of one who has been moving in great and grave emotions.

Arnold spoke with an involuntary quickness: " But you've heard, haven't you, about his giving up all his Colorado . . ."

Sylvia flushed a deep crimson and paid with a moment of bitter, shamed resentment for the other bygone moments of calculation. " Yes, yes, of course." She spoke with a stern impatience. " Did you suppose it was for his fortune that——" She paused and said humbly, " Of course, it's natural that you should think that of me."

Arnold attempted no self-exculpation. He sat down by her, his riding-crop across his knees. " Could you—do you feel like telling me about it? " he asked.

She nodded. It came to her like an inspiration that only if she opened her heart utterly to Arnold, could he open his sore heart to her. " There's not much to tell. I don't know where to begin. Perhaps there's too much to tell, after all. I didn't know what any of it meant till now. It's the strangest thing, Arnold, how little people know what is growing strong in their lives! I supposed all the time I only liked him because he was so rich. I thought it must be so. I thought that was the kind of girl I was. And then, besides, I'd—perhaps you didn't know how much I'd liked Felix Morrison."

Arnold nodded. "I sort of guessed so. You were awfully game, then, Sylvia. You're game now—it's awfully white to fall in love with a man because he's rich and then stick to him when he's——"

Sylvia waved her hand impatiently. "Oh, you don't understand. It's not because I think I *ought* to—Heavens, no! Let me try to tell you. Listen! When the news came, about this Colorado business—I was about crazy for a while. I just went to pieces. I knew I ought to answer his letter, but I couldn't. I see now, looking back, that I had just crumpled up under the weight of my weakness. I didn't know it then. I kept saying to myself that I was only putting off deciding till I could think more about it, but I know now that I had decided to give him up, never to see him again—Felix was there, you know—I'd decided to give Austin up because he wasn't rich any more. Did you know I was that base sort of a woman? Do you suppose he will ever be willing to take me back?—now after this long time? It's a month since I got his letter."

Arnold bent his riding-crop between his thin, nervous hands. "Are you sure now, Sylvia, are you sure now, dead sure?" he asked. "It would be pretty hard on Austin if you—afterwards—he's such a square, straight sort of a man, you ought to be awfully careful not to——"

Sylvia said quickly, her quiet voice vibrant, her face luminous: "Oh, Arnold, I could never tell you how sure I am. There just isn't anything else. Over there in Paris, I tried so hard to think about it—and I couldn't get anywhere at all. The more I tried, the baser I grew; the more I loved the things I'd have to give up, the more I hung on to them. Thinking didn't do a bit of good, though I almost killed myself thinking—thinking—— All I'd done was to think out an ingenious, low, mean compromise to justify myself in giving him up. And then, after Judith's cablegram came, I started home—Arnold, what a journey that was!—and I found—I found Mother was gone, just gone away forever—and I found Father out of his head with sorrow—and Judith told me about—about her trouble. It was like going through a long black corridor. It seemed as though I'd never come out on the other side. But when I did—— A door that I couldn't ever, ever break down—somehow it's been just quietly opened, and I've gone through it into the only place where it's worth living. It's the last thing Mother did for me—what nobody but Mother could have done. I don't want to go back. I couldn't if I wanted to. Those things don't matter to me now. I don't think they're wrong, the ease, the luxury, if you can have them without losing something finer. And I suppose some people's lives are arranged so they don't lose the finer. But mine wouldn't be. I see that now. And I don't care at all—it all seems so unimportant to me, what I was caring about, before. Nothing matters now but Austin. He is the only thing that has lived on for me. I'm down on my knees with thankfulness that he just exists, even if he can't forgive me—even if he doesn't care for me any more—even if I shouldn't ever see him again—even if he should die—he would be like Mother, he couldn't die, for me. He's there. I know what he is. Somehow everything's all right—because there's Austin."

She broke off, smiling palely and quietly at the man beside her. He raised his eyes to hers for an instant and then dropped them. Sylvia went on. " I don't pretend to know all the ins and outs of this Colorado business. It may be that it was quixotic on Austin's part. Maybe it *has* upset business conditions out there a lot. It's too complicated to be *sure* about how anything, I suppose, is likely to affect an industrial society. But I'm sure about how it has affected the people who live in the world—it's a great golden deed that has enriched everybody—not just Austin's coal-miners, but everybody who had heard of it. The sky is higher because of it. Everybody has a new conception of the good that's possible. And then for me, it means that a man who sees an obligation nobody else sees and meets it—why, with such a man to help, anybody, even a weak fumbling person like me, can be sure of at least loyally *trying* to meet the debts life brings. It's awfully hard to know what they are, and to meet them—and it's too horrible if you don't."

She stopped, aware that the life of the man beside her was one of the unpaid debts so luridly present to her mind.

"Sylvia," said Arnold, hesitating, "Sylvia, all this sounds so—look here, are you sure you're in *love* with Austin?"

She looked at him, her eyes steady as stars. "Aren't there as many ways of being in love, as there are people?" she asked. "I don't know—I don't know if it's what everybody would call being in love—but——" She met his eyes, and unashamed, regally, opened her heart to him with a look. "I can't live without Austin," she said quickly, in a low tone.

He looked at her long, and turned away. "Oh yes, you're in love with him, all right!" he murmured finally, "and I don't believe that the Colorado business or any of the rest of what you're saying has much to do with anything. Austin's a live man and you're in love with him; and that's all there is to it. You're lucky!" He took out his handkerchief, and wiped his forehead and the back of his neck. Sylvia, looking at him more closely, was shocked to see how thin and haggard was his face. He asked now, "Did you ever think that maybe what Austin was thinking about when he chucked the money was what you'd say, how you'd take it? I should imagine," he added with a faint smile, "that he is hard to please if he's not pretty well satisfied."

Sylvia was startled. "No. Why no," she said, "I thought I'd looked at every single side of it, but I never dreamed of that."

"Oh, I don't mean he did it *for* that! Lord, no! I suppose it's been in his mind for years. But afterwards, don't you suppose he thought . . . he'd been run after for his money such a terrible lot, you know . . . don't you suppose he thought he'd be sure of you one way or the other, about a million times surer than he could have been any other way; if you stuck by him, don't you see, with old Felix there with all his fascinations, plus Molly's money." He turned on her with a sudden confused wonder in his face. "God! What a time he took to do it! I hadn't realized all his nerve till this minute. He must have known what it meant, to leave you there with Felix . . . to risk losing you as well as—— Any other man would have tried to marry you first and then——! Well, what a dead-game sport he was! And all for a lot of dirty Polacks who'd never laid eyes on him!"

He took his riding-cap from his head and tossed it on the dried pine-needles. Sylvia noticed that his dry, thin hair was already receding from his parchment-like forehead. There were innumerable fine lines about his eyes. One eyelid twitched spasmodically at intervals. He looked ten years older than his age. He looked like a man who would fall like a rotten tree at the first breath of sickness.

He now faced around to her with a return to everyday matters. "See here, Sylvia, I've just got it through my head. Are you waiting here for that five-fifteen train to West Lydford and then are you planning to walk out to the Austin Farm? Great Scott! don't do that, in this heat. I'll just run back to the village and get a car and take you there in half an hour." He rose to his feet, but Sylvia sprang up quickly, catching at his arm in a panic. "No! no! Arnold, you don't understand. I haven't written Austin a word—he doesn't know I'm coming. At first in Paris I couldn't—I was so despicable—and then afterwards I couldn't either,—though it was all right then. There aren't any words. It's all too big, too deep to talk about. I didn't want to, either. I wanted to *see* him—to see if he still, if he wants me now. He could *write* anything. He'd feel he'd have to. How would I ever know but that it was only because he thought he ought to? I thought I would just go to him all by myself, without his knowing I was coming. *I* can tell—the first moment he looks at me I can tell—for all my life, I'll be sure, one way or the other. That first look, what's in him will show! He can't hide anything then, not even to be kind. I'll know! I'll know!"

Arnold sat down again with no comment. Evidently he understood. He leaned his head back against the rough bark of the pine, and closed his eyes. There was a painful look of excessive fatigue about his whole person. He glanced up and caught Sylvia's compassionate gaze on him. "I haven't been sleeping very well lately," he said very dryly. "It breaks a fellow up to lose sleep." Sylvia nodded. Evidently he was not minded to speak of his own troubles. He had not mentioned Judith.

She looked up thoughtfully at the well-remembered high line of the mountain against the sky. Her mother's girl-hood eyes had looked at that high line. She fell into a brooding meditation, and presently, obeying one of her sure instincts, she sat down by Arnold, and began to talk to him about what she divined for the moment would most touch and move him; she began to talk about her mother. He was silent, his worn, sallow face impassive, but she knew he was listening.

She told one incident after another of her mother's life, incidents which, she told him, she had not noted at the time, incidents which were now windows in her own life, letting in the sunlight her mother loved so well. "All the time I was growing up, I was blind, I didn't see anything. I don't feel remorseful, I suppose that is the way children have to be. But I didn't see her. There were so many minor differences between us . . . tastes, interests. I always said hatefully to myself that Mother didn't understand me. And it was true too. As if it matters! What if she didn't! She never talked morality to us, anyhow. She never talked much at all. She didn't need to. She was herself. No words would express that. She lived her life. And there it is now, there it always will be for me, food for me to live on. I thought she had died. But she has never been so living for me. She's part of me now, for always. And just because I see the meaning of her life, why, there's the meaning of mine as clear as morning. How can poor Father crave those ' messages ' from her! Everything is a message from her. We've lived with her. We have her in our hearts. It's all brightness when I think of her. And I see by that brightness what's in my heart, and that's Austin . . . Austin!" On the name, her voice rose, expanded, soared, wonderfully rang in the ensuing silence. . . .

Arnold said slowly, without opening his eyes: "Yes, yes, I see. I see how it is all right with you and Austin. He's big enough for you, all of you. And Felix—he's not so bad either—but he has, after all, a yellow streak. Poor Felix!"

This brought up to Sylvia the recollection of the day, so short a time ago when she had sat on the ground thus, much as she now sat next to Arnold, and had felt Judith's body rigid and tense. There was nothing rigid about Arnold. He was relaxed in an exhausted passivity, a beaten man. Let what would, befall. He seemed beyond feeling. She knew that probably never again, so life goes, could they speak together thus, like disembodied spirits, freed for once from the blinding, entangling tragic web of self-consciousness. She wondered again if he would find it in his heart to speak to her of Judith She remembered something else she had meant to ask him, if she could ever find words for her question; and she found that, in that hour of high seriousness, they came quite without effort. "Arnold, when I was in Paris, I met Professor Saunders. I ran across him by accident. He told me some dreadful things. I thought they couldn't all be true. But I wondered——"

Arnold opened his eyes and turned them on her. She saw again, as she had so many times, the honesty of them. They were bloodshot, yellowed, set deep in dark hollows, but it was a good gaze they gave. "Oh, don't take poor old Saunders too seriously. He went all to pieces in the end. He had a lot to say about Madrina, I suppose. I shouldn't pay much attention to it. Madrina's not such a bad lot as he makes her out. Madrina's all right if you don't want anything out of her. She's the way she is, that's all. It's not fair to blame her. We're all like that," he ended with a pregnant, explanatory phrase which fell with an immense significance on Sylvia's ear. "Madrina's all right when she's got what she wants."

The girl pondered in silence on this characterization. After a time Arnold roused himself to say again: "I mean she wouldn't go out of her way to hurt anybody, for anything. She's not the kind that enjoys seeing other folks squirm. Only she wants things the way she wants them. Don't let anything old Saunders said worry you. I suppose he laid all my worthlessness at Madrina's door too. He'd got into that way of thinking, sort of dotty on the subject anyhow. He was terribly hard hit, you know. I don't deny either that Madrina did keep him strung on hot wire for several years. I don't suppose it occurred to her that there was any reason why she shouldn't if he were fool enough. I never could see that he wasn't some to blame too. All he had to do—all they any of them ever had to do, was to get out and stay out. Madrina'd never lift a finger to hinder. Even Saunders, I guess, would have had to admit that Madrina always had plenty of dignity. And as for me, great Scott! what could you expect a woman like Madrina to do with a boy like me! She never liked me, for one thing; and then I always bored her almost more than she could stand. But she never showed her impatience, never once. She's really awfully good-natured in her way. She wanted to make me into a salon sort of person, somebody who'd talk at her teas—converse, don't you know. You see *me*, don't you! It was hard on her. If she'd had you, now—I always thought you were the only person in the world she ever really cared for. She does, you know. All this year you've been with her, she's seemed so different, more like a real woman. Maybe she's had her troubles too. Maybe she's been deathly lonely. Don't you go back on her too hard. Madrina's no vampire. That's just old Saunders' addled wits. She's one of the nicest people in the world to live with, if you don't need her for anything. And she really does care a lot for you, Sylvia. That time out in Chicago, when we were all kids, when I wanted to go to live with your mother, I remember that Madrina

suggested to her (and Madrina would have done it in a
minute, too)—she suggested that they change off, she take
you to bring up and I go out to live with your mother."
He stopped to look at the woman beside him. "I don't
know about you, Sylvia, but I guess it would have made
some difference in my life!"

Sylvia drew back, horrified that he was even in thought,
even for a moment robbing her of her mother. "Oh, what
I would have been—I can't bear to *think* of what kind of
woman I would have been without my mother!" The idea
was terrible to her. She shrank away from her aunt as never
before in her life. The reminiscence brought an idea, evidently as deeply moving, into Arnold's mind. The words
burst from him, "I might now be married to Judith!" He
put his hands over his eyes and cast himself down among
the pine-needles.

Sylvia spoke quickly lest she lose courage. "Arnold!
Arnold! What are you going to do with yourself now?
I'm so horribly anxious about you. I haven't dared speak
before——"

He turned over and lay on his back, staring up into the
dark green of the pine. "I'm going to drink myself to
death as soon as I can," he said very quietly. "The doctors
say it won't take long."

She looked at his wasted face and gave a shocked, pitying exclamation, thinking that it would be illness and not
drink which was to come to his rescue soon.

He looked at her askance, with his bloodshot eyes. "Can
you give me any single reason why I shouldn't?" he challenged her.

Sylvia, the modern, had no answer. She murmured
weakly, "Why must any of us try to be decent?"

"That's for the rest of you," he said. "I'm counted out.
The sooner I get myself out of the way, the better for
everybody. That's what *Judith* thinks."

The bitterness of his last phrase was savage. Sylvia cried
out against it. "Arnold! That's cruel of you! It's kill-
ing Judith!"

"She can't care for me," he said, with a deep, burning resentment. "She can't ever have cared a rap, or she wouldn't be *able* to——"

Sylvia would not allow him to go on. "You must not say such a thing, Arnold. You know Judith's only reason is —she feels if she—if she had children and they were——"

He interrupted her with an ugly hardness. "Oh, I know what her reason is, all right. It's the latest fad. Any magazine article can tell you all about it. And I don't take any stock in it, I tell you. It's just insanity to try to guess at every last obligation you may possibly have! You've got to live your life, and have some nerve about it! If Judith and I love each other, what is it to anybody else if we get married? Maybe we wouldn't have any children. Maybe they'd be all right—how could they be anything else with Judith for their mother? And anyhow, leave that to them! Let them take care of themselves! We've had to do it for ourselves! What the devil did my father do for me, I'd like to know, that I should die to keep my children unborn? My mother was a country girl from up here in the mountains. Since I've been staying here winters, I've met some of her people. Her aunt told me that my father was as drunk as a lord on his wedding night—— What did he think of *his* son? Why should I think of mine?"

He was so evidently talking wildly, desperately, that Sylvia made no attempt to stop him, divining with an aching pity what lay under his dreadful words. But when he said again, "It's simply that Judith doesn't care enough about me to stick by me, now I'm down and out. She can't bear me in her narrow little good world!" Judith's sister could keep her silence no more.

"Look here, Arnold, I haven't meant to tell you, but I *can't* have you thinking that. Listen! You know Judith, how splendid and self-controlled she is. She went all through the sorrow of Mother's death without once breaking down, not once. But the night before I started to come here, in the middle of the night, I heard such a sound from Judith's room! It frightened me, so I could hardly get my breath! It was Judith crying, crying terribly, so that she couldn't keep it back any more. I never knew her to cry before. I didn't dare go into her room—Mother would— but I didn't dare. And yet I couldn't leave her there alone in such awful trouble. I stood by the door in the dark— oh, Arnold, I don't know how long—and heard her—— When it began to be light she was quiet, and I went back to bed; and after a while I tiptoed in. She had gone to sleep at last. Arnold, there under her cheek was that old base- ball cap of yours . . . all wet, all wet with her tears, Judith's tears."

Before she had finished she was sorry she had spoken. Arnold's face was suffused with purple. He put his hand up to his collar and wrenched at it, clenched his fists, and finally, flinging his riding-crop far from him, hid his face in his hands and burst into tears. "Isn't it damnable!" he said over and over. "Isn't it damnable!"

Sylvia had nothing more to say. It seemed indeed damnable to her. She wondered again at Judith's invincible force of will. That alone was the obstacle—no, it was something back of Judith's will, something which even Arnold recognized; for now, to her astonishment, he looked up, his face smeared like a weeping child's, and said in a low tone, "You know, of course, that Judith's right."

The testimony was wrung out of him. But it came. The moment was one never to be forgotten.

Out of her passionate pity was born strength that was not to be denied. She took his hand in hers, his dry, sick man's hand. "Arnold, you asked me to give you a reason why you should get the best you can out of yourself. I'll give you a reason. Judith is a reason. Austin is a reason. I'm a reason. I am never going to let you go. Judith can't be the one to help you get through the best you can, even though it may not be so very well—poor, poor Judith, who would die to be able to help you! Mother wasn't allowed to. She wanted to, I see that now. But I can. I'm not a thousandth part as strong or as good as they; but if we hang together! All my life is going to be settled for me in a few hours. I don't know how it's going to be. But however it is, you will always be in my life. For as long as you live," she caught her breath at the realization of how little that phrase meant, " for as long as you live, you are going to be what you wanted to be, what you ought to have been, my brother—my mother's son."

He clung to her hand, he clung to it with such a grip that her fingers ached—and she blessed the pain for what it meant.

CHAPTER XLVII

" . . . AND ALL THE TRUMPETS SOUNDED!"

THEY had told her at the farm, the old man and the old woman who had looked so curiously at her, that Mr. Page had gone on up the wood-road towards the upper pasture. He liked to go there sometimes, they said, to look at the sunset from a big rock that stood in the edge of the white birch woods. They added, in extenuation of this, that of course somebody had to go up there anyhow, once in a while, to salt the sheep.

Sylvia had passed on, passed the great, square, many-chimneyed house, passed the old-fashioned garden, and struck into the wood-road beyond the bars. The sun was so low now, almost below the edge of the Notch, that the rays were level and long behind her. So she had walked, bathed in luminous gold at Versailles, on the day when Austin had first told her that he loved her, on the day she had told him the truth. From the first moment she had seen him how he had always brought out from her the truest and best, finer and truer than anything she had thought was in her, like a reflection from his own integrity. His eyes that day, what clear wells of loyalty and honor . . . how her mother would have loved him! And that other day, when he said farewell and went away to his ordeal . . . she closed her eyes for an instant, pierced with the recollection of his gaze on her! What was she, what poor thing transfigured to divinity, that such passion, such tenderness had been hers . . . even for a moment . . . even if now . . .

She looked timidly up the green tunnel of the arching trees, fearing to see him at any moment. And yet how she hastened her steps towards where he was! The moments were too long till she should find her heart's home!

After a time, there came a moment of such terrible throbbing of the heart, such trembling, that she could not go on. She sat down on a rock beside the road and pressed her shaking hands on her cheeks. No, it was too awful. She had been insane to think of putting everything, her whole life, to the test of a moment's shock. She would go back. She would write him. . . .

She looked up and saw her mother's gallant figure standing there before her. She smiled, and started on. Strange that she had thought her mother could be dead. Her first instinct had been right. Her mother, *her* mother could not die.

The road turned sharply to the left. She came out from the white birches. She was in the edge of the pasture, sweet-fern at her feet, a group of sheep raising startled heads to gaze at her, the sun's rim red on the horizon below her. And up there, the sunlight on his face, above her, stood Austin.

The sight of him was like a great burst of music in her heart, like a great flood of light. Her doubts, her uncertainties, they were gone out, as utterly as night goes before the sun. Her ears rang to a sound like singing voices. For a moment she did not feel the ground under her feet. . . .

Austin looked down and saw her. He stood like a man in a dream.

And then he knew. He knew. And Sylvia knew. He gave a great cry of welcome which was to ring in her ears for all her life, like a benediction. He ran down to meet her, and took her in his arms.

THE END

NOTES AND SUGGESTIONS

NOTES

Page 3.—Arcadia: An ideal spot where "rustic simplicity and plenty satisfy untutored hearts and where ambition and its crimes are unknown."

Page 4.—A gold sheepskin: The story of the Argonauts.

Page 21.—Promethean: Prometheus, it is said, stole fire from heaven and brought it to earth. Thereupon Zeus punished him by having him chained to a mountain where daily his liver (which grew again each night) was consumed by an eagle.

Page 26.—Benthamism: Jeremy Bentham (1748-1832) was an utilitarian philosopher.

Byzantine: A style of architecture.

Alexandrine: Ancient school of art.

Page 27.—Franco-Prussian War, 1870-1871.

Page 38.—Ceres: Goddess of grain and harvest.

Diana: Goddess of the moon and of the hunt, and protectress of her sex.

Hall of the Mountain King: A musical composition by Edvard Grieg.

Page 48.—Vulture: See note to Promethean, page 21.

Comme le diable . . . : Like the devil, they are always well.

Page 49.—*wie eine blume . . .* : like a flower, so beautiful and lovely.

Page 51.—*comment ça roule:* how goes it?

Schubert: Franz Schubert, 1797-1828, is noted for the lyrical quality of his songs.

Page 62.—Olympian: Mount Olympus was the reputed home of the Greek gods and goddesses.

Page 68.—*cul-de-sac:* blind alley.

Page 73.—Koran: the sacred book of the Moslems, or Mohammedans.

Page 80.—" Meechin' ": subservient, ingratiating.

Page 103.—*mit der flachen Hand schlagen:* spank.

Page 110.—Kreutzer Sonata: composed by Beethoven and dedicated to Kreutzer.

Loyola: Ignatius de, 1491-1556. Founder of the Society of Jesus, an organization for the conversion of infidels and a counteraction of the Protestant Reformation.

Page 112.—Hannibal: Noted Carthaginian general who, when nine years old, was taken by his father to the altar of the gods and made to swear eternal enmity against Rome.

Page 115.—Ionic: One of the three orders of Greek Architecture, in style between the simple Doric and the ornate Corinthian.

Page 139.—Olympian: See note to page 62.

Page 141.—Götterdämmerung: Twilight of the Gods. The fourth opera of the Ring Cycle composed by Richard Wagner.

Page 142.—Volsung: Characters in Norse literature.

Eroica: The third and greatest of Beethoven's symphonies.

Siegfried: The hero of Wagner's Ring Cycle.

Durch Leiden, Freude: Suffering brings joy.

Page 143.—Moses: See Exodus iii, 1 to 6.

Page 145.—Phi Beta Kappa: A collegiate scholastic honor.

Page 159.—Diana: See note to page 38.

Page 170.—Haydn, Joseph: 1732-1809. A composer noted for his severe technique, one ill suited to satisfy the vague longings of youth.

Chopin: Frederic François, 1809-1849. A composer whose works are more lyrical in quality than Haydn's.

Page 171.—Kreutzer Sonata: See note to page 110.

Page 173.—Athens: The home of cultured ease opposed to Sparta, the home of effort and bleak sparseness.

Pater: Walter Horatio, 1839-1894. English stylist who wrote of art and literature.

Page 202.—Brünnhilde: The heroine of Wagner's Ring Cycle, at times stormy and untamed as well as athletic.

Page 237.—Capua: An ancient city of Italy famous for its wealth and luxury.

Carthaginian: Capua opened its gates to the Carthaginians opposing the Romans.

c'est son métier: That's her way.

Page 243.—*Et vera . . . :* And by her walk is manifest the real goddess. (From Virgil.)

Page 251.—Chardin: Jean, 1699-1779. A noted French painter of still life.

Whistler: James M'Neill, 1834-1903. Distinguished American painter and etcher. He is best known to the layman for his portrait " Mother."

Page 261.—Chopin: See note to page 170.

Page 262.—Am Meer: By the Sea.

Page 263.—Thibet: A land in central Asia.

Page 265.—Bach: Johann Sebastian, 1685-1750. Great composer of church music.

Bizet: Alexandre César Léopold, 1838-1875. French composer best known for his opera Carmen.

Page 267.—Seneca: A celebrated Roman Stoic philosopher.

Page 269.—*arrière-pensée:* idea.

Debussy: Claude Achille, 1862-1918. A French composer noted for new methods of expression and new harmonic combinations.

Masaccio: Tommaso, 1401-1429 (?). An Italian painter sometimes called the father of modern art.

Page 270.—Socrates: A famous Greek philosopher who ever searched after a knowledge of virtue.

Page 271.—*confession intime d'un enfant du siècle:* intimate confession of a child of the world.

Renaissance: A period covering part of the 15th and 16th centuries when a new interest in art and literature was awakened.

Page 273.—Liszt, Franz, 1811-1886. A Hungarian composer. Liebestraum: Love dream.

Page 277.—*Il faut . . . :* One must howl with the wolves. *Hurlements:* howlings.

Page 282.—*Beau rôle:* Fine part.

Page 287.—*Mais bien sûr:* Why, yes, indeed.

Page 296.—Valkyrs: In Norse mythology, handmaidens of Odin who rode through the air to battle, decided which soldiers were the heroes to fall, and conducted them back to Valhalla, the warrior's paradise.

Page 317.—Marathon: A plain near Athens where battle was waged between 100,000 Persians and 10,000 Athenians aided by 1,000 neighboring Platæans, and ended in a Greek victory which kept Asiatic civilization from prevailing in Europe to-day.

Page 319.—Oscar Wilde: 1856-1900. A British writer, clever in the use of epigram.

Page 322.—Marie Antoinette: 1755-1793. The Queen of Louis XVI of France.

Page 324.—*En tête-à-tête:* By the two alone (free trans.).

Page 333.—Buddha: A name meaning "enlightened," taken by the founder of Buddhism; here applied to an image of the god.

Zuloaga, Placido: a well known Spanish metal worker.

Page 334.—Ming dynasty: In China the ruling dynasty from 1368-1648, preceding the Manchu dynasty.

Page 335.—Midas: The legendary lover of gold.

Page 336.—Henry James, 1843-1916, a novelist, American born, European bred, and later a British citizen.

Page 339.—Saracenic: Moorish.

Beauvais: A French town north of Paris, noted for its tapestries.

Louis XVII: 1785-1795.

Page 340.—Jacques Cœur: A noted French financier.

Page 344.—Cassandra: A legendary Greek prophetess whose predictions, though true, were never credited.

Page 350.—Etruscan: pertaining to ancient Etruria, now Tuscany.

Page 358.—Revue Bleue: Blue Magazine.

Page 370.—Huysmans, Joris Karl: 1848-1907. French writer.

Versailles: Suburb of Paris, noted in history and art. Here are the *Grand Trianon,* a palace built by Louis XIV for Madame de Maintenon, and the *Petite Trianon,* a palace built by Louis XV and later the favorite abode of Marie Antoinette.

Page 370.—Madame de Maintenon: 1635-1719. A woman of insignificant birth who later, as the second wife of Louis XIV of France, exerted a powerful influence at court. She lived with rigid care for propriety.

Page 375.—Edict of Nantes: Issued in 1598 by Henry IV of France, granting certain political equalities to the Huguenots.

Page 380.—*Toujours perdrix:* Everlastingly the same thing.

Page 394.—Louvre: The famous palace in France now used as a museum and art gallery.

Ribera, Jusepe, 1588-1656. A Spanish Neapolitan painter.

Winged Victory: The well known statue of the Victory of Samothrace.

Botticelli, Sandro, 1447-1510. An Italian painter.

Page 395.—*"Ces dames":* "The ladies."

Page 396.—Titian: Tiziano Vecellio, 1477-1576. The greatest painter of the Venetian School, noted for his shades of red.

Da Vinci, Leonardo, 1452-1519. The famous Italian artist best known for his The Last Supper and his Mona Lisa.

Venus of Melos is the most admired single existing Greek statue.

Page 399.—*Petit four:* Small cake.

Page 400.—Life, life eternal . . . : A quotation from Bunyan's *Pilgrim's Progress.*

Rubens, Peter Paul, 1577-1640. A celebrated Flemish painter noted for the voluptuous figures of his women.

Juno and her peacocks: Juno, the wife of Jupiter, had several sacred birds, among them the peacock.

Tuileries: Formerly a royal palace in Paris. It is connected with the Louvre by wings.

Place de la Concord. A square in Paris, noted for its intimate connection with French history.

Page 401.—Chabrier, Alexis Emmanuel, 1841-1894. A French composer of operas.

Page 404.—Athens: See note to page 173.

Page 405.—Palissy, Bernard, 1510-1589. A French potter and enameler.

Page 409.—Wicket Gate: A reference to Christian's journey in *Pilgrim's Progress.* At the Wicket Gate he was to be rid of his heavy burden.

Apples of Hesperides.—Apples of gold according to Greek mythology.

De la crème, fromage à la crème. Cream, cream-cheese.

Page 411.—Talleyrand-Périgord, Charles Maurice de, 1754-1838.
Noted French statesman and diplomat of the time of the French
Revolution.

Page 413.—D'Indy, Vincent. 1851-   . A French composer,
leader of the radical modern French school.

Page 418.—Panthéon: Famous Parisian church noted for its
beautiful Corinthian columns. See note on page 115.

Page 421.—Messalina: Wife of the Emperor Claudius, and
known for her vices.

Page 422.—Puvis de Chavannes, Pierre: 1824-1898. A French
historical and decorative painter.

Page 423.—Rodin, Auguste, 1840-1917. A French sculptor best
known for his statue, " The Thinker."

Allons, ma belle! Come on, my dear!

Page 434.—Bastile: A celebrated state prison of pre-Revolu-
tionary times in Paris. The anniversary of its fall on July 14,
1789, is now the national birthday of the French Republic.

SUGGESTIONS FOR STUDY

BOOK I

Chapter 1.

Notice the choice of words in the first paragraph. Why is this paragraph sketchy? What sentences, what incidents show the character of the persons of the novel? Describe the home life as portrayed in this chapter. Why is Aunt Victoria introduced here? List the characteristics of the mother.

Chapter 2.

What is the author's opinion of social life in a University circle? Contrast the childhood of Sylvia and Judith with that of the ordinary child, as to (1) atmosphere, (2) reception of crises, (3) mode of life. Notice the figures of speech on pages 20, 28, 45 and 60.

Chapter 3.

Make a list of topics from which the Marshall children gained a wide education through family discussion. Why did Victoria exasperate her brother? Contrast the home life of Judith with that of Arnold. What does the sentence "Madrina doesn't know what . . . lessons" (page 34) tell us of Arnold's upbringing?

Chapter 4.

Contrast the two pictures of Lydford. What do they tell us as to the character of the sketchers? Can you picture Mr. Marshall as a young man?

Chapter 5.

Notice (page 44-45) the author's portrayal of feminine and masculine self-consciousness. Contrast the Sunday evening in this chapter with the more usual type described on page 19 ff.

Chapter 6.

Notice the choice of words pages 56-7. Contrast Victoria and Barbara Marshall in appearance and humaneness.

488

Chapter 7.

A study of American democracy. Is it an ideal picture? Sum up in two paragraphs the author's opinion of the American school. What is the individual and social gain derived from an attitude of tolerance and understanding between races and classes? List what you now know of Sylvia's character; of Judith's. (Note especially page 84.) Contrast the reaction of Sylvia with that of Judith when they hear the news of the Fingal girls. Is this significant? Sum up in one sentence Mrs. Marshall's idea of democracy.

Chapter 8.

Does Mrs. Marshall approve of the punishment inflicted by the principal? What does the home atmosphere gain by her silence? Is the reader in doubt as to her attitude? Do you think the punishment was wisely selected? What has the incident contributed to Sylvia's character development? To Judith's?

Chapter 9.

Comment on the school children's change in attitude toward the Fingals on the next Monday. Does this affect your idea of their democracy? Why was Sylvia glad to be educated at home? How is her awakening individuality most clearly shown? What shows the author's appreciation of the emotional reaction of Youth to the settled ways of Maturity? Where does she show that the father and mother do not yet realize that Sylvia is growing up? Which side of Sylvia's nature is coming to the front? What shows it?

QUESTIONS ON BOOK I

Notice the ends of the chapters. Are they transitional in effect? If so, does the novel gain thereby? Study the figures of speech on pages 84, 85, 87, 94, 106 and 160. What policies of the Marshall home tend to bring broad-mindedness? Family happiness?

BOOK II

Chapter 10.

Make the following words a part of *your* working vocabulary: discrepancy, receptivity, nonchalance, askance, physiognomy, Ionic, utilized, welted, substantial, casual, deference, perception, diverse, lavishness, covetousness, abysmal, confronting. Pick out the words and sentences on page 116-121 which seem to give significance to the characters.

Chapter 11.

Note the grim irony of the "educational trip" page 123. Do you find anywhere in this chapter sentences that show the author's sense of democracy? Her knowledge of the adolescent boy? Why did Victoria refuse Arnold's request to live at the Marshall home?

Chapter 12.

Notice the descriptions of (1) the ride on the elevated train, (2) the poor section of the city, (3) the hospital wards. Notice the author's use of contrasts: (1) the attitudes of Sylvia and her mother toward the poor; (2) the attitudes of Sylvia and Judith toward the hospital; (3) the troubles of a society woman and those of suffering humankind.

Chapter 13.

What lines emphasize the respect, understanding, and love in the Marshall home? Comment on the author's ability to describe the emotional reaction to music. Why was there "relief in Mrs. Marshall's voice" (p. 144)?

Chapter 14.

What do you think of the author's opinion of college fraternities? What paragraphs or phrases in this chapter are especially satiric?

Chapter 15.

Contrast Colonel Fiske's democratic ideals with those of Mrs. Marshall. Contrast Mrs. Draper and Mrs. Marshall as to (1) conversational ability, (2) worth of character, (3) charm of manner, (4) purpose of contact with people, (5) ideals, (6) interests, (7) effect on youth.

Chapter 16.

What is the author's idea of student social life "as planned by the pioneer fathers"; by the faculty; by the students? Of the student's response to faculty effort? What is her idea of finishing schools? Pick out the significant words on page 169. Which seem to you the best worded sentences on pages 167, 170, 173, 175?

Chapter 17.

Describe Mrs. Jermain Fiske. Contrast Sylvia's opinion of her home with Mrs. Fiske's opinion of it. What incidents in this chapter further reveal Mrs. Marshall's character? What do you think of the "Marshall theory"? What elements in Sylvia's life and character presage a right solution to her present problem?

Chapter 18.

Why did the author introduce the unnamed young man who bought the chocolates? List the incidents and omissions that show Colonel Fiske's character and his home life.

Chapter 19.

Had Mrs. Fiske overheard the library scene between Jerry and Sylvia? Was it a sense of courtesy that compelled Mrs. Fiske to accompany Sylvia to the trolley?

Chapter 20.

List examples of Mrs. Marshall's tact. What do you think of Mrs. Marshall's theory as to confidences (p. 219)? What adjective describes Mrs. Marshall's philosophy of life? What describes Mrs. Draper's? Which resulted in true home happiness?

Chapter 21.

This is a transition chapter. Have you found any other thus far in the book? Why did Sylvia resent the deep glowing content of her father and mother?

QUESTIONS ON BOOK II

What minor characters have been well drawn in a sentence or two (see pages 120, 132, 135)? Discuss Jerry Fiske as one type of college-educated youth. Contrast him with the student mentioned on page 145. Try to picture both fifteen years later. Notice the significance of chapter titles. What are the characteristics of a good title? What of significance to the plot has happened in this book? What incidents have brought out character? Of what value to the story is Jerry Fiske? Mrs. Fiske? Colonel Fiske? Notice the figures of speech on pages 117, 119, 120, 132, 133, 160.

BOOK III

Chapter 22.

Does this chapter help you to form an opinion as to coeducation in colleges? Discuss Arnold's opinion of Morrison. List evidences of Sylvia's posing.

Chapter 23.

Contrast the reaction of men to Morrison with that of women. In the first half of this chapter is Morrison "handing Sylvia a full cup of his irresistible fascination "? What sentences in the second half explain Arnold? Does he appeal to you?

Chapter 24.

What is the secret of Morrison's fascination? Is Sylvia's evaluation of her home sincere? Is it true? Is sophistication desirable? List its advantages and disadvantages.

Chapter 25.

Is Sylvia generous in giving up Morrison? Do you admire Morrison? Have Molly and Morrison a safe basis for future happiness? Have Arnold and Judith?

Chapter 26.

What is Victoria's idea of a suitable marriage? What would be Mrs. Marshall's idea? What was troubling Molly? What effect did need for action have on Molly? Notice descriptive words on pages 293, 294, 296.

Chapter 27.

Do you find any possible foreshadowing in this chapter? Make the following words a part of *your* working vocabulary: lassitude, suppositions, aromatic, tepid, adroit, carping, strictures, swart, incongruity, stagnant, murky, limpid, ablutions, pique, indissolubly, acrid, pungency, astringency, lustration, grotesque, candid, rueful, parapet, vaporous, beatitude.

Chapter 28.

Do you recall other examples of Morrison's "cameo of small talk"? Explain the meaning of the paragraph on page 314 and 315. Does Sylvia recognize that Morrison's act was despicable? Is her brain trying to readjust to a new situation or to remold her ideals and opinions?

Chapter 29.

List the sentences and incidents that show the struggle between the two sides of Sylvia's character.

Chapter 30.

Contrast the beginning and the end of the chapter. What is the purpose of this chapter? How does the chapter further the plot?

Chapter 31.

Contrast the topics of conversation between Morrison and Sylvia with those between Austin and Sylvia. Contrast Austin's definition of beauty with Victoria's. Discuss the tragedy of Arnold's life. Memorize " In this modern maze . . . proportion " (page 343); " encounter with death . . . live on " (page 345); " If you've . . . humanity " (page 345).

Chapter 32.

Do you agree with Victoria or with Sylvia as to letting Judith know of Arnold's weakness? Why? Notice the emotional, illogical working of Sylvia's mind when she is under stress. Is this art on the part of the author? Give instances or phrases that show Victoria's lack of understanding and of sympathy with those persons not in her social set. The last sentence in many chapters points onward; notice and comment on the last sentence in this chapter.

Chapter 33.

Is a jarring note given to the account of the wedding by the description of the women (page 366 and 367 and 368 top)? The wedding is described from what point of view?

Chapter 34.

Was it a patriotic sentiment or was it a love of nature " unimproved " by man that made Page prefer Vermont scenery to Versailles scenery? Notice the peaceful atmosphere of the chapter. Contrast the marriage proposal of Jerry Fiske with that of Page. In this connection notice on page 382 the sentence " She wondered . . . hair's-breadth of pretense."

Chapter 35.

Memorize " It's only people who *do* something who have anything to say." Make the following words a part of *your* working vocabulary: emanation, modulated, mediocre, explicitly, retentive, promiscuity, amenity, loquaciousness, deprecatory, portentous, divination.

Chapter 36.

What kind of chapter is this? Notice the effect of the short choppy sentences at the end of the first paragraph. How does the author gain sympathy for Felix Morrison? Does she leave you with the feeling that Molly's death was accidental? Has Sylvia doubted this at all? Prove your answer by words from the text. By what means does the author give the impression that time is passing? Notice the sharp irony of the horror of Sylvia's thought and Mr. Perth's fondness for chocolate éclairs.

Chapter 37.

What sentence makes the second paragraph a unit? Do you agree with Felix Morrison's point of view on social questions? With Austin Page's? Or with neither? In the argument Page keeps his temper better than Morrison. Does this indicate (1) that his cause is juster, (2) that his arguments are better worked out, (3) that his mind is broader, or (4) that his nature is less high strung? What is the purpose of this chapter? Does Morrison's "spray of diamond-like trills" enhance Page's deep sincerity (page 407)?

Chapter 38.

Study the descriptions on page 409-410. Notice especially the appeal to the sense of taste in the last paragraph of page 410. Why do we not get Austin's letter complete? Memorize (page 414) . . . "there is another kind of beauty . . . lived at its best." Also "It's true that . . . misery of others."

Chapter 39.

Why is the meeting with Saunders introduced and why introduced here? How does Saunders sum up Victoria's character (pages 419-422)? What part has Saunders played in the story? How does the author get the effect of Sylvia's weariness on pages 424-425? Is Sylvia's reaction to easeful life cowardly?

QUESTIONS ON BOOK III

Contrast the setting of Book III with the setting of Books I and II. Contrast the tone of conversation in the two social groups, direct openness and subtle fencing. List the good figures of speech on the following pages: 246, 262, 276, 279, 281, 288, 291, 320, 322, 327, 341, and 342. What characteristics of Molly did the fire bring out? List Parisian places of human and artistic importance that Sylvia and her friends had not visited. Why had they not? Notice the endings of chapters. Do you find here a characteristic of the author? Discuss the author's perception, portrayal and opinion of society life. Study the descriptions on pages 261, 308-310, 371, 382-3.

BOOK IV

Chapter 40.

Notice on page 434 a good example of a very long sentence. The description on page 435 is from whose point of view? What contrasts do you find in this chapter? What is the effect of real trouble upon Sylvia's relationship to Morrison? Does their relationship now seem to have a basis for future happiness? What is her relationship to others with hearts softened by sorrow?

Chapter 41.

What type of paragraph is the first on page 440? How are the characters of Sylvia, Judith, Lawrence and Mr. Marshall affected by Mrs. Marshall's death? What does this add to your conception of Mrs. Marshall's character?

Chapter 42.

The healing power of Mrs. Marshall's spirit is how shown? What indications do we get of the author's religious convictions? Which is more alone now, Sylvia, shut out from her father also, or Mr. Marshall, who realized at the same time Sylvia's sympathy and yet her inability to recognize his personal loss?

Chapter 43.

Notice the lessening of Sylvia's self-interest and her increasing thoughtfulness for others. What incidents show this best? Would the vision of Felix Morrison (see page 455) have been a rock of strength to Sylvia now?

Chapter 44.

Does it seem inconsistent that Mr. Marshall, ever opposed to spiritualism, should embrace the faith now? What purpose had the author in having him thus change? Does she accomplish it, and if so, how?

Chapter 45.

This is a wind-up chapter. Is Judith's nature cold or is it strong? Was she right in her decision? List instances that show Sylvia's growth in humanity and sympathy. Notice the significant similes on page 464. Memorize "It seemed to her ... integrity" page 465.

Chapter 46.

Why can Arnold be called decent? Contrast him with Jerry Fiske (pages 473-477). Memorize "Those things don't matter ... something finer" page 469.

Chapter 47.

Have Austin and Sylvia a basis for true happiness in marriage? What words bring this out?

QUESTIONS ON BOOK IV

Contrast Sylvia's two great romances. Does the author keep the interest and suspense to the end? Look up what is meant by a strophic circle. By having this story end in Vermont do you find any evidence of a strophic circle from the point of view of setting? atmosphere? character?

GENERAL QUESTIONS

PLOT: List episodes that develop the plot. Do some also portray character? Did you expect Austin to give his wealth to the State and provide for uplift work? If so, what led you to expect it? List the incidents that show the effect of Sylvia's home-training on her character and on her actions. What part did the following play in this story: Cousin Parnelia, Mrs. Draper, Saunders, the Fingals? List the sub-plots.

CHARACTER: List the episodes that portray character. Write character sketches of Sylvia, Judith, Arnold, Professor Marshall, Mrs. Marshall, Victoria, Austin, Molly, Felix, Mrs. Draper. Contrast the characters of Eleanor Hubert and Molly, Felix and Austin, Jerry and Austin, Jerry and Arnold, Judith and Sylvia, Sylvia and Victoria, Victoria and Mrs. Marshall. Contrast the effect of Victoria and that of Mrs. Marshall upon those with whom they come in contact. How was Sylvia affected by such contact? How would Arnold have differed if as a youth he had gone to live at the Marshall home? Could Victoria's influence be bad when even her enemies admitted that she wanted to harm no one? Explain your answer. Compare Judith's directness with Sylvia's hesitating uncertainty.

SETTING: Contrast Sylvia's home life with that of Victoria as a girl. Does a varied setting add to the interest of any story? What is the effect of her home life on Sylvia's development? The effect of her college life? Of her months with Victoria?

GENERAL: Compare Sylvia's life with the life of girls you know. Is she representative of the modern girl? Is the story true to life? What is the author's opinion of modern life? What can you learn of the author by reading this book? What is the significance of the title "The Bent Twig"? Do you think this story will live? If so, why?

TOPICS FOR THEMES

BOOK I.

Visitors at the Marshall home.

Arnold's first taste of child life.

A conflict of natures (chap. 4).

The effect of Victoria's personality on Sylvia as a child.

The upbringing of Sylvia and Judith contrasted with that of Arnold.

Description of the Marshall home life.

BOOK II.

Sylvia's first contact with strict conventions.

Sylvia's growing absorption with the non-essentials of life.

Factors which contributed to Sylvia's growing alienation from her family.

The tragedy of Mrs. Fiske's life.

BOOK III.

The effect of Arnold and Judith's engagement.

The Parisian drawing room as a setting for Austin's sincerity.

The author's opinion and treatment of the "social art."

BOOK IV.

The effect of real trouble upon Sylvia.

Sylvia's three possible futures.

SELECTIONS FOR CLASS READING

Pages 292 (end) to 298.

Pages 431 to 434.

Pages 440 to 442.

Chapter 42.

Page 472 (the last paragraph).

kaleidoscopic
divergencies
contrapuntal?
archaisms
chiaroscuro
anachronism
phenomena
accelerandoes
reprehensible
dolichocepalic